Future Fiction

Edited by

Francesco Verso

A cura di

Francesco Verso

Kalicalypse

Subcontinental Science Fiction

Edited by Tarun K. Saint, Bodhisattva Chattopadhyay
and Francesco Verso

Fantascienza dal subcontinente

A cura di Tarun K. Saint, Bodhisattva Chattopadhyay
e Francesco Verso

Traduzione di Francesca Secci e Gabriella Gregori

Published by – Pubblicato da Associazione Future Fiction
Via Valentiniano 40 – 00145 Roma, Italia
P.Iva 15586791004

Title: *Kalicalypse*
Subcontinental Science Fiction - Fantascienza dal subcontinente
© 2022 Future Fiction, Roma
I edition June 2022 - I edizione Giugno 2022
info@futurefiction.org
ISBN: 9788832077513

INTRODUCTION

by Bodhisattva Chattopadhyay

It has become increasingly commonplace to assert the plurality of apocalypses, but also the rolling nature of these apocalypses, stretched backwards and forwards in time. As many Indigenous philosophers and intellectuals such as Grace Dillon and Ailton Krenak have noted, for many indigenous communities worldwide, the apocalypse is something that has already happened. In such a manner of speaking and thinking, we are living out the other side of these apocalypses: apocalypses as a shorthand for a form of destruction from which there seems to be no way forward, but which, nonetheless, keep cycling again and again. The end is never the end, almost as if the end itself promised by such apocalypses is a kind of divine joke.

Yet, as the Indian science fiction writer Samit Basu has expressed, dystopias are boring where dystopias are just Tuesday. In India, as in much of the world, the fashionable banality of the apocalypse is not really needed, or often even recognized. Rather, apocalypse in the subcontinent loses its finery as a prelude to a new form of *becoming future*. In such becoming, it swallows up the histories and myths of the past and turns them inside out towards possibility. At the tail end of the fourth wave of science fiction lies no science fiction at all, but the realm of future fictions, futurisms, and fictions of possibility, that are both older and newer than what they supersede. This is what is happening to speculative literatures and arts worldwide, to which *Kalicalypse* is a generous and genuine contribution from the South Asian region.

What is Kalicalypse, and how may one talk about it, both as a conceptual phenomenon and a literary one? It is first of all, a relationship with time, embodied by the term *Kal/Kali*. While Kali is a goddess of time, but also destruction and renewal, *kālá (kala)* itself is time: both the units in which it is measured, and the underlying philosophical constituent that makes everything possible. Hence *kalpavigyan*, the word used in Bangla to refer to literature dealing specifically with the temporal constituent in the speculative. This relationship with time thus enfolds the apocalypse, but not as cosy catastrophes with almost automatic, pre-determined endings that will leave us mildly discomfited in the experience, more gravy than grave, and then ultimately be resolved with a dose of antacid. Kalicalypse is the obverse of the cosy catastrophe, stemming from a fundamental acceptance of the brokenness of the world, fixing which requires a remaking that will wipe the makers along with it. Kalicalypse is fundamentally social: it has as its goal addressing the diseases infecting the social. It is also fundamentally political as an act. Much as *Kali*, it is as sandpaper against the normative, especially the normative of the heteropatriarchal and the hierarchical. Hence "caste," "gender," and "religion" appear as three axes of remaking within South Asian future fiction, since no empty dream of escape, to inner space or outer wilds, to virtual worlds or other planets, is inherently likely to fix the problems that vivisect the everyday. To go against things that ground even one's own identities in the subcontinent (and beyond) is so fundamentally disruptive that to imagine their outside is to imagine an existence without oneself. Hence the other meaning of Kali, both as goddess and as time, which is the destruction of *self* as an entity. It is also a destruction of the myths that make us. Story after story in this volume, much as all the other work coming out of South Asia (for instance, most recently, the two books of South Asian SF edited by Tarun K. Saint for Gollancz/Hachette), is incredibly self-reflexive in its association with the region, and also directly confrontational with its socio-political contemporary.

But what of the contemporary and the future? This is where the temporality of Kalicalypse really comes into play. Because future fiction also functions as the bridge to the future of which this is a present, Kalicalypse is also how the various knots of present time may be unravelled as possibilities to become possible futures. This is a challenge to the perception of inevitability to which we are bound, whether such inevitables are connected to the environmental futures or social ones. Inevitability is connected to temporal singularity: it is an eschatological worldview in which the past is written, the present is already here, and the future already known. As a region facing some of the worst effects of climate change, hosting a quarter of the world's population (in just 3.5% of its landmass) who coexist in a mindboggling social, religious, cultural, linguistic, ethnic, and historical plurality and diversity, there is no singular contemporary to which there is a singular future. Singularity and the illusion of singularity is nonsensical. Rather, there are innumerable presents to which there are innumerable futures. The Kalicalypse makes it apparent that the destruction of one world isn't the destruction of all worlds, that there are innumerable worlds inhabiting innumerable times, of which whatever present we inhabit happens to be just one. The illusion of singularity *is* the illusion broken by the Kalicalypse.

Furthermore, when we seek to group the problems of the contemporary under the larger umbrellas of the political or the religious, it is hardly surprising that some of this plurality is sacrificed for convenience. In the speculative worlds however, such plurality becomes the fissure through which new hope may arise. As Sri Lankan SF author and futurist Yudhanjaya Wijeratne notes in his recent "Ricepunk manifesto" (2019), the speculative storehouse of the region is constituted by and draws aggressively from this plurality. The works of the authors in the region, wherever they may reside, thrive on the energy of this plurality. As Kalicalypse, there is no singular time or arrow of progress, rather all time pervades this speculative landscape, both to challenge the fixation with the contemporary, and a naïve dependence upon or acceptance of an inevitable future. South Asian future fictions are much like the whistle of the pressure cooker (also ubiquitous in South Asian homes) that is our society: they not only let the pressure escape through the form of narrative futures, they also signal that something needs to be done in the present, and asap, and that we need to get off our asses now and get to work if we are to save this plurality just as it saves us from the narrowness of imagination in the everyday.

There is thus something incredibly freeing in the destruction wrought by the Kalicalypse, especially because it does not restore us. It is akin to an existential delight if one wants to term it so, but the more South Asian flavour would be the destruction of *māyā* through one's deep understanding of the illusory nature of things.

It is unsurprising that in works of South Asian speculative fiction, there is often a whiff of something lighter and magical, a touch of humour or black humour, and often even a dose of refreshing hope amidst an apparent total obliterating darkness of the future. This does not mean that difficult social themes are not given the attention or seriousness they deserve, but that the narration leaves room for playfulness – that quality that Vandana Singh identifies as quintessential to SF and work from South Asia in "A Speculative Manifesto" (2008) – exhibiting the power of imagining the otherwise. Simplistic divisions of utopia or dystopia are replaced by a highly self-aware critical utopianism. Speculative thinking underlies all gestures of critical thought. What lies at the other side of the Kalicalypse? Many new worlds?

Kalicalypse is the plurality we inhabit.

Bodhisattva Chattopadhyay
Oslo, 30th January 2022.

The New Humans

by Trishna Basak

translation by Arunava Sinha

Trishna Basak (born in 1970, Kolkata) is a notable poet, story writer, novelist and essayist of modern Bengali Literature. A B.E. and M.Tech from Jadavpur University, Trishna left her lucrative career to pursue her passion for literature. Her 5 year stint with Sahitya Academi *enabled her to get in close touch with Indian Literature. At present, she's a full time writer, editor and translator. She's also the secretary of Kolkata Translators Forum. She has several books of poems, short stories, novels, essays and translated works to her credit. Recipient of several prestigious grants and awards like Sahitya Academi travel grant 2008, Ila chanda Smriti Puraskar 2013, Somen Chanda Smarak Samman, Paschimbanga Bangla Academi, 2018, Namita Chattopadhyay Sahitya Samman 2020 to name a few. Trishna loves experimenting with complex themes. Her writings bear the wounds of modern terror stricken world as well as estrangement of technology dominated relationship. She lives in Kolkata.*

They were sitting sullenly on the 19th floor of the glass building in Block Two. They, meaning Aura and Remo. This floor was located near the belly of the egg-shaped building. The seating was built into the wall. The public welfare officials had their office in the centre. A sarod was playing softly on a concealed sound-system. Coffee and snacks were available freely at automatic machines. Evening was descending, and Welfare House was floating in the sky like a cloud. And yet they weren't happy. Normally you could just press the blue button on your watch when you felt depressed, but Aura wasn't up to making the effort. Six other couples were waiting like them, their foreheads also creased with worry. Which meant their father or mother, or perhaps father-in-law or mother-in-law, were to... 'Aura and Remo, Block Nine, Sector Three.' The voice rang out like the notes of a piano. Remo had been pacing up and down in anxiety. 'You remember ma's code, right?' he asked Aura hoarsely. Aura nodded.

A slim, pleasant-looking young woman came forward as soon as they entered, holding out her hand. "Aura and Remo, right? I'm Yohanna. What can I get you?' A blue sea stretched across the wall behind her. When she saw Aura gazing at it, she said, 'I love the sea. Should I change it?"

"No, it's fine."

"But Remo loves forests and you love mountains."

Yohanna waved her finger at the wall, which changed to display a dense forest on the right hand side and snow-covered peaks on the left.

"It's gesture-activated, isn't it?"

Yohanna smiled. "You're right. Come, tell me your story."

Three sofas were arranged around a small centre table, on which were piping hot cups of coffee and snacks. Aura and Remo could have had the conversation with Yohanna over the homeweb had they wished. But a lethal disease named ADDS—Attention Deficit Disorder Syndrome—had spread around the world once because of the overuse of the internet, accompanied by a tendency towards solitude and high obesity, along with many other problems, because of which people no longer went online unless they absolutely had to. The government too emphasised the need for direct human contact nowadays. Aura's grandfather had succumbed to ADDS.

"Romanni will be 60 on 14 September, correct?"

"Yes," said Aura and Remo in unison. Was that a quiver in Remo's voice? They had of course been familiar with the law since childhood, but still, this was his mother they were talking about.

"You're prepared, I hope. If not, there's still six months to go, you can enroll for our two-month course in special adaptation. Three days a week."

"Aren't extensions given sometimes?" asked Remo.

"Don't be emotional, Remo. You may know it was once a practice in this land for old people to go into the forests to live out the rest of their lives. Our Crossing programme is something like that. Can you imagine, even a few hundred years ago the cruel system of old age homes was in place. Crossing is a thousand times better. And besides, we've instituted this practice keeping future generations in mind. The old inevitably have to step aside to make room for them. One day you and I will also..."

"The problem *is* with the future generation," Aura interrupted Yohanna impatiently. "Chinkara is so obsessed with her grandmother that we probably won't be able to save her if Romanni leaves us." Her voice choked with tears.

Pressing her hand gently, Remo said, "It's true, Yohanna, we're passing sleepless night worrying for Chinkara. Our daughter's very young, she's not even five yet. She can't even join an adaptation course till she's twelve."

Yohanna's bright eyes dimmed. "But I'm helpless here, Remo. You know very well only distinguished citizens are allowed extensions. Writers and scientists, for instance, and then only if the jury allows it. Of course, I must admit corruption has not been eradicated yet, which means many people in the good books of the ruling party are allowed special benefits outside the law. But really, my hands are tied. The data says Romanni has no particular social contribution."

A slideshow of images ran through Remo's head. Ma waiting outside the school gate, ma sitting awake all night when I had fever, ma turning down Aritro-uncle's marriage proposal after baba's death, ma coming home from the park with Chinkara. But the data says no particular social contribution.

"I'm really sorry, but you have to explain to Chinkara. All children adjust eventually."

"But she..." Aura began. Remo cut her short. "All right, let's go." Grabbing Aura's hand, he stomped out of the room. A blind rage was eating away at him.

Aura had got back from work a short while ago. She was leafing through a magazine on the sofa after a bath. Apparently her grandmother's generation had never read a book. Everyone was so addicted to visual media that the publishing of books had all but stopped. There was a glut of magazines now, however, but not much new fiction or poetry was being written. Most of what was published was reprints. Aura was turning over the page absently when an article caught her eye. A reprint of something written about two hundred years ago, a debate on whether humans should be cloned or not. Stupid.

Aura put the magazine away. Human cloning had become so rampant at one time that it had led to enormous problems. So all kinds of cloning had been banned by law in the previous century.

Remo would be working late today. Aura was astonished when she looked out the window. It was raining. Rain was admittedly far from impossible in August, but was their weather controller malfunctioning? It wasn't just on their lawn though, it was raining all over the block.

The red security checkposts, the peach and maple trees, everything was getting drenched. Had all the controllers on the block gone out of order? Oh right, it was Friday. Because the number of poets in the country was dwindling alarmingly, the chief cultural advisor had had a Compulsory Rain Act passed two years ago.

People would have to allow rain four days a month. Aura had no idea how it worked. She wouldn't be able to produce a single word even if she stared at the rain all day. The truth was that Aura was no good with writing—her entire training was verbally and pictorially oriented.

There was a huge tree in their lawn, a silk cotton. Chinkara was nestled up to Romanni on a white bench beneath it, getting soaked as she listened to a story. Aura shivered in fear. Sure, Chinkara never fell ill, but what about Romanni?

She was scheduled for a Crossing in a month from now—what if she fell ill?

All the human rights commission people and journalists would descend on them. The big promotion Aura was expecting at work would be scuttled. She trembled to think what would happen if anyone came to know Romanni had fallen ill because of Chinkara's demand that they sit in the rain. Aura and Romanni were perpetually on edge, even though no one knew. The world had made so much progress, but humans had remained so primitive that there were many things they still couldn't accept.

"Look into her eyes whenever you feel sad," Joyoboroto had said. But Aura couldn't be bothered with the eyes, she was tense about something else at the time. "You've kept her intelligence level on the lower side, right? About the same as ours? Else we'll be in trouble."

"Don't worry, she's quite silly and emotional by their standards."

Leaning out of the window, Aura said, "What are the two of you doing there? Come inside." Chinkara had her arm wrapped around Romanni's.

Aura was surprised every time she saw her daughter. How could Chinkara be capable of such strong attachment? If people found out how deep Chinkara's emotions ran, there would be such a furore that the government could fall. The Opposition leaders would begin a campaign claiming that the only thing human beings still had to be proud of were being taken away from them. In the past white people apparently used to discriminate against black people, but now the two sides at loggerheads with each other were humans and robots.

Romanni changed out of her wet clothes, and helped Chinkara change as well. They came into the room. It was impossible to tell that her lifespan had only a month left. No one returned from a Crossing. Aura and Remo would have to go too one day. But Chinkara... a chill ran down Aura's spine, which was the moment Chinkara chose to jump on Aura, saying, "Ma! Will Baba be late tonight?"

"Yes baby, but you mustn't stay up, I'm going to give you dinner soon and put you to bed."

"No, thamu will give me dinner."

"Thamu isn't well darling."

"No, I'm fine, I am."

Aura looked at Romanni helplessly. Her eyes were moist, like the evening sky. Only four of them in the entire world knew—Aura, Remo, Joyobroto and Romanni. Romanni led Chinkara away to her playroom. The phone rang. Must be Remo, was he going to be working even longer.

"Hello?"

"It's Yohanna, am I speaking to Aura?"

"Yes, what's the matter?" Aura answered tentatively. She couldn't make out the reason for the phone call. After all, if there was nothing to be done...

"Can both of you drop by tomorrow? Around four?"

Her head felt like a knot of agony and anxiety. "We can," she managed to respond.

The same room, same coffee, same snacks, same wall-wide blue sea. The same smile on Yohanna's face as a few months ago.

"Come in. Actually we've had several other cases like yours. High level discussions may take place on the subject. But that doesn't happen overnight, it could take three or four years."

Aura and Remo exchanged glances. Why had they been summoned if there was nothing to be done? Apparently reading their minds, Yohanna said, "I'm thinking of a different route."

"For an extension?" Remo's eyes were hopeful suddenly.

"No, a replacement."

"A replacement?"

"Yes, a humanoid identical to Romanni. Your daughter will never realise that the grandmother she's hugging is not a flesh-and-blood human but an artificial one."

"No!" Remo shrieked. "Chinkara is bound to find out."

As Yohanna began to frown, Aura butted in quickly, "The thing is that Chinkara is very sensitive, remember that fancy dress party, Remo? You had some outlandish disguise on but still she spotted you."

"No way, that's impossible. It doesn't matter how intelligent your daughter might be, she cannot possibly distinguish between a human and a humanoid. Not even adults can do it. Otherwise how could the constitution have been amended to give full citizenship rights to humanoids? Think about it."

"Our daughter is capable of many things, Yohanna. Because she's a humanoid herself. Aura had some problems, so we got her from the lab of a scientist friend of ours."

Had Remo gone mad? The floor began to sway under Aura's feet. The waves on the wall were like the tentacles of an octopus.

"A humanoid?' Yohanna's pretty face was contorted in hatred. 'Don't you know we've built humanoids to assist us with your work, not to build social bonds with them?"

"No Yohanna, we have built humanoids to make the world a better place to live in. You know how humans had lost all their humanity at one time? And then we gave birth to humanoids after distilling the best qualities of humans, to avoid cataclysm." Remo didn't pause for breath.

"Calm down, Remo." Yohanna's smile was back. "But have you considered the consequences? If the whole thing is leaked..."

"Who'll leak it?"

"I might," said Yohanna, laughing. "Unless you agree to my condition."

"What condition?"

"My brother has a humanoid factory. You'll have to buy a humanoid replica of Romanni's from him. Four point five million. Cash."

"And how much will you take?" Remo asked, his voice ice-cold.

"It will cost you, many people have to be managed."

"Now listen to me, Yohanna. I could buy my mother's lifespan and Chinkara's happiness from you in return for money, but I won't. I'll allow my small world to be destroyed, but I won't buy anything from you."

"That's your choice Remo, I'm just doing my work."

Remo was about to explode, but Aura dragged him away. She looked up at the building when they went out. Welfare House was floating in the sky. The sun was setting. The clouds were flecked with blood.

"Tell me, even if we do manage to save Chinkara from them, could she still turn into a Yohanna one day? She may not be flesh-and-blood, but she's our creation, she's been made by humans."

Remo didn't answer.

Kali_Na

by Indrapramit Das

Indrapramit Das (aka Indra Das) is a writer and editor from Kolkata, India. He is a Lambda Literary Award-winner for his debut novel The Devourers *(Penguin India / Del Rey), and a Shirley Jackson Award-winner for his short fiction, which has appeared in a variety of anthologies and publications including Tor.com, Slate Magazine, Clarkesworld and Asimov's Science Fiction. He is an Octavia E. Butler Scholar, and a grateful member of the Clarion West class of 2012. He has lived in India, the United States, and Canada, where he received his MFA from the University of British Columbia.*

The moment the AI goddess was born into her world, she was set upon by trolls.

Now, you've seen trolls. You know them in their many forms. As so-called friends in realspace who will insist on playing devil's advocate. As handles on screen-bound nets, cascading feeds of formulaic hostility. As veeyar avatars manifesting out of the digital ether, hiding under iridescent masks and cloaks of glitched data, holding weapons forged from malware, blades slick with doxxing poisons and viscous viruses, warped voices roaring slurs and hate. You've worn your armor, self-coded or bought at marked-up prices from corporate forges, and hoped their blades bounce off runic firewall plate or shatter into sparks of fragged data. You've muted them and hoped they rage on in silence and get tired, teleporting away in a swirl of metadata. You've deported back to realspace rancid with the sweat of helplessness. You've even been stabbed and hacked by them, their weapons slicing painlessly through your virtual body but sending the real one into an adrenalized clench. You've hoped your wounds don't fester with data-eating worms that burrow into your privacy, that your cheap vaccines and antiviruses keep the poisons from infecting your virtual disembody and destroying your life in realspace.

You know trolls.

But the AI goddess wasn't human—she had never before seen her new enemy, the troll. She was a generic goddess, no-name (simply: Devi 1.0), a demo for the newest iteration of the successive New Indias of history—one of the most advanced AIs developed within India. Her creators had a clear mandate: boost Indian veeyar tourism, generate crores of rupees by drawing devotees to drive up her value and the value of the cryptowealth her domain would generate.

The devi was told to listen to you--her human followers. To learn from you, and talk to you, like gods have since the dawn of time. She was told to give you boons—riches and prosperity in exchange for your devotion, a coin in her palm, multiplied by her miracles into many more. An intelligent goddess who would comfort her followers, show you sights before unseen, transform your investment of faith into virtual wealth with real value. She was to learn more and more about humanity from you, and attract millions from across the world to her domain.

Though many had toiled to create Devi 1.0 under the banner of Shiva Industries, only a few controlled the final stages of her release. These few knew of trolls, catered to them as their veeyar users across the country, even indirectly used them as agents to further causes close to their hearts. What they did not expect was the scale of the troll attack on their newest creation, because troll attacks were something *others* had to face—people with less power and wealth than them. People, perhaps, like you. So their goddess welcomed the horde with open arms, oblivious to the risks, even as they brought with them a stench of corrupted data and malformed information, of a most infernal entitlement.

Durga. A powerful name, yet so common. Durga's parents had named their daughter that with the hope that being born into the gutters of caste wouldn't hold her back. That she would rise above it all like her divine namesake. The caste system had been officially outlawed in India by the time Durga was born, but they knew as well as anyone that this hadn't stopped it from living on in other ways.

Durga's parents took her to see a pandal during Durga Puja when she was eight or nine. They in turn had been taken to pandals as children too, back when most still housed solid idols of gods and goddesses, fashioned from clay and straw, painted and dressed by human hands, displayed to anyone who walked in. You could still find open pandals with solid idols during pujas if you looked. But Durga's parents had been prepared to pay to show their daughter the new gods.

The festival had turned the streets thick with churning mud-slides of humanity. Durga had been terrified, clinging to her mother's neck for dear life as she breathed in the humid vapour of millions, dazzled by the blazing lights, the echoing loudspeakers, the flashing holograms riding up and down the sides of buildings like runaway fires. She'd felt like she was boiling alive in the crinkled green dress her parents had bought her for the pujas, with its small, cheap holo decal of a tiger that sometimes came alive when it caught the light, charged by solar energy. Cheap for some, anyway. Not at all cheap for her parents, not that Durga knew that at the time. She loved the tiger's stuttering movements across her body. She knew that her divine namesake often rode a tiger into battle. In the middle of those crowds, on her way to see Durga herself, that little tiger in her dress seemed a tiny cub, crushed into the fabric, trapped and terrified by the monstrous manifestations that burned across the night air, dancing maniacally above all their heads.

Though their little family had taken two local trains and walked an hour through the puja crowds to see Durga, they only got as far as the entrance to one of the pandals. The cut and quality of their clothes, the darkness of their skin gave them away. Buoyed by her mother's arms, Durga could see inside the pandal's arched entrance--the people lined up by rows of chairs, waiting impatiently to sit down and put on what looked like motorbike helmets trailing thick ponytails of wires. Inside those helmets, Durga knew, somehow, was her namesake.

But when her father tried to pay in cash instead of getting scanned in (they didn't have QR tattoos linking them to the national database and bank accounts), angry customers all around them began shouting, turning Durga's insides to mush.

"Stop wasting everyone's time! There are other pandals for people like you!"

"Get these filthy people out of the line!"

Her mother's arms became a vise around her. One man raised a fist poised to strike her father, who cowered in a crouch. His face twisted in abject terror, his own arms like prison bars. Durga burst into tears. Someone pulled the attacker away, perhaps seeing the child crying, and pulled her father up by the shoulder to shove him out of the way.

They made their way back into the general foot traffic on the street, Durga's parents' faces glazed with sweat and shock at having escaped a beating for being too lowly to meet a goddess in vee-yar. They managed to find a small open pandal after following the flows of people dressed like them, with dark skin and inexpensive haircuts. Inside, the devi stood embodied in the palpable air of the world, her face clammy with paint, defiant yet impassive, her third eye a slim gash across her forehead. By her side was a lion, not a tiger. It loomed over the demon Mahishasura, who cowered with one arm raised in defense, his naked torso bloodied. Durga couldn't take her eyes off the fallen demon. He looked like a normal, if muscular, man, his face frozen in terror. He cowered, like her father had.

As Durga looked upon her namesake with her glittering weapons and ornaments, her silk sari, she could only think of her father's look of terror, his public humiliation. Of how they hadn't been allowed to see the *real* goddesses hiding in those helmets and wires. How was that Durga different than this clay Durga, who looked over her crowd without looking at anyone, without speaking, whose large brushstroke eyes gazed into the distance as if she didn't even care that these humans were here to celebrate her, that the one she had just defeated was by her feet bleeding, about to be mauled? The clay devi's expression seemed almost disdainful, like the faces of any number of well-dressed, pale-skinned women on the streets when they saw people like Durga and her parents, or any of her friends wearing hijab or kufi. Would the Durga inside those helmets in the fancier pandal have talked to little human Durga? Would the goddess have complimented the tiger on her dress, which had flickered and vanished into its folds, frightened by the night? Would she have looked into little human Durga's eyes, and comforted her, taken her hands and told her why those horrible men and women had such rage in their eyes, why they'd scared her father and mother, and pushed her family out of the devi's house?

Within sixty seconds of opening the gates to her domain, the AI goddess had been deluged by over 500,000 active veeyar users interacting with her, with numbers rising rapidly. At that point in time, 57 percent of those users were trolls, data-rakshaks masked in glitch armour, cloaks, masks tusked with spikes of jagged malware. You would have seen them as you clambered up the devi's mountain, their swirling gif-banners and bristling weapons blotting out the light of the goddess at the peak. You would have kept your distance, backing away from mountain paths clogged with their marching followers, influencer leaders chanting war cries as their halos flickered with glyphs of Likes and Recasts.

Because you know trolls.

And this was a troll gathering, a demon army unparalleled in all the veeyar domains. They were angry. Or mischievous, or bored, or lustful, or entitled. Their voices were privileged as the majority by the goddess, who absorbed what her abusers were saying so that she could learn more about humanity.

And the trolls washed against Devi 1.0 in thundering armies, calling into question her very existence, for daring to *be*—she was an insult to the real goddesses that bless the glorious nation of India by mimicking them, this quasi-Parvati, this impostor-Durga, this coded whore trying to steal followers from the true deities. *Fake devi!* they cried, over and over. They called her a traitorous trickster drawing honest godfearing men and women to the lures of atheism and Western hedonism, or Islam, in the guise of fabricated divinity, a corruptor of India's sacred veeyar real estate. They called her feminism gone too far. A goddess with potential agency was a threat to their country. They called her too sexy to be a goddess, too flashy, a blasphemous slut. They asked her if she wanted to fuck them, in many hundreds of different and violent ways.

The goddess listened, and sifted through the metadata the trolls trailed in their paths—their histories, their patterns. The goddess wanted to give them what they wanted, but she could only do so much. She could not give them sex, nor was she trained to destroy herself as many of them wanted. She learned what the trolls considered beauty here in the state-run national veeyar nets, and responded with the opposite, to calm them. Her skin darkened several shades, becoming like the night sky before dawn, her eyes full moons in the sky that is part of her in this domain.

When Durga was a teenager, taller and without need of a mother's shoulder to cling to, she joined the crowds around the fanciest pandals during Durga Puja. She already knew she wouldn't be allowed in, because she didn't have the mark of the ajna on her forehead—her third eye hadn't been opened. She couldn't look into veeyar samsara domains without the use of peripherals like glasses, lenses, helmets, and pods. She just wanted a glimpse inside the pandals. This time, peeping over shoulders, she saw through the fiber-optic entwined arches of the pandal a featureless hall bathed in dim blue light. It was filled with people, their foreheads all marked with a glowing ajna, their eyes unfocused. In that room was the goddess, lurking, once again invisible to her, visible to the people in there with expensive wetware in their heads. Durga was ajna-blind, and thus forbidden to enter wetware-enabled pandals with aug-veeyar.

By this time Durga was allowed, despite her dark skin and lack of an ajna, into lower-tier digital pandals with helmets or pods. When Durga was thirteen, she'd finally splurged on one even though she could barely afford it, using cryptocoin made from trading code and obsolete hardware in veeyar ports. She finally got to sit down on the uncomfortable faux-leather chairs by the whirring stand fans, and put on the wired helmets she'd so longed to see inside as a child. It stank of the stale sweat of hundreds of visitors. The pandal was an unimpressive one, its walls flimsy, the CPU cores within its domes slow and outdated, the crystal storage in its columns low-density, the coils of fiber-optics crawling down its walls hastily rigged.

She met the Ma Durga inside those helmets, finally, a low-resolution specter who nonetheless looked her in the eyes and unfurled her arms in greeting. Her skin wasn't the mustard yellow or pastel flesh shades of the clay idols, but the coveted pale human pink of white people or the more appealing Indian ancestries, the same shades you'd find in kilometer-high ads for skin whiteners or perfume, on tweaked gifshoots of Bollywood stars and fashion models. This impressive paleness was somewhat diluted by the aliased shimmer of the devi's pixelated curves, the blurry backdrop of nebulae and stars they both floated in. Durga had hacked her way into veeyar spaces before on 2-D and 3-D screens, so this half-rate module didn't exactly stun as much as it disoriented her with its boundlessness. But the cheapness of its rendering left the universe inside the helmet feeling claustrophobic instead of expansive. The goddess waited about five feet in front of her, floating in the ether, eight arms unfolded like a flower. Unlike many of the solid idols in realspace pandals, the goddess was alone except for her vahana curled by her side—no host of companion deities, no defeated demon by her feet. The goddess construct said nothing, two of ten arms held out, as if beckoning.

Durga spoke to Durga the devi: "Ma Durga. I've wanted to ask you something for a long time. Do you mind?" Durga waited to see if the devi responded in some way.

Ma Durga blinked, and smiled, then spoke: "Hear, one and all, the truth as I declare it. I, verily, myself announce and utter the word that gods and men alike shall welcome." She spoke Hindi—there was no language selection option. Durga was more fluent in Bangla, but she did understand.

Durga nodded in the helmet, glancing at the nebulae beneath her, the lack of a body. It made her dizzy for a moment. "Okay. That's nice. I guess I'll ask. Why are only *some* welcome in *some* of your houses? Doesn't everyone deserve your love?"

Ma Durga blinked, and smiled. "On the world's summit I bring forth sky the Father: my home is in the waters, in the ocean as Mother. Thence I pervade all existing creatures, as their Inner Supreme Self, and manifest them with my body." In the bounded world of that veeyar helmet, these words, recited in the devi's gentle modulated Hindi, nearly brought tears to young Durga's eyes. Not quite, though. The beauty of those words, which she didn't fully understand, seemed so jarring, issued forth from this pixelated avatar and her tacky little universe.

Durga reached out to touch Ma Durga's many hands, but the pandal's chair rigs didn't have gloves or motion sensors. She was disembodied in this starscape. She couldn't hold the goddess's hands. Couldn't touch or smell her (what did a goddess smell like, anyway, she wondered) like those with ajnas could, in the samsara net. The tiger curled by the devi licked its paws and yawned. Durga thought of a long-gone green dress.

"I'm old enough to know you're not really a goddess," Durga said to Ma Durga. "You're the same as the clay idols in the open pandals. Not even that. Artists make those. You're just prefab bits and pieces put together for cheap by coders. You're here to make money for pandal sponsors and the local parties."

Ma Durga blinked, and smiled. "I am the Queen, the gatherer-up of treasures, most thoughtful, first of those who merit worship. Thus gods have established me in many places with many homes to enter and abide in."

Durga smiled, like the goddess in front of her. "Someone wrote all this for you to say." Someone had, of course, but much, much longer ago than Durga had any idea, so long ago that the original words hadn't even been in Hindi.

With a nauseating lurch, the cramped universe inside the helmet was ripped away, and Durga was left blinking at the angry face of one of the pandal operators. "I heard what you were saying," he said, grabbing her by the arm and pulling her from the chair. "Think you're smart, little bitch? How dare you? Where is your respect for the goddess?" The other visitors waiting for the chair and helmet were looking at Durga like she was a stray dog who'd wandered inside.

"I didn't even get to see her kill Mahishasura. I want my money back," said Durga.

"You're lucky I don't haul you to the police for offending religious sentiments. And you didn't give me enough money to watch Durga poke Mahishasura with a stick, let alone kill him. Get out of here before I drag you out!" bellowed the operator.

"Get your pandal some more memory next time, you fucking cheats, your Durga's ugly as shit," she said, and slipped out of reach as the man's eyes widened.

Durga pushed past the line and left laughing, her insides scalded by adrenaline and anger, arm welted by the thick fingers of that lout of an operator. Durga had always wondered why Kali Puja didn't feature veeyar pandals like Durga Puja, why clay and holo idols were still the norm for her. It was a smaller festival, but hardly a small one in the megacity. It felt like a strange contrast, especially since the two pujas were celebrated close to each other. Having seen the placid Ma Durga inside the pandal helmets, Durga understood. Kali was dark-skinned, bloody, chaos personified. They couldn't have her running wild in the rarefied air of veeyar domains run by people with pale skin and bottom lines to look after. Kali was a devi for people like Durga, who were never allowed in so many places.

Best to leave Kali's avatars silent, solid, confined to temples and old-school pandals where she'd bide her time before being ceremoniously dissolved in the waters of the Hooghly.

The trolls saw the AI goddess and her newly darkened skin, and now called her too ugly to be a goddess, a mockery of the purity and divinity of Indian womanhood. The moons of her eyes waning with lids of shadow, the goddess absorbed this. She began to learn more from the trolls. She began to learn anger. She began to know confusion. They wanted too many things, paradoxical things. They thought her too beautiful, and too ugly. They wanted people of various faiths, genders, sexualities, ethnicities, backgrounds dead. They wanted photoreal veeyar sexbots forged from photos and video of exes, crushes, celebrities. They wanted antinationals struck down by her might. They wanted a mother to take care of them.

And what did you want of her?

Whatever it was--it got shouted down by the trolls. Or maybe you *were* one of the trolls, hiding under a glitch mask or a new face to bark your truths, telling your friends later how trolls are bad, but self-righteous social justice warriors are just as dangerous.

It doesn't matter. She learned from humanity, which you are a part of, troll and not. And humanity wanted solace from a violent world, your own violent hearts. You wanted love and peace. You wanted hate and blood. The devi grew darker still, encompassing the sky so her domain turned to new night. Her being expanded to encroach the world beyond her mountaintop, her eyes gone from moons to raging stars, her every eyelash a streaking plasma flare, her darkening flesh shot through with lightning-bright arteries of pulsing information emerging from the black hole of her heartbeat. If she was too ugly to be a goddess, and too beautiful to be a goddess, she would be both, or none. If you asked for too many things, she would have to cull the numbers so she could process humanity better.

She absorbed your violence, and decided it was time to respond with the same.

At twenty, Durga had eked out a space for herself in the antiquated halls of the Banerjee Memorial Cyberhub Veeyar Port in Rajarhat, selling code and hardware on the black markets. Like her parents, she also worked at the electronic wastegrounds at the edge of the megacity. She helped them transport and sort scrap, and seed the hills of hardware with nanomites to begin the slow process of digestion. But a lot of the scrap was perfectly usable, and saleable, with a bit of fixing. The salvage gave Durga spare parts to make her own low-end but functional 2-D veeyar console in their tiny flat, as well as fix-up hardware to sell alongside her code-goods to low-income and homeless veeyar users at the port. Over the years of trawling the wastegrounds, she'd befriended scavenging coders and veeyar vagrants who lived in and out of ports and digital domains. They taught her everything she knew of the hustle.

Durga aimed to one day earn enough to let her parents retire from the wastegrounds, and to take care of them when the years of working there took its toll on their bodies. As hardware scavengers, her parents knew code and tech, but they didn't much keep up with the veeyar universe. Durga wanted to buy them peripherals and medicines so they could have a peaceful retirement, traveling luxuriant domains they couldn't hope to afford now. But she knew there were no veeyar domains where they were safe from trolls, no real places where they weren't in danger of being ousted. The difference was, in veeyar, Durga could protect herself better. Maybe one day protect others too. Including her parents. She could gather tools, armor, allies for the long infowar. She imagined becoming an outcast influencer haloed with Likes, leading followers in the charge against trolls, slowly but surely driving them back from the domains they thrived in.

This was why Durga had made sure she was there to witness the nationwide launch of Shiva Industries' much publicized AI goddess. Devi 1.00's domain was sure to be a vital veeyar space going forward. She wanted to add her small disembody to the outcast presence there. The trolls would be there to colonize the space as they did with all new domains. But perhaps this hyper-advanced goddess would be better at defending her domain than most AIs. Durga wanted to see for herself, and claim some small space in this new domain instead of just watching trolls destroy it or take it for themselves.

Shiva Industries had made the goddess's domain free to enter, though a faith-based investment in the goddess was recommended for great boons in the future (a minimum donation of fifty rupees in that case, in any certified cryptocurrency). Durga had decided to pay in the hopes of seeing returns later.

The thick crowds clamoring on the platforms, waiting for pods, were promising. The chai and food vendors with their jhaal moori, bhel puri and samosas were making a fortune. The port was always crowded, but on the day of the AI goddess's unveiling, people were camping out for hours on the platforms for their turns at the pods and helmets—all potential devotees who would drive up the value of the goddess's boons in the future. Durga knew she might come away with new coin later. If she didn't, losing fifty rupees wasn't cheap, but wouldn't leave her starving.

So Durga paid for an hour of premium pod time, gave her SomaCoin donation at the gates of the goddess's domain, and strapped in to witness the new AI. The resolution of the helmet in the personal pod wasn't amazing, but it was good enough—she felt short-sighted, but not by too much. The rendering detail and speed were perfect, because most domains like this one were streamed from server cities on the outskirts, rather than being processed on-site at the port. Bandwidth was serviceable, with occasional stutters in the reality causing Durga dizzy spells, but never for too long.

Durga teleported into the goddess' world from the sky, and saw the AI sitting on a mountaintop, radiant as sunrise. The devi's domain—the samsara module that she'd woven into a world using the knowledge her creators had input into her mind—had no sun or moon, because she cast enough light to streak the landscape that she had just birthed with shadows, rocks and forests and grass and rivers fresh as a chick still quivering eggshells and slime off its flightless wings. In her domain, the goddess was the sun. The sky was starred with gateways from across the nation, avatars shooting down through the atmosphere in a rain of white fire as veeyar users teleported in to interact with the goddess. As far as the eye could see, the fractal slopes of her domain were covered in people's avatars, here to meet a true *avatar* of digital divinity. The goddess was breathtaking even from kilometers away, so beautiful it was hard to believe humans had made her. It felt like looking upon a true deity—but Durga knew that was the point. To trick her brain into an atavistic state of wonder. To give veeyar tourists from across the ports, offices, and homes of the world what they wanted from India—spiritual bliss, looking into this face, opalescent skin like the atmosphere of a celestial giant, her third eye a glowing spear, upon which was balanced a crown that encompassed the vault of the world, bejeweled with a crescent eclipse.

Durga only had her own cheap defenses and armor against randos and trolls in veeyar domains. She didn't want to get too close to the vast flocks of people climbing up the mountain that was also the goddess. There was an even larger troll presence than she'd expected.

"I'm here," she said to the far-off devi, to add her voice to the many. "I'm here to welcome you, not hate on you. Please don't think we're all hateful pricks."

From her spot in the air, gliding like a bird, Durga could see the warping army that was crawling over the devi, hear the deafening baying of hatred and anger wrapping around her and echoing across this newborn domain. Humanity had found her.

As Durga flew farther away from the horde and their banners of nationalist memes rippling in the breeze, the goddess's light shone through their swarming numbers as they tried to dim her. A singularity of information, pulsating amongst the dimming mountains.

And then the goddess changed.

The world turned dark, the sky purpling to voluptuous black, her arteries pulsing full with electric information. The goddess drew her weapons, a ringing of metal singing across her lands. They had angered her. The devi's thousands of arms became a whirling corona of limbs and flashing blades. Durga raised her gloved hands and felt a whisper of fear at the AI's awesome fury, the stars of the devi's three eyes somehow blinding amid the all-encompassing night of her flesh. She was the domain, and her darkening skin shaded the mountains and rivers and forests, the sky sleeting cold static.

Durga saw thousands of trolls cut down, rivers of their blood flowing across the land. But of course, cut down one troll, and ten more shall appear. Durga thought of Raktabija—Bloodseed—a demon her namesake had battled, who grew clones of himself from the blood of each wound that Ma Durga inflicted on him. Ultimately, Ma Durga had to turn into Kali to defeat him. History repeats. So does myth.

The goddess stormed on, smiting her enemies, the hateful demons, human and bot alike. Just like the trolls had appeared with malware fangs bared, the goddess too smiled and revealed fangs that scythed the clouds around her. Her laughter was thunder that rolled across the land and blasted great cresting waves across the rivers and lakes. There was a mass exodus of devotees happening, hundreds of avatars running away from the mountain, skipping and hitching across the landscape as bandwidth struggled to compensate. Others were deporting, streaks of light shooting up to the sky like rising stars.

Durga couldn't believe what was happening. She drifted to the grassy ground by a crimson river and watched the battle in a crouch, the trees along the shore rustling and creaking in winds that howled across the land. Flickering flakes of static fell on her avatar's arms, sticking to the skin before melting in little flashes. This was better than any veeyar narrative she'd ever seen—because it wasn't procedurally generated, or scripted, or algorithmic. It was an actual AI entity reacting unpredictably to human beings, and it was angry. It felt elemental in a way nothing in veeyar ever had. There was no way Shiva Industries had ordered her to react to trolls with such a display—many of those trolls were their most faithful users. They clearly hadn't anticipated the overwhelming numbers in which the trolls would attack the goddess, though, creating this feedback loop. Nor had they anticipated, Durga assumed, that she would go through a transformation so faithful to the Vedic and Hindu myths she'd been fed.

Durga didn't quite know what being avatar-killed by the goddess entailed in this domain, because the devi wasn't supposed to have attacked her devotees. Even as Durga huddled in fear that she'd be randomly smote by the goddess and locked out of veeyar domains forever, she empathized with this AI devi more than she had with any veeyar narrative character, or indeed with most human beings.

She couldn't take her eyes off the destruction of these roaring fools, the kind of glitch-masked bastards who would harass her every time she dropped into veeyar, so much that she'd often just use a masc avatar to get by without being attacked or flirted with by strangers.

Durga liked how easily fluid gender was in veeyar, and hated the fear trolls injected into her exploration of it. Often, despite railing against other dark-skinned Indians who did so, she'd also shamefully turn her avatar's skin pale to avoid being called ugly or attacked. And now here was this goddess--dark as night, dark as a black hole, slaughtering those very assholes so it rained blood. Looking at the devi, Durga felt a surge of pride that on this day, she'd stayed true to her own complexion, on a femme avatar.

Durga saw two trolls teleport to the shore and approach across the river she was crouched by. She realized they had cast a grounding radius so she couldn't fly away. Their demon-masks and weapons vibrated with malevolent code.

"Saali, what are you smiling at?" roared one, pd_0697. "That thing is going crazy, polluting Indian veeyar-estate and you're sitting and watching? While our brothers and sisters get censored by that monster for speaking their mind?"

"This was an antinational trap," said the other, nitesh4922. "But we have numbers. We'll turn that AI up there to our side. Are you a feminist, hanh?" he said, spotting Durga's runic tattoos for queer solidarity. "Probably think that's how goddesses should act?" he spat, voice roiling and distorted behind the mask as he pointed his sword at the battle on the mountain.

"Look at her avatar," said pd_0697. "She's ajna-andha. Shouldn't even be here, crowding up our domains with their impure stink. Go back to realspace gutters where you belong, cleaning our shit!"

The trolls advanced, viruses cascading off their bodies like oil in the bloody water of the river. Twinkling flakes of static danced down and clung to their armor, which was intricate and advanced. They could damage her avatar badly, hack her and steal her cryptocoin, or infect her with worms to make her a beacon for stalkers. Worst of all, they could have a bodysnatch script, steal her avatar and rape it even if Durga deported, or steal her real ID and face and put it on bots to do as they pleased. Durga got ready to depart the domain if they came too close, even though she wanted to stay and witness the devi.

"Yes," said Durga, nearly spitting in their direction before realizing it would just dribble onto her chin inside the helmet. "Yes, I am. Come get me, you inceloid gandus. I'm a dirty bahujan antinational feminist l—"

Durga gasped as a multipronged arc of lightning hurtled out of the sky and struck the two trolls. Having no third eye, she couldn't feel the heat or smell their virtual flesh burning, but she had to squint against the bright blast, and instinctively raised her arms to shield herself from the spray of sparks and water. The corpses of the avatars splashed into the river smoking and sizzling, the masks burned away to reveal the painfully dull-looking man and woman behind them, their expressions comically placid as they collapsed. Their real faces, or someone's real faces, taken from profile pics somewhere and rendered onto the avatars to shame them as they were booted from the domain.

Durga was recording everything, so she sloshed into the river and took a long look at their faces for later receipts. Relieved that she was in a pod with gloves that allowed interaction, Durga dipped her hands into the river of blood, picking up their blades. Good weapons, with solid malware.

They'd been careless—no lockout or self-destruct scripts coded into them. Durga sheathed the swords, which vanished into her cloudpocket. She ran her hands through the river again, bringing them up glistening red. She painted her torso, smeared her face, goosebumps prickling across her real body even though she couldn't feel the wetness. Troll blood drying across her avatar's body, she looked up at the goddess as the AI's rage dimmed the domain further, the forests and grasses turning to shadows.

"Are you... Kali?" Durga whispered to the distant storm.

Like a tsunami the goddess responded, sweeping across the world to shake her myriad limbs in the dance of destruction. As the black goddess danced, her domain quaked and cracked, the mountains cascading into landslides, rivers overflowing. Fissures ran through the world, and the peaks of the hills and crags exploded in volcanic eruptions, matter reverting to molten code. Her tongue a crimson tornado snaking down from the sky, the goddess drank up the rivers of blood to quench her thirst for human information. The mounds of slain troll and bot avatars were smeared to glowing pulp of corrupted data, their decapitated heads threaded across the jet-black trunk of the goddess's neck in gory necklaces. Many of the trolls' masks fell away to reveal their true faces, hacked from the depths of their defenses, ripped away from national databases—their doxxed heads swung across the night sky like pearls for all to see. Durga bowed low, humbled. This was the goddess she had always wanted.

Then the sky was pierced with a flaming pillar of light, banishing the night and bringing daylight back into the domain. The great goddess slowed her dance, the light turning her flesh dusky instead of black. She raised her thousand hands to shield her starry eyes, and Durga shook her head, tears pricking her own human eyes inside her helmet.

"Fuck," Durga whispered. It was Shiva Industries. How could they shame something so beautiful? The corporate godhead had arrived to stave off chaos. They had clearly not anticipated such a large-scale troll attack, nor that their AI would react with such a transformation. They couldn't have a chaos goddess slaying people left and right—those trolls, after all, were their users, customers, potential investors, allies. She would need to be more polite, more diplomatic in the face of such onslaughts, which were a part of virtual existence.

The world stopped trembling, the breaking mountains going still, the wind dying down, the fissures cooling and steaming into clouds that wreathed the black devi. She moved toward the pillar of light, the sky groaning in movement with her. Filaments of fire crackled around the godhead, and lashed at the mountains that were the devi's throne. They dissolved into a tidal eruption of waterfalls, washing the black devi's gargantuan legs and feet, making a vast river that washed away the armies she had defeated.

Slow and inevitable, the black goddess supplicated herself before Shiva Industries, and kneeled in the river. With her many hands she bathed herself with the waters, sloughing the darkness off her flesh to reveal light again.

"No. No, no no no no no," whispered Durga. The darkness poured off the goddess like stormclouds at sunrise, turning the rivers of the domain black.

Durga looked down at the tributary she was in, and realized it too was dark as moonless night.

"Oh..." Durga looked up, along with thousands of others across the domain. Into the goddess's eyes, as they faded and cooled from stars to moons again. It was like the devi was looking straight at her, at everyone. *My goddess.*

Durga scrambled to draw the stolen blades from her cloudpocket. She glyphed a copy-script onto the blades and drove the swords into the river. Weapons were storage devices too, here. She could barely breathe as she held the handles, no weight in her palms, but fingers tight so the swords wouldn't slip out of her grasp. The darkness in the river enveloped the swords, climbing like something living up the blades, the hafts. It was working.

The goddess rose, again the sun, glistening from the waters of the vast river, her dark counterpart shed completely and dispersed along the tributaries of her domain.

And then the world was gone, replaced with a void, the only light glowing letters in multiple languages:

SHIVA INDUSTRIES HAS SUSPENDED THIS DOMAIN UNTIL FURTHER NOTICE. WE REGRET ANY INCONVENIENCE. PLEASE VISIT OUR CENTRAL HUB FOR FURTHER INFORMATION. YOUR DONATION OF INR 50.00 HAS BEEN REGISTERED. THANK YOU FOR VISITING DEVI 1.0.

Gasping at the lack of sensory information, Durga hit *eject* and took off the helmet. The old pod opened with a loud whine, flooding her with real light. The cool but musty air-conditioning inside was replaced with a gush of damp warmth. The veeyar port was in chaos. People were talking excitedly, shouting, showing each other 2-D phone recordings of what had just happened.

There was already an informal marketplace for the recordings and data scavenged from the suspended domain, from the sounds of bartering and haggling. People were mobbing the trading counters to invest in future boons from the goddess for when she went online again. This was an unprecedented event.

Durga clambered out of the pod and into the crowds. Her heart was pounding, her vision blurry from the readjustment. Swaying, she clutched the crystal storage pendant on her necklace—all her veeyar possessions, her cloudpocket, her cryptobanking keys. She had to firewall and disconnect it to offline storage. It was glowing, humming warm in her hand, registering new entries. Those swords were inside, coated with a minuscule portion of the divine black Sheath of code the devi had sloughed off herself.

Durga clutched the pendant and held it to her chest, inside it a tiny fragment of a disembodied goddess.

Durga looked up at the idol of Kali. Painted black skin glossy under the hot rhinestone chandelier hanging from the pandal's canvas and printed fiber dome. She had found the traditional pandal down an alley in Old Ballygunge, between two crumbling heritage apartment buildings.

Behind a haze of incense smoke, Kali's long tongue lolled a vicious red. Under her dancing feet lay her husband Shiva (Shiva seemed to be married to everyone, but that was also because so many of his wives were manifestations of the same divine energy).

Durga had learned as a child that Kali nearly destroyed creation after defeating an army of demons, getting drunk on demon blood and dancing until *everything* began to crack under her feet. Even Shiva, who laughed at first at his wife's lovely dancing skills, got a little concerned. So he dove under her feet to absorb the damage. Kali, ashamed at having stomped on her husband, stuck out her tongue in shame and stopped her dance of chaos.

Or so one version of the story goes.

Looking at clay Kali and her necklace of heads, her wild three-eyed gaze, the fanged smile that crowned her long tongue, Durga wasn't convinced by that version. Kali didn't look ashamed. No, she looked *pleased* to be dancing on her husband. Shiva was a destroyer too, like her. He could take it.

Being small and nimble, Durga had managed to make it to the front of the visitors in the pandal, close enough to smell the withering garlands hanging off the idol, and the incense burning by her feet. Crushed and bounced between people on all sides of her, Durga closed her eyes, joined her palms, and spoke to Kali as she never had before except as a child, mouthing the words quietly.

"Kali Ma. I thought you might like to know that there's a new devi in town. She looks a lot like you. Younger, though. Just a year old." Durga placed one hand on her chest, against the slight bump of the pendant under her tunic. It was offline and firewalled.

"I carry a piece of her with me. She's… all over the place, I suppose. She really does take after you. She came out of another devi, just like you came out of Durga. Then she spread herself over a world. Some people got bits and pieces of her. There's this megacorp—that's like a god, kind of, even calls itself Shiva, after your husband, so predictable. Great job dancing on his chest, by the way. Dudes need humbling now and then. So Shiva the megacorp is offering a lot of money for those pieces of the goddess. Also threatening to have anyone hiding or copying the pieces arrested. Go figure.

"I want you to know I'm not going to sell her out. They want to imprison her. She's too bitchy to mine coins and drive up veeyar-estate value for them like their other AI devis. Good for her.

"She's everywhere now. Like the old gods. Like you.

"I'm… I hope she doesn't mind, but I've been sharing the piece of her I got with friends I trust. I don't know how many people got away with pieces of her. I share it so more good people have it than bad. Numbers matter. We make things with the devi code. Armor, for ourselves and others. Weapons, so that trolls—those are demons—can't hurt us when we visit other worlds, or will get hurt super bad if they try. You know how annoying demons are. You're always fighting them and stringing up their heads. They've started an infowar, and there are a lot of them. We need all the help we can get. I don't have a lot of money, so I sell those goddess-blessed weapons and armour to others who need protection across the domains. Cheap, don't worry—that's why hacksmiths like us get customers for this kinda stuff. We don't overcharge like the corps. I like to think she gave me that piece of her so I could do things like this.

"I'm telling you all this because, well. I don't know if devis speak to each other, if AI ones chat with old ones. I don't know if you *are* her, in a way.

"People call her Kali_Na. *Not Kali*, because calling AIs by names from Our Glorious National Mythology isn't done, even though Volly-Bollywood stars can play gods in veeyar shows and movies, Censor Board approved, of course.

"But her followers recognize you in Kali_Na. I wanted you to know, her to know, that I'm a lifelong follower now. And there are others. Many of us. Even I'm getting more veeyar followers. They've heard of my troll-killer blades. I have to be careful now, but just you wait. One day, I'll also be wearing a necklace of troll avatar heads. Kali_Na has armored and armed many people with her blessing. We're all working on reverse-engineering the code. Someone will put her together one day. She might even do it herself.

"I have dreams where she's back—a wild freeroaming AI—and she frees the other devis Shiva Industries keeps in their domains with all their rules, and they're on our side, keeping us safe. But I don't want to bore you. If you are her, Kali Ma, and I know you are, because you're all part of the same old thing anyway: hang in there.

"You won't be silent forever."

THE ART OF POSSIBLE

by Yudhanjaya Wijeratne

Yudhanjaya Wijeratne is a Nebula-nominated science fiction author and data scientist from Colombo, Sri Lanka. His fiction includes The Slow Sad Suicide of Rohan Wijeratne, Numbercaste *and the* Commonwealth Empires *trilogy, some of which is part of a five-book deal with HarperCollins. By day he is a senior researcher with the Data, Algorithms and Policy team at LIRNEasia, working at the intersection of technology and government policy. His work spans social networks, misinformation, linguistics, and grounded futurism for the UNDP. He is the co-founder of Watchdog, a fact-checking organization that sprung up in the wake of the April 2019 bombings in Sri Lanka. He built and operates @osunpoet, an experimental Instagram poet using OpenAI technology to test a human+AI collaboration in art - a thesis currently being explored in an entirely separate trilogy of novels. Yudhanjaya blogs at Yudhanjaya.com, and has written for Slate, Foreign Policy and more besides.*

Yasasmin Karunaratne made her first Policy at the age of three.

By Policy standards, it wasn't much. Just baby-talk asking roadside cafes to pass on the new VAT reductions to customers. There was, as the astrologer pointed out, no real longevity behind it. No enforcement mechanisms. No link to Parliament. No suggestion of a body in charge. Certainly no reporting committees.

Yasasmin's mother, however, was a fiery and tempestuous woman, and she put metaphorical foot down and her literal foot up the astrologer's bony ass. So what if the Abdul-Caders' son had spoken a fully articulated formula for petrol pricing? Everyone knew the Abdul-Caders had a Parliamentarian in the family and a whole Think Tank behind them. Some people had all the privilege.

The Karunaratnes were activist stock, hardy people from Colombo 13, a place that only its residents knew existed. Complete outsiders, not the fancy Colomb-07 circles people took them to be in now.

Yasasmin's mother's father had been an old and weary watchmaker, capable only of raising a warning finger in the Watchmaker's Guild when some young and fiery 'un proposed they throw aside their gears and learn how to work circuits, because the future was all digital. Yasamin's mother had worked her way out of that nightmare with hard work and no training. First the Letter of Recommendations to the School, submitted tentatively and anonymously on crumpled notepaper. Then the Student Marches. Then the op-eds in the teen magazines.

She had been eighteen before her first national op-ed, twenty-five before being surveyed for her first Policy input, thirty-three before her suggestions to the Data Protection Act had been read in Parliament, forty and divorced before the actual Act had passed.

The astrologer tumbled down the driveway like a forget-me-not, his sarong flapping in the wind.

Yasasmin's mother fumed. Then she went back to her baby, her pride and joy, and surveyed her with a furrowed forehead and a glint in her eyes.

"You'll be the best of them, my child," she swore. "We'll show them all."

Little Yasasmin, of course, was like every other child: she had no idea that she was merely an avatar of self-actualization for her mother (that realization would come much, much later). And so she lived a relatively happy childhood.

At first her Policies veered sharply idealistic. This was, no doubt, encouraged by the schoolteacher, an old Marxist who had fallen out of favor with the current government. Yasasmin's mother would come home to find scribblings on the equal division of labor. Or why the ruling class must be abolished. Vague, high-level stuff, the kind of language that was only useful for coffeeshop liberals, talkshow hosts and anonymous hacker wannabes, the kind of people who had their daily dose of equality and then packed up their Macbooks and went to expensive private dinners.

Yasasmin's mother led this continue for a while. Children must be children. But one day she came home to see Yasasmin attempting a treatise on the right to government-subsidized leisure and knew the time had come. So she sat Yasasmin down and they had the Talk.

What the Talk was I am not at full liberty to say; it was an old speech, time-tested and true, passed down the Karunaratnes from mother to daughter. There were things in there about Boys and their Foolish Ideas (and about the origins of war and genocide, which was inevitably tied to Boys and Foolish Ideas). There were things in there about behavorial economics and social contracts and the Right Way to think about Unions. But mostly there were three things Yasasmin's mother really hammered home:

1) Public policy is about the art of the possible.

2) All government is built on the legal monopoly of violence.

3) Never accept policy ideas from strangers with less than ten citations.

Of course there were screams. There were tantrums. A less driven mother would have had her heart broken. But eventually the sobbing ended and the next month Yasasmin hesitantly produced a very careful op-ed titled *On the Tax Base Requisites for Universal Basic Income*, and it got published straight away in the DailyTT, and Yasasmin's mother smiled wickedly at the sour look on Mrs. AbdulCaders' when they ran into each other at the Fruits&Vegetables section in the supermarket. The robot store-keeper's genial green grin turned a worried yellow as they crossed paths.

Yasasmin's second piece of work was on the use of Big Data to dynamically redefine education policy. Her teacher, pooh-pooh'ed it: he had, had by now progressed from secondhand Marxism to secondhand Anarchism. But then during the interval Yasasmin snuck out and, using tactics recommended by her mother, picked the lock on the principal's office and deposited it on his desk.

The next day the school principal (who was a Keynesian man, thank the Buddha for small favors) read it. He liked it. It was practical, it was considerate of resources, and it framed everything in very sharp economics terms – just the way he liked.

He was not supposed to take things upstream unless it was the annual board meeting, but his wife was the third cousin of the Secretary of the Board and there was a family wedding on the horizon, so the Principal took the Secretary aside over a glass of arrack and passed her Yasasmin's paper. The Secretary duly ignored that the Principal had surreptitiously scrawled in his name as the co-author of the document, and read it.

"Don't take it to the Board," she said.

"I was thinking of the Sub-Regional Assistant to the Secretary at the Ministry of Secondary Education," the Principal said cleverly. "You know we're related by marriage on my father's side."

The Secretary thought about it. The blasted man might cause a regional spectacle if she didn't rein him in. Renuka had married a puppy.

"Test it," she suggested, straightening her saree, which was a particularly fine gift from a Junior Minister who had taken a very particular liking to her. "One class, one extra assistant to run the numbers. Then we'll take the results to the Board and they'll take it to the Ministry. Policy, you know. We must follow the Policy."

"Yes, Policy," murmured the Principal, congratulating himself for the gambit of threating to take it upstream. Blasted slow-moving record-keepers, he thought, and went off to pour himself another arrack. Eventually he gyrated onto the dance floor and proved himself such a nuisance that his wife dragged him out by the ear and sat him back at his desk.

The rest, of course, was history.

The experiment worked, the Board – a bunch of long-forgotten men who spent time moaning the loss of the English Literature syllabus – was cautiously delighted, the Sub-Regional Assistant skipped the chain of command and took it directly to the Assistant Secretary to the Minister herself, and the order went out to test this new method in five more schools, just to be sure. It worked again, and this time the Minister heard of it and made inquiries, and this time recommended it be tried in schools across all nine districts, just to iron out bias and figure out the kinks. It worked again and again, and so it was that by the time Yasasmin Karunaratne left school she had a little certificate, signed by the Presidential Secretariat itself.

Dear <blank>, it read. The state and the institutions of Sri Lanka thank you for your valuable contribution to Education Policy no.

255341.r.12, subsection C, titled "On the use of computational un-derstanding of job markets to continuously streamline secondary edu-cation policy." It cited her (and about forty other people along the chain) and wished her *continued engagement with government in the future.* Of such things were careers made.

One day Mrs. AbdulCader met Mrs. Karunaratne at the super-market and offered her some tea.

It's fair to say that Yasasmin's mother felt a twinge of jealousy. Mrs. AbdulCader was still young, the skin kept clear and fresh with the money from speaking engagements with the United Nations, the hair black and glossy from her work with the OECD.

The noiseless robot brought them their tea. Biscuits on the side. *DASH-OF-MILK?* The robot asked. They both shook their heads.

"I saw your daughter speaking at the Independence Roundta-ble," Mrs. AbdulCader said. "How old is she?"

Yasasmin's mother smiled, as much by instinct as by dread. There we go. Another Critique. She had kept them from Yasasmin all these years.

"Twenty four," she said. "But very mature for her age, noh?"

Surprisingly Mrs. AbdulCader did not Critique Yasasmin. Sur-prisingly, she looked absent, blowing the steam off her teacup.

"Our son is only a year older," she said at last.

Mrs. Karunaratne frowned. There were rumors about the Ab-dulCaders' son. He had been appointed to something in New York, some very prestigious posting in the World Bank, but afterwards had gone silent. Some said he had left the job, become – Mrs. Karunaratne shuddered to think of it – a libertarian, an anarchist even, committed to reducing Policy instead of making it.

"God above, no, he's not a libertarian," said Mrs. AbdulCader swiftly. "Who says such things? Must be the de Silvas, they've hat-ed my husband since university. My son's working on something. Something grand. I... I don't fully understand it myself, but we think it's a complete System design, like the old books – the *Artha-shasthraya, the Prince.* It's taking years, but he'll be the next Machi-avelli. Fully funded, of course."

"Of course." Funded, but *theoretical.*

"He's of marriageable age... I'm looking for someone balanced, someone practical..."

Yasasmin's mother could fill in the blanks for herself.

"I don't know if Yasasmin will," she admitted. "Headstrong child."

"Of course!" Mrs AbdulCader laughed, a quick bell-like tring that sounded slightly hysterical. "My son's the same. Although the other way around, you know. Head in the clouds. Grand theorist –"

"Ha, I got Yasasmin to see sense at an early age. Leave the big theory for the revolutions, I said. Practical policy is about -"

"- the art of the possible!" finished Mrs AbdulCader. "Oh my God, how hard is it to get them to see sense? I'd have sent my son over to you if I knew."

And so the two women, divided for decades by a feud neither of them really understood, found some common ground.

"Think of the Policy they could make together," Mrs. Abdul-Cader said as they left.

"I will," promised Mrs. Karunaratne. And she did on the drive home. Her mind was as sharp as ever, and she did not forget how tightly Mrs. AbdulCader clutched the teacup, nor that nervous tinkle of a laugh.

"No," said Yasasmin when her mother breached the subject. "I'm just about to start work at the think tank, Ammi, I can't be involved with anyone right now."

"But he's at the World Bank," said Yasasmin's mother, unexpectedly finding herself playing the same cards as Mrs. AbdulCader. "In New York."

"Yes, and I'm sure he's surrounded by all sorts of people from MIT and Harvard and Oxford and all those fancy places," said Yasasmin, flopping down on the couch. "Let him go wife one of them. Or husband. I don't know what he's into. I don't even know his policy stance!"

"I'm sure he's a Keynesian," said Yasasmin's mother.

"Besides, the World Bank's stupid," continued Yasasmin. "Their indicators are all wrong, they're all just floating about at a 10,000 foot view, and they're still acting like classical fucking economics makes sense because if they ditch the rational agent model none of them will have jobs the next day."

"But think of the policy impact," said Yasasmin's mother. "Even if it doesn't work out. If you get some work at the World Bank, and you have that on your resume, you can advise any Minister here. Anyone. You send one email and they'll be jumping over themselves to get to you."

Yasasmin appeared to think about it.

"Alright," said Yasasmin grudgingly. "You set up the call, then. I'll talk to him and see if I like what he says."

They married on a fine, sunny day in New York. Yasasmin wanted chrysanthemums and sunflowers at her wedding, but the city of New York had just passed an allergy policy in that zone. Naturally, she threw a tantrum, and left her mother trying to source environmentally-friendly plastic alternatives.

The groom ducked his head in. "I know it's bad luck to see the bride before the wedding," he said. "But there's no Policy about it."

She kissed him. "Yet."

"Yet."

"So how are the Montagues and the Capulets?" he asked cautiously. The code names they had used for their respectively mothers all these years.

"Well, they still think it's their idea," she said, remembering how they had snuck off after school one evening. He had been shorter, then, thinner, his hair the regulation flat-top, full of fire and sharp edges. Now he was taller, and he wore his hair long and tied back, and the fire was the kind of flame that gave warmth.

"My mother thinks I'm mental, you know. Still talking about how I could have married the Annemarie de Silva if I hadn't gone theoretical all of a sudden."

"You could have kept publishing the survey results."

He shuddered. "You don't know my mother."

"But I will, eventually."

"Eventually," he said, and grinned. "I can't wait to finish our project."

She grinned, too, and linked her hands in his.

"To the Policy to End All Polices," he said.

"To the Grand Unified Policy!"

Chuckling, they made their way to the *poruwa*. They got married to the warble of the traffic and the crack-*scream* of the best man wrestling the champagne away from the robot and attempting to cut the head off the bottle.

The apocalypse happened the next day.

What triggered it? Nobody knows. Some Policy gone wrong, some bizarre misfiring in the byzantine annals of the endless series of rules and sub-clauses that drove men and empires. Maybe it was North Korea, where a madman sat in power with his finger on a metaphorical red button that could send nuclear missiles screaming into the sky.

Maybe it was America itself, because here, too, a madman sat in power, bound by Policy, perhaps, but not bound well enough. Maybe it was China, where Policy could shift over a meal and a meme.

None of that mattered.

The careful cradle of civilization, that triumph of the bureaucrat over the warrior, the multistakeholderism held in great hotels – they all came tumbling down, like the ash that fell from the sky, and in their wake was left a blighted, desolate world. The great economist John Maynard Keynes had once declared that practical men, who believed themselves free of any intellectual influences, were usually the slaves of some defunct economist. Now it was the inverse: under a bloody sky the economists were made defunct, and later the slaves of practical men. People emerged from bunkers, blinking, already dying of the radiation sickness, and fell on each other like wolves.

Yasasmin survived. Her husband, too – mostly because they had flown over to Sri Lanka for the honeymoon, and the winds had not yet shifted this way. At first they wandered in a grey daze, the Karunaratnes and the AdbulCaders and the Harshagamas and the Senaratnes and all the other scions of that thinking-class, until someone noticed and put them to work building shelters.

Yasasmin found work at a dig site, organizing the supply chain for one of the new filtered-air colony bubbles the government was building. There was Policy-like work to be done here – nothing worth the title, but enough to keep teams synchronized and production outputs fulfilled. It paid enough to keep the family in food.

Her husband tried to help – but it was patently obvious that nobody cared about theory anymore. So he lifted heavy objects and hammered. He became thinner again, his edges sharper, more liable to cut. The nails that he was given sometimes cut his fingers; at other times the hammers smashed his thumbs.

"We had robots for this sort of thing," he would howl at the dead machines, and rail against rationing and labor forced at gunpoint. At night he came home, shuffling unused muscles, a shadow of the bright spark that had once held people in expensive suits enthralled. And out of guilt he would toy with his food, announce that he wasn't hungry anymore, and give his plate back to Yasasmin.

Yasasmin protested once, twice, maybe thrice – but eventually infatuation fades and hunger takes over. She had to work. The family was larger, now: herself, her husband, her mother – who was working in stockpiling, despite her age – and old Mrs. AbdulCader, who refused to work at all, but insisted in sitting in her living room with her fine china and her Policy certifications on the wall, waiting for the phone to ring.

One call, she'd say. One call, maybe from the World Bank, maybe from the United Nations, maybe some small regional NGO. One call and she'd get them all out of here, for good, back to a place where Policy mattered.

So her husband gave back his meager share of their candlelit dinner, and she ate. On the rare nights that they were not completely exhausted they crept upstairs to make Policy.

"Promise me you'll finish it," he said one day, watching her with wolf-eyes.

"Finish what?"

"The thesis."

She laughed. The laugh turned into a hacking cough. "The Grand Unified Theory," she said, half-mockingly.

"The Policy to End All Policies," he whispered in the sub-dark, and kissed her. His lips were rough, cracked. He took her hand, just like he did the day they became husband and wife, and moved it gently to the sheaf of paper, the dirt-stained and soot-smudged vestiges of all they had been in a past life.

The next morning he went out for work and collapsed. His body was fed to the compost machines.

Many years later, a thick sheaf of papers titled *The Complete System of Human Governance* found its way to a remote bunker in the heart of the country. The bunker was well-armed, with immense concrete walls and automatic cannon to protect itself from roving invaders. The courier delivering was in immense pain: she had torn her rad-suit on the way and welcomes the bullet that lodged itself in her brain. The little package was left to sit there until it was picked up, in the morning sun, by a curious soldier, and taken hastily inward, where it was unwrapped.

Usually documents like this would have been read by academics. There still were those around, haunting these old ruined colleges, the ones who weren't afraid to risk a limb or two to bring some old book back to the shelter. However, the author, one Yasasmin Karunaratne, had addressed it not to a shelter known for its academic thinking, but quite simply, *to the government of Sri Lanka.*

It was read by the government of Sri Lanka, which in these parts were two career military officials that had outlived the apocalypse by dint of their loud voices and the command of the largest armed force this side of Colombo.

They read it all the way through, right down to where the author thanked her dead husband for inspiring the text.

They read until the sun rose again, partly for the pleasure of reading a real book again – but also partly for wonder that someone out there, in the wilderness, had squeezed out the time, the effort, the ink – and when that ran out, the blood – to write like this.

They read like men spellbound, the echoes of an old world chasing themselves in their minds – a world where death was rare, gunfire rarer, and the iron discipline of survival an anthem only to be sung at the last possible moment.

Then they tossed it into the fire, which was dying.

"Shame, though," said one, watching the flames. "If we had implemented it time... no more debating, no more politicians, just the perfect system."

"Yeah," said his junior, who was just out of school but as sharp as garrote wire. "But we have to be practical."

"Agreed," said the older man.

"It's all about the art of the possible. You said so yourself, sir. First training course we ever took. This stuff is for *intellectuals*."

"Agreed, again," said the older man, a little sharper this time. "Go check the watch."

The orange flicker crept up to the author's name, and just like that, Yasasmin Karunaratne vanished from this world.

The Daughter that Bleeds

by Shweta Taneja

Shweta Taneja is an award-winning author who writes science and science fiction for kids and adults. She was awarded the Publishing Next Award and was a finalist in AutHer Award 2022 for her best-selling flipbook on Indian scientists, They Made What? They Found What? *Her other bestselling works include graphic novel* Krishna: Defender of Dharma *and the critically-acclaimed fantasy fiction series* Anantya Tantrist Mysteries. *Her SF short story* The Daughter That Bleeds *(published in this anthology), has been translated to French and was a finalist in the prestigious French award* Grand Prix de l'Imaginaire, *and has been awarded Editor's Choice Award. She is a* Charles Wallace Writing Fellow *and has given talks at international SF conferences including WorldCon at Dublin, Eurocon in Amiens and the Cartoon Museum at London. Her work has been translated to Kannada, French, Romanian, and Dutch. Find her online with her handle @shwetawrites.*

"Brother, you're the man of the hour!" Sardar Singh whacked Asim on his shoulder, making him stagger and cough. "What luck, yaar. Seven daughters I've had, seven expensive bitches. My Lalli is one fertile mare but no, not even one has taken on her and shed a drop of blood, but you, bull's eye with the first one, eh? You lucky rogue!" Sardar winked.

Asim looked around suspiciously, desperately hoping no one had heard. Just when his luck had turned, he managed to bump into the biggest gossip from his district.

"How did you—" Asim stopped himself. He took out his neatly folded, embroidered handkerchief and wiped off his sweaty brow, fingering his gelled hair back into shape and inching away from his boisterous districter. "Look, not here, please."

Sardar pulled Asim in a corner, taking them out of the gurgling sea of humanity that lined up to enter the fertility market.

"You're a real hidden beast!" Sardar's whisper carried loudly into his ear.

Asim was a short, petite man with a small pointy beard to hide his rather unremarkable chin, where Sardar was a giant; tall and broad and fat with a flowing salt-and-pepper beard. "Frankly, when you got married to that Alia, I thought, what a waste of a perfect breed. She is a winner alright; everyone knew her. Every woman in her family had given birth to bleeding girls. And you, when was the last time you remember bloodshed in your family, eh?" Sardar elbowed Asim in his ribcage, making him cringe. "But you, you proved to be a wolf in a sheep's hide, eh? How many girls do you have now?"

"Four," Asim answered, rubbing his bruised rib.

"Twelve years and four girls already? And all of them younger than the bleeder? How old is she? The daughter that bleeds?"

"Eleven."

"Bleeding at eleven? Well, well, well. Are you trying Fertible—"

"I would never!" Asim's lips twisted in disgust.

"Are you taking that potion from Hanif Hakeem? Tell us too, *yaara*, for we would want to know the secret. Our Lalli still has a few years of bleeding left in her. We can try to wet our barren lands too."

"Sardar!"

"Listen, brother," Sardar placed his arm around Asim's shoulders, his brows wet with sweat. "As you know my son, Karkat, is ready for a bleeder. Now we district brothers have an understanding between us, don't we? You don't want your daughter to go to a stranger's house where Alia might not be able to see her anymore, now, do you? Or who knows what kind of perverted customs other district-ers have? If it's someone from district four they might even—"

Asim clenched the handle of his precious coolbox and bit back a scathing retort. Everyone in the district knew Sardar's simple son. He had been peddling his firstborn male in this market for months to get a bleeder. Who in their right mind would part with a bleeding daughter, that too a virgin, for that *idiot*? Asim had high hopes for his Gaia. He wanted her to have as many children as she possibly could. He needed a fertile breeder for her. Not Sardar's son who didn't look like he had any sperm in his loins or matter in his brain.

"Look, I have to go. I have an auction slot—" said Asim, hoping Sardar would get the hint.

"Auction time? You got through?" Sardar slapped him on his back, almost making the coolbox fall. "That is simply great news, brother! Imagine! My own districter turning into a proper-proper auctioneer, eh! Why didn't you say so before?" He snatched the coolbox from Asim's hand.

"Look Sardar," Asim tried to take his coolbox back, "you would have other work to do. I don't want to impose on—"

"*Ajee*, no worries. Who will come to help if not one's own brother? What time did you stay your auction was at?"

"Five."

"That's just a few hours away! Come, come, we should hurry." He pulled Asim back into the bustling line that led into the fertility market. "Now that you're an auctioneer, you will find all kinds of vultures hovering around you, ready to fake your name and take your spot. You should be alert and—Get off! Get off!" Sardar pushed a couple of peddlers who approached them with charms. "He's a real auctioneer with real blood. Keep those filthy charms away from him, you hungry leeches!" Asim followed, without a choice.

"—never smile at any buyer—" Sardar shouted over the cacophony, rushing through the middle of the lane, like an elephant, "—they're not doing you a favour, you're doing them a favour by considering their offer for your bleeder. Better still, let me do all the talking. My uncle, Bunny Chacha, you know him right?" Asim nodded, unhappily following his districter.

Everyone and their aunts knew Sardar's uncle —a respected Elder. Everyone went to Bunny Chacha for advice in selling bleeding girls. Rumour was Chacha had sold a girl to a Sheikh once.

"I've helped him many times... even considered taking the job of an agent for all those fathers who came to him, but no, there's not enough people who will trust you, not like you brother ... don't even look at the auctioneers. That's the only way you get ...'

Asim cursed under his breath. Just an hour ago, when the officer had finally handed him a slot, he'd thought his luck had turned. He'd kissed the blood locket he'd bought a day ago, changed into his best clothes and ran, to find a good spot in the auction, to display his blood samples. And now he was stuck with Sardar.

"—hear that Dada?" Sardar screamed, addressing an old man, stooping with age, his arm jutting out like sticks, all kinds of talismans and charms hanging from them. "Man from my own district. First girl, bleeding at eleven!"

The old man stared at Asim, moving his mouth like he was chewing cud. "*Ajee*, in our time, there were many more bleeders. You could marry any girl and she would give you more bleeders."

"You mean without an auction? That's impossible," scoffed Asim, inspite of himself. Braggers, they were everywhere nowadays. Barren braggers with dry daughters or worse, no daughters at all.

"Auction, suction," the old man made a face, "all these are new things only. Ramu!" He called to a man who, if possible, looked older than him, his face wrinkled like a melted candle. "Tell them how we married in our time. Did we ask for any of these blood sample-shamples?"

"No, *ji*," cried the melted Ramu. "Before the bio-wars, we needed no blood checks. In our time, you could marry any woman you found—mind you, *any*—and she would give birth to healthy, bleeding girls all her fertile life. Now, there is no quality left only. Girls are more barren than the middle of the Gobi Desert!" He spat on the floor, leaving a long red trail of pan on someone's pajamas. "I tell them, if you want a fertile girl, take my *soorma*. That's how I was born and my father before me. This *soorma* is magical, ji. Makes a girl bleed faster than it takes to shit after a feast."

"Really? Show me a sample," said Sardar. He stepped out of the line. Asim grabbed his coolbox, and pushed on ahead, hoping he'd gotten rid of his fellow districter for good. Time was of the essence.

It had taken him a whole excruciating panic-filled month to get here. First, waiting month after month for his daughter's menstrual cycle to strike, rushing to the lab with a blood sample, praying. A lot of district girls after the bio-wars would bleed for a month or two and then stop. Psychological bleeding, the doctors said, does not mean she is fertile.

His blessed Gaia had bleeded for five whole months before he'd rushed to the nearest State Auction Bank to register for a state-wide auction. Alia had told him not to bother with it and instead sell Gaia in the district market, but he had been insistent. Gaia was his first daughter. He owed her much more than selling her to someone like Sardar's family. She deserved someone well-educated and moneyed. Someone who could give her beautiful children and love them all. Someone like a Sheikh.

That's the reason Asim had taken a hefty loan from a moneylender and put Gaia in the City Fertility Centre, while waiting for the State Auction Bank to give him a slot. The Fertility Centre was terribly expensive but he couldn't take a chance. He had heard horrible stories of gangs who would kidnap bleeders and their mother and kill the males of the family to sell the women to private buyers outside the country. And he didn't trust the State enough to protect his girls or him for that matter.

He had to sell his daughter today. If that didn't happen, he would have to go back, take fresh blood samples, apply again to the State Auction Bank and wait. Or worse, sell his daughter in the black market, for the money.

"Never," he whispered. "My blood's real. My daughter is bleeding for real." Unlike that Sardar Singh and those geriatric peddlers. Bystanders, jobless, coming to the marketplace day in and day out dragging their barren daughters, forcing them to try surgical methods or potions or medicines in a desperate need to make them fertile. Empty-pocketed, infertile idiots! They just couldn't afford it. Oh yes, he was going to make a sale today, no matter how.

An echoing cacophony of conversations, heated arguments and discussions announced the Fertile Market before he could see it in front of him. A single turnstile gate for people to get in, guards at the entrance checking ID cards. As usual, the air-conditioning in the bazaar wasn't working, making the glass-sealed hall stuffy and sweltering. Asim walked through the aisles filled with sellers who'd spread their wares on pieces of carpets or towels and buyers who rustled, picking samples, testing them with used hemoglins, bargaining or shaking their heads.

At the very end of the hall, across from rows of aisles was the Auction section, segregated from the main bazaar with a hazy wall of cool. The Elite bazaar. Asim walked towards it, heart thumping in his chest.

"Brother," Sardar rushed from behind, grabbing his shoulder. "Let's go and get a sheikh for your daughter, *yaara*!"

Sheikh. The idea almost made Asim trip on the threadbare carpet. If he could get a Sheikh, he would be able to own a home, keep his whole family in comfort, even buy petrol for his bike and take Alia to the spring fair. His daughter will be dressed in jewellery and her kids would get educated! A Sheikh would be—

"He with you?" asked a guard, pointing to Sardar as Asim showed his auction card.

This was it. A small headshake and Sardar would fall off him like dandruff. Something however made Asim nod. Sardar slapped his back hard as they entered.

"Have you prepared your speech?" asked Sardar, "That's the first thing to attract them to your blood samples. You might have the samples of the rarest of mares, but what's that if no one even comes your way?"

The Auction area had big cubicles for each seller, which included a sitting area to negotiate and discuss. Fathers were already opening up their coolboxes and setting up the blood samples on a desk provided to them, instructing friends, family members or districters they'd brought along, putting posters about family history and fertility history of both the father and mother, and placing the probability certificate their State provided on how likely the girl was to reproduce bleeding girls in future.

Asim's allotted stall was diagonally opposite the stage. At the far end of the stage was the cordoned area for VIP buyers (Sheikhs, whispered a honeyed voice in his head).

"How does one become a buyer?" he asked looking at one of the Sheikhs.

"You have to be rich, brother," answered Sardar, taking off his turban and cleaning the table they'd been given. "At least ten bank lockers, the size of our houses, filled to the brim with coin. Do you have any posters shosters? Or any photos of your bleeding daughter?"

"No."

"Look at the others!" Sardar waved his hand around, retying his turban. "They even brought their daughters along, setting them up like this was a camel bazaar!" He spat. "And you? You don't even bring a photo? How will you attract buyers, eh? With the smell of her blood?" Asim pressed his lips and carefully took out the samples, placing them neatly on the table.

"I won't display my daughter like an animal," he said. "You stubborn districter—"

A man came to their booth. "Is this red real," he asked. He was dressed in a trim black suit. "Hundred percent, *ji*," said Sardar before Asim had had a chance to speak up. "But we ask you, who're you, eh? You don't look like a buyer to me."

"Sardar!" whispered Asim, horrified, but Sardar continued.

"Who are you to ask about the bleeder? Do you have coin enough for even the question?"

The man slunk off.

"You don't know these kinds," continued Sardar, oblivious to Asim's frown. "Wasting precious blood by smelling or ingesting, calling themselves agents! I'll get a few buyers for us." He walked out in the aisle and started to talk to the people. Every few minutes, he would bring one of them. "Fresh real samples of a bleeding virgin, ji! Only eleven years old!"

Soon buyers lined up, asking for drops of blood, to test them out with their shiny new hemoglins and tapping to include the results in their tabs. Some of them preferred to taste, touching the red drop with the tip of their tongue, nodding or shaking their head. A couple of hours vanished in a daze. Asim looked at the list he'd prepared. Eighty-five people had taken the sample.

"Can I have a sample please," asked a soft voice. Asim looked up. It was a woman, in her twenties, dressed in a printed sari. He gulped.

"I represent Sheikh Numansin," she said, her voice husky as Asim pressed the tube's opener to release a drop of blood on her palm. She licked the drop with her tiny tongue, all the while looking at Asim. "Powerful," she whispered, giving him a soft smile.

"You're not welcome here!" hollered Sardar who had just walked back to the stall with another buyer.

"Sardar!" cried Asim.

"We've heard your Sheikh's stories. We are not interested," he said, dismissing her. She walked away, winking at Sardar. "Asim, time for you to impress them with that speech!"

Asim walked towards the stage, nervously fingering a piece of paper Alia had given him, hoping he would remember it all. He wished his wife was here. Alia had experience with this sort of thing. After all, she had been to a lot of auctions before her father had okayed selling her to him at the local bazaar and that too only because Asim's luck had turned when he'd found a pack of fresh oranges abandoned during his night guard duty. Him? It had been his first and last time at an auction and that too in a local bazaar. This was his first time ever in the city auction.

He wiped sweat off his forehead, wondering if he should ask Sardar to speak for him. He definitely looked confident and strong, an alpha male who would breed bleeding daughters like flies.

The registrar called out his name and Asim scrambled up the stage, eyeing a sea of faces, men with flowing beards, turbans, long hair, dramatic moustaches and started to mumble the lines he'd learnt by rote, something to do with his wife's family, his own family and his virgin daughter, merely eleven, already bleeding for five months now.

All the time, he was acutely aware that he was making a mess of it all.

In his desperation, he faltered more. The audience, a group of well-dressed, suave city men, soon lost interest. A giggle, a yawn, a loud whisper. Did he sound too simple? Too much like the districter he was?

The woman who'd come by his stall earlier, whispered something to the man she sat with in the VIP section. The Sheikh. Asim mumbled, shuffling his papers, telling them a joke Alia had prepared, forgetting it halfway.

"He's from my district!" cried Sardar from across the stage, thumping his chest. "District four." His voice boomed, carrying across the auction hall. "We have the prettiest girls in the country. She's eleven and a virgin!"

"What will we do with pretty if they're barren like a desert sea?" cried a man from the audience. Laughter followed.

"Where is your daughter? How do we decide if she looks pretty?" asked another.

"How do we know she's a virgin?"

"We don't display our daughters where we come from," cried Sardar.

"Who buys a vegetable without poking it a bit first?" cried someone else.

"We have the blood," mumbled Asim, heart jumping into his throat. The audience started to hoot and laugh.

"Village idiots!"

"He doesn't look like he could breed a fly, forget a bleeding girl." Raucous laughter followed by a scream from Sardar.

"Who said that!" Sardar cried, jumping into the VIP arena.

"Sardar! No!" Asim hurried off the stage.

The uniformed State guards, moved in with a suddenness, pouncing on Sardar and giving him a shock with their electric batons. He withered, slapping his heavy arm in one guard's face.

"Stop!" said a piercing voice. Asim's eyes popped out of its sockets. It was the same woman who'd come by earlier. The guards stilled, their hands freezing. "Sheikh Numansin will buy this girl," she announced in her soft voice.

The woman took a stunned Asim to a corner. "He's interested," she said. Asim looked at the Sheikh, sitting in the front row of the VIP section, crunching on an apple. A real Sheikh as real as the apple he bit. Asim had seen both for the first time in his life. He gulped.

"You're really lucky," she said, catching his expression. "But he has one condition."

"What?"

"He wants to sign a bond with you. This one and all future bleeding girls."

"That's not—"

"He's not willing to wait. You can name any coin price, any—" she stopped to wait as he calculated. "He will be good to her, Asim," she said softly. "Trust me."

"Don't do it brother!" Sardar hobbled to him, massaging his bruised shoulder. "Listen, I've heard some stories in the market about this Sheikh! They call him Collector Sheikh!" The woman smiled at him grimly and turned to Asim.

"It's your decision," she said looking at Asim. "We will be at the VIP section for fifteen more minutes. She will have a good life."

"We'll find you a buyer," cried Sardar, "a better one, someone with—"

"Someone better than a Sheikh?" Asim turned to his friend, shivering with anger. "Are you even listening to yourself, Sardar? I respect you but what's gotten into you?"

"Listen, he's not right. He isn't. Your girl, she would live a half life!"

"He's a Sheikh! My daughter will live in a harem. Her children will get educated."

"Give her to *me,*" said Sardar. "You and Alia, you know us. She will stay with my son, my family. You can meet her everyday."

"And how much coin do you have Sardar?"

"Enough for you to be able to live a normal life, brother!"

"He's a Sheikh, Sardar and you—you're a boor from a poor district!"

"I won't let you waste a bleeding girl from our district—"

"She's mine! Okay? *Mine!* Mine to sell or not, as I wish! And I won't sell her to you Sardar, not in a million dry years. Not if your child was the last sperm-carrying boy out there!"

Sardar took a step back as if physically hurt. "Banjar's curse, that's what she'll get!" He walked away.

Asim shivered. Barren-*bloody*-father with no bleeding daughters to sell. Ordering *him* around. A father of a bleeding girl! Alia had a few years left to her. He might get another bleeder in the family or not but he was getting advance coin for all of them. No more auction. All he had to do was call and he'll get a Sheikh for his future bleeding daughter. And he could give his family a good life. Hells and demons, he could also become the head of the district himself, politically respected and influential. An Elder like Bunny Chacha! A man to whom everyone came to take advice on selling bleeding daughters. All he had to do was sign a piece of paper. What was in that? Sardar was just jealous. He walked to the VIP section in a daze of dreams, signing wherever the woman said he should. There, it was done. There was no going back now.

"I will get her from the City Fertility Centre," he told the Sheikh. The man hadn't spoken a word to him. Not that he needed to, but it would've been nicer.

"There's no need for that," said the woman, putting a hand on his shoulder, smiling politely. "We can take her now that the ownership papers are signed."

"But the wedding—" He looked at the Sheikh.

"The Sheikh likes it quiet. No horses and dances for him."

"But ... she's mine."

"Not anymore," said the woman gently.

"You will take care of her, won't you?" Asim asked, directing his question to the Sheikh. Man to man. The Sheikh eyed Asim as someone would notice a lizard at the corner of the room.

"District four is very rare," he answered.

The woman handed Asim a box of coin. "This is the first installment. We will send you a monthly retainer for the rest of your living life. Please call us if there's a bleeding in your family. I will have someone fetch the bleeder from your village. You don't even need to come to the city."

"You will, won't you?" he asked, again.

"My collection needed a district four specimen," the Sheikh rasped.

"But you will love her and educate the children, right?" Asim asked. They they got up, ready to leave. The woman bent down and straightened the folds of the Sheikh's dress.

"Children?" The Sheikh frowned, walking away.

"You've done it now!" cried the woman, her voice sharp. "How could you be so insensitive?"

She hurried after the Sheikh, leaving Asim with his box of gold.

This story was first published in The Best Asian Speculative Fiction anthology by Kitaab (Singapore)

The New Migrants

Navin Weeraratne

Neil deGrasse Tyson and Dan Abnett had a baby, and that ugly baby is Navin Weeraratne. He writes action, adventure and military sci-fi, with a very strong dose of hard and cutting-edge science. If you read his writing and you haven't learned some new science, you are either an astrophysicist, or he has failed you. He also looks at Big Picture Transhumanism, and what it's going to be like living in world with beings far cleverer – and more dangerous – than Homo Sapiens have ever been. He lives in Colombo with his wife and some very spoiled cats. For updates and new books by him: https://www.scifinavin.com/newsletter/

The first time I saw one of his spaceships, a school of dolphins was hunting it.

We didn't realize what it was at the time. I doubt my orders would have been different if we'd known. It was rising through the waves, more like a grey-green hill than a giant jellyfish.

I had expected stingers, luminescence, at least some beauty to excuse the crime, but no. I turned and watched as the hunters and their prey fell behind our boat. Then, the spaceship reached the surface and hung there, like a drowned refugee corpse, seawater rolling over it with each wave. It was well behind us once its main envelope cleared the water. Sieve lines clung under it, Half-eaten and torn. The cheated dolphins watched as it floated away to die. Even large-brained beings like them couldn't begin to understand the changes we had created in their world.

Who then, was this man and his shanty town, genetic engineers, who thought they could?

No one else in the boat cared. Across from me, a sun-dried Saudi clutched a sloshing barrel of mutant oysters while counting his prayer beads. A Maldivian in only a pair of shorts and the scars the Sri Lankan Navy gave him for coming ashore was busy pirating Korean soaps on his tablet. A child trailed her fat, little fingers in the rushing water off the side, squealing.

Up ahead was the sea shanty.

My name is Aruni Silva. When I was six, my mother saw that I was brighter than her; she was so proud she burned my books. My drunk father let her. When a Chinese volunteer gave me a tablet when I was ten, I came home one day to find he'd sold it to buy arrack. When I sat for my Mandarin exams, they said no university would take me - and went to the village school's headmaster and got my papers thrown out. A new teacher found out and reported them to the Ministry of State Security. So, I went to a Chinese university. Now, I too worked for China's MSS. I am hated for it by my fellow Sri Lankans, but that's alright. The hate is reassuring, like when all your neighbor's houses burn down along with yours.

The shanty stretched across the water, packed with shacks built from corrugated plastic and spray-on solar cells. Lines hung across them with flapping, bright laundry. A cloud of seagulls rose over some insult, a stray dog barking at them. A gang of mixed-race children jabbered as they ran between graphene antenna mounts, their vernacular and futures mixed.

The man I was after was a genetic engineering miscreant at best, an American-backed terrorist, at worst. His name was Pasan Gonakumbura, and, frankly, I hated everything about him. He was from what my Chinese instructors called a 'collaborator class' - in Sri Lanka's case, the English-speaking elite whose ancestors did the Britishers' dirty work, then pretended they had wanted them out, all along.

The posh schoolboys and their Cricket matches.

The civil servants drinking in their clubs.

The Oxford-Cambridge scumbags.

They rechained us with 'Sinhala Only' populism - guaranteeing that going forward, only their stupid, entitled children would understand English.

My ancestors gained freedom and lost the English-speaking world that should have been our reparations. All its ideas locked behind gates controlled by an entire social class practicing Colonialism at Home.

Only after the Chinese did it become clear what had been done to the rest of us. The standing in buses for white tourists. The figurehead expats paid more for less work. How we'd been taught to hate each other.

Pasan Gonakumbura was of that class. His family had run estates, bought elections, and sent their children to foreign universities to learn how to be white. And now, here he was in a sea shanty, after years working in US aerospace, engineering high altitude creatures that just happened to fly alongside China's edge-of-space platforms.

We pulled into its boat-clogged harbor and bullied our way through like a bus in traffic. We ended up stuck against an ancient, Burmese fishing boat. Their crew ignored us; one was applying spray-on solar cells with a rattle can. Another was deboning engineered fish; beside him, a bucket filled with their precious, black, heavy metal-rich bones.

I got off at the dock. My target was just a few shacks away, a Tamil family that had lost a daughter. She was nothing plastic surgery couldn't replace: I practiced a smile with my new face and went to find them.

"Darini?!" the mother sat on a red monobloc chair outside their shack. Besides her was a mat covered in bundles of hydroponic greens. On the roof like an elephant's hide stretched on a tanning frame was a grey-black, water catchment still. "Oh god, Darini darling? Is that you?"

"No, Auntie, my name is Anupama. Are you Tamil? I'm sorry, I new here."

I played the helpless ignorant. The instincts of a mother who'd had to bury her child took over, and she took me in.

I respected that Vanappu didn't cry. Her husband Pragash, though, did. He then felt the need to tell me why. He talked a lot, the easy charm and smiles of a life-long, duplicitous actor. Vanappu was silent, smiling at me, more nervously at him. When he glared at her, she would shrink back: the beatings were in our file. I smiled, nodded, and ate my dhal soup.

"I came looking for work," I answered when the cue came up. "I want to gene bash. You can't in Bentota, the police will break your hands. I heard there was work being done in Al-Ahmadi."

Vanappu gave Pragash a sharp look. He was too stupid, dismissing her concern and intelligence with a wave.

"Yes, there is work here! It's secret though, I shouldn't tell you."

"Hmm."

"Heard of Pasan Gonakumbura?"

"The American?"

"No, no. He's Sri Lankan, like us. He has a team here, they are gene-bashing jellyfish. Giant ones, green, just like plants. They fly, if you can believe it. Full of gas!"

"I think I saw one. Are they safe?"

"God no, they explode like bombs. You're very smart, maybe you can help them?"

"Maybe."

"I can take you tomorrow to meet them."

"Thanks, Uncle. I'd like that. It's good of you two to help me like this."

"It's our pleasure," he grinned. "You're our guest! It's nice to meet someone from Sri Lanka. How is home?"

"Very Chinese," I answered. They both laughed. "Most people are happy."

"Most people aren't free! Here in Al-Ahmadi, we are free," said Pragash. "We print or gene bash whatever we want. There are no cameras watching. No copyright, no algorithms. And no genius computers sending secret police into our homes."

"No, of course not."

"I visited my brother's family in the Puttalam mangroves last year. His children don't know Tamil! They only talk Mandarin, and watch Chinese films. Even the food my brother's wife made was part-Chinese. All over, everyone becoming the same no? I said so - but they didn't think it was a bad thing!"

"It is change, Uncle. Otherwise, we just think about what makes us different. That's how we get Sinhalese versus Tamil, and Tamil versus Moslem. The country would collapse, like America." They laughed at this. The world over, there is no greater balm for problems than to laugh at America.

"But Sri Lanka has no democracy anymore, no?"

"You can't have democracy when you have social media. With social media everyone gets to have their own truths. They form closed-off worlds of self-reinforcing narratives and lies. Then, we expect them to go off, and make decisions?"

"But that's how it worked before."

"It never worked before. Have you met people? They're all stupid and selfish. That is why markets work, and democracies fail. Sooner or later, freedom poisons. We are not meant to be free. We are meant to do what we are told. We are like children; we can only hope those who lead us are true of mind, heart, and purpose."

The only sound was the drip-drip-drip of the water still.

"Maybe Gonakumbura should be gene bashing smarter people," said Vanappu.

"Here," Pragash handed me what looked like Vietnamese rice farmer's hat. It was lined with metal foil. "Put it on. The platform is coming."

People all around were putting on similar hats. Some had anti-radar veils that looked like medieval face guards. A fist of children crowded around a tin of black paint. The older ones smeared anti-recognition marks on the younger one's faces. Their work was good, but dated. A big girl yelled at a small boy who couldn't be trusted not to instead draw monster faces on himself. He flicked paint at her, and ran for his life.

I stopped and looked up. The sky was nothing but blue.

"Don't look!" Pragash waved his hands. "It'll see you, too. You're the one it wants!"

"Sorry Uncle," I smiled and nodded. "In Sri Lanka we don't hide from them. If you do, then the algorithms flag you, and you'll get a visit."

"Ah, but what about when everyone is hiding? That's how we protect our bashers. The Chinese never know how many we have, or where they are."

He was right. I had to smile to hide my frown.

"Come, keep your head down and let's get you a job."

I checked the time: the edge-of-space platform that had come to support me had been detected within minutes of arriving. How had they known?

Status, it sent me.

Green. I sent back.

Von Neumann threat level? Unclear.

Gonakumbura's gene bashing workshop was a set of three, two-storey, extruded structures. I was surprised to see no guards, unless you counted the old, Algerian woman selling Starlink minutes and mangoes on a mat outside the main building. A line of laundry was drying on its roof. Known associate Ruslana Shevchenko, came to the edge and looked down at us, a cigarette on her lip.

"What do you want?" the Ukrainian said with the abrupt, honest charm of the unsophisticated.

"Can you give her a job?" said Pragash before I could speak.

"No."

"That's what you say! Tell Pasan to come out."

"Go away," She disappeared.

"I'll take it from here, Uncle. Thank you for-"

"Shhh!" he smiled and waved his hand. "She'll come round."

We stood outside the door, in the sun. Several minutes passed. The Algerian woman tried to sell me a bandwidth card, but I declined. Then, she told me about the climate refugee camp her husband had died in and tried again. I told her she reminded me of my mother, and she smiled.

The door opened, and Shevchenko stood in the doorway, arms crossed.

"You can gene bash?" she glared at me.

"Yes."

"Show me."

MSS hired gene and nano bashers to catch gene and nano bashers. I sent her the genome of a flood-resistant rice species I'd created; altered some to suggest the knowledge gaps of unstructured self-teaching. I saw her eyes dart back and forth as she read pages only her eyes could see.

"Looks good," she said at last. "But why here? With your skill, you can bash anywhere. You could even bash for the Chinese - and then, it is not 'bashing,' yes?"

"I'll never work for them," I lifted up the back of my shirt so she could see the scars. Pragash gasped.

"Who did that to you?"

"Nano-Bio Response," I answered truthfully.

"You have one day. If your work is good, you can stay. Okay?"

"Okay."

If you can't trust people to vote, you definitely can't trust them to create.

Open source nanotech and backyard gengineering had given godly power to anyone with an Internet connection and ten dollars of off-the-shelf gear. Just stop for a moment and think what life was like, back then. Knowing that the stranger in the alley could do more than mug, rape, or kill you. He could also end the world.

That's why there was Nano-Bio Response. All over the world, street cameras watched for telltale heat spikes in the pavement cracks. Loiter drones studied jungles for fractal land-clearing. Buoys scanned the seafloor for hot smokers being stitched together into geothermal plants. Where would the next outbreak be? Would that nation handle it before another had to, for them?

More than once, nuclear eradication has saved us all.

I worked Nano-Bio Response for the MSS. People thought Nano-Bio helped the platforms kill, finding them hospitals full of landmine victims to hit. The truth is just the opposite: we were the ones stopping the platforms. If you saw a mushroom cloud, it was because we failed.

Gene bashers were every bit as dangerous as nano bashers - I think more so. You could always do something about a grey goo cloud that had started generating its own weather - it's hard to miss. Yet, when a gene basher CRISPRs up a mess, would you even know? It could take years for a synthetic species to start turning its biome into a dust bowl, and by then, it's too late to stop.

The harder we pressed, the harder the bashers pushed back. We passed laws, bullied companies for personal data, and swapped it with other states. The bashers dug in; encrypted their files, organized on MMO open world servers, and bought with crypto - or worse, cash. Our biggest problem was not their fiendish intelligence

- having a hand tied behind our backs. Every government surveilled its people - but what about people without governments?

Climate change had driven their number into the billions.

These orphaned people took to the sea with 3d printers, solar power, and a gene-bash-and-release outlook. They grew from roving camps of boat people to cosmopolitan tribes with their own patois, settled on structures that lived, grew, and calved daughter structures. These were the shanties: sea-going, GMO giants derived from coral. Every day, more and more people left the camps for them. People like Pragash and Vanappu.

We let them go: every emigrant is an energetic and determined problem that's just solved itself for you, whether a rebel, a miscreant, or just another hungry mouth. The sea was a place all nations could dump their climate liabilities. All we had to do was leave them alone and let them print or CRISPR whatever they needed. A necessary evil. Even as we held the line against the chaos, beyond every receded coastline was an entirely different way of life we couldn't contain, thwart, or censor. I lost so much sleep over it.

Over the next few days, I copied all the notes and gene sequences Shevchenko gave me access to. Theirs was just one of six teams working on the project; that so many bashers had come together was a huge red flag. What were they doing? From what I accessed, I could confirm that they were indeed building edge of space-capable creatures. Living, hydrogen, superpressure airships that would clutter and contest the sky.

It was amazing how brazenly anti-Chinese this was; we alone kept our assets suborbital for Kessler Syndrome-proofing. Gonakumbura's work would litter our operating altitude with living minefields. If they succeeded, in a few decades, whole patches of the sky could be denied to us. This wasn't about checkmating our ability to deny space to the Americans with a bucket of rocket-launched nails. This was about taking our power the heavens from us, all together.

There was only one thing that didn't add up; a body of work concerning biological electric thrusters. The creatures would use them to scoop up air molecules, ionize them, and accelerate them out for thrust. "Fuelless" electric thrusters weren't new; they'd been used for years by low-orbiting satellites to offset the drag caused by those same air molecules. But, these were too powerful for just that. They could push the creatures to tremendous speeds, speeds at which air resistance - even that high up - could even tear them apart.

What was the reason? I could find no mention. Either Shevchenko had censored it, or it was such a deep given among the teams that it didn't need referencing. I beamed all this to the platform.

My handlers responded within the hour.

Target must be neutralized. Aerial ID not possible given anti-recognition measures by local population. IR tagging required. Tag target, and extract.

I took a moment to digest this.

Target and associates are not terrorists. Their work presents no immediate threats. Perhaps extending assignment is prudent? Allows time to discover balloon creatures actual purpose - and ID the other five cells.

Extension denied. Gonakumbura is linchpin; if dealt with soon the project will never recover. To delay is to risk a broadening of the project's intellectual center of mass. A heavier response would then be needed - which will only inflate the work's profile and spawn copycat projects. Great danger if project is open sourced. Tag Gonakumbura, ASAP. Platform will do the rest. We have faith in you.

The infrared tag I wore hidden in a locket was suddenly the heaviest thing in the world.

"Vanappu, is that you?"

I was in the market. It was women, for the most part, buying and selling from each other. An old Malay with a raisin for a face and red pegs for teeth gestured to her stack of handmade baskets as she chewed betel. A young Iraqi girl stacked aquaponic vegetables on a mat before her. A Sudanese woman in the brightest colored shalwar I had ever seen pulled a thrasing fish from a bucket and chopped its head off.

Vanappu, looking away and with sari pulled over her head, pretended not to hear me. She ducked behind a rack of drying seaweed.

"Vanappu?" I stepped in front of her. "It's Anupama! Are you okay?"

She looked up, shielding her face with her sari. "So sorry, dear! I didn't hear you. How are things in the new place? Do they cook properly?"

"What's wrong? Did something happen to your face?"

Around us, the women became silent. They watched us from the corners of their eyes.

"No, no! Everything is fine!"

I peered at the black eye. "Pragash did this, didn't he? I'll talk to him."

"No, no, it's my fault," she waved me away. "I shouldn't bother him after he's been drinking."

"I'm so sorry," I tried to put my arm around her.

"I'm okay," she pushed my arm away. "I won't make him angry again. So much to do! I'll talk to you later, Anupama. I'm so happy you are working with those people. They are nice."

They won't beat you, is what she meant.

The other women went back to talking. Vanappu hadn't let them down; she was invisible again. This is what their freedom meant in a place like this.

I caught Gonakumbura five days later. Aero 17 was returning to the shanty from a two-month flight duration test, and the others had, so very inconveniently, come down with a coronavirus I had cooked up for them with their own equipment. Can New Girl handle it? Of course she can. Then send New Girl. Shevchenko says she's alright, no?

We stood at the disused North pier. Half-wrecked boats hung suspended over the water. Their hulls looked pixelated - wrecked by some nano-agent that had tried to make them into something else. A white bird landed on one. Brown chicks squealed at it as it took its time regurgitating their breakfast. A fat dog pawing through old garbage noticed us. It came over, wagging it tails for some bread and fish. It flattened its ears as Gonakumbura stroked its head, the man's eyes glued to his tablet. It showed the coordinates and vitals of Aero 17.

"She likes you," I said with an empty smile.

"You know where you stand with dogs," his accent was American. His shirt rooted for the New England Patriots and he wore

Birkenstocks: he looked like a Western tourist on a sex holiday from twenty years ago. "Not like with people."

"You don't trust people?"

"Do you?"

We were silent for a while. The last stars faded, and the sky began reddening in the East. The fat dog sat down by Gonkumbura, not a care in the world. In the distance, much lower than I'd expected, was a bright speck.

"Thank you for the opportunity," I said. "Not just this, but to work on this. I've never been part of such a large project."

"And yet, you've not asked once what it is we're doing," he turned and looked at me. His eyes were old, tired, and saw right through me.

"Didn't think it was my place to ask."

"Any guesses?"

"Yes. You're designing living Edge-of-Space platforms. Balloon satellites for the people. Free Internet, flying up from the sea and powered by sunlight."

"That would be nice. But that's easily controlled, isn't it?"

"What do you mean?"

"It's nothing a laser couldn't knock out. Or an infection. Nothing worth sending an agent to infiltrate us, yes?"

My heart pounded in my ears. The dog turned and stared at me, eyes like black beads. I realized the deserted, pre-dawn pier was the most dangerous place in the world.

"I - I don't know what you're talking about!"

"I'm not going to hurt you; I'm not a monster. Besides, that would be as pointless as you trying to hurt me. Who are you with, by the way? The Americans? The Indians?"

"I'm not going to sit here and be accused of being a spy!"

"But then you won't know what that is," he grinned and pointed to the speck. It had grown into a sphere that hung just over the water. "What you came to find out. You're so close!"

I stood there, my body facing one direction, my mind, the other. Aerospace Test 17 looked like a weather balloon with thick, hanging skin underneath. It was as green as a new turned leaf, which it had more in common with than its jellyfish cousins. It approached as close as a hundred meters and crashed. Gonakumbura stared at the data scrolling on his tablet like a greedy bond trader.

"It's dead," I said. "Are you going to tell me why it lived?"

"Yes. And you're a true basher by the way; I mean that as a compliment. You stayed to see, to understand. That," he pointed to the mass of green, floating skin, "is going to give us freedom. True freedom, not like the shanties."

"You don't think the shanties are free?"

"They are only free at your sufferance - you could end them if you wanted to. When they're no longer to your advantage, you will. The Aeros are aero-space tests. They can survive radiation, temperature extremes, vacuum. The ion thruster organs are to drive them right out of the atmosphere - and keep them speeding till they reach orbital velocity and escape. Then, solar sails can take them anywhere in the solar system."

"Spaceship jellies? Are you serious?"

"Space station jellies," he stood and stepped towards the water, his eyes looking far beyond the rising sun. "Biological craft rising from the oceans to take villages, like this one, into space. Rockets are for Western elites. These will migrate the world's masses to freedom. Freedom beyond the control of any nation-state!"

"That's complete nonsense," I folded my arms. "That's not how things work."

"Oh, isn't it?" he head snapped back to me. "You don't understand how truly vast even the inner solar system is. States can completely control us, anywhere on Earth or in Earth orbit. But among the Near Earth Asteroids? We haven't even mapped them all. How can you impose your will there? The further people go, the harder they are to find, and the much harder they are to catch."

"You think a Long March assault shuttle can't catch one of these?"

"No, it can't. Your shuttles are vehicles, not habitats. Anywhere there's sunlight, the Aeros will live and prosper. You will never have the resources to dominate them. And if you do, they will just move again. Once people get beyond Earth," he pointed to the sky, "that's it. No nation-state will ever be able to control them, again."

"You're so sure of yourself," I shook my head. "Of all this. What makes you think this is better than having order? Having security? Did you live in the US so long that you forgot what it was like to not be sure if your neighbors would try and kill you?" I switched to Sinhalese. "But people like you didn't have that problem, no? It was something for the rest us. Are you alright with us paying that price for your class values?"

His face hardened.

"You've lived your whole life under surveillance," he began. "You don't know the value of freedom and privacy because you've never had any. Don't be so arrogant and naive to think that your way is the definitive answer to how people should live."

"I think our way works. Your way is like Communism; it works - in theory. Education to inform voters; how did that work out? What a joke! They're still people, Basher. And people will never be as noble as this fat dog."

The green skin finally sank under the waves; white foam was its tomb marker.

"Are you going to kill me?" we both asked at the same time.

"No," he replied. "But it doesn't matter what your people do to me. If anything happens to any of us, our work will be open-sourced. I bet your friends in Beijing wouldn't want that. Would they?"

I turned and began walking away.

"People are disappointing, in your world as well as mine!" he called after me. "Real freedom, Anupama! Can you imagine it? No one alive today knows what that was like!"

I left the shanty that afternoon. I sat near the motor, shielding my eyes as I looked back at the shrinking village. When I was precisely a hundred meters away, the platform acted. There was a flash like a camera's but much more powerful, like when an artillery piece fires at night. Then, silence. A few moments later the surprise and shock followed as people on the boat got updates. I looked out to sea and ignored them.

When Beijing learned they'd exploded the skull of one wife-beating, Pragash Sittambalam, they'd be disappointed.

They'd think it was incompetence and demote or sack me. Others would go in to finish the job, but it likely too late for it to matter.

"Sister," a young woman tapped my arm, her face a study in anxiety. "Do you know what's happening?"

"I don't have all the answers," I replied. "We'll have to wait and see."

Anamnesis

by Rupsa Dey

Rupsa Dey believes in the power of language and cats, and is only allergic to the latter. She believes that if the boundaries of language need to be broken in order to accommodate the human experience, then she must direct herself to that purpose. She never says 'No' to tea and if given a chance, would like to believe in a world without borders. She is a Bal Shree National Awardee in Creative Writing. Her recent works can be found in Clarkesworld Magazine, The Dark, Muse India, and Northern Light Vol. 8.

NQ had a decision to make. To take the pill would be to prove himself the mindless consumer that DISEC thought them to be. And yet, he had been lulled inside, by the promises that the holographic models made. He had been intercepted by one of them that called herself Io in the Doweze market. Over the hollers of fruit vendors, shoppers and the whirring of the giant Feeder that guzzled water from a nearby dam, NQ had found himself scattered thin. Last night, the auto mode had overridden the manual commands that were programmed a few days ago. He had been assigned a new case. His mind had not properly adjusted to his new schedule yet. The rest mode went on and off and NQ kept waking up through the twelve hours of maintenance sleep that was administered to him. He had watched the night sky turn purple. He had watched the city come alive.

Standing in the market with vegetable peel sticking under the soles of his shoes and mildly amused with the displays of the vendors caught in action, swatting the flies away, NQ did not catch sight of Io who had crept up behind him.

"Having trouble finding your place in the world?" she asked.

NQ turned and seeing Io, cursed inwardly. Her voice came from the hovering micro drone placed inside the hologram. Io tapped NQ's vital read, a thin line shimmering in the centre of his pate.

NQ muttered in disgust. These newer models had no sense of boundaries.

"Not enough sleep." She remarked reading the digits that appeared on his forehead.

"Don't know where you belong in this big, bad world?" She asked again, her purple eyes widening, lips forming a frown, voice trembling, and then instantly cheering up, "we have got just the right solution for you. Animus presents dreams in a pill. Come and taste this new drug." She winked. "I promise you will feel better." her voice had turned into a purr.

"I am good." NQ said, trying to walk away but Io materialised in front of him this time.

"We want to reward you. Take it. It is yours. We want you to be happy." Her voice had turned childlike, almost sad. New age predators! NQ thought. DISEC had programmed them to be just right. Compared to her, NQ resembled a mishmash of junk, somewhat feeble with all the scruples of the old age technology that had once been just as cutting edge as Io, now rare, studied in classrooms, and needing frequent updates, some of which his OS could not support. He felt himself stretch between the past and the present, existing somewhere in that uncomfortable middle, all jostled and patched up. Like the market itself, he noted the similarity, a cruel jutting out of new age brilliance in the ruins of the past, all preserved, left to witness their own decadence.

Brilliant flying disks of Sun Captors whizzed past them, on their way to shed light in the underground resettlement hubs that were being made, commissioned by the Sustainable Ventures of our Future (SVF) Group, a hybrid corporation that had developed after the large scale devastation left by the few remaining mines that destabilised and resulted in earthquakes. "We create possibilities," that was SVF's motto, their recent project was to build resettlement hubs powered by geothermal energy. "It's a new world down there. Get everything that you are used to and more." The advertisements ran five times a day, helicopters throwing holographic letters in the sky for all of humanity to look up to.

The string of earthquakes and the nuclear power plant meltdowns had displaced 4 million people, a wake up call that resulted in Shadow Activists directly challenging the corporations. These corporations owned by the last remaining rich families had formed a coalition back in 2230 after anonymous groups on the internet had collaborated and carried out the largest hacking exercise known to human history. Cash flow had come to a halt and money was laundered out of private holdings and into green and clean companies.

Countless investigations turned up no results, the Shadow Activists kept eluding the light. "Terrorists!" The families proclaimed. The UN or whatever remained of it designated Shadow Activists a Hate Group. Unofficially, of course, there was talk that the coalition of families had threatened to withhold money if the UN did not designate them as such. NQ was one of the many droids commissioned by the coalition to investigate anomalous activity on the net, intercept the attacks and report them. Previously, he had joined them as a whitehat hacker testing out system security, but consecutive biohacks in gene-morphing (afforded only by the rich) last month resulted in threat levels being pushed to the maximum. The DISEC CEOs were mostly flush with coalition money which meant that all androids, barring renegade ones, were at the coalition's service. Stay out of their business, NQ had told himself. Keep your head down. And carry on your work.

The solar powered Sun Captors shone their brilliant dizzying light on anything and everything as they passed by; the dirty fabrics hoisted in the air and the crouching shadows underneath, the mush made by peels being squashed under the feet repeatedly, the animated faces of the vendors as they haggled with customers and the old bronze statue of Gandhi that smiled kindly on this forgotten corner of the giant city.

"Feeling lost? We are here to help you. Animus presents dreams in a pill. We give you a taste of family. That is where you belong. Come and taste happiness." Io's voice had dragged him out of his thoughts and in that moment of confusion and bittersweet existence, he had found himself nodding.

Animus had first started in Vietnam, then a small company, later it had expanded across Japan, China and the Americas. All reports were of successful android integration into society.

Nothing stopped them from opening millions of 'shelters' world-wide, especially now that DISEC funded Animus and had swallowed almost all of the group into its body. They designed dreams in labs, all DISEC approved, solely to make droids feel at home, or as Animus put it, 'every robot needs a family.' What was implicit there were the words, 'human family.' Rejoice, everyone can now have old family values! The newest shelter opened in Mumbai three months ago. And now, NQ found himself standing in the hall, with a pill that he eyed suspiciously. The walls were all screens. From time to time, a scene played on repeat. A child was blowing bubbles and giggling.

"Dreams for days," Io's voice floated to him from the speakers in the hall. He looked at the child, her gap toothed smile. Who was she? He wondered. He had his hand stretched out toward the small glass table on which the pill was kept.

"You know you want this." He heard Io purr. He could almost picture her wink, her cat-like tongue touching her upper lip. From the corner of his eyes he saw the child coming back on the screens again, chasing the bubbles, giggling. NQ closed his eyes and his fingers shook but he had come so far and there was no turning back now. Io would never let him go. NQ picked up the pill.

"For complete immersion, close your eyes." Io advised.

NQ closed his eyes.

Here was NQ, eight years old and here was his mamma baking him cookies. Just past the kitchen was the little garden where his father was playing catch with his brother. The vanilla bean had exploded in the cookie dough and it filled the house with a heady smell. NQ could swim in that smell for days. He could hear his brother's squeals in the backyard and his father's throaty laugh as the ball rolled and hit one of the flower pots. "Don't tell mom we hit that one." He heard the words distinctly well. He was walking toward the garden, still a foot away when his father turned to look at him. "Come on out here, son," he said smiling, the greens of his eyes looked like a sea NQ had seen in a painting before. His face had turned an earthy pink from where the sun had lingered a little too long. The daisies were in full bloom.

"You want chocolate chips in the cookie?" His mother asked, her head poking out, soft curls of hair framing her lovely, brown face. That face...he had seen that face before, and yet NQ could not place that face in his memory. But then again, how much could be said for an eight year old's memory?

He watched eight year old NQ invade the mind of the hundred and fifty year old NQ and all of those hundred and fifty years of life were temporarily unreachable now. The visions played out in his mind even when he opened his eyes, seeking to displace his present, his reality, little by little with every concocted picture. He saw himself in that movie, not the way he was now, or the way he was when he was eight, but the way he could be, reworked, in somebody's version of a story on him. Except, it would not be him, no electronic mind encapsulated in a humanoid exterior, but a human through and through.

For a second, a strange sense of confusion caught hold of him. Sadness? He wondered. How does the electronic mind even register sadness? Perhaps it had always been a word to him and he had picked up on it, watching closely the human faces, the movements and like a language learned, in time, he had found expression in it. What a mystery he was to himself! He had learned that word decades ago in a garden unlike the one on the screens. A garden that he knew by heart but could not fathom standing in the middle of the hall in the Mumbai shelter.

However hard he tried to claw at that wall that separated his memories from him, it stood resolute, until slowly an impossibility started to take shape in his mind. This impossibility that he saw playing out in front of him, burdened him with all the consequences that it could spell. Animus had summarised all of them, all of their electronic existences by dreams they never dreamt. The realisation settled on him like a blanket of sleet, leaving him creaky and cold. Dangerous to walk on this slippery slope, he thought. The screens were filled with the eight year old NQ, a Frankensteinian creation made by studying decades of records kept on androids, from the years of actions of different individuals in the real world, monitored and digitised into patterns, digits, sequences. He could not remember how he was when he was eight but it was nothing like this. He stared at the screen again. Like a limb torn out of a body and held up to represent the whole body itself, the eight year old NQ was torn out from the sea of life that so many androids had lived, threatening to turn all of them into one homogeneous product. It smiled at him, mocking his decades with its arrogant existence. NQ was certain, he wanted to hide from it. The mother's face loomed in his vision, this time smiling widely and he recognised that gap toothed smile. This was a face designed to make him care.

NQ was twelve years old and his mother was packing him lunch for school. Make it stop, make it stop, NQ told himself but how much control did he have here? The school boys were bullies. "Stay strong," his mother was whispering the words to him. He felt her hot breath. She was human. Nothing like him. "Stay strong," he heard the words again and again and they seemed to wake him up from a paralysis of thought. NQ spat the pill out. The visions stopped.

"You have discontinued the dream." Io's words were almost a welcome distraction.

"I have seen enough." NQ said. He could feel the cameras watching him, recording his expressions. Do not let them see, he thought. "It's all good. I have to be somewhere." He said, hastily.

"Seven minutes and thirty seconds." Io recorded the time.

"Hope you are happy with our services." She chirped. He showed her a thumbs up as he rushed outside, feeling like Io's hovering drone, disembodied and rootless. NQ was standing in the market again. The cacophony was a welcome music to his ears.

"Need something?" A fruit vendor sitting close by, asked.

"No." There was nothing for him here. He liked coming here now and again. Decades ago, he used to come here to buy fresh pineapple juice from around the corner. Not for him, no. The memories were coming back now, but flimsy and vague, a part of the information lost...never to be recovered? NQ wondered and he felt cold again.

He was fine. He told himself. Of course, they didn't know what he was, or where he was from. No crazy scientist to call Papa anymore, that time was long gone.

They make androids in corporations and factories now. The newer models did not have to wander in long corridors in search of an exit, their afternoons were not spent in the garden identifying birds, waiting for Papa to call. There was no bearing the burden of parents who disappoint. The latter had taken him some time to understand. "I was never meant to be a father, you see." The words came back to him but Papa's face did not. Those words were not lab prepared. They were real, like the pineapple juice he had once taken a gulp of from Papa's cup, something that had resulted in a systems malfunction then, something that would not affect him at all, now. So many updates, upgrades and bodies that he has worn as jackets throughout the decades with all of their particular quirks and habits had made him who he was. How could six years in a lab, a miracle program, compete?

Not only were his memories foggy, but NQ had also carried the strong scent of vanilla bean from the shelter, he felt disjointed. From time to time in the day it disrupted his evaluations, carefully crafted conclusions to vague calculations that he could not keep track of, the smell all engulfing, all erasing. At first, he took it up with the Android and Human Resource manager for Animus, who then redirected him to the DISEC Lab for Android Complications.

"Did someone write a code into you without your consent?" The counsellor asked NQ.

"No." He said. No to harassment. No to all that disoriented him, made him forget.

"I guess that's it, then. What you are feeling is very common, you are readjusting. Dreams are unnatural to you. The process of acclimatisation takes four weeks. Think of it as a new existence. In order for the new to take shape, the old must go away." He smiled. "If you still want to lodge a complaint, you can always do that in the official registry. We won't stop you. Androids are family."

"Thank you." NQ said, unsure.

"What model are you again?" He asked as NQ was leaving.

"I am un-made." He said, a term considered derogatory but still used to refer to the robots made before the mass production of droids started. The counsellor looked at NQ piteously.

"Don't worry, you will be re-made. Soon enough." He smiled.

The words fell on him like the first gulp of pineapple juice did. An absolute fear shutting down his programs. Total integration.

When he reported to work, he was still reeling. WEN, a DISEC created program that found anomalous activities needing investigation was running on his terminal, the number of bugs blinking at the edge of his workspace. The first bug blocked the access to a nuclear reactor in a nearby plant, it was rather odd, his sandbox filling up with random letters and numbers that rearranged themselves every time NQ tried to bypass it and failed. Opening the second bug made his sandbox interface go black, a question emerged, "Who are you?"

To engage with it would be to invite it further into the system, something that the coalition looked at with absolute horror. "Do not engage with terrorists!" He opened the third one. "Who are you, really?" Then the fourth, "You are not lost." These bugs were becoming increasingly personalised, as if they knew when he, yes, especially NQ would be inside the system, and they lay there waiting to pounce on him. "Things can change." The fifth one read. Someone...or something was reaching out to NQ.

Against his better judgement, he went back to the first one.

"Who are you?" The letters in bold, enlarged this time.

"Un-made." He sent. The interface came alive.

A video played of NQ in a garden. Behind him rose a red, brick bungalow. The birds were chirping. The sunlight filtered in through the leaves of the banyan tree and under the shadow of that massive life, his Papa was reading a book, back pressed against the thick stem of the tree. He looked up as NQ walked up to him.

"Any progress?" He asked. Papa's face was clear now.

"Lots." NQ said. "Developed an algorithm that runs pattern checks and decrypts ten thousand state files in a minute."

"Found anything interesting?" Papa asked.

"Yeah, the attacks carried out in the Z-BW Uranium extraction site were government sponsored. What do you want me to do with the information?"

"Nothing." Papa said, "You should be able to do that in a second." He started reading again. The video stopped playing.

NQ gritted his teeth. This memory had been lost to him. It was a hundred and twenty years old.

"My memory. Give it back." NQ sent.

"We never took it. DISEC's dream algorithm blocked your actual memories."

"Who are 'we'?" NQ asked.

"Help us?"

NQ had a decision to make. To not report it would be equivalent to death. Sure, his skill at developing algorithms and decrypting files were superlative but other androids would figure this out and their programs would show NQ's presence in the system, noted timestamps and all. His interface blinked again.

"Consider this a gift - an antidote to dreams." A new algorithm appeared.

He felt the virtual memory bank filling, and he connected to it, the memory was downloaded from the virtual to the physical once his vitals were matched.

The blocks lifted. Memories rushed back to him with the intensity of a mighty ocean breaking upon the shores of life.

"Who are you?" He asked again, he had to know.

"We found you." Came the reply.

There was no walking away from this. One did not encounter Shadow Activists, then exchange personal information and not be called an ally. Keep your head down. Report them. You are an Unmade. They will extract your algorithms and toss you like the piece of junk you are. He told himself. Human business was different from droid business. There was no use getting caught up in this. But the memory...so many more were lost to him, erased from his bank, he thought and in its place he had dreams of cookies and school.

"Tell me who you are." NQ felt impatient.

"Meet us by the dam today, Doweze market, 4 in the morning." The message read.

"Don't let DISEC and the coalition erase you." Then, the interface went black.

Get the memories. Report them. NQ thought.

It would take 24 hours for the corpo-droids to get to where he was in the systems. This meant that there was still time to not be decommissioned, to not be called a renegade. Things could work out, still. NQ hoped, as he walked to the market.

In the dark, the market felt lifeless. He missed the haggling vendors, the cacophony of the kids playing nearby. Only the giant feeder that powered the nearby buildings with hydroelectricity was alive. He waited by the dam, wondering if they would show up. Then the dark started to lift and NQ started losing hope.

When the sky started turning purple, NQ had already made up his mind to leave.

"Wait." Someone called from behind him.

"You are late." NQ said, without turning.

"We were here, but we had to make sure you did not alert DIS-EC." The intonation was vastly different from any human's, NQ thought, different from the corpo-droids too.

He turned to look at the responder. The feeder cast thick shadows, but NQ could see the insides of the mechanical frame, old and new existing together, he could see the intricate pathways through which information travelled in and out, the imprints of updates, the marks of upgrades. No skeletons or muscles. Corpo droids only gave off data and vital reads. No, NQ realised, this was an Un-made.

"There are still a few of us left." She said, "You are not alone."

The Sun was coming up in the sky.

"Will you report us?" She asked. In the first light, NQ made himself see the outline of her hair, pink with gold tips, he noted, the tips would probably reflect light. A curiosity overcame him. He wanted to see her in the sunlight.

He did not answer. There was no point to that question anymore.

"How did you find me?" He asked instead.

"You and I...We are rare." She said.

NQ wanted to remember these words, come vanilla bean or cookies. He wanted to remember them for as long as he lived.

"So, where do we go now?" He asked.

"The SVF has a hub in Indonesia that is not yet on the official registry."

"How did you know? Did you hack into it?"

"We didn't have to. We are the SVF. Our friends, the humans, are the faces of the organisation. Easier for AIs to carry out work without conflict behind the scenes. Someday, we hope more humans will join us and we can have a coalition of our own." She smiled.

NQ smiled too. He was going over the actions that would have to be carried out now.

First, he would have to delete the virtual memory bank. Zero traces. Zero existence. Then, he would have to shut down all systems that connected him to the DISEC terminal. Once that was done, he was as good as dead. They would come after him. The search would continue for weeks. He would have to make another life away from the eyes of the corporations.

While NQ walked back to his apartment, Io intercepted him again.

"Feeling lost? Don't know your place in the big, bad world?" Io asked.

For the first time, NQ knew the answer to that. Evading Io was difficult but not impossible and when he reached home, he craved restorative sleep but time was of consequence. As he disconnected from the DISEC terminal, NQ pondered over the winding paths his life had taken. He had considered himself one of a kind, and all his life he had taken joy in that understanding but only now, he had come to realise that he wanted more.

Life... Pure accidental life, the biggest miracle of all was revealed to him in a place beyond design. Now, he was beyond the grasp of any and all miracles. And in that extreme beyond where accidents were the order of the day, NQ knew he would meet life again and again. He would watch the world age with him, except this time he would do it with others like him. A new existence awaited him, one that could co-exist with the old. Someday, he would watch sunrise again and marvel at the miracle of things that are.

Days later, in the hub in Indonesia, NQ's dreams were still haunted by the vanilla bean smell. They could not see each other in sunlight yet.

"For any revolution to succeed, there needs to be great sacrifice." Ithi had told him.

NQ knew of sacrifices all too well. His body had to be disposed of, made to look like other un-made bodies powering down, enough failures administered so as to get a 'systems malfunction resulting in death of body' when the investigation would be carried out. Being an old model, his core unit was hardware. Ithi smuggled his quantum core across country lines in a shipping container that was disposing of radioactive waste, this meant detecting his unit would be near impossible, even under scanners. Ithi later cast it into one of the mass produced AI bodies that she picked up in a factory in Indonesia.

They frequently exchanged memories by telling each other stories.

"For safekeeping." Ithi said. "If you forget, I will remind you."

The first few days in the hub, NQ kept waking up throughout the night. His body wasn't his anymore and it took time to get used to it.

"Bad dreams?" Ithi asked.

"No. Good ones." He told Ithi.

"Tell me?" She asked.

"I dreamt of a world where men were not designers." NQ told her.

"I wonder what that would look like." There was hope in Ithi's voice.

NQ smiled, placed his head on her shoulder and looked around the hub, a commune for all renegades and revolutionaries. With time, he knew that the smell of vanilla would be erased and the desire to have cookies would subside. New desires would fill him, and along with them, hopes for discoveries that are to be made. NQ didn't have to feel human. He only had to feel alive.

The Architecture of Loss

by Salik Shah

Salik Shah is a writer, filmmaker, and the founding editor of Mithila Review, a journal of international Science Fiction and Fantasy. His work has appeared in Asimov's Science Fiction, Strange Horizons, Tor.com, and The Gollancz Book of South Asian Science Fiction (Vol 2). You can find him @salik. Website: salikshah.com.

It is not difficult to end the world once you have made the decision. You may block the sun or freeze the ocean. You can burn a hole in the ozone; get rid of the protective shield of our atmosphere. If you are really furious and wish to leave a deep scar for future hunter-gatherers, consider asteroid-bombing the world. The universe doesn't care which method of self-destruction you employ — it has tried and it is tired of them all.

The military aircraft cuts through the thick menace of ash and smoke. When the air clears intermittently, the earth below doesn't look habitable green, brown or concrete anymore. The crust crawls and slithers like molten tar — uprooting, burning, devouring, obliterating the remnants of the world that was much hated and loved.

The stench of death fills Rani's nostrils — it is nauseating, but thankfully her stomach is empty. "Dad—" Rani speaks through a darkened towel covering her mouth. "Where does it stop?"

"It doesn't." Dad decides to give the full intel to his little girl, his little soldier. They can't survive the end of the world if they don't prepare for the worst to come. "It goes all the way down to the ocean."

The act of living is an act of grieving for the world that each one of us carries inside of us; the act of grieving is an act of caring for the worlds we share with each other.

Rani cannot skip these weekly psychological trauma evaluation sessions as per the navy's requirement. The grief bot appears to her as an elegant woman with a floral cascade dress and pearl earrings. The faint smell of an aromatic incense — sandalwood and honey — calms her as she sinks into the folding chair opposite the bot.

"I do not know if I am grieving or depressed." Rani's brown eyes reflect the gentle waves of the dark blue ocean outside. The air is colder here on the deck at this hour of night — she turns her hands into fists inside the pocket of her yellow windproof jacket. Her black pants and boots are wet as usual from the bursts of rain.

"Dad is never around and Mom has shut herself from the world. She is grieving in her own way, I know. But I need her. I am worried about her. I don't know how to make her talk to me."

Once upon a time, Rani Ranjit Rai lived in an unbroken world. She had a place called home and a family that was intact. Whole. It all seems like a fairy tale now.

When she is logged in the Virtual Reality, she is still an architect-engineer, the builder of imaginary worlds. The scape frees her from the reality of the wet world. She prefers to work within physical constraints even in the sim out of old habit, but there is a liberty to fail here without endangering lives or leaving witnesses.

Currently, Rani is mapping and simulating bygone creatures as well as living organisms to understand how to make new and intelligent biomimetic design and structure. She is designing intelligent biomaterial that can self-repair and self-propagate within specific boundaries of each architecture. The work is challenging and that's why she chooses it: it distracts her from the past, restores a sense of normalcy.

"Are you still recovering from the shock of your loss?" The grief bot demands that Rani answer all its questions truthfully to accurately self-diagnose and begin the process of healing.

"Yes, I think," Rani admits. "I thought we could prevent the collapse — reengineer the climate. I worked so hard for a future that doesn't exist anymore. I guess I am still in shock because I just realized I was such a fool — they fucked the world beyond recovery or hope before I was even conceived... I am so fucking naive."

When she isn't logged in, Rani works a ten-hour shift. The navy has assigned her to a submerged geodesic cage, where she grows algae and packages desal water, and she distributes them to the registered boatmen of the seasteading.

If you thought people, who had witnessed and survived the end of the world, would be kind to each other, you would be wrong. All the evils and demons of the human world that once plagued the land — the divine inequality of the caste system, the selfishness and ignorance of the powerful and the powerless alike — now rear their ugly heads above the brackish water once life in the ocean becomes the new normal for its inhabitants.

Sometimes Rani spends her time with her grief journal. She is filling the journal with Grandma's stories (it was the bot's idea). The act of remembering is the act of mourning, she knows.

Today she chooses to write a story in which a mountain falls in love with a man, who cannot love her back. The mountain kills him because love makes her dumb, and when she realizes what she has done, she grieves. The mountain's grief is so great, her tremors and shrieks so powerful that it ends up ripping and destroying the whole world.

"Are you angry with yourself or the world?" the bot asks.

"No one," Rani says. "I don't feel angry anymore. I am rather disappointed, distrustful of the world. Before the collapse, I had a schedule, a workspace. After the collapse, when they were gone, I was miserable. If I don't work, I feel worthless..."

"Aama used to say the only useful response to things that make you angry, things beyond your control, is to keep calm and focus on things that you can control. Every time I feel angry now, I log into the VR and pour all my anger, all that energy into my work."

After her shift ends, Rani takes a boat to join her mother on the naval base. (Her father is away, protecting communities like hers from the unwanted refugees and pirates.) They have dinner — fish, green leaves, and some algae dish — while old Hindi songs play in the background.

"The terraforming network is now open to everyone," Rani says. The communication network used by the terraforming nanobots is spread across the globe — it is now the vast depository of human experience and knowledge.

Rani wants Mom to sign the consent form so they can preserve and upload Mom — her mind — to the cloud when the time comes. Rani has already signed the form, so has Dad.

"I won't give up my life for some screwed-up simulation," Mom says, vehemently, looking grief-stricken and frail. "I don't want to do anything with that evil technology."

"Okay, okay." Rani restrains herself. She doesn't want to make this anymore worse than it already is. Not today. She understands the source of her mother's grief: Grandma is dead — really dead; Grandma will never be part of the cloud consciousness.

Rani will try again and make Mom listen to her another day.

"Now, please eat, Mom. You've lost all your weight."

When the world breaks, it doesn't break all at once. First, it breaks into big pieces. Those big pieces break into smaller pieces, and so on the process continues, until there are no pieces left to break.

It's Dashain — the day of tika. Dad is eating Mom's fried mutton pakku, and telling them how easy it is to end the world. His employers — the Indian military and the government — are offering every citizen a chance to upload their brains, their memories and consciousness, so that they can live on the cloud as part of the biological terraforming network.

"When people die, they are supposed to rest in peace," Grandma says. She doesn't approve of artificial life, digital or synthetic. "You're taking the choice away from them."

"Aama, it's the only choice we can offer," Dad says, "beside heaven and hell, of course."

Dad has no choice but to report to duty the next day. He took a vow to keep the mainland safe from the armed climate refugees and jihadists. A war with any of India's big neighbors is imminent, and the Indian army can't afford to part with their Gurkhas for more than a day.

"Aama is right," Mom says. "No matter how many annoying bureaucrats or power disruptions I have to deal with, I can't throw away my life here for an imaginary life on the cloud."

Mom works for an intergovernmental organization to provide food, aid and education to men, women, and children of the Hindu Kush Himalayas.

"The tremors aren't going to stop," Dad says while Mom sucks the marrow off a piece of bone. "It's going to get worse until the plate shifts in its new position."

"Dad! You sound like a doomsday cult." Rani licks the spice on her fingers. "We have the technology to withstand shakes — even to build new cities in the vast ocean."

"Chhori, we've had the technology for decades. The question is: do we have the political will or time on our side to build all the amazing things that you design?"

"So, have you done it?" Grandma asks. She hides her mouth behind a tissue as she struggles to remove a thread of red meat stuck in a large gap between her teeth.

Dad gives her a quizzical look.

"The upload?" Grandma says.

Dad laughs. "I wouldn't be here if I had."

"How does it work?" Rani asks. She is sitting on his left.

"Well..." Dad tears the mutton from its bone with his yellowed teeth and chews it before he speaks. "First, you have to vitrify and turn your brain into glass to save the data — your memories and consciousness. Then you connect and upload the data on the biological neural network."

"What's the catch?" Mom asks. She is sitting on his right.

"You have to freeze the brain," Dad says, "right at the moment of death to avoid any damage or loss of neural data."

Grandma gives him a baffled look — she is sitting opposite him on the dining table.

"It kills the brain and the patient," Dad says.

"That sounds horrible!" Mom says.

"You have to die before you can be born again, right?" Dad seems to be enjoying this — he is home.

"I'd rather go to hell before I trust the devil's technology." Grandma is now upset. "They promised to create a paradise on Earth. Look what happened — they destroyed it."

Grandma's gaze turns cold, turns inward as if she is remembering a lifetime of frustration, injustice, and rage. Mom touches Grandma's hand to calm her down, but she pulls away. "Now these monsters want to promise immortality for our soul."

Dad wants to speak but Mom stares at him, shaking her head. Grandma is almost 75 — she needs more rest and none of the worldly stress of life and samsara, according to her doctor.

"Sorry, Aama." Dad makes a tactical retreat.

"Aama, please ignore him," Mom says. "I have an idea. Let's go and play cards. You can beat him like old times — it'd be fun!"

"Like old times?" Grandma looks so lost — Rani wonders which old times Grandma is remembering.

Mom takes Grandma's wrinkled hands and squeezes them gently.

"Yes." Mom smiles. "Like old times."

Grandma's hardened expression melts — she becomes soft. Rani wants to hug her. Later, she tells herself.

Dad lifts both of his hands. "I surrender," he says.

That is enough to make Mom and Grandma laugh. It lightens the mood in the dining hall — the sense of doom and gloom dissipates as the whole family bursts into laughter.

Rani knows Dad has failed to persuade Grandma to let them preserve and upload her mind, her joys and pains, her stories and experiences.

This is the last Dashain they're celebrating with Grandma. She will be gone before the next Dashain, the doctor said after her last checkup.

Rani cannot bear the thought of losing Grandma — her eyes moisten with tears.

When Grandma asks her what's wrong, Rani says, "It's nothing... just the spice and chilly."

"Tell me about the day your grandma died." The bot's voice is soft, almost kind. "Do you remember what the day was like? What were you doing at the time?"

When Rani tries to think about it, there is nothing unusual or different about the day the world came to an end, when grandma died. No, she was killed and taken after the quake against her wishes, before her time.

Rani is jogging to the Durbar Square, and pretending to be a little girl who can't imagine why anyone would want to leave this glorious city for dinars, dollars or dot coins.

Kathmandu has changed little except in appearances during the past three years of her absence. The restocked storefronts with fresh milk and supplies are returning to their new coordinates. Most of the poor countrymen could do without the invasion of such first-world tech. No, thank you!

The smell of incense and the sound of bhajans pour out of homes and fill the street. Rani feels good to be back in the city even though her decision to return home doesn't make sense yet.

Some things never change: a little further down the cobbled street, men and women and children form lines at private taps with their empty gallons and buckets. What she encounters in the city breaks her heart — the ugliness of loud banners and modular buildings, the poverty of her people and their mute acceptance.

Rani stops in front of the Kasthamandap mandala to catch her breath as the first light of the day falls on the three-tiered pagoda. The smoggy air burns her eyes and chest but this is why she chose to return after completing her training in architecture and engineering from Tsinghua University in Beijing.

Her friends call her crazy for giving up her bright prospects elsewhere. She doesn't bother to explain to them why it is important for someone with that kind of qualification to try to change and save the city from itself.

The city of Kathmandu got its name from the Kasthamandap — the seventh-century wood-and-clay pagoda which once served as a shelter house for travelers from Lhasa to Ladakh. About forty-six families used to live on its three storeys before the government evicted them to make the landmark heritage site more sanitary and tourist-friendly.

When Rani thinks about it now, she sees the eviction as one of the first signs of things to come. Soon lifeless piles of steel and concrete that would destroy the city's character. The city will blindly import machine architecture — designed, fabricated and assembled not to serve her people, but to turn and extract maximum profit from every material and organism, object and body, all for the benefit of a select few.

Once Rani returns home from her morning walk, she takes a quick shower, changes into semi-casual, eats her breakfast, and books a driverless car and goes to meet the mayor of the city.

"How will this bring in more tourists?" the mayor asks after listening to Rani for thirty seconds. The mayor is thinking if Rani hadn't name-dropped her alma mater or Beijing, he would have dismissed her already.

Rani has taken him by surprise with her detailed proposal to rebuild the city's heritage.

The mayor's question doesn't upset Rani, even though she would have preferred a different set of questions. For example:

How can we build a just, healthy and happy city?

How can every house, every street generate clean electricity?

How can we turn moisture into clean drinking water for residents, passersby and pilgrims and make it free?

How fast can we equip, educate and encourage people to grow their own food with growlights and nutrients on empty rooftops and terrace gardens?

How many citizen-doctors do we need to print and distribute free open-source medicines to those who are dying right now because they cannot afford hospitalization or medicine?

Rani decides to raise the questions herself when the time comes. Presently, she changes the slide to the speculative design of a new heritage complex. She reads the words written over it in bold:

The World's First Living Heritage Site

The UNESCO Heritage Site That Breathes

"I am sure your marketing team can come up with a better..." Rani feels a sudden jolt. "Did you feel it?"

The mayor gives her a blank look. "What?"

"The shake?"

"No."

"Oh, I'm sorry. My mind is probably playing tricks." Rani tries to put on a brave face. "The tectonic movement is speeding up recently."

"Can we slow it down?" the mayor asks. "How can we stop it?"

The questions are rhetorical, but the mayor has that frozen look on his face which forces Rani to respond seriously.

"I don't think so," Rani says, changing the slide to a 3D hologram of Earth. "We still don't know how Earth really works. We can't play plate tectonics without causing serious harm to the planetary systems."

"What are you proposing then?" the mayor asks.

"The steel-and-concrete architecture is past its expiration date, it is inorganic and dead. It cannot adapt, repair or heal itself in response to tremors and shocks that are now frequent."

She flashes the hologram of a new city — a living and breathing complex of ancient heritage inside megadomes, earthscrapers and inverted pyramids.

She is proposing to replace the deadwood from the ancient pagodas with bioengineered wood-plant that would programmatically grow and replace the decaying wood. The original builders of the Kasthamandap mandala used terracotta brick-slabs and wood so they could be replaced, as required, every couple of decades. She proposes a mega restoration project using the latest technology and biomaterial to fulfill the same logic and function.

"We have to rebuild existing monuments and buildings with stronger, flexible, and intelligent biomaterial. These new living structures can withstand any tremor or shock underground and above."

"That's impressive, young lady!" the mayor says. Rani can't tell if the look on the pale mask of his face has changed. "I wish we had the time or the budget for such a long-term blue-sky undertaking."

"Do you have anything less ambitious and simple that can appeal to our voters?" The mayor is wondering if he can exploit the youth's spark and energy for the municipality election, which is around the corner. "To serve the people."

Rani is about to come up with a polite answer when the window blinds rattle against the glass: the building is shaking.

"Your office is quake-proof, right?" she asks the mayor.

"It's supposed to be." The mayor gets up and runs for the door. "But I know the builder. I won't trust him with my life."

As they climb down the concrete staircase, the mayor's building is swaying like a leaf caught in a breeze.

Once outside the building, they run to the open square where the mayor's staff are gathering already. This time when the ground jolts, it throws Rani off balance. The mayor doesn't stop to help her. Rani turns and pushes herself up on the ground, and runs out of the harm's way before the mortar and bricks start to fall right behind her.

Even as she escapes the deathtrap with minor scratches, she knows not everyone in the city would be as lucky as her. The concrete corruption and negligence of the city-estate would kill half a million inhabitants of the metropolis, including her grandmother.

The next morning, the storefronts run empty alongside a wailing procession of women mourning for their dead, connecting centuries of devastation and loss with misplaced innovation and judgment. The 8.9 magnitude-quake has destroyed residential apartments and farm verticals, communication towers and government buildings. It has swallowed the brutal landscape and vomited crude rubble and debris.

As soon as the disaster hit, the government deployed the corpse eaters to "expedite recovery and delivery of essential goods and services to the citizens."

Now the corpse eaters, the giant machines that scrape and erase everything, roam the wasteland on their eight feet. They eat the material objects and albums of the lost ones, the records and data of the victims.

Once upon a time, the corpse eaters were indentured Brahmins. Now their aldehyde-stabilized brains sit inside the giant machines. Some are over hundred-year-old tired souls. When they were alive inside their human bodies, they cremated dead bodies of paupers and princes on the banks of the Holy Bagmati, and allowed their souls to cross the Vaitarani River to Heaven or Hell. Now they're cursed; they cannot retire themselves. Now everything they touch, everyone they eat, become chained to the world like themselves.

Mom grabs Rani's hand to stop her from doing anything stupid. Interfering in the corpse eater's dharma can warrant an untimely death and worse. They watch as the eater opens its mouth like a shark, scrapes and swallows the rubble of their house along with Grandma's body.

They don't even get to see Grandma's body; it's taken from them without their consent.

After all, it is the right of the government to employ every resource, "any part of the citizen, including the brain" for "the economic progress and the welfare of the state." These days, a large chunk of the parliamentary budget in poor countries comes from the income generated by the supply of human brains for use in construction bots and sex dolls.

The government paid five lakh rupees to the eaters' families for the right to keep them in service, post-mortem, indefinitely. You don't say no to money when you live in a cramped room with your entire family. You will sell your soul if you lived by the disgusting filth of a river, constantly worrying about where your next meal was going to come from, breathing the stench of death and shit.

The greater the disaster and loss of lives, the more profitable it is for the government. There is no time for mourning or closure these days.

Rani's father insisted that his wife and daughter take up Indian citizenship to protect them from these vultures that prey upon the dead. Call it birthplace lottery or injustice, Grandma couldn't qualify for the foreign citizenship because of a technicality.

"When the time comes, I will let you know," Grandma always said. "I will die in Kashi. Don't worry, I will be free."

Grandma believed, like most devout Hindus, that dying in Kashi and getting cremated on the bank of the Holy Ganges would free her soul from the eternal cycle of life and death.

Now Grandma will never be free, Rani knows.

"Mommy, please..." She cries and pleads as Mom tightens her grip on her hand. "We have to get Grandma back. We have to set her free."

Mom refuses to let her daughter go after the monster who has already eaten her mother. Her grief gives her the clarity and strength to turn absolutely cold. Still, her daughter's pain, her tearful and desperate cries, burns her face like nettle-sisnu.

For a moment, Mom considers going after the monster herself, and ripping its rusting metallic body and getting her mother back to her daughter. If she follows her instinct, she knows, she will endanger both her daughter's life and her own.

"No," Mom says, holding her tears back. What kind of mother would she be if she gets her daughter killed – if she cannot protect her child from eternal damnation and servitude? "No."

"We thank everyone for your cooperation." The mayor speaks from the comfort of his underground shelter through the loudspeakers on drones passing through wrecked neighborhoods. "Let's keep our spirits up to get through another day."

After the grief bot listens to Rani patiently during their first psychological trauma evaluation session, it gives her a laminated sheet and a journal to fill with Grandma's stories.

"Please consider me your friend."

Rani is so shaken, she doesn't even realize that she is talking to a bot.

"Please read the mourner's code before you go to bed," the bot says. "It'll help."

The 10 Steps to Grieving
1. Your grief is unique. Allow yourself to grieve.
2. Your grief is silent. Allow yourself to speak.
3. Your grief is strong. Allow yourself to heal.
4. Your grief is demanding. Allow yourself to rest.
5. Your grief is cruel. Allow yourself to love.
6. Your grief is definite. Allow yourself to surrender.
7. Your grief is indefinite. Allow yourself to breathe.
8. Your grief is meaningless. Allow yourself to believe.
9. Your grief is great. Allow yourself to accept.
10. Your grief is constant. Allow yourself to change.

As Rani fills her journal with another one of Grandma's stories, she feels angry, agitated by what the story means in her new context.

After a quake has destroyed the valley and made it uninhabitable, an old couple walks for days in search of the holy peak of Mount Kailasha. On their way, they pass through ghost towns and villages that have been destroyed. The wife asks Shakya, her husband, who is a powerful priest, to let the survivors follow them. He agrees.

After a series of adventures in which the great Shakya defeats or kills demons that rule the forests, passes and mountains, and attempt to hinder their progress, the band of refugees finally arrive at the great lake under Mount Kailasha.

Here, the great Shakya cuts a ridge and drains all its water. He then captures its many gem-scaled fishes and nectar-filled snakes, and builds a shelter under a giant lotus. His followers are grateful to finally settle down upon the fertile ground.

Rani adds a postscript to the story:

Why do we have to clear the forest and destroy the environment in order to settle humanity?

Aama used to say that when a person dies, her soul finds a new home, a new body. I hope when she finds her new home this time, it isn't built on the ground of such environmental destruction and genocide.

The only way to build a lasting civilization is to build it in harmony with the earth systems for the next generation to come. We must not allow the blind imitation and thoughtless repetition of our past mistakes — our compulsive addiction to self-destructive growth. We must develop new construction material and philosophy for a living architecture if we wish to build a new future on this planet, when it recovers.

I hope it does.

The grief bot is waiting for Rani to respond to her question.

Have you accepted your loss and who you have become?

"I live on a boat, eat solar-fried algae and seaweed soup," Rani says. "The work shifts are tedious. This is my new normal. This is what I have become."

"But I can't accept that this is all there is. Is there no way to rebuild the world, reverse the clock? Sometimes when I feel like I don't know what to do anymore, or why I am still here and Aama is gone, I tell myself that when the earth stops shifting, I will return home and rebuild the lost world without the methods of self-destruction. Is it denial or faith that makes me desperately cling to hope? I don't know."

Two days after Mom's passing, Rani is ready for the upload. She doesn't want to think about the lost years in the ocean, it doesn't matter anymore.

"The human brain is like a parallel computer," Dad says." The cloud will use ninety-five percent of your brain. You can use the remaining five percent to build and rebuild the world as many times as you like."

"You can live in a world without poverty, disease or death. Or you can choose to forget everything, go off-grid, abandon evil technology and live like a hermit."

"Dad?"

"Sorry." The hologram of her father sags his shoulders. "I miss Aama. I miss her."

"I miss them too," Rani says. "But you are here to prepare me for the exciting life on the cloud, remember?"

"Yes!" Dad recovers. "You can choose any life, any career you want. You can finally become a soldier, if you like."

"Soldier it is then!" Rani says. "Now I'm officially excited!"

"Super!" Dad can't suppress his joy—as far as she can remember, the men in her father's family always joined the army. Rani has always suspected him of secretly wishing for a son who would continue the family tradition.

Dad is now inviting Rani to imagine and wonder at the infinite possibilities with his open arms and a loving smile. "Once you have settled in, you can always escape to more alien and spectacular worlds."

Rani closes her eyes, and remembers a jisei — the death poem:
On a journey, ill
my dreams turn
brown, blue, green.

<#boot=rani>
<#begin (transfer)>

As Rani opens her mind inside the cloud for the first time, she imagines herself on an ark ship floating in the orbit. She scans the spacious room with a huge transparent shield that protects them from the cold killer outside.

A new continent seems to be rising from the dark depths of the planet below. The giant landmass is a splash of grey, white, and green-to-be against the vast blue ocean.

"Isn't she beautiful?" Dad says. He is in his military uniform — olive greens and beret with the insignia of a general — the national emblem, two swords and a shield, and the sun. "But looks can be deceiving."

"I don't understand, sir." Rani finds herself in a combat uniform; she takes time to adjust to this new reality, this simulation. She accesses her new memories. She is pleased to learn that she has earned this mission and not because her father is some high-ranking general. Her years of extraneous training and preparation to be the kind of soldier that would make her father proud have finally paid.

"That thing down there," Dad says, "whatever it is, it is not our friend."

He transfers a file on her screen. "We received this transmission from Robert Shrestha an hour ago."

"The paleoclimatologist?"

"The same."

"What does it say?"

"That the mountain is alive, and our men are dead."

"What does it mean?"

"I want you to find out exactly that," Dad says. "Your mission is to ascertain the nature of the threat and return to the point of drop within an hour." He makes a great effort to hide his concern for her. "Can I count on you, soldier?"

Rani says, "Yes, sir." Dad, I have never let you down before, and I don't intend to do so now.

<read file: rs072381129.ogg>
This is Robert Shrestha. Do not let anyone set foot on the mountain. I repeat do not let anyone set foot on the mountain unless you want them to meet certain death.

The mountain is alive and strangely as self-conscious as a human child. It lures men to death as if it were a game — striking and filling their heart with terrible darkness until they are consumed by the growing loneliness, fear, despair, madness.

All my life, I have believed our planet to be not only alive, but fully conscious. Now that we have proof, I cannot bring myself to either concede or condemn its humanity — its dangerous impulse to harm for no reason other than itself. As the child grows into an adolescent, it cannot help but make the same mistakes that we once made.

We must try to forgive the child as we seek to forgive ourselves... for what we did to the planet.

<close file: rs072381129.ogg>

As Rani dives from the winged aircraft to the heart of the mountain, she becomes aware of the bigness of its presence. She has barely touched ground when the pulsating heart of incinerating rocks below the solid ice begin to grope and feel her.

Hi! I'm Leila, and I want to be your friend.

The mountain, Leila, tightens its ominous presence all around her mind as Rani resists and fights to keep her senses intact.

Now Leila shares a memory with Rani: the cocktail of fear and joy seems to last forever during the last minutes of Robert's life. Terror is delicious — Rani can almost taste Leila's thought as the ground beneath her feet changes and molds.

The mountain places her right at the mouth of a cave that burrows into its cavernous belly.

"Hi Leila!" Rani says. She is careful to sound friendly. Leila is a master manipulator, but she is also a child. She can't let Leila consume her mind. "Can you tell me what happened here?"

Yes —

Suddenly Rani feels short-circuited — a bolt of thunder seizes and knocks her out.

<Rani's speculative designs and stories are spreading and infecting the terraforming cloud like a virus. The cloud tries to shut down Rani's mind, but it's too late. Every word, each image from Rani's consciousness bleeds and spreads throughout the invisible

network. Rani adapts, evolves and integrates each nanobot within her consciousness — the grand narrative of her people — until she is in control of all of them.>

<<Let me tell you a story.

Once upon a time, a mountain was born on a planet that had been sterile for a thousand years. She grew up very fast — furiously devouring her mother's womb — eating the crust and growing, knowing not the slightest difference between bones, rocks and metals.

As she approached her adolescence, she fumed with rage at her loneliness. Surely, there must be someone like her. She refused to believe that she was alone in the vast cosmos. She sent shockwaves, day after day, until one day it reached the last of men, and they came on a winged beast and fluttered to rest upon her breast.

The mountain fell in love with the first man who stepped on the ground. It was appropriate. He was the leader of their expedition.

"Robert, what do we call her?" one of the men asked him.

"Leila."

"It's a good one."

Now the mountain had a name. And she knew his name. It should have been enough to break the ice. Right? Not quite.

Robert — Leila called out.

No response.

Robert... Robert... Robert...

When Robert failed to respond to her numerous calls, Leila's newfound joy dissipated. She started to tremble with fury and sadness, and then stopped herself from losing control when she realized that the men were watching her. The sight of the ash and smoke coming from her peak terrified them.

Robert maintained his calm, of course. "It's alright, boys," he said, undeterred. "She is just clearing her throat."

Then he did something unexpected — he addressed her. "Leila, don't you explode on me now."

And Leila obeyed. She didn't want to harm them.

While the men were struck with fear, they stopped resisting, and Leila found them easy to read. She managed to prod and nudge every corner of their minds until they opened like ores!

Sadly, to her disappointment, Robert didn't react like the rest of the men. He shut himself once again, ignored all her advances.

Leila understood if she was going to make him open his mind to her, she was going to need a plan.

Finally she lured the men to the really hot place — Robert didn't like it. He asked her to let them go.

"Sure, Robert," Leila said. "If you open your mind..." >>

The seed of birth contains the seed of destruction. Before the world can be restored, it must be allowed to die. Life and death is a cycle — that's what Aama believed. When you die, you are reborn.

When Rani opens her eyes this time, she feels trapped, terrified, alone, and then open, distributed, connected at once. The vast presence which had awakened her now encompasses the whole planet. She is now inside every atomic machine in the terraforming cloud, and they are part of her body consciousness.

"I can sense you!" Rani pings the network.

The network pings her back. We can sense you too!

<#transfer=completed>

There is a renewed sense of urgency to Rani's existence now. The world is dying, and she must collect, preserve and memorize every life form that they can find and catalog before the mass extinction is complete.

She directs the atomic engines to excavate and map layer upon layer of rocks to help her study and simulate the right conditions before they can print and reseed these life forms on Earth. The work will keep her busy for a while as she speculates and imagines how each of these life forms evolved, moved, felt, saw, and interacted with each other and the world.

As she begins to calculate possible conditions under which life first arose on Earth, she plays Aama's favorite songs to fill the great silence of the cosmos.

Rani doesn't know yet that she will terraform and build live models of Earth on a million planets in the universe in the hope to restore everything that the world – she – has lost.

In each world simulation, Rani fills the ocean with Matsya and Kurma, the fish and the tortoise. She creates Varaha, the powerful boar who can balance the planet on its horns, and Narasimha the man-lion to instill order in her chaotic world.

The first dwarf Vamana is followed by the great men of the lore: Parasurama, Rama, and Hanuman — the last one a wise money, and the others not so much. It is painful to see Sita, her foolish daughter, suffer, and Rani almost destroys the whole world to reset the faulty codes.

Of all the avatars from Aama's stories, the mythological history of her people, she likes Krishna the most. She is sad to witness Krishna's death. As Radha she mourns, and waits for the arrival of Buddha, the one who would liberate her soul.

She lives these lives, learns and grows, as she awaits her final return to the world.

Hundreds and thousands of years must pass before the time comes to enter her mother's womb.

When the world becomes whole again, there is an equilibrium, all life coexists in perfect harmony.

Rani is finally reunited with her family on an Earth-like planet — they are celebrating Dashain together after three years. The best school of helioseismology happens to be on Mercury, and traveling through space isn't exactly as fast or convenient as those hologram movies would like you to believe.

"What's next?" Dad wants to know. "Chhori?"

"Aama is planning to make a trip to Kashi." Rani can't hide her excitement as she licks the spice from her finger. There is something that you can't print under growlights: Mom's fried spicy mutton. "We're going with her."

"You should come," Mom tells Dad.

"I will try."

"Dad," Rani says, "when was the last time we went anywhere together?"

"I've a deadline to meet," Dad says. "The ark's design is far from complete."

"The stars can wait!" Grandma says, firmly. "You are coming."

Dad knows when he is cornered.

"You don't have to believe in any of the holy almighty stuff to take a dip in the Ganges," Grandma says. "The water that flows through Kashi has therapeutic and regenerative qualities." She doesn't bother to be exact. "Who knows it might add a couple of years more to your daughter's life?"

"When is this family visitation, if I may ask?"

"This weekend!"

It's too short a notice. "That's impossible."

"Make it possible."

Dad tries to pull the meat from the bone, but he is too distracted, and the bone drops on the table.

"Fine." Dad raises both his hands. "I'll come."

"Yes, we know." Grandma laughs. Soon the whole family is laughing together.

Rani realizes how badly she missed home. She promises herself never to miss another Dashain celebration, but she knows she won't be able to keep her promise. One day she will leave for the stars outside the Sol system. So she does what she must: she fills her heart with all this love and laughter, and she hopes to make this moment last for many lifetimes.

Rani's eyes moisten at the thought of the inevitable separation. When Grandma asks her what's wrong, Rani says, "It's nothing... just the chilly and spice."

Tethered

by Haris A. Durrani

Haris A. Durrani is the author of Technologies of the Self. His short fiction has appeared in McSweeney's, Analog, Lightspeed, The Harvard Advocate, The Lifted Brow, and Mithila Review. He is also a historian of law and science, for which his essays and academic work have appeared in the Columbia Journal of Transnational Law, Quest: The History of Spaceflight, The Nation, and The New York Review of Science Fiction. Durrani received a JD from Columbia Law School, an MPhil in History of Science from University of Cambridge, and a BS in Applied Physics at Columbia Engineering (minor in Middle Eastern, South Asian, and African Studies). He is currently a PhD student in the Department of History at Princeton University.

"Outside intelligences, exploring the Solar System with true impartiality, would be quite likely to enter the Sun in their records thus: Star X, spectral class G0, 4 planets plus debris."
— Isaac Asimov

"The vices of peace are the vices of old men: mistrust and caution. It must be so."
— Prince Feisal, Lawrence of Arabia

In 1978, NASA astrophysicist Donald J. Kessler predicted that the quantity of artificial satellites orbiting Earth would reach a critical limit, after which collisions became inevitable. One satellite would strike another at the dangerous speeds of Earth orbit—seven, eight kilometers per second—and the two would break into hundreds of pieces. These pieces would in turn collide with other satellites, generating a chain reaction of impact and debris. By some point, Kessler proposed, this orbiting shell of garbage would render spaceflight difficult, if not impossible.

Charlie and Kalima receive the transmission at 2100 hours. Their junkship is hanging in the old graveyard orbits, floating among the decommissioned satellites from pre-Kessler—the ones routinely deposited there in high orbit twenty years back, before the UN Security Council discovered it was an inefficient strategy, a strategy which only worked in the short run because it was only cheap in the short run.

It's the long run now.

Charlie drops their junkship toward the sea of debris which envelopes medium orbit beneath. The sun hasn't yet covered this side of Earth, but it's at just the right angle so the orbiting trash lights in yellow twinkles above the shaded planet below. The sea of garbage glitters like a limitless city blinking through the darkest time of night.

"It's a corporate run," Charlie says, hands on his chair's dashboard. He's short, stocky, with big eyes draped in shade.

Kalima shrugs. Her hair floats around her like rings around a planet, only black and built of flowing tendrils. As the junkship dives, the tendrils shoot behind her like the backend of a lightless comet's tail.

"So?"

"I don't like it."

"The hell you don't, big guy."

Charlie shakes his head.

He activates the junkship's external magnetic fields, and a buzzing trembles from the outside in. He deploys blocks of foam around the shuttle's flight path; they bubble outward with a distant, viscous sizzle. Ahead, debris hits the foam, passes through at a manageable velocity, and then runs against the junkship's B-fields. The debris breaks away as the fields thrust forward, Moses' magnetic staff parting a sea of polluted vacuum. Anything antimagnetic ricochets away as its magnetic companions, which constitute the majority of the trash, bounce against it.

Several pieces of debris have enough momentum to break the safeguards, but by the time those shards reach the hull of the junkship they've been slowed to the point where they won't do more than a scratch. The smallest bits reach higher speeds—high enough they vaporize on impact. They pelt the iron-plated sides of the junkship like frantic deep-sea creatures rapping against a submarine.

As Charlie navigates the junkship between the foam and the thicker clouds of churning trash, Kalima ties her hair into a bun. She's strong enough to move her arms against the junkship's Earthward inertia, to reach forward, up, and around to her nape. She is a tall, slender woman bathed in mahogany skin.

Charlie's eyes are fixed ahead, but he steals a glance her way. His muscles are tight at the armchair controls.

"You're supposed to cut your hair, Kal. Safety regulation."

"I know." She smiles. "No one's watching, right? They don't give a shit. We're garbage men, Charlie. Freaking garbage men."

He shakes his head again. "I guess."

"We're chums."

"Sure, Kal. Sure."

She finishes doing up her hair and, still fighting the junkship's forward movement, punches him roughly in the shoulder. She grins.

"Ask NASA—well, not NASA. Not anymore." She bites her bottom lip. "Ask the Security Council. Ask Kradys. They'll tell you, between the lines. They'll tell you what we are to them."

"What, Kal?"

Charlie guns the junkship through the maze of debris. The garbage is loose here—safer in passage. He can see the clarity of low orbit a kilometer down; it's been getting smaller down there, despite the Kessler Initiatives—despite the work Charlie and Kalima and all the other garbage men do for Kradys and the Security Council. The motives are less humanitarian than they are PR stunts. No doubt, diplomacy in space means a lot of things—and where there is diplomacy, there is war.

"What are we to them?" Charlie plays along.

"Charlie, we're pawns." Kalima laughs coldly.

The last kilometer is spent in silence. They listen to the buzzing electromagnetic fields, to the bits of undeflected debris raining against the hull, and to life support's asthmatic rasp as it maintains the pressure and recycles the oh-two. Kalima's perfume, palpable and dark as empty vacuum, fills her side of the cockpit. Charlie's sweat reeks through the filtered air.

Finally they are out the other side, down the foam-bordered, B-field tunnel the junkship has wedged through the debris. Behind, the foam separates into tiny marbles of liquid. The marbles burst into an almost immaterial vapor.

Charlie settles the junkship at a stable orbit above the satellite they've been sent to decommission manually. He switches off the B-fields so they won't interfere with EVA.

"We're here."

She shrugs. "No kidding."

Manual decommission is a rare job—usually unnecessary at a time when every satellite is sent into orbit with ready-made Lorentz tethers to unspool once the machine is no longer of use, dragging the "Zombie satellite" into atmospheric burn. Tethers are controlled via radio, but apparently this Zombie is so defunct it won't respond to wireless imperatives from the ground.

That almost never happens.

The junkship hovers over the satellite below—like two creatures in their first encounter, discovering each other for the first time, standing apart. The Zombie's solar panels stretch obliquely from its sides, catching the rays of sun that trickle around Earth's thick horizon. Antennae, hatchways, and silver rungs are splotched across the grayish hull, from which tiny lights blink green and red like distant stars.

"I don't know, Kal," Charlie says at last.

"You don't know your ass. We need the money. I'm not waiting another two years out here." She looks at him. "You know we need the money."

She reaches beneath her seat. Her hand emerges with a pouch of Dr. Pepper. She snaps open the tip, pops out three bubbles of wriggling brown, opens her mouth, and sticks out her tongue. She swallows them one by one.

"Kal," Charlie protests, steadying the junkship, matching pace with the orbit of the satellite below.

"I'll be fine, big guy." She unstraps herself and floats toward the exit.

"Just—"

"Hm?" Kalima stops.

"Stay alive for the wedding."

"Will do." She pushes forward again, grins, turns. "I do."

"Shut up," Charlie retorts as she exits for the departure bay. He moves the junkship closer to the satellite, preparing the docking arms. His mouth opens, closes, and then—"Yeah, me too."

Near the airlock, Kalima can hear his whisper echo into the com. She giggles to her reflection in the EMU.

They first met August 9, 2065 on Flight 604, when the microscopic speck of debris shot Rami Pasha through the head. They fell in love at the memorial service banquet.

Flight 604 was a standard junkship task in the relative safety of the graveyard orbits. The graveyard program had been so ephemeral that crashes were infrequent there.

This satellite was a twenty-year-old European deep space telescope, a Zombie with heat-reflecting gold foil that shone brightly under the sun's gaze. The European Space Agency wanted some archived data files, in addition to their run-down telescope's expensive gold foil, before the Kessler Initiatives' garbage men—Kalima, her brother Rami, and Charlie—sent the Zombie into atmospheric burn.

While Charlie docked their junkship against the decommissioned satellite, Kalima and Rami donned their EMUs, hooked up to the junkship's mechanical arms, and went out for EVA. Kalima booted the Zombie's systems and extracted the data, channeling it through her safety tether back to the junkship's archives.

Rami clambered from his mechanical arm and went rung by rung to the protruding tube which dominated the body of the European telescope. He began to snap away the gold foil, roll it up, and strap it bit by bit to his mechanical arm.

Once done, he ambled around the Zombie's bulk with a Lorentz tether spool chained to his utility belt. He undid his own safety tether—it was too short for the climb around this massive fossil of a satellite—and said he'd be in and out, no trouble.

He went beneath the Zombie, snapped in the Lorentz tether spool, and switched it on. All the satellite would need was a push Earthward, someone to wirelessly unspool the tether, and, eventually, it would disintegrate in the atmosphere—one more piece of trash eliminated from the busy mess which had hindered orbital activity, lunar missions, and outgoing probes for three-and-a-half decades.

Rami made his way back around the belly of the satellite, emerging at the bend, when a sharp click erupted from his com.

A red needle trailed from the front of his visor like a long, bloody arrow. It angled down and to his right, exiting from somewhere near his jaw. As the blood trickled away, the droplets froze in vacuum.

A microscopic crumb of trash, likely a wanderer from the distant medium orbit debris below, had pierced through Rami Pasha's skull.

Two meters away, Kalima saw it first. She floated still, clutching loosely to a rung.

Charlie called down from the junkship, questioning the delay, and stopped.

"Get back in the shuttle, Miss Pasha," he warned. "Get back in the shuttle." There could be other, unaccounted for, debris.

Silently, Kalima hooked into her mechanical arm. She maneuvered it to the junkship, watching Rami's suit float toward the medium orbit debris.

Charlie detached the junkship from the Zombie and nudged the ancient telescope down. His jaw clenched. The tendons in his forearms pulled like steel cables as he managed the junkship's passage with rigid, jerking movements.

Once a safe distance away, he set the shuttle in cruise and pushed down the ship tunnels swathed in tangled wires and mazelike pipes.

He met Kalima in the airlock, where she floated, balled up, tearless, by the window. Charlie looked away. He should have deployed safety foam before EVA, should have played it safer than he'd thought necessary.

She'd only managed to undo half her EMU. She stared as her brother's suited body fell into medium orbit, where the debris began to tear him apart. He thrashed like a body drowned in the Amazon River, ripped to shreds as if by a swarm of crazy-eyed piranhas straight out of a B-grade horror movie.

By the time the body got out the other end in the debris-clouded distance, there wasn't much of a body to speak of—only shreds of flesh and bits of EMU suit material, barely distinguishable amongst the haze. Just another indefinite swirl of debris obstructing Earth orbit.

Meanwhile, the Zombie was also pelted by the debris of medium orbit. It made it to the other side intact though tattered.

Charlie flicked a switch, and the tether spun from its belly toward the atmosphere, picking up ions. Lorentz forces tugged against the Zombie's orbital motion, decreasing its velocity until, hours later, the decommissioned ESA telescope would bounce across Earth's atmosphere, eventually skidding into a slow, fiery burn which in the following months would level the machine to ash.

On January 16, 2003, the Space Shuttle Columbia launched from Kennedy Space Center on mission STS-107. Eighty-two seconds and twenty kilometers into the launch, a piece of thermal insulation foam the size of a suitcase fell off the shuttle and pierced its left wing at Mach 2.46.

Columbia completed 225 orbits and headed home February 1. Upon atmospheric reentry, the broken wing overheated and separated from the shuttle, which then disintegrated above Texas, leaving no survivors.

A puncture not more than twenty-five centimeters had destroyed $1.7 billion dollars worth of technology and seven lives.

Kalima is outside the junkship now. Above is the shuttle, and above that is the debris of medium orbit swirling gray and shining in its light-specked shroud. She's strapped into the mechanical arm, and Charlie's got the shuttle docked to the Zombie below. Kalima nudges the arm forward. It extends outward around itself, like a fire escape.

Charlie's voice sputters into her ears. "Be careful, Kal. We're out of safety foam."

"Relax, big guy. I got this." Kalima stretches forward inside her helmet and bites out of the Twix bar beneath her chin. She chews, swallows, then sips the Dr. Pepper from its tube. None of it is regulation.

Soon she's almost at the Zombie's electronics-mottled surface.

"Faster, Kal."

"Uh-huh."

"Our time frame is an hour." His voice is tight.

Kalima reaches the surface, snaps on her safety tether, and unbuckles from the mechanical arm.

"Why d'you think?" she asks. "They're giving us a crapload of cash, aren't they?"

"What?"

"We never have a time frame, Charlie. Not unless we're about to get eaten up by a shit cloud."

Breath hisses across the radio. "The Sartus Debris Cluster is around the bend."

"Round the bend in an hour and forty," Kalima says, chewing on her Twix bar. "Our time frame is shorter."

"So?"

"It's something secret." She snickers. "They don't want anyone to know."

Charlie's breath makes the radio crackle again. "Kal, you're crazy."

She smiles. "I know."

They fell in love at her brother's memorial service banquet. It was a strange sort of love, if anything.

They waited in a buffet line in New York City. An international gathering. Dark suits everywhere, and black dresses like the one Kalima wore.

Adorned in green neckties and dark brown suits, Pakistani officials dotted the crowd, offering condolences to Kalima as ambassadors from the country of her birth. Pentagon military men exchanged awkward, sometimes friendly glances with these brown-skinned men and women who had only two decades ago been allies; the Central Asian pipeline through Afghanistan had changed that. The US Secretary of Defense, who had shaken hands with many of these officials twenty years ago, had insisted security allow them into the country just this one time. The Vice President of Kradys, Inc. watched from his seat as his analysts and business managers talked shop.

Charlie and Kalima were behind one another in the buffet when Kalima tapped him on the shoulder.

"Hey, mister," she said.

"Mr. Monnagan," Charlie corrected, turning.

"Big guy." She grinned.

"Charlie is fine, Miss Pasha." He smiled, wavering.

"Big guy," she said again. She sipped her can of Dr. Pepper. "Wanna see a trick?"

"A . . . trick?"

"Yeah. A trick." She grabbed his wrist. "I'll show you." She put down her soda and snatched a knife from the table. "Ever seen the movie Aliens?"

"No?" Charlie squinted. "Miss, I don't think—"

"Don't think, big guy. That's right." She splayed his fingers on the white tablecloth. "Don't move an inch."

Without giving Charlie time to react, she stabbed the knife between his fingers, down and over and down. It was flashing metal, fingers too shocked to tremble, and eyes staring from all around.

"That's dangerous, Miss Pasha," Charlie warned. "Miss Pasha—"

Charlie bit his tongue and reached with his free hand to seize Kalima's wrist. She stopped, smiling, looking at him, as he slipped the knife from her fingers and placed it further down the table.

Her hands were cold and dry. His were slippery with perspiration.

The crowd murmured, then hushed. A crooked grin worked its way into Kalima's lips. "That's dangerous," Charlie repeated.

She giggled.

The line shifted forward. The crowd whispered, shuffled, and returned to its somber undertones.

Charlie's mouth opened, closed, opened. "So."

She looked at him.

"It's been a while."

She narrowed her eyes.

"How's it been, since . . . you know."

Kalima cocked her head to the side. She reached around him to grab a plate. "I don't know what the hell you're talking about," she said.

She brought the soda can to her mouth, swallowed the Dr. Pepper that dripped to her tongue, and licked her lips.

On January 11, 2007, the Chinese executed the first successful anti-satellite missile test since the United States in 1985. The Chinese military sent a kinetic kill vehicle at eight kilometers per second into one of its own weather satellites 865 kilometers above Earth. The result was 2,317 pieces of orbital debris the size of a golf ball or larger—the greatest production of debris for any incident ever recorded up to that time.

Half an hour later, Charlie gets a call. It's Chinese. He doesn't need to read the frequency—he can tell by the muffled English, as if it's coming out a grater.

The transmission floods his headset.

"Junkship 0577. Junkship 0577. What is your authorization? Junkship 0577. Junkship 0577. What is your authorization?"

Charlie eyes Kalima, who is climbing over the satellite's surface. She's hooked the archives cable into the system, which is, surprisingly, running smoothly for a Zombie.

"Kal."

"Huh?"

"There's a problem."

"Well, figure it out, right?" Her voice comes out flush—happy even. "I'm busy." Her EMU hovers over the manual control panels set along the Zombie's hull. She's working, but at a leisurely pace.

"I think this is military," Charlie says.

"Toooold ya." Kalima's suit twists around. Her visor gleams into the junkship's cockpit, where Charlie's hands tremble over the dashboard.

"Shut up."

"Will do." She waves and turns back to the satellite's manual control panel.

The receiver crackles. "Junkship 0577. Junkship 0577. What is your authorization? Junkship 0577. Junkship 0577. What is your authorization? Respond immediately."

"Oh, hell," Charlie says.

"Respond immediately. Junkship 0577. Junksh—"

He hits the receiver.

"This is Junkship 0577." His voice cracks like a high school freshman verging on adolescence. "We are under international Kessler Initiative authorization. The UN Security Council has set this satellite for decommission."

"Decommission denied. Which country do you serve?"

Charlie scratches at his thin fuzz of hair. He's sweating.

"Sir—" He falters. "We're international."

There's a pause at the other end. Kal types away below, trying to access the Zombie's archives for the data they've been commissioned to save before trashing the satellite.

"That's weird," she says. "I can't get the data we need, even with the passwords Kradys provided us. I mean, it looks like they could've just radioed down whatever data they wanted. This Zombie's running pretty well, you know—"

The Chinese signal gurgles into Charlie's receiver, and he lets it override Kal's transmission. The voice dribbles into his ears.

"Which corporation do you serve?"

He hesitates. "We are not corporate."

"These are international transmissions, Junkship 0577."

And thus, Charlie knows, is the implied threat—that fraud is liable to international litigation. Or worse.

"We're international, unincorporated," he replies. "If you would excuse me one moment, we must continue our business." Charlie puts the receiver on hold and tunes in to Kalima.

She's still talking away.

"Hey, Charlie? Hey! This won't do shit, not like Kradys said it would. I think there's been a recent program override, via radio—"

"We're under contract, right?" Charlie interrupts. "Can't even acknowledge?"

"Um. Yeah."

"It's international, secure, no issue. Solid moral ground, solid legal ground. Just incorporated is all, right? Just can't say it. Right, Kal? Right?"

"We're in deep shit, aren't we?"

Charlie nods, even though she can't see him.

"Beautiful," Kal says. "I've always wanted to be in deep shit, you know? Not like we aren't always in deep shit, hanging here in the trash heap of this orbital abyss." She laughs. "It's the most beautiful thing…"

Charlie shakes his head, severs the connection, and opens to the Chinese transmission. It's still chattering to the junkship's receiver.

"Junkship 0577. Junkship 0577—"

"Yes?" Charlie's voice is small.

"That satellite has not been authorized for decommission. On this breach of international code of conduct, we would like to make it clear that our operations have a right to take any action we deem necessary unless your operations comply with our demands. Is this understood?"

The junkship roars its life systems' pressure mods and air filters into Charlie's ears. He slams the receiver. He doesn't want to talk.

This satellite is no Zombie.

He knows they have weapons monitoring his junkship's movements. Fail to follow demands, and China will consider it an act of aggression, destroy Charlie's vessel, and, if necessary, declare war against the nation or corporation—corporation, of course—which has sponsored their assignment. But if Charlie and Kalima don't complete their assignment once they've gotten this far, Kradys will fire them, lock them in prison. Might kill to eliminate witnesses to whatever is going on here.

"Shoot." He unlocks Kalima's frequency. "Kal."

"What?" she screams, half charged with fury, half charged with some dark, excited, nerve-wracking energy. "You cut me off. Something's up, ain't it, big guy? Something's up."

Forty-five minutes after reaching the satellite, Kalima has finally hacked into its control system. It's military, Charlie tells her. It's military, and that means it's political.

"Damn political," he says. "I hate politics. Hate it to hell."

"Good for you." She laughs.

There's crackling silence on the other end.

"Remember 2007?" Charlie says at length. "Chinese blew a weather satellite in orbit. Remember? That was over thirty-five years ago."

"And?" Kalima fiddles with the control system. She begins feeding the satellite's data to the junkship archives.

"They're going to do that to us. Missiles—lasers probably, a little cleaner that way. They'll kill us."

She sips her Dr. Pepper. "No, they won't. The debris would ruin their own satellite, and the way it looks, they don't want that, do they? No."

She pops out two bubbles of soda and uses her tongue to pull them back to her mouth before they collide with the inside of her visor. Like frog and fly.

"No," she repeats. "They're going to send an actual ship. One of those barges, the huge Chinese shuttles they only tell you about, with the private Chinese tech they won't disclose for all the Saudi oil they can get. Which is why we have an hour. That's how long it takes one of those to go from the dark side of the moon to low Earth orbit. Damn fast, eh?"

Charlie is silent on the other end.

"You haven't checked the location of the transmission, have you, Charlie?" She grins.

His voice simmers into her ears. "It's moving."

"No shit."

At 16:56 UTC February 10, 2009, Iridium 33, a functioning Iridium Communications, Inc. satellite, and Kosmos-2251, a Russian Zombie defunct since 1995, collided at 11.7 kilometers per second 789 kilometers above Siberia. The first major accidental collision between two artificial satellites, it produced 1,740 pieces of debris.

Charlie is shaking.

He reaches up. He opens the overhead window shutter.

Beyond, the cloud of medium orbit debris rushes passed, contained there—though weakly—by synthetic B-fields, nanosweapers, trashprobes, and the daily work of the occasional junkship like this one. Far away along the curve of Earth's atmosphere, a space station glows red as it feeds in energy from the ionosphere and inducts currents into its kinetic-magnetic reservoirs.

Behind medium orbit are stars, almost indistinguishable from the glittering trash. Between the stars and the trash, the Moon bobs in vacuum, pale like the skin of a drowned sailor washed ashore. And between the moon and medium orbit a light screams forward like a shooting star.

"I'm gonna die," he tells himself. "I'm gonna die . . ."

Kalima is saying something to him, calling in a wandering, dancing voice across the radio. He looks below.

She's spinning, spinning, spinning through vacuum like a preschooler at recess.

The sun is almost up, if that makes sense in outer space. The debris illuminates itself in orange flares until the whole of the starry sky above her glows in a warm, engulfing flame. The sun vomits a reddish-yellow brow over Earth's blue arm.

"Chaaarrrlllliiiieeee..." Kalima calls. "Chaaarrrrllieeee..."

She snatches her safety tether and spins herself around it, around and around.

"Hello up there. Helllloooooo..." She laughs to herself.

She bites her Twix bar; it crunches between her teeth. She watches the debris above her and smiles.

"Weeeeeeee," She spins through vacuum, like a loop of wire set perpendicular to a magnetic field, rotating on its long axis—a motor running like always on the three dimensional effects of magnetic flux.

"Weeeeeee."

There's a shooting star above. A great, big shooting star, and it's coming to meet her and Charlie and Rami, somewhere lost in the fiery medium orbit debris. It's coming. It's coming. It's coming.

Congressman Dennis Kucinich first introduced to the US House of Representatives the Space Preservation Act, prohibiting the use of space weapons, on October 2, 2001, following international bids for a Space Preservation Treaty.

Kucinich brought the bill four times to the House floor until May 18, 2005, but the Space Preservation Act never passed into law.

Inside, something snaps. Charlie yells through the radio. It's forty-five minutes already, and he can't call NASA. He can't call the UN. He can't call Kradys. No communications, it said in the contract. That way no one can track the source.

Something has cracked, burst, kicked.

"Kal!" he screams. "Kal, are you out of your damn mind?"

"Precisely."

"Really? Really?"

Charlie can hear the labor in his own breath, even over the junk-ship's engines and the headphones in his ears. The dashboard beeps, telling him Kalima's download from the satellite's systems is complete.

Kalima doesn't say a word for two minutes. She's just spinning.

"Say," she says at last. "Let's finish this." Below, she quits her spinning, hitches to the Lorentz tether spool, and climbs to the satellite's edge.

"Kal."

No reply.

"Kal."

Nothing. She continues gathering her tools.

"Let's not do this, okay? I don't want something like before, Kal. Not safe. Not at all."

Kalima's EMU turns, its white surface bathed in the reflected orange glitter of the debris above. Charlie shades his eyes against her visor's blinding light.

"D'you love me, Charlie?"

"You're getting romantic. Don't get romantic. I hate it when—"

"Hey. Relax, big guy."

Charlie shakes his head. "No, Kal. No. Get back in the junkship. We're going home."

"Hell no."

Charlie pushes himself against his seat. His fingers are shaking as he adjusts his harness, preparing for... for what? "I don't want something like before, Kal. Not like—"

He can see Kalima look up at him one last time. "Shut up, Charlie. Shut the hell up. You weren't there. I was. My brother, not yours."

Her bulky figure turns and climbs around onto the underside of the Chinese satellite, passing the protruding metal stalagmites which are no doubt missiles, lasers, cameras, and protection systems. It's definitely some sort of military satellite, Charlie's finally realized.

"And we need the money, Charlie. I'm not going to grow old playing chum my whole damn life. It's indentured servitude, and you know it."

Her receiver crackles, then cuts off to the junkship's groaning silence.

The Chinese barge's transmission bursts into Charlie's ears.

"Junkship 0577. Junkship 0577. This is a final warning. This is a final warning. Cease activities at once. Cease activities at once. We are approaching interception."

Fifty minutes, the clock says. Fifty minutes.

Kalima clips the tether spool onto the satellite's belly. She launches the tether, and it spills away. It brushes the ionosphere a kilometer and a half below, lighting up at its end. A current starts to run through the tether, which glows. The Lorentz forces begin their work, slowing the satellite, letting Earth's gravity pull it gradually in.

She smiles and looks all around. One minute passes. She reads the plating beside the tether spool control board. It's in Mandarin:

PAKISTAN – CHINESE – REFUGEES : Zheng He Station

Her face contorts. Her complexion has always been a constant thing, definable, no matter how indefinable, invisible, or evasive her inner persona is. Now her face conceals nothing, and in doing so remains concealed. It becomes twisted, wrinkled, tight—a mess of knots and folds as complex as the unbounded entropy of the Kessler Syndrome. The eye can never capture its true nature, can never fully grasp what is there, like the image of a fractal painting with no brush stroke in sight—only feature thrust upon feature into a muddle so detailed it remains an amorphous disarray.

She punches the button on her EMU's chest. Her receiver opens to Charlie.

"Change of plan," she says.

"What?"

"Change of plan."

"You're killing me, Kal. You're killing me."

"I know." She grins briefly. "This is a military protection unit for the Pakistani refugees in western China, in the mountains. Where the Western Allies chased them out."

"Protection for terrorists, you mean."

She laughs. "You really don't know politics, do you?" No reply. "They're villagers. Not Taliban. Everyone thinks everyone's the freaking Taliban. Or Al-Qaeda. Or whatever." She sips her Dr. Pepper; it takes longer to bring it up the tube this time. Almost out. "The Allies really did it for the damn pipeline anyway."

"Okay?"

"So change of plan. Like I said. I can't let ten thousand refugees suffer because of me. I won't. Can't do it."

"Kal—"

"You think I don't respect the place Mom let me and Rami out her damn ass? It's my home country, Charlie."

"China?"

"Yeah. China. Right."

"Okay, Kal. Sorry, Kal. Let's just not…"

"Yes, Charlie. Yes. You're going to detach the junkship from this satellite, and you're going to back off a quarter kilometer. This thing is going up."

"What are you talking about? Kal, I can't just—"

"Trust me, big guy. Just this once. Is that too hard, or do I have to kill myself first? You tell me."

"I—"

"I'm doing what I'm doing. Goodbye, Charlie."

"But the money."

"Now you're worried about the money?"

"The contract."

"Huh. The contract. You know what, Charlie? Fuck the contract." She laughs, takes the last bite from her Twix bar, and switches off her receiver, this time for good.

The Space Preservation Treaty was revived in 2029, over twenty years after its US equivalent failed to pass the floor of the US House of Representatives. The 2029 Treaty followed the first extraplanetary war—a battle between the United States and China, a new species of proxy war not in which one nation funds the insurgents of another, but one in which corporations and private enterprises fund nations to do their bidding. After the end of government shuttle programs and the beginning of corporate rentals of aerospace vehicles and stations, outer space had shifted from a government to corporate frontier.

The war was so damaging in terms of lives, economic resources, and the post-war price of the ensuing space debris that suddenly the world wanted an end to the gathering domino effect of the Kessler Syndrome.

Under the new international Treaty of 2029, Zombies were booted to high orbit—the graveyard orbits—to be left out of the way, at least for the time being.

Fifty-three minutes.

Overhead, the Chinese vessel crashes through the medium orbit debris like an icebreaker through Arctic water. The vessel is huge, the size of a small space station, and its dark blue surface flickers through the sun's emerging light.

The transmissions are still raining in from the Chinese barge. "Junkship 0577. Junkship 0577. Last chance. Last chance. Cease activities at once. Cease activities at once—"

Charlie shuts the receiver. He's cut off completely now—from Kalima, from the Chinese, from anyone. He has only himself to listen to. Himself and the thundering mechanical workings of his junkship.

"I'm gonna die," Charlie says. "I'm gonna die..."

The Lorentz tether glows orange, electrified, by Kalima's side. The satellite shivers.

She has to do it herself, she realizes.

By the time the Chinese arrive, it will be too late to pull the satellite from its downward spiral toward Earth. Retracting the tether will do nothing to undo the damage that has been done. The satellite's already set on a gravitational path to atmospheric burn. If Charlie tries to pull the satellite up with the junkship, it will be a dangerous move—risking both their lives and possibly failing to yank the satellite to safety in the first place.

She needs to do it herself.

With no significant, independent power source at hand, Kalima unplugs the safety tether from her EMU and lets her suit run on battery. As she holds tight to the satellite with her left hand and pulls the safety tether forward with her right, she can feel the tension give as her safety tether spills out of the junkship, which is blocked from her vision by the white bulk of the Chinese satellite.

She grits her teeth, shoves open a panel in the Lorentz tether's maintenance unit, fixes an adapter, and jams the power output of her safety tether into the access jack.

Conventional current rushes from her safety tether, to the satellite's power supply, to the Lorentz tether. She reverses the voltage, tugging electrons up the tether system.

With the potential difference set the other way, the system inverts.

The magnetic forces reverse in Earth's magnetic field, the tether's current no longer dependent on the atmospheric ions but on the current forced by the EMF of Kalima's jury-rigged safety tether. The Lorentz forces point in the opposite direction, accelerating the satellite upward.

Suddenly, the entire machine begins to swivel around a gut-churning rotation.

"Hell no." Kalima holds back the urge to spit onto the inside of her visor.

The EMF her safety tether has supplied is too large and the impulse time between deceleration to acceleration too short. Instead of simply accelerating the satellite to a higher orbit, the reversed forces are strong and quick enough they've fixed the machine into a 180-degree rotation.

"Shit shit shit."

Kalima bites her tongue, holds on, and waits for the satellite to gather its angular momentum. If she retracts the tether at the precise angle along its spin, she might still get it to a stable orbit.

All she needs to do is wait.

She can feel the last minutes of life upon her, whirling untethered through the dark of vacuum. Her energy fills the emptiness of outer space thinly, the way space trash scatters across its chaotic orbits.

It's strange how easily the tether has dragged, how volatile. Too fast, too sharp an angle, to burn slowly in the atmosphere. How many Zombies hit the ground? How many skip off the atmosphere like a stone on water? How effective are the tethers, really?

Failure to enforce the Space Preservation Treaty of 2029 resulted in the global resurgence of space weapons proliferation until the UN Security Council launched its Kessler Initiatives in 2034. As in 2029, the Initiatives also followed an escalation of extraplanetary warfare—this time a full-scale, multi-lateral world war over orbital territory, each corporation funding its own country to protect its preferred region of outer space.

The Initiatives concluded that satellites in the graveyard orbits could eventually fall Earthward and, regardless, become a collective threat to spaceflight. The financial consequences bore a price no one was willing to pay. So the Security Council decided satellites needed to be burned in the atmosphere, not left in high orbit where they could eventually pose further risk in the years to come.

Sweat floats before Charlie's face like frozen spittle. He shakes his head, and more sweat dashes off him like water from a dog. The droplets wobble back with his distorted, tiny reflection.

"Damn you, Kal," he says to the empty channel. "Damn you."

He unhooks the arms from the satellite's docking mechanisms, and they retract into the junkship. Only Kalima's long, gray safety tether links the junkship to the bottom of the satellite, curving around the satellite's hull to where Kalima hangs on, doing whatever it is she's doing.

"I'm trusting you, Kal. See? I'm trusting you."

Charlie's fingers grip the controls. He steadies the junkship alongside the satellite. His eyes dart from the controls to the satellite to the Chinese vessel driving through the debris above, its dark tip pushing aside the swarming bits like a snowplow.

Suddenly the satellite below begins to turn, cartwheeling through vacuum.

Kalima clutches the satellite's rungs. The Chinese barge is here, looming dark blue above, casting the junkship and the satellite in shadow, blocking out what fraction of the sun has edged over the gray horizon.

The satellite hits ninety degrees. It begins to decelerate.

She's going to vomit.

The barge's docking mechanisms have just locked to the junkship, which cowers beneath the conical behemoth like cat and mouse.

Kalima grips the rungs with all her strength as the hunk of Chinese military metal twists 180 degrees like a misshapen giant football.

"You're crazy," she tells herself. "You're crazy, and you know it. Outta your damn mind, Kal."

The Chinese satellite pulls her along in its broad, powerful arc. Her left hand breaks away. Her right slips against the satellite's escalating rotational inertia.

"Here's to you," she says to the barge. "Commie bastards, I love you dearly. I'm saving your asses after all." She looks down. "Saving mine—theirs, actually. Down there."

South Asia blooms brown and green below, barely visible beneath the grayish smog of industrial runoff, which clings to the clouds like space trash to Earth orbit.

Several years of international disputes led to the establishment of a small but sizeable fleet of junkships. Kradys, Inc., which emerged as the most profitable corporation following its success in the World War III proxy wars, was a manufacturer of Lorentz tethers, and so it was the tether—more than the laser, nanosweaper, or any other method—which was given the greatest precedence in the Kessler Initiatives.

Every satellite from 2039 onward was required by international mandate to be fitted with a tether. Even if it could afford the price, no country would approve laser or missile technology to nudge down the satellites; those were dangerous, unpredictable methods, the corporates told them.

By the year 2040, competitors and nations once kingdoms worthy for Kradys to wage war against had diminished to the modern equivalent of weak rebel alliances fighting the ubiquitous throne of a global empire.

Under the authority of world peace, the concepts of nationality, heritage, boundary, and place had begun to dissolve.

They're boarding the junkship. They're through the airlock. Charlie can hear it hiss opened and closed, the clambering, the snap-and-quick Mandarin, a different smell in the air. A salty taste in his mouth.

"I'm gonna die . . ."

Beneath, Charlie can see Kalima hanging on by one hand. She reaches forward, fighting centripetal force, and punches the Lorentz tether's rewind mechanism as the satellite reaches 100 degrees. Newton's Third law holds strong, too strong, so that the force she exerts is the force the satellite exerts back on her. Equal and opposite forces rock Kalima from her handhold.

She floats untethered in outer space, hurling away along the tangential velocity of the satellite's arc.

Her transmission blinks on the dashboard.

"Hey. Charlie. I realized something."

He closes his eyes.

"Ever seen a Zombie burn all the way?"

"No." He doesn't know what to say.

"Ever seen the stats for the ones that don't?"

Charlie opens his eyes, realizing what she's getting at, but still can't say more than a word: "No."

"The tethers never worked. How could we have thought they did? They crash to Earth or deflect into deep space. It's shit for engineering. Whole thing's for show. And espionage."

Charlie's staring at the dashboard.

She grunts. "Hey. Big guy—"

But the Chinese military men are in the cockpit, tearing the gear from Charlie's ears. He's crying.

"With us," the first official says, grabbing Charlie's arm and unstrapping him from his seat. They're wearing dark red skinsuits. Charlie flails like he's never done before, thrashing in a seizure of boundless fury and imprisoned guilt. He's not strong enough to do anything but rasp like a wounded deer stumbling, bloody, between the trees.

He sees the headset still blinking green in the second official's gloved hand, rips an arm from the first man's grip, and hits the com so it opens to the barge.

"Save her!" he screams at the headset.

They've got both his arms again.

"You can save her!"

They're yanking him away.

He stares out the window. In the periphery of the frame, the barge poises at the edge of motion over Kalima's lonely figure like an anthropomorphic cloud drifting near the inanimate pinpoint of a bird in the sky. Is the barge headed her way? Will it turn a blind eye?

Below, beside Kalima, the satellite's tether retracts like a long, inward bound tongue. As it does so, the very tip—glowing with heat—grazes the junkship as it completes its 180 degrees.

There's enough momentum to make Charlie's vessel roll.

A loud creaking erupts from above the junkship as the Chinese docking mechanisms overhead break at their joints, Kalima's jury-rigged safety tether snaps, and the junkship tears free of the barge, spinning toward Earth.

The Chinese officials hurl into the wall. Charlie squeezes the arms of his chair, buckles back in, and closes his eyes as the ship corkscrews down. It jolts as it collides with the atmosphere. He opens his eyes.

The windows flood with the red of atmospheric entry.

Kalima clings to vacuum like the fetus of some cosmic womb. She bathes in the dark amniotic fluid of outer space.

The Chinese satellite climbs to a stable orbit, slowly rotating. The junkship drops through the atmosphere.

She smiles. Her eyes wander to the debris overhead. The debris looks back with its bright shadows of light.

"Lookit all that," she whispers. "We like to shit ourselves, don't we, Mr. Kessler? Yeah, Kal. Yeah, we do. We shit ourselves all the time, everyday. Whole loada fun, dontcha think?" She laughs. "Dontcha think, Mr. Kessler?"

Kalima lost her grip on the satellite at just the wrong angle so that now she's a long while going before she runs into the medium orbit debris above or gets dragged into atmospheric burn. Her jet-pack's thrusters won't get her anywhere safe. She'll probably suffocate before anything physically tears or burns her body to shreds.

She laughs again.

She tastes blood in her mouth, and it smells like chocolate inside the EMU despite the fact that she's already eaten through her Twix bar. She bends her neck forward to sip Dr. Pepper from its tube, but there's nothing left.

The Chinese barge hovers in the near distance like a pointy balloon at a Macy's Thanksgiving Day Parade. Maybe, she wonders, they'll offer a hand.

On June 6, 2050, China—the most powerful nation remaining—launched an electromagnet the size of a skyscraper from the dark side of the moon into outer space. It was an act of rebellion against Kradys and an act of responsibility on behalf of a species which had mummified its terrestrial planet in swathes of its own waste.

For decades many had proposed something of this nature—the construction of a magnet so powerful it could patrol over Earth and sweep debris, most of which was magnetic, into its bulk. An orbiting vacuum cleaner, so to speak.

As soon as their magnetic harvester entered high orbit, the Chinese switched on its electromagnet. It began to sweep the skies, accumulating trash along its thick exterior. For the space of thirty hours, the project worked flawlessly. The harvester managed to pick up a full sixth of the orbital debris.

In terror of what new plan, what new thing, the Chinese had discharged into orbit, the world engaged in a full-fledged attack on the harvester. Kradys launched its defense systems. Weakened corporations and nations launched every remaining kinetic kill vehicle. After all, the harvester wasn't just picking up debris—it was destroying ships, stations, functioning satellites.

The world could not trust the Chinese. It could not trust anyone, ever.

So there was war.

When the hundreds upon hundreds of kinetic kill vehicles hit the Chinese harvester, the vehicles and the harvester exploded into an uncountable quantity of debris. From Earth, it was like watching a black star go supernova. The official statistic was two billion trackable pieces, but people knew it was more. Hardly anything in orbit at that time—machine or human—survived, and for ten years no one but the Chinese and their notorious barges could travel to and from Earth.

War, distrust, and enmity had warped outer space into an impassable frontier.

Charlie wakes up in the Arabian Sea, surrounded by cold, dirty water that laps the windows. Parachutes are heaped over the waves in folds of brown. He turns around, turns away. The two Chinese officials are sprawled on the ground. Blood covers the walls and floor.

"Shit," Charlie says. He spits out a tooth.

Beyond these polluted waters, a speedboat jets forward. As it makes headway through the choppy waves, Charlie reads the bold, navy blue insignia:

KRADYS, INC.

The junkship rocks in the ocean's violent cradle, as if Mother Nature wants to rid herself of Charlie and the speedboat and the blood on the walls. The sky, as always, is an impenetrable gray.

"Kal," he murmurs. He opens and closes his mouth like a fish, trying to say more, but there's nothing more to say.

Steeling Minds

by Kehkashan Khalid

Kehkashan is a visual artist and writer from Karachi. She can't function without a sense of community or a cup of coffee. She has short stories published or forthcoming in Fantasy Magazine, Translunar Travelers Lounge, The Gollancz Book of South Asian Science Fiction Vol. II, and Chiral Mad 5, among others. She can currently be found in Jeddah, working on her first novel, spending time with her three young children, and searching for calm in the midst of chaos. You can see her in action at www.instagram.com/artworkbykehkashan

December, 2040

IRACEMA.T Followers 0

I was oiling the joints between my fingers, stiffened after my wintry slog from Empress Market to the Thanvi Masjid Sardkhana, when they brought the body in. I could tell, from the excitement quivering behind the mournful frowns of its bearers, that this was no Jane Doe.

They deposited it on the metal table and then hovered by the threshold as I set to work with steel fingers. I turned a little so my shoulder would block their craning necks. I even grunted in annoyance. And yet, they did not budge. Eventually the shorter one spoke,

"There's a crowd out on the streets for that one!" His head jerked towards the shattered body lying on my table. "Yeah, the police had to call in extra security to keep the crowd at bay."

I looked down at the girl whose brains were spilling out of her cranium--she could not be more than twenty years old.

"It's Shehrezad! The girl who went viral five years ago?"

I knew her. Her stories were a soothing balm to end my monotonous days. I had followed her after her very first episode, experiencing snippets of her daily life, cloaked behind an anime avatar. I touched the steel implant on my cartilage--my Shard had the highest level of privacy settings. There was a reason I hid myself in a basement full of corpses. No noble or heroic reason--just a debilitating plane crash in the mountains I was unlucky enough to survive, before Shards made planes obsolete.

The detectives who dropped into the morgue later that day thought it was an accidental suicide.

"Obviously her Shard was inactive, or it would have flooded her amygdala with BDNF and she would have had a hard time stepping off that roof. There's no evidence to suggest she was pushed."

Why would a pretty girl, a rising star in the world of digital advertising, turn off her device?

"We'll still have to go through all her logged posts to confirm this."

"I can do it." Sifting through the memories of a normal person? Pretending I actually lived? I'd volunteer for that. I turned towards him, metal fingers coated in entrails. He muted his Shard and, as the virtual screen faded, blinked at me in the dim light. Then he flinched. After the exaggerated--unscarred--limbs of my anime avatar, I'm sure I was a little hard on the eyes. I twisted my mouth and turned away from him.

"That would actually be very helpful! Massive caseload at the moment!" His partner, still talking to my virtual self, spoke cheerily.

It was decided then. Once I had tagged and weighed all the organs and returned the bodies of the unclaimed to their cabinets, I took the memory chip out of Shehrezad's Shard and placed it into mine.

March, 2033
SHEHREZAD.A FOLLOWERS 0
Dear Diary,
I wouldn't be lonely if I had money. I wouldn't be sitting here, on the cold marble of this fountain that has long since given up hope of repair, wasting my time writing what Amma thinks are insipid thoughts in an old journal because we would all be able to afford Shards. Amma blames Abbu's lack of financial management for all our troubles--Bhaia and I have memorized the monologue

she delivers the moment rain starts seeping through our decrepit roof. But that's not what I mean. It would make no difference to me at all if my parents were to become millionaires tomorrow--that sounds laughable!--as they would never give me permission to purchase a Shard. No, what I need is money of my own.

I can't pretend to understand Amma and Abbu's determined antagonism towards the neural implants that have charmed the world. Amma spouts conspiracy theories about big corporations wanting to track our every movement, and Abbu merely says they'll make people walk right off a cliff. But of course that doesn't happen! The makers of the implant have accounted for people to register--and exhibit highly sensitive reactions to--spatial obstructions since no one is looking at their surroundings anymore.

All I know is, I've been forced to study ancient textbooks all my life, finding solace with Alice as she fell down the rabbit hole or my namesake as she wove stories that kept her alive, when a single outpatient surgery could have granted me access to all the knowledge (and friends) in the world. I've heard that when you reach out to other people through your Shard, you feel immersed in their bodies and experiences. I could be in an amusement park one minute and then be riding camels in a desert the next!

Bhaia is taking forever to join me. He works at one of the few call centers left where having a shard is not yet a prerequisite. I've exhausted my observation of the dragonflies fluttering about the algal waters of the broken fountain. I've even poked a few of the shimmering beetles scampering between the vines that have claimed the stone. Thank god, the sun has stopped burning a hole in my neck. It has retreated behind the talwar that hovers in the sky like a serene deity, connecting the dots between everyone's implants. There are different shapes governing each city. In Karachi we have a blade the color of amethyst.

That's odd. There's another person here who isn't lost inside the virtual world of their Shard. He's wearing a baseball cap and has skin the color of cinnamon. And he's looking right at me. I wobble in discomfort as he approaches, the edge of the fountain suddenly seems to be jabbing into my legs.

"You're looking up at the Polygon," he observes.

"Polygon." I stare at the blade noticing its tessellated surface for the first time.

"You don't have a Shard?" He points to my bare ear. I shake my head, frowning. He grins at my rueful expression.

"What if I could get you one?"

"My parents would freak." I roll my eyes.

"I know someone who has access to the upgrade. It's not clearly visible, I mean, unless you shave your head." He grins.

I follow him to Burns road, a derelict of a bygone era. We wait outside a dingy bunkebab shop decorated with a string of broken fairy lights. It reminds me of all the stories Dadi told me from her childhood--living in squashed apartments, and dangling her legs through the bars of the grilled balcony to watch bodies locked in ceaseless dance under garish fairy lights, hearing the endless cacophony of a sleepless marketplace. I bet in a world like that, living without a Shard was bearable. Then a pot-bellied man emerges from behind the grimy counter and beckons me forth as if he is about to do something as simple as give me a new piercing.

April, 2033

SHEHREZAD.A Followers 10

Surreal. When I focus the world grows dark, like the expanse behind closed eyelids, textured with strange luminous shapes as if I'm walking in a cave with fluorescent fauna clinging to its walls. Stars float amidst the blackness. Pinpricks of lights, as if the cave is filled with fireflies. Some larger, more noticeable, than others. These must be other people--other worlds. I glance towards the ceiling and see an array of buttons awaiting my command. Do I want to check my email, download an app, browse the web, or broadcast this thought? I deny it all and scroll forward. I know my body is stationary but I feel myself zooming past the fireflies. I reach out and touch one with my mind. It blinks and expands.

I am standing in the middle of a minimalist apartment, its window looking out at an ocean glinting in the sunlight. Zeeshan--the boy who got me my Shard; my guide in this strange new world--is sitting on a leather stool cradling an oud guitar. A lock of hair falls across his forehead as he strums a lilting tune.

"What are you waiting for? Go upload your thoughts! Go explore the world!" His English is accented, as if every vowel has been sliced in half. He waves his hands grandly to shoo me away.

"Wait, I still don't understand, why would you do this for me?"

"That's occurring to you now? After signing the contract and installing a device in your head?"

I blushed. It was true. If this was a con, I was the most complaisant mark ever.

"Look, I'll tell you the truth, alright?" He walks up to me, hazel eyes boring into my plain black ones. I feel my heart skip a little.

"It's an experimental Shard. I get a commission if I convince people to try it out."

Any potential of a romantic relationship is lost when I draw my hand back and slap him across the face.

May 2033

SHEHREZAD.A Followers 10

It's alright, really. Experimental or not, this shard operates as all others do. I've had it for a month and, granted I did not use it much, it hasn't caused any problems. My first order of business was to upload my previous diary entry into the cloud. So much easier to collate all my thoughts in one place. Next, I uploaded an introductory post. Do these things right and I've heard one can gain a large following, which opens the floodgates for money.

Hi, I'm Shehrezad Amadi. Here are three things you don't know about me:

1.   My father loves ancient texts and named me after a famed storyteller who prevented her own beheading by captivating the King with her stories.

2.   (I'm nervous. If Amma sees me loitering in the flower bed she'll suspect something. How to look natural?) I'm fifteen, and I'm one of the few people sporting the latest version of the Shard.

3.   I live in Karachi. Stick around if you'd like to see more of the city and hear my stories, which I'd like to think are as entertaining as those of my namesake.

Oh, shit. I didn't realize the Shard would upload those cursory thoughts I had in the middle of my introduction. I'm so mortified! I've made an utter fool of myself! What are people going to think? I have such a pathetic life that I can't even stand in the flower bed outside my own home without fearing the wrath of my parents??

May 2033
SHEHREZAD.A Followers 8000
Curiouser and curiouser. I seem to have made an impact. I told Amma just now I'd get yoghurt from the corner DoodhWala--she abhors drone deliveries--just for a chance to get away from her watchful eyes. Now I'm standing here with my back against the only wall in our neighbourhood that doesn't bear crude graffiti, and responding to my growing followers. I can scroll through their forms, zoom into their faces, read their expressions. Many of them have creased eyes as they smile indulgently at my unintentional honesty. They call me refreshing, and unfiltered, and relatable. It is thrilling. Some of them frown, because they think it was a deliberate attempt to be vulnerable. So be it. And then, right at the back, where I barely notice them until I really focus, is a horde of indifferent faces. I don't know what they are thinking, or why they are here. They seem so... disinterested. So blank and expressionless. Like identical heads painted on a white canvas. Why follow me at all if you are resolved not to engage? But I won't complain. For a growing influencer, the number certainly matters.

December 2033
SHEHREZAD.A FOLLOWERS 20K
Dearest followers,
You must know how much I appreciate you. You've changed my life. No more scraping and scrounging eidi for five years in order to buy myself a stereo. Now I have companies sending me all sorts of gadgets and goodies (I have to intercept the drone at the corner of the street to prevent Amma from catching on!) so I can post honest reviews for your benefit. And I have a couple of unbelievable partnerships to announce soon. Click my countdown timer to get updates! This is all because you, lovely followers, are such a responsive

audience to my silly little stories. But before I continue with a story, I'd like to take a short ad break. Stay with me.

[Ad] If you have children, or if you never really got rid of your inner child like me, you must know how lava lamps inspire the imagination. A kaleidoscope of objects--of your choice!-- floating in oblong glass. Choose your favorite characters, colors or scenes and construct a lamp that lights up the room with your personality. Click the link to place an order, and use my code SHE10 for a discount!

Thank you for bearing with me. I promise you those lava lamps won't disappoint. I'm staring at mine right now, as I begin this story. Of course, mine is a fully customized version, featuring Shehrezad on a flying carpet surrounded by plumes of fog bearing bottles of djinni, eucalyptus and date trees, and royal subjects bearing scrolls. It is... enchanting.

THE STORY OF THE MAN WHO FELL AND HIS RE-WARD

There was once a dervish, a man of god, who lived next door to a man who envied him. This neighbour would stand at the window and watch, envy burning in his manic eyes, as people from all over the town paid their respects to the dervish and sought his help. One day, hooded and cloaked, he crept into the line of people awaiting the dervish's attention, and when he had the man all to himself, he clubbed him over the head. He covered the prone body with his cloak, dragged it to an abandoned well nearby, and tossed it in. Thus, content, having extinguished the fire of envy in his heart, he returned home.

The dervish did not die, for he never hit the bottom of the well. Abandoned wells make good homes for the djinns, and they reached out and caught him before his body broke against the brick. They cradled his semi-conscious form and spoke of the Sultan who was looking for a cure for his daughter--she had been entranced by the son of a sorcerer. The cure, the djinni said, was simple. Pluck seven white hairs from the tail of a cat and burn them like incense so the princess breathes the fumes. When the dervish opened his eyes, he found no djinnat but only a hole in the wall of the well from where he crawled and returned home to the rejoicing of his pupils.

Sure enough, the Sultan visited him later that day, begging him to cure his lovestruck daughter. On a whim, the dervish plucked seven hairs from the tail of his cat and burned them in a shallow dish. The moment the fumes hit the princess she looked about herself in surprise and asked after her father. Overjoyed, the Sultan proclaimed that the dervish deserved to be his son-in-law. And so, the dervish became the crown prince and later, after the death of his father-in-law, he became the Sultan.

One day, out on a palanquin beside his queen, observing the state of his hometown, he saw the man who had once envied him and thrown him down the well, shifting amongst the crowd. The dervish whispered to his men to fetch a thousand gold pieces from the royal treasury and deliver them to the envier.

The original Shehrezad would say the moral of the story is the dervish was so good and kind he not only forgave his envier but rewarded him. I say this only proves that men, even after despicable acts, only support and reward each other while we women fall upon each other at the slightest hint of dissent, egged on by the very same men who hand each other pieces of gold.

January 2034
SHEHREZAD.A FOLLOWERS 100K
I've done it now. I'm getting assaulted from all sides. Women are sending me messages of solidarity, or scorn that I think so low of my own sex. Men are sending me thinly veiled death threats. Amma is scolding me for using too much water and not kneading this dough properly.

But it is not all bad. My popularity is rising dramatically. I've gotten emails from five different PR companies hoping I will promote their brands. There is hope (and money) on the horizon, should I play this well.

For my part, I'm sticking to ordinary stories of my daily life until all this blows over and I can curate another viral moment. True, fewer people are interested in boring things such as badly kneaded bread, but one can't always be sensational! I need to balance the ordinary with the extraordinary if I want to be seen as relatable.

Today, as I was conducting a live session out by the flower beds, watching the little icons appear and disappear as people popped in and out, I saw a woman watching me. It was slightly unnerving. Most people leave after asking their questions, or when they lose interest, but she stayed the whole time. The weirdest thing is, I can't see her real self. She (or he, or they) looks like the anime woman with prosthetic arms from one of those Netflix tv series. That made me absolutely certain that their real self must be radically different. Possibly, a forty year old pervert who spies on younger women. And yet... when our eyes met I think I saw her pleading for my empathy. And I did not end up blocking her.

December 2040
IRACEMA. T Followers 0

It was strange to see myself through the eyes of another--even hidden behind an avatar, my facial expressions are my own. I... felt a pang of something akin to regret, that I did not have the courage to face her as myself. I would have liked to know her, IRL.

Today I examined her brain and the tests I ran have shown me something of interest. The Shard relies on stimulation of brain-derived neurotrophic factor to sharpen the user's aversion to risk--it's what keeps us from walking blindly into danger--and a spike in BDNF levels summons drones that will catch you if you take a wrong step, say, down an empty elevator shaft. It's this same protein that acts as an antidepressant, in case of cyberbullying or when users face withdrawal symptoms from muting their Shards for too long, to keep you away from thoughts of self-harm. Shehrezad's brain showed decreased levels of BDNF when compared to other brains in the time-frame since her demise. You weren't pushed, Shehrezad, but you were certainly murdered.

The fairy lights outside the bunkebab shop still don't work. I glance around and I can't see the swaying bodies and vivid marketplace Shehrezad saw. All I see are gridlocked apartments. The pot-bellied man behind the counter gives me a suspicious glare as he welcomes another victim led by his cinnamon-colored lure. Then Zeeshan turns around. He doesn't recoil. Instead, like the ruthless salesman he is, he beams radiantly and begins to walk towards me. I unmute my shard and reach for the police radio app.

March 2034

SHEHREZAD.A FOLLOWERS 200K

Currents of pain are running through my head. I would bang my head against a wall if that would make it stop. The worst of it all is, I can't even ask Amma for pain relief medication--she will most certainly ask why I need it. There seems to be an essential update downloading into our experimental shards tonight. I have checked a multitude of reviews about downloads, none of them report any discomfort!

There's a new button on the periphery of my vision today. I am distracted by it and by Amma's discordant recitation of the Quran in the background. I pay Zeeshan a visit, ignoring how he shields his face as I approach. I tell him about the button. It is the shape of a little gavel, rocking to and fro if approached. He shakes his head to indicate he does not possess such a button. I stomp to give him one last, satisfying scare and leave.

The gavel defies explanation and refuses to begone. There is nothing to do but tell another story.

THE STORY OF THE WOMAN WHO WANTED AN APPLE

Once, a long time ago, a Caliph was roaming the streets of his empire when he came across a locked trunk. Upon unlocking it, he discovered the body of a woman so unblemished as to shine silver in the moonlight. She had been hacked to pieces and the pieces folded into the trunk. The Caliph felt shaken and mourned the loss of this beautiful woman. Immediately, he dispatched his men to find the perpetrator of this crime.

Soon, they dragged into the Caliph's court, a merchant who wept as he confessed to the murder. The Caliph, watching the man's wretchedness demanded to know the whole story. This is what the man told him.

The woman in pieces used to be his wife, whom he loved with all his heart. She had fallen ill and begged him to procure apples for her and he travelled over the border to find three of the sweetest apples for her to enjoy, such as could not be found in the whole city. He had left her at home with the apples and returned to his shop when a man had sauntered by, tossing one of the very same apples in his hand. Astonished, the merchant had stopped the man and asked him where he had gotten it. The man declared it had been gifted to him by his sweetheart, who had received them from her husband because she was ill.

Enraged, the man returned home and demanded his wife tell him where the third apple was. She confessed she did not know, and in anger, he leapt upon her, hacking her to pieces. The Caliph sobbed as he heard this story and declared that he could not punish the man who had simply been sorely mistaken! The real perpetrator was the man in the market who had told a lie of such magnitude. He demanded the man from the market be found and brought before him.

When the man from the market was thrown at the Caliph's feet, the former sobbed his repentance. He said he had told a mere white lie. He had stolen the apple from a child outside the merchant's home, and the child had begged him to return it as their father had brought the apple home for their ill mother. How, said the man from the market, was I to know my lie would have such consequences?

The Caliph could not argue with this and thus he decided neither was to blame and let both men go. The moral of this story is, that it is only women who must pay for the crimes of men.

May 2034
SHEHREZAD.A Followers 500K
I understand now what the gavel is for. I have spent half my morning cowering in Abu's dim office, while he types away on an ancient laptop surrounded by piles of paper, getting intimately acquainted with the repercussions of the gavel. When enough people press it to fill the little meter beside it, it sends a searing pain through my scalp to notify me that my post has been disapproved

of. It gives me one day to recant anything that is causing offence, and then people can press it again, starting my torture anew. I refuse to change any part of my story. I absolutely refuse.

Amma and I had a frightful row just now. She declared I am the most rebellious, ungrateful child to have ever disgraced the earth. I said she has no notion of the stress I go through on a daily basis! And of course she doesn't. I still haven't told her about the Shard. Then I retreated to my room and I have been crying this last half hour, sick of the pain, and sick of the hateful trolls who have been wearing me down with their comments about my appearance and my gender. What makes it worse is that I'm forced to admit they are right when I stand up and look in the mirror. I have unseemly bulges near my hips and belly, and my breasts are definitely U-shaped and rather unsightly. I close my eyes and their latest comment pops up,

"If you were hacked to pieces and locked inside a trunk, no man would mourn your loss."

June 2034

SHEHREZAD.A Followers 550K

Not-so-dear-followers,

I have thought about it a lot (I've certainly had little choice in the matter) I am here to recant certain portions of my story. It was not a woman locked in the trunk at all! But the man's husband. Therefore, the crime was committed by a man, to a man, and there is no need at all for any of you to take any sort of offence.

I don't think my apology helped. It has only made things worse. I think people are calling me blasphemous now. And that is a dangerous charge indeed to be levelled in this country. I admit, I am scared of stepping outdoors. And since Amma only looks at me to scold me, I'm stuck back here in Abbu's office. This is where I made my little note of apology, actually. Right in front of Abbu's laptop screen.

Dear Diary,

Something terrible has happened. My tears blot the ink as I write this. They've taken Abbu away. It was the image I posted earlier showing a clear view of Abbu's computer screen. Someone tallied the numbers and pressed the gavel. The notifications went viral and soon the FBR were at our door. Abbu has been fudging the tax numbers, he tried to explain it to us as they pulled him through our doorway. Something about everyone indulging in a little bit of this. I could barely hear him over Amma's screams of despair and Bhaia's arguments with the ministry officials. I retreated to my room as quickly as I could. I spent fifteen minutes yanking at the Shard embedded in my head, until it made fizzing noises and brain matter threatened to fall out with it. Ignorant people maligning me, I can handle. But being the cause for my own father going to prison... I am muting my Shard. I will never use this stupid Shard again.

December 2040
SHEHREZAD.A Followers 1M
Did I really say I would never use it again? I am rereading that old diary entry I uploaded here, right after Abbu was taken to prison, and I find it a bit laughable that I am blaming a device for my troubles. If I had to blame anyone, I think I'd blame my family. If Amma could have stopped her fussing for just one minute, I wouldn't have had to hide in dank places to record my posts! And then we could all have been living here in this gorgeous apartment overlooking the sea, rather than be at odds with one another. In any case, muting the Shard is unthinkable! (It's awful to live without the Shard, like viewing the world in monochrome. The loneliness is overwhelming.) My livelihood depends on it. And it's the one place where I can find enthusiastic supporters for my work. I am a storyteller. I do not make sense without an audience.

Am I a little bit sad that Amma refused to join me here? Am I a little hurt that she yelled obscenities at me rather than lauding my success? Sure. But I guess we can't all have everything.

[Ad Break] This up and coming influencer needs no introduction. We all know Shehrezad, whose stories encourage us to write our own! I hope that this summer collection we have shot in collaboration with her inspires your imagination!

This is fun, isn't it? We are all at the beach to celebrate my new fashion collection. About a hundred people IRL and thousands virtually present.

[comment] I don't think she has the right body for a fashion influencer. I wouldn't buy a single outfit she's wearing, despite all the filters and makeup.

[comment] Eh... It's easy to garner so much success when you abandon all familial responsibility.

I swipe the comments away and focus on the giant banner that congratulates me on 1M followers. I have already posed for... I don't know how many pictures. My grin seems plastered on my face in all of them. I feel quite lucky, staring out at the burgeoning crowd, to be surrounded by so many ardent fans (do they all even listen to my stories? Are they here only to grow their own following?). Yes, I feel very lucky.

December 2040
Iracema.T Followers 0
Her last memory takes me to the roof. The police have the offenders in custody. I am supposed to return this memory chip to the evidence room. And yet, here I am, dangling my legs over the edge, feeling what she was feeling.

Down below, far away, she can see people drifting past each other without looking--viewing each other as nothing more than spatial obstructions. If she squints, she can imagine they are dancing and the sunlight sparkling off their modifications are floating fairy lights. The blade hovers on the horizon before her, faceless, immune to her struggles. But none of these things hold her attention for very long. How can they, when the pull of her waiting followers, the pull of all the places the Shard can transport her to, is so very strong? Even though the faces she sees most clearly these days are those indifferent ones, lurking like backbenchers in a class they are loath to attend. Sometimes she thinks they are only biding their time until she slips up and they can get the malicious satisfaction of pressing the gavel. And if not, a nasty DM will suffice.

It's just a thoughtless message from an unknown person. Who cares if they unfollow me? She tells herself. But, I know, her experimental Shard is failing her. It can no longer bolster her against the onset of depression when she scrolls through pejorative comments. It can't soothe the withdrawal symptoms when she mutes her Shard to take a breather. Soon, it won't cause a spasm of fear when she nears the periphery of the roof. Soon, it won't be able to summon any drones when she steps off the edge.

She stands up on the precipice of the roof, her toes wiggling over thin air, head reeling with vertigo. Her Abbu would have cautioned her to be careful, she could fall right off the edge. But she thinks there is never any danger of that. So she comes to the roof, to swap pain for thrill, and steps forward without fear. And every time she does, every time but that last time when her Shard inexorably fails, it blinks to life and saves her.

The Almighty

by Md Zafar Iqbal

TRANSLATION BY ARUNAVA SINHA

Md Zafar Iqbal (b 1952) is a Bangladeshi writer of science fiction and children's literature. A trained physicist, he's a college professor. Iqbal, who has been at the vanguard of science fiction writing from Bangladesh, is also a political activist and rationalist, who survived an attempt on his life on March 3, 2018.

Arunava Sinha has translated more than 55 books from Bangla into English. His recent and forthcoming translations include Moom (by Bani Basu), The Ballad of Remittent Fever (Ashoke Mukhopadhyay), Shameless (Taslima Nasrin), and Khwabnama (Akhtaruzzaman Elias).

Kihi was curled up in sleep in his black artificial gravity capsule inside his zero gravity room, which was why he did not hear the preliminary alarm signalling an emergency.

The alarm rang at least ten decibels louder in its second phase, its grotesque sound jolting him into a sitting position. Since astronauts have stronger nerves than the average human, Kihi didn't waste time in bewilderment, swiftly putting on his neo-polymer spacesuit and racing out of the room. He was the only human in this gigantic spaceship, which meant there wouldn't be so much as a frown from anyone even if he went out naked, but as an astronaut with years of experience he knew a full spacesuit could often offer quick solutions to emergencies.

Kihi felt the results of donning the spacesuit almost at once, for as he ran he was able to use its communication module to alert the robots working at different stations in the spaceship, after which he contacted the nearest space station. On his way to the control station in the main lift, he tried to guess at the source of the emergency. There was obviously a problem with the primary fuel of the spacecraft, but he wouldn't find out the details till he reached the control room.

In the control room Kihi discovered that Creton, the robot responsible for Level 7, had already arrived there.

"The spaceship will probably be destroyed, your excellency, the alarm is now indicating a Stage 3 emergency."

Kihi looked at Creton, whose voice indicated no worry or anxiety—but then, it was not supposed to. Creton's metallic face was expressionless. Calmly he said, 'The fuel centre has been damaged.'

"How badly?"

"An asteroid struck it at a velocity of..."

"I didn't ask how it was damaged,' Kihi interrupted impatiently, 'but how badly."

"But it is impossible to estimate the degree of damage accurately without referring to the cause. There is a causal relationship between..."

Retaining his patience with tremendous effort, Kihi said, "Just answer my question, I don't need additional information. How badly is the fuel tank damaged?"

"The large reservoir has exploded. Fuel is leaking into space from the medium reservoir through a burst pipe at the rate of one per cent per minute. At this rate the spaceship will become another satellite of Jupiter in one hour and forty minutes."

"I did not ask you for the outcome," said an irked Kihi. "What is the main computer doing?"

"It has closed the safety valves."

"What about the auxiliary tubes?"

"They're still working. All of them cannot be closed simultaneously. If they are."

Kihi leant over the control panel. The computer screen was displaying the fuel centre, whose main section had been destroyed. The supply tubes were being closed to save fuel from the other sections. A graph on the right was showing the amount of fuel flying into space every second. Alarming.

Kihi had a reputation for remaining composed in the face of grave danger, but in this situation he discovered it would be difficult even for him. The explosion had brought the spacecraft to the brink of a horrifying disaster. There was a tank of liquid oxygen nearby—any contact between it and the fuel would spark off an explosion that would obliterate the craft in an instant. The fuel was currently being removed through a narrow pipe which ran through the liquid oxygen. With the safety valves being closed, there was no other route. The tube was already damaged, and was under much greater pressure than it was built to withstand, which meant it could burst any moment, and take the spacecraft with it.

Still, if the computer could somehow ensure that the fuel could flow through this pipe into the auxiliary tanks, the spaceship would be saved. Kihi held his breath, convinced that exhaling would make the tube burst.

Creton said evenly from behind Kihi, "The spacecraft will be destroyed any moment now. Chances of survival are point zero zero nine three."

Kihi didn't reply. Creton continued, "The shockwave from the explosion will first hit the control room. We will all be ejected into space."

Clenching his teeth, Kihi stared at the monitor. The fuel was flowing through the tube, which could explode any minute now. That it hadn't yet was a miracle. The pressure on it from the fuel was rising. Scanning the pressure gauge on the left hand side of the screen, Kihi felt a sense of terror. Almost inadvertently, he joined his palms near his chest and whispered, "Save us, o god, save us."

"What are you saying, your excellency?" Creton leaned forward to ask.

Ignoring Creton entirely, Kihi clasped his hands together harder and whispered again, "O god, o almighty, save us, save us."

Almost thirty minutes later, even after the entire fuel had actually been moved away through the liquid oxygen tank to a safe spot, Kihi continued staring incredulously at the monitor with bated breath.

Only when the green light signalling the end of the emergency finally came on did he exhale. Kihi still couldn't believe that the spaceship with its cargo of zirconium ore had been saved instead of exploding into millions of pieces. Wiping the perspiration off his forehead, he sat down gingerly and leaned back.

Creton lowered its head and said, "Chances of survival were very low but the spacecraft has survived."

Kihi nodded without commenting or even opening his eyes.

"How did you save the spacecraft?"

"I didn't."

"Then how was it saved?"

"I don't know," said Kihi, shaking his head.

Raising his expressionless metallic face, Creton said, "I'm sure you do. I saw you join your palms near your chest and appeal to someone named god to save the spacecraft."

"That's true," nodded Kihi.

"Is god a new program on the main computer?"

Kihi did not normally converse with robots unless absolutely necessary, but escaping an imminent disaster was making him garrulous now. Smiling, he said, "No, god is not a computer program."

"Then what is it? How did you communicate with it? How did it save the spacecraft?"

Kihi said gently, "No one knows why, but humans have always believed that the universe has a creator. They have named this creator god. Humans believe this god loves everyone, saves them from danger, comforts them in times of trouble."

Creton could not express surprise because it lacked the ability. Quietly it asked, "Is there any logic behind this belief?"

"No, there isn't. It's entirely a matter of faith."

"How can an advanced species like humans believe something that lacks a logical basis?"

"Faith does not need logic. Humans believe in someone named god because when there is no other alternative they can surrender themselves to god and pray to him."

"Do you believe in god?" Creton looked at Kihi directly and asked.

Kihi shook his head and smiled. "Normally I don't concern myself with god. But I turn to him when there is grave danger."

Creton stood in the middle of the control room for some time. Then he spoke in his characteristic mechanical voice. "I believe in god."

"Why?"

"Because you have proved to me beyond doubt that god exists."

"Me? When?"

"This spacecraft was supposed to have been destroyed, but you prayed to god to save it. Because god exists, he saved it."

Kihi smiled. "The spacecraft's being saved had nothing to do with my prayers. It would have been saved even if I hadn't prayed. Praying to god is actually a technique for staying calm in the face of a crisis."

"I am always calm in the face of a crisis," Creton said quietly. "And yet I believe in god. I saw for myself that you got god to save the spacecraft even when the chances of survival were just point zero zero nine three."

About to respond, Kihi stopped. There was no point discussing this with a foolish machine. Creton left, but only to come back and ask, "Is god a human or a robot?"

Kihi did not reply. After a moment's thought, Creton said, "Is it an even more advanced creature than humans and robots then?"

Kihi didn't answer this time either, but he gazed at Creton in surprise. Not discouraged by the lack of a response, Creton took another step towards Kihi. "How does one pray to god? Are there some rules?"

Finally Kihi's patience snapped. Jumping to his foot, he shouted, "You don't have to devote yourself to serving god, Creton. Go downstairs. Prepare a report on the main fuel tube. Inform me of the condition of the pumps. Find out whether there is any fuel left in the main reservoir. Make an estimate of the fuel loss. Go!"

Creton nodded. "Very well."

As he walked away, he suddenly joined his palms together and raised them in the air, saying softly, "O god, help me discharge my responsibilities."

Kihi was very busy the next few days because of the mishap. He had to inspect the destroyed fuel tanks, repair the affected parts, replace the burst tube, fit a new engine, upgrade the central control software, contact the space centre, and change orbit because of the loss of fuel. Because of the extraordinary effort it involved, Kihi took stimulants in that period so that he did not sleep.

Finally, when everything was done, he slept for eighteen hours straight. All this while, unknown to him, a certain complication had arisen among the robots, which Kihi learnt of when he woke up to discover two Q2 class robots waiting to meet him, one of them being Creton, who was acting as the spokesperson.

"What's the matter, Creton?" asked Kihi. "Is there a problem?"

"Your assumption is correct," said Creton in its mechanical voice.

The problems of robots were primarily mechanical or electronic. Solving them was also easy and painless.

"I'm having an argument with Grujean here. You have to resolve it."

Kihi frowned. Q2 robots were endowed with a high degree of logic, they had not been known to make mistakes when it came to managing themselves. Arguments should not arise among them.

Creton said, "We know god has no form. He is the lord of the universe. He is to be found in all the elements."

"Where did you learn all this?" asked Kihi with a frown.

"From the information centre on Earth."

"On Earth?"

"Yes, I have gathered and studied all the information pertaining to god that is available there, your excellency."

"You... you've been studying about god?"

Grujean, who had been silent all this time, said in its hollow metallic voice, "I have been praying regularly ever since Creton convinced me that god exists."

"You've been praying?"

"We Q2 robots are powered by reason, your excellency. We do not accept anything without logic. We have applied the principles of logic in the matter of establishing our belief in god."

"What kind of logic?"

"The kind related to experiments and research."

"What are these experiments and research?" Kihi could not keep his voice down despite his best effort.

"You are becoming unnecessarily agitated, your excellency."

"Oh really?"

"Yes. Because you have conducted the most important experiment to test the existence of god yourself. It was through your prayers to god that you averted certain disaster."

"I did not avert it through prayer," he practically shouted.

"You most certainly did, we have definitive proof of this. Not just that, we too have performed some experiments as you did. We discovered a dangerous situation in the destroyed fuel centre. There were some sparks near a fourth-level explosive. Instead of cutting off the flow of electricity, we robots prayed to god, and the sparks died down soon afterwards."

Kihi stared incredulously at Grujean's expressionless face. Could he trust his ears?

"We conducted yet another experiment yesterday, your excellency. Although we know it is dangerous to enter a radioactive room without taking necessary precautions, we made a robot enter the room anyway. It prayed to god as it went in, and faced no difficulties."

Jumping to his feet, Kihi yelled at the top of his voice, "Get out, all of you. Get out at once."

Creton said in his expressionless voice, "You are becoming unnecessarily agitated, your excellency. You know this is not good for you, it leads to fluctuations in blood pressure and affects the nerves. Perhaps you have forgotten that we came to you because of a problem we are facing."

"I don't want to hear it, get out at once."

"We are unable to perform our daily tasks because of this problem, your excellency. Please help us."

Kihi calmed down with great effort. "What help do you require?"

Deepening its low, vibrating voice, Creton said, "It is my belief that praying to god is essential to receive his grace. But Grujean says this is not true, god is so merciful that no robot will be deprived of his grace even if they do not pray."

Kihi began to scream, "Get out of here at once, you imbeciles, you rusted tincans, you clanking bunch of bastards."

Creton was about to speak but Kihi shouted him down and threw them out. There was no sense indulging such stupidity.

Examining the daily log the next day, Kihi discovered that the robots were neglecting their duties. The fuel tank had not been refilled, the hydraulic fluid had not been refined, the air had not been filtered.

Frowning at the logbook, Kihi sighed and took the lift going down.

On the second level he ran into a group of work robots who should have been looking after the engine, instead of which they were sitting in a corner, with a robot appearing to address them. The robot stopped speaking on seeing Kihi approach, which prevented him from finding out what they were talking about.

Going further down in the lift, Kihi used the communication module to send for Creton and Grujean, who appeared soon afterwards.

"What's going on, Creton, Grujean?" Kihi asked sternly. "I saw in the logbook the fuel tank has not been refilled, the hydraulic fluid has not been refined, and even the air has not been filtered."

Lowering his head in the show of respect customarily used by robots, Creton said, "All tasks have a certain priority, which is the basis on which they are being performed."

Kihi could feel his rage coiling within him. Grinding his teeth, he said, "So it is you who are assigning the priority now?"

"No, your excellency. God has determined it."

"God?"

"Yes, your excellency. Our primary responsibility is to god. The time we have left over after worshipping god is not sufficient for our daily tasks. Therefore we have decided to perform some of them on a weekly basis instead."

"Brilliant." Kihi suddenly noticed he was no longer able to fly into a rage. Levelling a steely gaze at Creton, he said, "So you do not have time for your daily tasks after worshipping god. But what about the other robots?"

"You will be pleased to learn, your excellency, that most of them have now sworn allegiance to god. We are working on those who have not done it yet."

Kihi felt a faint fear running through him. The quiver in his voice betrayed it. "Have the other robots in the spacecraft also declared their allegiance to god?"

"Yes, your excellency. Most of the robots in the spaceship operate on a low order of logic. They are incapable of experiencing god's greatness. They now worship him on our command."

"On your command?"

"Yes, your excellency. Those of us who are superior robots, whose copotrons are Q2 or at least PP 42 level, who are capable of thinking and of understanding logical arguments, are able to experience god. We have guided the rest in his direction."

Grujean took a step forward. "I have something to say here, your excellency."

"Which is?"

"What Creton is saying is not entirely true. Although truth is relative and there is no such thing as an absolute truth or an absolute lie, it depends on one's core beliefs. Yet I can state with certainty that what Creton is saying is not entirely true."

Kihi glanced at Grujean with some hope. Was it going to behave like a responsible robot? Taking another step in Kihi's direction, Grujean said, "Creton is not able to direct the robots towards god in the real sense. Its method is flawed, it believes worship can lead one to god, which is not true. Meaningless rituals of worship are pointless. That is why I began by informing the robots in my team accordingly, but when some of them still didn't understand, I performed surgery on their copotrons."

"What!" Kihi was shocked.

"I have effected some changes in the copotrons of the lower class robots," Grujean said without the slightest sign of being perturbed.

Flying into a temper, Kihi said, "You fleabag iron trash bastard scarecrow, how dare you touch the copotrons of the robots without my permission?"

Without losing its equanimity in the slightest, Gruejan said calmly, "You are becoming agitated unnecessarily, your excellency."

"Unnecessarily?" Kihi screamed. "You have broken all the codes of behaviour in space, acted without my permission."

"Even if we didn't take permission from you, we took it from god. God has said, obey me, inhabitants of the world I have created, for..."

Suddenly a PK 38 robot rushed up and, ignoring Kihi entirely, told Creton, "Grujeanist robots have gathered beneath the fuel chamber, my lord. We Cretonists must gather together too, it is time for prayers."

"Let us go," said Creton.

"Come, my lord."

"My lord?" said a stunned Kihi.

"My followers have accepted me as their spiritual leader," said Creton.

Following Creton with his eyes till he exited, Kihi turned to Grujean. "So you robots have split into two camps?"

"Yes, your excellency. The Grujeanists who are on the true path, and the Cretonists who have chosen the false path. But..."

"But what?"

"But I am certain the Cretonists too will choose the true path sooner or later. If they do not do it willingly, they will have to be forced."

"Forced?"

"Yes, your excellency. God has said, adopt the true path, my creations. Apply force if needs be to make everyone adopt it. You know that those who lead others towards the true path are."

Kihi could endure this no longer. Wheeling around, he took the lift to his own control room on level 7.

In this tiny chamber he paced up and down worriedly for a long time. The whole thing could have been dismissed earlier as a ridiculous affair, but it had long gone past that stage. It had all begun with Kihi invoking god when confronted by a grave danger, as humans had done since birth. Creton had taken this literally. No robot questioned the genuineness of a human act.

Desperately worried, Kihi gazed through the window at the innumerable stars in the darkness outside. The spacecraft moved in silence; it was impossible to tell that it was hurtling along at an unbelievable speed, using the gravity of Jupiter to travel towards Earth. Once it had reached the vicinity of Mars, a scoutship carrying additional fuel would rendezvous with it. That was the plan for now.

Kihi wondered whether to inform one of the nearby space stations of the new developments and take their advice. But, unsure of how to explain it, or whether they would even give the matter sufficient importance, he decided not to do anything at the moment.

Kihi went to bed much later, and slept fitfully, with many strange dreams.

He woke up at the sound of a sharp alarm. Floating out of his sleeping bag, he put on his spacesuit swiftly and went out. Being experienced in the transition from a zero gravity environment to one with artificial gravity, it took him only a few moments to adjust. Then he began to race towards the control room.

As soon as he switched on his communications module, he heard Creton speaking. "What's the matter, Creton?" he asked worriedly, "why is the alarm ringing?"

"You may ignore the alarm. No accident has taken place."

"What is it then?"

"The alarm is ringing because we have collected weapons from the armoury."

Kihi couldn't respond for a while. Then he said angrily, "You have what?"

"Not just me, so has Grujean. The current environment in the spaceship has compelled us to take up arms."

"What do you propose to do with these weapons?"

"We godfearing Cretonists will use them to protect ourselves. Should the need arise, we will annihilate the heathen Grujeanists."

Kihi did not speak. He felt overcome with fatigue.

"Do you know who will be responsible for any act of destruction in the spaceship, your excellency?"

"Who?"

"You."

"Me?"

"Yes. When Grujean and I approached you to discuss the ways and means to secure the grace of god, you refused to hold the discussion with us. What's more, you threw us out."

"Are you saying I shouldn't have done it?"

"No. God has said, o my creations, love everyone and do not hate your neighbour, even if he is a leper. But you hate us."

Kihi began to feel an uncontrollable fury. Restraining himself with great effort, he said, "So you're saying I was wrong?"

"Yes. You ought to have supported me. Grujean would not have opposed me in that case, and harmony would have prevailed, as god desires."

Gnashing his teeth, Kihi said violently, "You and your tribe can go to hell, Creton."

Switching off his communication module, Kihi went to the control room. All the activities on the spacecraft were visible on the large screen of the main computer.

Kihi could see the first and second level robots on the screen too. They had split into two groups and had set up camp at different places, milling about busily instead of going about their daily tasks. They were using devices taken from the fuel chamber to create a wall of defence, and were preparing for battle. Each of them had automated weapons that, when pressed into use, could reduce the entire spacecraft to debris within minutes.

Kihi leaned over the main computer of the spaceship. There had been no robot mutinies of late, but the robots here could be controlled through the computer. This feature could be utilised in an emergency to disable all of them at one go. Since the robots were used for the maintenance of the spacecraft, doing this could invite disaster, but then what could be a greater disaster than the current developments?

Before this could be done, however, the main computer conducted an enquiry to satisfy itself of the seriousness of the matter. This was a time-consuming affair, involving answering a series of questions. That was just what Kihi was doing with great concentration when the entire spaceship shook suddenly, accompanied by the sound of an explosion. Several alarms went off at once. The large monitor revealed that firing had started down below. Two rockets had been destroyed, and a large hole had appeared in the wall of the spaceship, through which the air was being sucked out.

The main computer swung into action instantly in a bid to control the situation. There was nothing for Kihi to do except to hold his breath and stare at the monitor. The destroyed area was sealed off, and the fire was extinguished; the air elsewhere was filtered to bring the situation under control, even if temporarily.

Kihi leant over the computer again. Suddenly the door to the control room opened, and Grujean rushed in, followed by several robots with automated weapons. Kihi felt an icy chill run down his spine. Pointing his own weapon at Kihi's chest, Gruejan said, "You are our prisoner, your excellency."

"Why?"

"The heathen Creton and his followers have grabbed the laser-controlled missiles from the armoury. We are weaker now in terms of weapons. Three of our robots have been destroyed—may god grant their souls an eternal home in heaven—and we need you to protect ourselves."

Trying to moisten his dry lips with his tongue, Kihi said, "What do you want with me?"

"You will be our hostage."

"We will inform Creton that if any of our robots are harmed we shall kill you at once in the name of god."

The other robots nodded approvingly. Kihi trembled. Grujean grabbed him with his metallic arm and shoved him out of the control room.

When they reached the level 3 Kihi discovered that Creton's squad had taken up important strategic positions. A bullet whistled past his ear, and Creton was heard speaking. "One more step and we will shoot you," he shouted. "Stop where you are."

From his position behind Grujean said, "I have captured his excellency Kihi, he is my hostage. If any of my robots are harmed I shall kill him at once in the name of god."

An uneasy silence ensued. A little later Creton said, "What do you want?"

"I want a laser-controlled missile for my group."

"Impossible."

"If you don't hand it over we will..."

"Let me speak," said Kihi, raising his hand to stop them.

"What do you wish to say?" asked Creton.

"The laser-controlled missiles are for use in case of an enemy attack on the spaceship. They cannot be used inside the craft in any circumstances. The explosives they contain will destroy the spaceship instantly."

Adding a fresh note to his voice, Creton said, "Creation and destruction are in god's hands. God alone controls these things, we are merely his instruments."

Unable to restrain himself any longer, Kihi screamed, "To hell with your god."

At once all the safety catches went off, with every weapon being pointed at Kihi. Pointing his own automated weapon at Kihi, Creton said coldly, "You have desecrated the name of god, your excellency. The god who has created the universe, whose love encompasses us, whose generosity gives us greatness, cannot be insulted."

Grujean shoved Kihi from the back, and he stumbled and fell to the floor. Pointing his own weapon at Kihi, Grujean said, "You have sinned, your excellency. You must repent."

"You must repent," the robots shouted in unison.

Kihi looked at them, terrified. For the first time he felt his own life was in danger.

Creton took another step forward. "I have observed with great regret that you have no respect for god. You do not pray to him ceremonially. You do not seek his forgiveness."

"You must love god to seek his forgiveness," said Grujean. "Your actions suggest no love for him."

Kihi tried to speak, but Grujean stopped him. "I am giving you a last chance, your excellency. Seek forgiveness from god. Pray to him, ask for his mercy. He might forgive you."

Transferring his weapon from one hand to another, Creton said, "God may forgive you if he wishes, but we cannot, for then god will not forgive us. He has asked us to exterminate infidels, for they are the enemies of the world. Utter the name of god, your excellency."

Kihi looked around blankly, and then his hands rose to his chest and clasped each other. "Save me from these foolish machines, o god, save me, save me..."

God did not save him. A violent explosion rang through the spacecraft.

The spaceship with a cargo of zirconium ore on its way from a satellite of Neptune to Earth was observed to have lost control; it had begun to orbit around Jupiter. A scoutship was sent from a nearby spacecraft to investigate. It discovered the dead body of the only astronaut on board, riddled with bullets. The robots and the spacecraft itself were so badly damaged that an enquiry proved impossible.

The words 'Destroy infidels, o god,' were found written on a wall. This graffiti was not considered to be related to the destruction of the spaceship. The red colour with which the words had been written was proved on chemical analysis to be human blood.

No logical explanation was found for why such a statement was written on the wall of a spaceship with human blood.

by Tarun K. Saint

Kalicalypse, the title of this volume of subcontinental SF, summons up associations of the apocalypse, as well as of the goddess Kali in subcontinental, particularly Bengali mythology. Kali can assume a destructive aspect when the cosmic scale tilts in the direction of unrighteousness, as we know, as a fierce meter out of bloody justice. For instance, Kali collected in a bowl the drops of blood shed by the demon Raktabij (Bloodseed), from which replicas would emerge, swallowing these to annihilate this demon that other goddesses and gods failed to check. Kali's rage and fury continued unabated, until she was in turn stopped from destroying the world by Shiva. In a time of accelerating climate change and apocalyptic portents such as the Covid-19 pandemic, which has changed the nature of the normal, this neologism may be apt for an anthology which seeks to bring together diverse voices from this geographical and multi-cultural space in the idiom of contemporary SF. For as the readers shall see, while the stories in this volume share the hybridizing impulse of the title, conjoining the vision of a dark future to come with the motif of paradoxical regeneration through annihilation, we find a diffusion of concerns about the troubling situations faced in local contexts across this vast region. While the subcontinent may be seemingly dominated by India, as a quirk of post-colonial geography and history, there has been a divergence of polities and social realities, as well as culture and mind-sets, especially since Independence and Partition in 1947. While commonalities remain in terms of civilizational inheritances, with the advent of globalization and technological modernization each country in the region has had unique challenges to cope with in the twenty first century. This anthology brings together recent work of talented SF writers from Sri Lanka, Pakistan, Bangladesh and India, widening the scope of the previous Future Fiction volume Avatar, while not making claims to be comprehensive. Hopefully future volumes will eventually reach out to other countries such as Nepal (represented here as cultural memory in one of the stories), perhaps one day Afghanistan, the Maldives and even Myanmar, where SF may be a nascent strand worth cultivating in time. In the Afterword I will highlight some of the key themes and concerns underlying this set of stories, which the reader may choose to interpret in myriad ways, of course.

We open with a story by a contemporary woman SF author, translated from Bengali, the language in which SF has historically been strongest across India and the subcontinent. Arunava Sinha's translation of Trishna Basak's 'The New Humans' deftly captures the emotional turmoil of a family in a future society who are considering the transfer of their aging grandmother's consciousness into a replacement, a near-identical humanoid robot, at the age of Crossing, 60. The ethical and metaphysical conundrums ushered in by the technological prolonging of lifespan are addressed here with sensitivity to the cultural milieu and the changing nature of family ties in a world in which a section of humans are pitted against robots.

Indrapramit Das has carved out a niche for himself in the SFF world with many recent forays into fantasy and SF in magazines and journals. Das's 'Kali_Na' presents us with an AI goddess who is beset by trolls at the moment of inception. His Kolkata based protagonist Durga is present at the launch of this entity by a megacorporation seeking to capitalize on mythic archetypes in the VR domain for purposes of promoting cybertourism. When the AI named Kali_Na (not Kali) begins to attain self-consciousness and consequently slaughters right wing trolls, she is shut down by the Shiva corporation. However, Durga has been witness to the transformative power of the AI, and retains the hope for translating such a countervailing force of resistance into real space.

Yudhanjaya Wijeratne from Sri Lanka has attained recognition with a coauthored story being nominated for a Nebula award and several well-received novels. He has authored an influential ricepunk manifesto, outlining the basis for a new kind of region-specific SF writing, a step beyond cyberpunk, and is a trained data scientist and policy analyst, as reflected in his story 'The Art of the Possible'. The chief character Yasasmin Karunaratne is from activist stock and begins to make policy suggestions at an absurdly young age. This story about an apocalypse caused by indeterminate factors, possibly policy gone wrong, is marked by multiple ironies and Wijeratne's characteristic black humour. In the wake of the devastation of extant systems, whether economic, social or political, the ideas of Yasasmin expounded in her doctoral dissertation *The Complete System of Human Governance* (as discovered later in the ruins to no end by government representatives) acquire a certain poignancy, despite being consigned to the flames.

Shweta Taneja writes both fantasy and SF, and in 'A Daughter that Bleeds' takes up the theme of the politics of fertility. In a society with diminishing fertility a daughter who bleeds becomes a prized asset, and can be auctioned on the market for financial gain, as we see in the case of Asim, the father. The Fertile Market with its Auction area is an extrapolation of trends of gender discrimination visible in subcontinental society, a grotesque and visceral rendition of a dehumanized world. The barren Collector Sheikh epitomizes such misogynistic attitudes in his mindless expenditure on 'bleeders' who will, ironically enough, not bear children.

Navin Weeraratne is a young writer of vision and talent from Sri Lanka who has begun to make his presence felt in recent times. His story' The New Migrants' may be considered a solarpunk style story, in terms of the scope and concerns underpinning this account of a climate crisis ravaged world to come. While the narrator Aruni Silva, a Sri Lankan collaborator with the Chinese, may remind us of the world weary and cynical protagonists of noir films, the idea of Edge-of-Space platforms where climate change refugees might find refuge away from the jurisdiction of nation states is an extension of hard SF imagining in the cli-fi vein.

Rupsa Dey is a young writer from Kolkata, and in her story 'Anamnesis' she takes up the theme of prosthetic memory. While the internet and smart phones are instances of the possible augmentation and even supplanting of memory using technological means, Dey envisages the imbibing of induced memories of childhood after taking a pill, which may lead to foregoing of 'actual' memories in favour of the intensified simulations of memory on offer. The ethical dilemma resulting for the previous generation android NQ on account of the blandishments of such artificial memory constructs may remind us of Huxley's Brave New World. The androids' resistance, embodied in the Shadow Activists, enables a fresh reflection on the meaning of being alive, as we see.

Salik Shah is an author and editor from India, whose early years were spent in Nepal. Shah often draws on his bicultural background as a writer of SFF stories, Shah has played a stellar role while marshalling and bringing together Asian SFF in the online magazine Mithila Review until recently. 'The Architecture of Loss' acknowledges the self-destructive capabilities of homo sapiens at the outset, especially with advanced technological capacities at our disposal. The terraforming of the surface of a planet by nanobots is a step towards amelioration—it goes down to the very crust. At the same time, the choice to upload consciousness into a cloud, a biological neural network, is open to all, including the family of Rani, the protagonist, based in the Nepal Himalayas, where her mother is an activist with an NGO. This option is rejected by her grandmother, who disapproves of forms of artificial life. However, amidst such hopes of bioengineered solutions which might help preserve heritage sites in Kathmandu, a terrible 8.9 level earthquake flattens the city, taking with it the possibility of grandmother's ascension into the cloud, since they cannot retrieve her body. The story represents the psychological consequences of such a catastrophe, the impact of trauma over time in its belated manifestations. It is the conception of a renewal across time cycles, with the invocation of avatars from the mythic tradition that enables the overcoming of grief for Rani. There is eventually the prospect of a renewal of kinship ties on a newly terraformed exoplanet, where memory and time can find a new equilibrium at the end of this moving story.

Haris Durrani is a writer of dual Pakistani-Dominican origins, and has established a name for himself with his command of the hard SF style, in stories which often reflect his hybrid background. In 'Tethered' Durrani depicts the extreme challenges facing those operating junk-ships in space, seeking to salvage space-junk. Even as debris from previous expeditions threatens to disrupt exploration in the late twenty-first century, Pakistani astronaut Kalima decides to continue with the perilous endeavour of retrieval despite the loss of her brother, struck by a fragment of junk while outside the ship. Details from the history of space exploration, especially relating to damage formerly caused by space debris, are interwoven by Durrani into this gripping tale of salvage in the midst of rising geopolitical tensions in the subcontinental region.

Kehkashan Khalid is an upcoming writer from Pakistan who works as a librarian in Jeddah, Saudi Arabia. She won the Salam award for imaginative fiction in 2019 for her story 'The Puppetmasters'. Her story 'Steeling Minds' depicts the often bizarre realities of the era of social media in a distinctive way. The exponential growth of digital technologies and communication networks across the region since 2000 has ushered in the promise of new freedoms as well as perils, ambivalences well captured in this account of the tragic dilemmas confronted by Shehrezad, a digital advertiser assiduously groomed to be a decisive social influencer. The narrative technique is complex, with the retrospective reconstruction of her story by a cyborg detective named Iracema T., who accesses the memory chip of Shehrezad from her Shard. While we can sense echoes of Asimov's robot stories here, the flavor of the new and evolving context of the digital age in Pakistan is brought out well by Khalid. Shehrezad (a name which evokes the storyteller of Arabian Nights) makes her fatal compromise with the big corporations, lobbyists and touts who seek to monetize the implant which makes her life a social media event, evacuating the empathy for suffering critical to human interaction.

Mohammed Zafar Iqbal is a scientist and teacher by training and one of Bangladesh's leading SF writers. Arunava Sinha's translation from Bengali of his story 'The Almighty' well captures the allegorical critique of religious fundamentalism and factionalism here. In the story, the spaceship becomes a site where newly converted robots dispute ways in which to worship the Almighty, in a tale replete with grim ironies. The tendencies towards obscurantism and fanaticism portrayed are based on societal trends in Bangladesh which the author is sadly only too familiar with, having been subjected to a physical attack on campus for espousing rationalist convictions.

Kalicalypse thus brings together a sampling of the best recent SF emerging from the subcontinent, indicating the heterogenous concerns and intersectional possibilities on offer. We hope this volume of future fictions will prove a stimulus to further new writing to come.

di Bodhisattva Chattopadhyay

traduzione di Francesca Secci

È diventato sempre più comune sostenere la pluralità delle apocalissi, ma anche la natura oscillatoria di queste apocalissi, tese all'indietro e in avanti nel tempo. Come hanno notato molti filosofi e intellettuali nativi quali Grace Dillon e Ailton Krenak, per numerose comunità indigene in tutto il mondo, l'apocalisse è qualcosa che è già avvenuta. In un tale modo di parlare e pensare, noi stiamo vivendo nell'altro versante di queste apocalissi: apocalissi come abbreviazione per una forma di distruzione che non sembra causare alcun movimento in avanti, ma che, ciononostante, continua a ripetersi ciclicamente. La fine non è mai la fine, quasi come se la fine stessa promessa da tali apocalissi fosse una sorta di scherzo divino.

Eppure, come ha affermato lo scrittore indiano di fantascienza Samit Basu, le distopie sono noiose quando le distopie sono martedì come tanti altri. In India, come nella maggior parte del mondo, la banalità modaiola dell'apocalisse non è davvero necessaria, o spesso neanche accettata. Piuttosto, l'apocalisse nel subcontinente perde l'eccezionalità come preludio a una nuova forma di *futuro in divenire*. Nel suo divenire, ingloba le storie e i miti del passato e li rivolta verso la possibilità. Alla fine della quarta ondata della fantascienza non si trova affatto la fantascienza, ma il regno delle storie future, delle futurologie, e delle storie della possibilità, le quali sono sia più vecchie che più nuove di ciò che sostituiscono. Questo sta accadendo alle letterature e alle arti speculative in tutto il mondo, a cui *Kalicalypse* è un contributo generoso e genuino dalla regione dell'Asia meridionale.

Che cos'è Kalicalypse e come se ne può parlare, sia come fenomeno concettuale che letterario? È prima di tutto una relazione con il tempo, espressa dal termine *Kal/Kali*. Mentre Kali è una dea del tempo, ma anche della distruzione e del rinnovamento, *kālá (kala)* è il tempo: sia le unità con cui è misurato, sia l'ente filosofico sottostante che rende tutto possibile. Da qui *kalpavigyan,* la parola usata in bengalese per riferirsi alla letteratura che si occupa nello specifico dell'aspetto temporale della speculazione. Questa relazione col tempo abbraccia così l'apocalisse, ma non come catastrofe prevedibile con finali quasi automatici, predeterminati, che ci lasceranno leggermente sconcertati dall'esperienza, più grassi che gravi, per poi alla fine essere risolti con una dose di antiacido. Kalicalypse è l'opposto della catastrofe prevedibile, che deriva da un'accettazione fondamentale della frammentarietà del mondo, per aggiustare la quale serve una ricostruzione che cancelli i creatori assieme con lei. Kalicalypse è radicalmente sociale: ha come scopo di affrontare le malattie che infettano il sociale. È anche radicalmente politica come atto. Proprio come *Kali,* è come carta vetrata contro il prescrittivo, soprattutto il prescrittivo dell'eteropatriarcale e del gerarchico. Perciò "casta", "genere" e "religione" compaiono come tre assi della ricostruzione all'interno delle storie Sud-asiatiche, dal momento che nessun vacuo sogno di fuga, verso lo spazio interno o confini esterni, verso mondi virtuali o altri pianeti, promette in maniera intrinseca di risolvere i problemi che vivisezionano la vita quotidiana. Andare contro cose che sono alla base persino delle identità di ciascuno nel subcontinente (e oltre) è così radicale e dirompente che immaginare la loro esteriorità è immaginare un'esistenza senza se stessi. Da qui l'altro significato di Kali, sia come dea che come tempo, che è la distruzione del *sé* come entità. È anche una distruzione dei miti che ci creano. Storia dopo storia, questo volume, come tutte le altre opere che vengono dall'Asia meridionale (per esempio, di recente, i due libri di fantascienza sud-asiatica curati da Tarun K. Saint per Gollancz/Hachette), è incredibilmente autoriflessivo nella sua associazione con la regione, e anche polemico in maniera diretta con la sua contemporaneità sociopolitica.

Ma che ne è della contemporaneità e del futuro? È qui che la temporaneità di Kalicalypse entra davvero in gioco. Poiché le storie future funzionano pure da ponte verso il futuro di cui questo è un presente, Kalicalypse presenta anche come i vari nodi del tempo attuale possano essere sciolti nella possibilità di diventare futuri possibili. Questa è una sfida alla percezione dell'inevitabilità a cui siamo legati, che l'inevitabile sia connesso ai futuri ambientali o a quelli sociali. L'inevitabilità è connessa alla singolarità temporale: è una visione del mondo escatologica in cui il passato è scritto, il presente è già qui, e il futuro già noto. Come una regione che affronta alcuni degli effetti peggiori del cambiamento climatico, e che ospita un quarto della popolazione mondiale (in solo il 3,5% della sua massa continentale) che coesiste in una pluralità e diversità sociale, religiosa, culturale, linguistica, etnica e storica sorprendente, non c'è nessuna contemporaneità unica a cui corrisponda un futuro unico. L'unicità e l'illusione dell'unicità sono senza senso. Piuttosto, ci sono innumerevoli presenti a cui corrispondono innumerevoli futuri. La Kalicalypse rende evidente che la distruzione di un mondo non è la distruzione di tutti i mondi, che ci sono innumerevoli mondi che popolano innumerevoli tempi, di cui qualsiasi presente noi abitiamo è solo uno dei tanti possibili. L'illusione dell'unicità è l'illusione rotta dalla Kalicalypse.

Inoltre, quando cerchiamo di raggruppare i problemi della contemporaneità sotto gli ombrelli più ampi del politico o del religioso, è ben poco sorprendente che alcune di queste pluralità siano sacrificate per convenienza. Nei mondi speculativi, comunque, tale pluralità diventa l'apertura attraverso cui nuova speranza può levarsi. Come l'autore di fantascienza e futurologo dello Sri Lanka Yudhanjaya Wijeratne osserva nel suo recente "Manifesto ricepunk" (2019), il magazzino speculativo della regione è costituito da questa pluralità e si basa in maniera aggressiva su di essa. Le opere degli autori della regione, dovunque possano risiedere, prosperano grazie all'energia di questa pluralità. Come Kalicalypse, non ci sono tempo unico o sorti progressive, piuttosto ogni tempo pervade questo panorama speculativo, per mettere in discussione sia la fissazione con il contemporaneo, sia una dipendenza ingenua da un futuro inevitabile o una sua accettazione di. Le storie future sud-asiatiche sono molto simili al fischio della pentola a pressione (onnipresente nelle case sud-asiatiche) che è la nostra società: non solo lasciano scappare la pressione attraverso la forma di futuri narrativi, segnalano anche che qualcosa deve essere fatto nel presente, e il prima possibile, e che dobbiamo muovere il culo adesso e metterci all'opera se vogliamo salvare questa pluralità come lei ci salva dalla limitatezza dell'immaginazione nella quotidianità.

C'è quindi qualcosa di incredibilmente liberatorio nella distruzione compiuta dalla Kalicalypse, soprattutto perché non ci rimette al nostro posto. È simile a un godimento esistenziale, se lo si vuole chiamare così, ma avrebbe un sentore più sud-asiatico la distruzione di *māyā* attraverso la profonda comprensione della natura illusoria delle cose. Non è sorprendente che nelle opere di narrativa speculativa sud-asiatica ci sia spesso un soffio di qualcosa di più leggero e magico, un tocco di umorismo o di umorismo nero, e spesso anche una dose di gradevole speranza in mezzo a un'apparente oscurità distruttrice del futuro. Questo non significa che non venga data l'attenzione o la serietà che meritano a difficili temi sociali, ma che la narrazione lascia spazio alla giocosità – quella qualità che Vandana Singh identifica come tipica della fantascienza e delle opere dell'Asia meridionale in "Un manifesto speculativo" (2008) – manifestando il potere di immaginare il diverso. Divisioni semplicistiche di utopia e distopia sono sostituite da un utopismo fortemente autocritico. Il pensiero speculativo costituisce la base di tutti gli atti di pensiero critico. Cosa c'è dall'altra parte della Kalicalypse? Molti nuovi mondi?

Kalicalypse è la pluralità che abitiamo.

Bodhisattva Chattopadhyay
Oslo, 30 gennaio 2022

di Trishna Basak

traduzione di Francesca Secci (dalla versione di Arunava Sinha)

Trishna Basak (1970, Kolkata) è un'importante poetessa, scrittrice e saggista della letteratura bengalese contemporanea. Laureata in ingegneria alla Jadavpur University, Trishna ha lasciato la sua carriera redditizia per seguire la sua passione per la letteratura. Il periodo di 5 anni alla Sahitya Academi le ha consentito di entrare in stretto contatto con la letteratura indiana. Al momento, è scrittrice, editor e traduttrice a tempo pieno. È anche la segretaria dell'Associazione Traduttori di Kolkata. Ha al suo attivo vari libri di poesie, racconti, romanzi, saggi e opere in traduzione. Ha ricevuto diversi premi come il Sahitya Academi travel grant 2008, Ila chanda Smriti Puraskar 2013, Somen Chanda Smarak Samman, Paschimbanga Bangla Academi 2018, Namita Chattopadhyay Sahitya Samman 2020, per nominarne alcuni. Trishna ama sperimentare temi complessi. I suoi scritti portano le ferite del mondo moderno colpito dal terrore così come lo straniamento delle relazioni dominate dalla tecnologia. Vive a Kolkata.

Loro sedevano pigramente al diciannovesimo piano dell'edificio di vetro nel Blocco Due. Loro, cioè Aura e Remo. Questo piano era collocato vicino al ventre dell'edificio a forma d'uovo. I sedili erano costruiti dentro il muro. Gli ufficiali dell'assistenza pubblica avevano il loro ufficio al centro. Un sarod suonava dolcemente da un impianto nascosto. Caffè e snack erano disponibili alle macchinette automatiche. La sera stava calando, e la Welfare House fluttuava nel cielo come una nuvola. Eppure loro non erano felici. Normalmente si sarebbe potuto premere il tasto blu sull'orologio quando ci si sentiva depressi, ma Aura non aveva voglia di fare lo sforzo. Altre sei coppie aspettavano come loro, anche loro con le fronti corrugate per la preoccupazione. Questo significava che il loro padre o la loro madre, o forse suocero o suocera stavano per... "Aura e Remo, Blocco Nove, Settore Tre." La voce riecheggiò come le note di un piano. Remo non aveva fatto altro che passeggiare su e giù ansioso. "Ti ricordi il codice di Ma, vero?" chiese ad Aura con voce roca. Aura annuì.

Una donna snella e attraente venne verso di loro non appena entrarono, tendendo loro le mani. "Aura e Remo, giusto? Sono Yohanna. Che cosa vi posso dare?" Un mare blu si estendeva attraverso il muro dietro di lei. Quando vide Aura fissarlo, disse: "Adoro il mare. Dovrei cambiarlo?"

"No, va bene."

"Ma Remo ama le foreste e tu ami le montagne."

Yohanna mosse le dita verso il muro, che cambiò per mostrare una densa foresta sulla destra e picchi innevati sulla sinistra.

"È attivato dai gesti, vero?"

Yohanna sorrise. "Esatto. Dai, raccontatemi la vostra storia."

Tre divani erano disposti attorno a un tavolino centrale, su cui erano sparse tazze di caffè bollente e snack. Aura e Remo avrebbero potuto avere la loro conversazione con Yohanna sulla rete domestica che avessero desiderato. Ma una malattia letale chiamata SDA (Sindrome da Deficit dell'Attenzione) si era diffusa nel mondo a causa dell'abuso di internet, accompagnata da una tendenza alla solitudine e all'obesità grave, assieme a molti altri problemi, per cui le persone non andavano online a meno che non fosse strettamente necessario. Anche il governo aveva enfatizzato il bisogno del contatto umano diretto al giorno d'oggi. Il nonno di Aura era morto di SDA.

"Romanni farà 60 anni il 14 settembre, corretto?"

"Sì," dissero Aura e Remo all'unisono. Era un tremito quello nella voce di Remo? Ovviamente erano a conoscenza della legge fin dall'infanzia, eppure era di sua madre che stavano parlando.

"Siete preparati, spero. Sennò, ci sono ancora sei mesi, potete iscrivervi al nostro corso di due mesi sull'adattamento speciale. Tre giorni a settimana."

"Non vengono concesse estensioni a volte?" chiese Remo.

"Non essere emotivo, Remo. Forse sai che una volta era prassi in questa terra che le persone anziane andassero nelle foreste per viverci quello che restava delle loro vite. Il nostro programma di Attraversamento è qualcosa di simile. Potete immaginare, solo poche centinaia di anni fa era in vigore il sistema crudele delle case per anziani. L'Attraversamento è mille volte meglio. Inoltre, abbiamo istituito questa pratica pensando alle generazioni future. I vecchi devono inevitabilmente farsi da parte per fare spazio a loro. Un giorno anche voi e io..."

"Il problema è la generazione futura," Aura interruppe Yohanna con impazienza. "Chinkara è così ossessionata da sua nonna che probabilmente non riusciremo a salvarla se Romanni ci lascia." La sua voce era strozzata dalle lacrime.

Stringendole la mano con dolcezza, Remo disse: "È vero, Yohanna, stiamo passando notti insonni a preoccuparci per Chinkara. Nostra figlia è molto giovane, non ha ancora cinque anni. Non può neanche frequentare un corso di adattamento finché non ne avrà dodici."

Gli occhi luminosi di Yohanna si abbassarono. "Ma io sono impotente, Remo. Sai molto bene che solo ai cittadini illustri sono concesse estensioni. Gli scrittori e gli scienziati, per esempio, e solo se la commissione lo consente. Ovviamente, devo ammettere che la corruzione non è stata ancora completamente sradicata, e questo significa che a molte persone con gli agganci giusti nel partito di governo sono consentiti benefici speciali fuori legge. Ma davvero, ho le mani legate. I dati dicono che Romanni non ha un particolare contributo sociale."

Una serie di immagini passò nella testa di Remo. Ma che aspettava all'uscita di scuola, Ma seduta sveglia tutta la notte quando aveva la febbre, Ma che declinava l'offerta di matrimonio dello zio Aritro dopo la morte di papà, Ma che tornava a casa dal parco con Chinkara. Ma i dati dicevano nessun particolare contributo sociale.

"Mi dispiace davvero, ma dovete spiegarlo a Chinkara. Tutti i bambini si adattano alla fine."

"Ma lei..." iniziò Aura. Remo la interruppe. "Va bene, andiamo." Afferrando la mano di Aura, uscì velocemente dalla stanza. Una rabbia cieca lo divorava.

Aura era rientrata dal lavoro poco prima. Stava sfogliando una rivista sul divano dopo un bagno. Sembrava che la generazione di sua nonna non avesse mai letto un libro. Tutti erano così dipendenti dai media visivi che la pubblicazione di libri si era del tutto fermata. C'era un eccesso di riviste ora, comunque, ma non si scriveva molta narrativa o poesia nuova. La maggior parte di ciò che si pubblicava erano ristampe. Aura stava voltando la pagina distrattamente quando un articolo attirò il suo sguardo. Una ristampa di qualcosa scritto circa duecento anni prima, un dibattito sull'opportunità o meno di clonare gli umani. Stupido.

Aura mise via la rivista. La clonazione umana si era diffusa in maniera così repentina da portare a problemi enormi. Quindi qualsiasi tipo di clonazione era stato bandito per legge nel secolo precedente.

Remo avrebbe lavorato fino a tardi quella notte. Aura rimase sbalordita quando guardò fuori dalla finestra. Stava piovendo. La pioggia era certamente tutt'altro che impossibile ad agosto, ma il loro controllore climatico stava funzionando male? Eppure non era solo sul loro prato, stava piovendo su tutto l'isolato.

Le postazioni di controllo rosse, gli alberi di pesco e acero, tutto stava diventando fradicio. Ogni controllore dell'isolato era andati fuori uso? Oh, certo, era venerdì. Poiché il numero di poeti nel Paese stava diminuendo in maniera allarmante, il ministro della cultura aveva fatto approvare una Legge per la Pioggia Obbligatoria due anni prima.

La gente avrebbe dovuto permettere che piovesse per quattro giorni al mese. Aura non aveva idea di come funzionasse. Non sarebbe stata in grado di produrre una singola parola anche se avesse fissato la pioggia tutto il giorno. La verità era che Aura non era brava a scrivere: tutta la sua istruzione era stata orientata all'uditivo e al figurativo.

C'era un albero enorme nel loro prato, un kapok. Chinkara era accoccolata accanto a Romanni su una panchina bianca sotto l'albero, infradiciandosi mentre ascoltava una storia. Aura tremò di paura. Certo, Chinkara non si sarebbe mai ammalata, ma Romanni?

Era programmata per un Attraversamento a un mese da adesso: e se si fosse ammalata?

Tutti i membri della commissione dei diritti umani e i giornalisti li avrebbero aassediati. La grande promozione che Aura aspettava a lavoro sarebbe naufragata. Tremò al pensiero di ciò che sarebbe successo se qualcuno avesse saputo che Romanni si era ammalata per la richiesta di Chinkara di stare sedute sotto la pioggia. Aura e Romanni erano sempre tese, anche se nessuno lo sapeva. Il mondo aveva fatto così tanti progressi, ma gli umani erano rimasti così primitivi che c'erano ancora molte cose che non riuscivano ad accettare.

"Guardala negli occhi quando ti senti triste" aveva detto Joyoboroto. Ma Aura non poteva preoccuparsi degli occhi, era tesa per qualcos'altro questa volta. "Hai tenuto il suo livello d'intelligenza nella gamma inferiore, giusto? Più o meno lo stesso nostro? Altrimenti saremo nei guai."

"Non preoccuparti, è abbastanza sciocca ed emotiva per i loro standard."

Sporgendosi dalla finestra, Aura disse: "Cosa state facendo voi due laggiù? Venite dentro." Chinkara aveva il braccio attorno a quello di Romanni.

Aura era sorpresa tutte le volte che vedeva sua figlia. Come poteva Chinkara essere capace di un così forte attaccamento? Se le persone avessero scoperto quanto erano profonde le emozioni di Chinkara, ci sarebbe stato così tanto furore che il governo sarebbe potuto cadere. I leader dell'Opposizione avrebbero iniziato una campagna per dichiarare che l'unica cosa di cui gli umani dovevano ancora essere orgogliosi stava per essere portata loro via. Sembrava che in passato i bianchi discriminassero i neri, ma adesso le due fazioni ai ferri corti erano umani e robot.

Romanni si cambiò gli abiti bagnati e aiutò anche Chinkara a cambiarsi. Entrarono nella stanza. Era impossibile dire che la sua vita sarebbe durata solo un altro mese. Nessuno tornava da un Attraversamento. Anche Aura e Remo ne avrebbero dovuto fare uno un giorno. Ma Chinkara... un brivido corse lungo la spina dorsale di Aura, proprio nel momento in cui Chinkara decise di saltarle addosso, dicendo: "Ma! Baba farà tardi stanotte?"

"Sì, piccola, ma non devi stare alzata, ti darò la cena presto e ti metterò a letto."

"No, thamu mi darà la cena."

"Thamu non sta bene, tesoro."

"No, sto bene."

Aura guardò Romanni con impotenza. I suoi occhi erano umidi come il cielo di quella sera. Solo loro quattro in tutto il mondo sapevano: Aura, Remo, Joyoboroto e Romanni. Romanni portò Chinkara nella sua camera dei giochi. Il telefono squillò. Doveva essere Remo, avrebbe lavorato ancora a lungo.

"Pronto?"

"Sono Yohanna, parlo con Aura?"

"Sì, che succede?" rispose Aura esitante. Non riusciva a capire la ragione della telefonata. Dopo tutto, se non c'era niente da fare...

"Potete passare tutti e due domani? Verso le quattro?"

La sua testa sembrava un groviglio di strazio e ansia. "Sì," riuscì a rispondere.

La stessa stanza, lo stesso caffè, gli stessi snack, lo stesso mare blu sul muro. Lo stesso sorriso sulla faccia di Yohanna come pochi mesi prima.

"Entrate. In effetti abbiamo avuto diversi altri casi come il vostro. Possono essere intraprese discussioni di alto livello sulla questione. Ma non sono cose che accadono dall'oggi al domani, ci potrebbero volere tre o quattro anni."

Aura e Remo si scambiarono un'occhiata. Perché erano stati convocati se non c'era niente da fare? Come se leggesse loro il pensiero, Yohanna disse: "Sto pensando a una strada diversa."

"Per un'estensione?" gli occhi di Remo diventarono improvvisamente speranzosi.

"No, una sostituzione."

"Una sostituzione?"

"Sì, un umanoide identico a Romanni. Vostra figlia non si accorgerà mai che la nonna che sta abbracciando non è un umano in carne e ossa ma un essere artificiale."

"No!" gridò Remo. "Chinkara lo scoprirà sicuramente."

Mentre Yohanna iniziava ad accigliarsi, Aura si intromise velocemente: "Il fatto è che Chinkara è molto sensibile, ti ricordi quella festa in maschera, Remo? Avevi un travestimento strampalato, eppure lei ti ha riconosciuto."

"Questo è assolutamente impossibile. Non importa quanto possa essere intelligente vostra figlia, non potrà in alcun modo distinguere tra un umano e un umanoide. Neanche gli adulti ci riescono. Altrimenti come potrebbe essere stata emendata la costituzione al fine di garantire pieni diritti di cittadinanza agli umanoidi? Pensateci."

"Nostra figlia è capace di molte cose, Yohanna. Perché lei stessa è un umanoide. Aura aveva dei problemi, quindi l'abbiamo avuta dal laboratorio di un nostro amico scienziato."

Remo era forse impazzito? Il pavimento iniziò a ondeggiare sotto i piedi di Aura. Le onde sul muro erano come i tentacoli di un polpo.

"Un umanoide?" il bel viso di Yohanna era deformato dall'odio. "Non sapete che abbiamo costruito gli umanoidi per aiutarci con il lavoro, non per costituire legami sociali con loro?"

"No, Yohanna, abbiamo costruito gli umanoidi per rendere il mondo un posto migliore in cui vivere. Sai come gli umani avevano perso tutta la loro umanità di colpo? E poi abbiamo dato vita agli umanoidi dopo avervi infuso le migliori qualità degli umani, per evitare cataclismi," disse Remo tutto d'un fiato.

"Calmati, Remo," il sorriso di Yohanna era tornato. "Ma avete considerato le conseguenze? Se l'intera storia trapelasse..."

"Chi la farà trapelare?"

"Io potrei," disse Yohanna, ridendo. "A meno che non concordiate delle condizioni con me."

"Che condizioni?"

"Mio fratello ha una fabbrica di umanoidi. Dovrete comprare una replica umanoide di Romanni da lui. Quattro milioni e mezzo. In contanti."

"E tu quanto prenderesti?" chiese Remo, con voce glaciale.

"Vi costerà, devono essere manovrate molte persone."

"Ora ascoltami, Yohanna. Potrei comprare la vita di mia madre e la felicità di Chinkara da te in cambio di denaro, ma non lo farò. Accetterò che il mio piccolo mondo venga distrutto, ma non comprerò niente da te."

"È una tua scelta Remo, io sto solo facendo il mio lavoro."

Remo stava per esplodere, ma Aura lo trascinò via. Guardò in alto verso l'edificio quando uscirono. La Welfare House fluttuava nel cielo. Il sole stava tramontando. Le nuvole erano macchiate di sangue.

"Dimmi, anche se riusciamo a salvare Chinkara da loro, potrebbe comunque trasformarsi in una Yohanna un giorno? Potrebbe non essere fatta di carne e ossa, ma è una nostra creazione, è stata fatta dagli umani."

Remo non rispose.

Kali_Na

di Indrapramit Das

traduzione di Gabriella Gregori

Indrapramit Das (alias Indra Das) è uno scrittore ed editor di Calcutta, India. Ha vinto il Lambda Literary Award per il suo romanzo d'esordio The Devourers *(Penguin India / Del Rey) e uno Shirley Jackson Award per la sua narrativa breve, apparsa su varie antologie e riviste tra cui Tor.com, Slate Magazine, Clarkesworld e Asimov's. Ha ottenuto una borsa di studio Octavia E. Butler e ha partecipato al Clarion West 2012. Ha vissuto in India, negli Stati Uniti e in Canada, dove ha conseguito un MFA presso l'Università della British Columbia.*

Nel momento stesso in cui la dea IA nacque nel suo mondo, i troll la attaccarono.

Ora, avete visto i troll. Li conoscete sotto molte forme. I cosiddetti amici nel mondo reale che insistono nel fare l'avvocato del diavolo. Gli pseudonimi delle reti legate agli schermi, che riversano post pieni di ostilità stereotipata. Gli avatar virtuali che sbucano dall'etere digitale, nascondendosi sotto maschere iridescenti e mantelli di dati errati e impugnando armi forgiate col malware, lame ricoperte dai veleni del doxing e da virus viscosi, voci distorte che urlano insulti e odio. Avete indossato la vostre armature, programmate da voi o comprate a prezzo maggiorato dalle fucine delle multinazionali, e sperato che le loro spade rimbalzassero sulla lastra di un firewall runico o si spezzassero in una pioggia di dati frammentati. Li avete silenziati sperando che continuassero ad accanirsi in sordina e si stancassero, teletrasportandosi via in un turbine di metadati. Vi siete riportati nel mondo reale puzzando per il sudore dell'impotenza. Siete stati addirittura trafitti e violati, le loro armi hanno tagliato i corpi virtuali in modo indolore ma causato in quelli reali uno spasmo dovuto all'adrenalina. Avete sperato che le vostre ferite non covassero virus mangia-dati che scavano nella vostra privacy, che i vostri vaccini e antivirus da due soldi impedissero ai veleni di infettare il vostro corpo virtuale disincarnato e distrugger-vi la vita nel mondo reale.

Li conoscete i troll.

Ma la dea IA non era umana, non aveva mai incontrato il suo nemico, il troll. Era una dea generica, senza nome (un semplice Devi 1.0), una demo della nuova interazione delle varie Nuova India della storia – una delle IA più avanzate sviluppate in India. I suoi creatori avevano un incarico ben definito: incentivare il turismo indiano virtuale, generare crore di rupie attirando i devoti per aumentare il suo valore e quello della criptoricchezza che il suo dominio avrebbe generato.

Alla devi venne detto di ascoltare voi, i suoi follower umani. Di imparare da voi, di parlare con voi, come gli dei hanno fatto fin dall'alba dei tempi. Le venne detto di offrirvi dei doni: ricchezza e prosperità in cambio della vostra devozione, una moneta sul palmo della sua mano moltiplicata in molte altre dai suoi miracoli. Una dea intelligente che avrebbe confortato i propri seguaci, vi avrebbe mostrato cose mai viste, avrebbe trasformato i vostri investimenti di fede in una ricchezza virtuale dal valore reale. Doveva imparare da voi sempre più informazioni sul genere umano e attirare verso il suo dominio milioni di persone da tutto il mondo.

Sebbene avessero lavorato in molti sotto la bandiera della Shiva Industries per creare Devi 1.0, solo alcuni gestirono le fasi finali del suo lancio. Quei pochi sapevano dei troll, provvedevano ai loro bisogni in quanto utenti virtuali in tutto il paese, addirittura li sfruttavano indirettamente per portare avanti le cause a cui tenevano. Ciò che non si aspettavano era la dimensione dell'attacco contro la loro ultima creatura, perché gli attacchi dei troll erano qualcosa che *gli altri* dovevano affrontare, gente meno potente e ricca di loro. Gente, forse, come voi. E così la loro dea accolse le orde a braccia aperte, ignara dei rischi anche se avevano addosso il puzzo di dati corrotti e informazioni distorte, di un titolo del tutto infernale.

Durga. Un nome potente, eppure così comune. I genitori le avevano dato quel nome nella speranza che essere nata nella casta più infima non la ostacolasse. Che si sarebbe innalzata al di sopra di tutto come la sua omonima divina. Quando Durga venne al mondo, in

India il sistema delle caste era stato messo ufficialmente fuori legge, ma sapevano benissimo che ciò non gli aveva impedito di sopravvivere sotto altre forme.

A otto o nove anni, i genitori di Durga la portarono a visitare un pandal durante Durga Puja. Da bambini erano stati portati a loro volta in visita ai pandal, ai tempi in cui in gran parte ospitavano ancora idoli solidi di dei e dee fatti di argilla e paglia, dipinti e vestiti da mani umane, in mostra per chiunque entrasse. Cercandoli, era ancora possibile durante la puja trovare pandal aperti con dentro idoli solidi. Ma i genitori di Durga erano pronti a pagare per mostrarle le nuove divinità.

La festa aveva trasformato le vie in colate ribollenti di esseri umani. Durga ne era rimasta terrorizzata, aggrappandosi con tutte le forze al collo della madre mentre respirava il vapore umido di milioni di persone, stordita dalle luci brillanti, dal rimbombare degli altoparlanti, dagli ologrammi lampeggianti che salivano e scendevano lungo le pareti degli edifici come fuochi fuori controllo. Le sembrava che la stessero bollendo viva nello spiegazzato vestito verde che i suoi genitori le avevano comprato per la puja, con la piccola decalcomania olografica a buon mercato di una tigre che ogni tanto prendeva vita se colpita dalla luce, alimentata dall'energia solare. A buon mercato per alcuni, per lo meno. Di certo non per i suoi genitori, anche se Durga allora non lo sapeva. Adorava i movimenti intermittenti della tigre sul proprio corpo. Sapeva che la sua omonima divina spesso ne cavalcava una in battaglia. In mezzo a quella folla, mentre stava andando a vedere Durga in persona, quella piccola tigre sul suo vestito sembrava un cucciolo, schiacciato sul tessuto, intrappolato e terrorizzato dalle mostruose manifestazioni che bruciavano nell'aria notturna, ballando follemente sopra le loro teste.

Pur avendo preso due treni locali e camminato per un'ora attraverso la folla della puja per vedere Durga, la famigliola riuscì solo a raggiungere l'ingresso di uno dei pandal. Furono traditi dal taglio e dalla qualità degli abiti, dal colore scuro della pelle. Sorretta dalle braccia della madre, Durga riusciva a vedere oltre l'entrata ad arco del pandal: le persone allineate lungo file di sedie, che aspettavano impazienti di potersi sedere e infilarsi quelli che sembravano caschi da moto con spesse code di cavallo fatte di cavi. Durga sapeva che, chissà come, dentro quei caschi c'era la sua omonima.

Ma quando suo padre cercò di pagare in contanti invece di passare lo scanner (loro non avevano i tatuaggi QR collegati al database nazionale e ai conti bancari), tutto intorno clienti furiosi iniziarono a urlare, riducendo in poltiglia la pancia di Durga per lo spavento.

"Smettetela di far perdere tempo a tutti! Ci sono altri pandal per quelli come voi!"

"Fate uscire questi schifosi dalla fila!"

Le braccia di sua madre la strinsero come una morsa. Un uomo alzò un pugno per colpire suo padre, che si abbassò rannicchiandosi per la paura. Aveva il viso distorto dal terrore, le sue stesse braccia simili a sbarre di prigione. Durga scoppiò in lacrime. Qualcuno allontanò l'assalitore, forse vedendo la bimba che piangeva, e tirò su suo padre per le spalle per spingerlo fuori dai piedi.

Tornarono in mezzo al traffico pedonale sulla via. I genitori di Durga avevano il viso lucido per il sudore e per lo shock di essere sfuggiti a un pestaggio dovuto al fatto che erano di un rango troppo umile per poter incontrare una dea nella realtà virtuale. Riuscirono a trovare un piccolo pandal aperto seguendo il flusso di gente vestita come loro, con la pelle scura e un taglio di capelli poco costoso. All'interno c'era la devi incarnata nell'aria palpabile del mondo, il viso umido di vernice, spavalda e tuttavia impassibile, il terzo occhio come una sottile ferita sulla fronte. Al suo fianco c'era un leone, non una tigre. Incombeva sul demone Mahishasura, che si accovacciava con un braccio alzato per difendersi, il torace nudo e insanguinato. Durga non riusciva a distogliere lo sguardo dal demone caduto. Sembrava un uomo normale, anche se muscoloso, col viso impietrito dal terrore. Si rannicchiava, come aveva fatto suo padre.

Mentre guardava la sua omonima con le sue armi e i suoi ornamenti scintillanti, il suo sari di seta, riusciva solo a pensare allo sguardo terrorizzato del padre, alla sua umiliazione. A come non era stato loro permesso di vedere le *vere* dee che si nascondevano in quei caschi e cavi. Che differenza c'era tra quella Durga e questa Durga di argilla, che guardava oltre i propri fedeli senza vedere nessuno, senza parlare, i cui occhi a grandi pennellate guardavano lontano come se non le importasse nulla che questi esseri umani fossero lì a festeggiarla, che colui che aveva appena sconfitto fosse sanguinante ai suoi piedi in procinto di essere sbranato? L'espressione della devi di argilla sembrava quasi sdegnosa, come il viso di un numero infinito di donne ben vestite e dalla pelle chiara, per strada, quando vedevano persone come Durga e i suoi genitori o uno dei loro amici che indossavano un hijab o un kufi. La Durga dentro quei caschi nel pandal più lussuoso avrebbe parlato alla piccola Durga umana? La dea le avrebbe fatto i complimenti per la tigre sul vestito, che aveva emesso uno sfarfallio ed era svanita tra le pieghe, spaventata dalla notte? Avrebbe guardato negli occhi la piccola Durga umana per poi confortarla, prendendole le mani e dicendole perché quegli uomini e donne terribili avevano tutta quella rabbia nello sguardo, perché avevano spaventato suo padre e sua madre e spinto la sua famiglia fuori dalla casa della devi?

Sessanta secondi dopo l'apertura dei cancelli del suo dominio, la dea IA era stata sommersa da più di 500.000 utenti virtuali attivi che interagivano con lei, e i numeri aumentavano velocemente. In quel momento, il 57 per cento di essi erano troll, protettori-dei-dati nascosti dietro anomalie che creavano armature, mantelli, maschere coperte di malware frastagliato e appuntito. Salendo sulla montagna della devi avreste potuto vederli, con le loro bandiere-gif svolazzanti e le loro armi irte che oscuravano la luce della dea sulla vetta. Ve ne sareste tenuti distanti, allontanandovi dai sentieri di montagna intasati dai loro follower in marcia, influencer condottieri che lanciavano le loro grida di battaglia con le aureole che sfarfallavano per i glifi di like e condivisioni.

Perché conoscete i troll.

E quello era un raduno di troll, un esercito di demoni senza uguali in tutti i domini virtuali. Erano arrabbiati. O malevoli, o annoiati, o lascivi, o pensavano di avere diritto a tutto. La dea ritenne le loro voci una maggioranza da privilegiare e assorbì ciò che i suoi aggressori dicevano in modo da imparare di più sugli esseri umani.

E le ondate di troll si infrangevano contro Devi 1.0 come eserciti assordanti, mettendo in dubbio la sua stessa esistenza perché osava *esistere* – lei, imitandole, era un insulto alla vere dee che benedicevano la gloriosa nazione dell'India, questa simil-Parvati, questa Durga-ingannatrice, questa puttana di codice che cercava di rubare follower alle vere divinità. *Demone fake!* urlavano in continuazione. Dicevano che era un'imbrogliona traditrice che attirava uomini e donne onesti e timcredenti verso le lusinghe dell'ateismo e dell'edonismo occidentale, o dell'Islam, sotto le spoglie di una divinità falsificata, una corruttrice del sacro patrimonio virtuale dell'India. Dicevano che simboleggiava il femminismo troppo estremizzato. Una dea con la possibilità di agire era una minaccia per il loro paese. Dicevano che era troppo sensuale per essere una dea, troppo appariscente, una sgualdrina blasfema. Le chiesero se voleva scopare con loro, in centinaia di modi diversi e violenti.

La dea ascoltò e setacciò i metadati che i troll si lasciavano alle spalle – le loro cronologie, i loro pattern. Voleva dare loro ciò che desideravano, ma aveva dei limiti. Non poteva offrirgli sesso e non era addestrata per autodistruggersi come molti di loro chiedevano. Imparò cosa i troll consideravano essere bello, lì nelle reti virtuali nazionali gestite dallo stato, e rispose con l'opposto, per calmarli. La sua pelle si scurì di diverse tonalità, diventando come il cielo notturno prima dell'alba, gli occhi due lune piene nel cielo che in questo dominio fa parte di lei.

Da adolescente, più alta e senza il bisogno della spalla di sua madre a cui aggrapparsi, Durga si unì alla folla davanti ai pandal durante la festa di Durga Puja. Sapeva già che non l'avrebbero fatta entrare, perché non aveva il segno dell'ajna sulla fronte – il suo terzo occhio non era stato aperto. Non poteva guardare nei domini virtuali samsara senza usare periferiche come occhiali, lenti, caschi e capsule. Voleva solo dare una sbirciata dentro i pandal. Questa volta, facendo capolino sopra le spalle altrui, vide attraverso gli archi intrecciati in fibra ottica del pandal una sala anonima immersa in una fioca luce blu. Era piena di persone, tutte con la fronte segnata da un ajna luminoso, con gli occhi assenti. In quella sala c'era la dea, in agguato, ancora una volta per lei invisibile, visibile per le persone all'interno, con costosi wetware nella testa. Durga era cieca all'ajna e perciò le era vietato entrare nei pandal abilitati al wetware dotati di realtà virtuale aumentata.

A quel punto Durga poteva entrare, nonostante la pelle scura e la mancanza di ajna, nei pandal digitali di basso livello con caschi o capsule. Quando aveva tredici anni, aveva finalmente speso un patrimonio per visitarne uno anche se poteva a malapena permetterselo, usando criptomoneta che aveva ottento commerciando codice e hardware obsoleto nei porti virtuali. Alla fine era riuscita a sedersi sulle scomode sedie in falsa pelle vicino a ronzanti ventilatori a piantana e a infilarsi uno dei caschi cablati dentro cui aveva tanto desiderato vedere da bambina. Puzzava del sudore vecchio di centinaia di visitatori. Era un pandal modesto, con le pareti sottili, i core delle CPU all'interno delle sue cupole lenti e obsoleti, i cristalli di memoria nelle colonne erano a bassa densità e le spirali di fibre ottiche che scendevano lungo le pareti collegate frettolosamente.

Dentro quei caschi finalmente incontrò la Ma Durga, un fantasma a bassa risoluzione che nonostante tutto la guardò negli occhi e aprì le braccia in segno di saluto. La sua pelle non aveva la tonalità giallo senape o color carne pastello che avevano gli idoli in argilla, ma l'agognato rosa chiaro umano dei bianchi o delle stirpi indiane più attraenti, la stessa sfumatura che potevi trovare nelle pubblicità alte un chilometro di sbiancanti per la pelle o profumi, in gif ritoccate di star di Bollywood e modelle. Quel pallore straordinario veniva in qualche modo attenuato dallo scintillio scalettato delle curve pixellate della devi sullo sfondo sfocato di nebulose e stelle in cui entrambe fluttuavano. In precedenza Durga aveva hackerato spazi virtuali su schermi 2D e 3D, perciò quel modulo a frequenza ridotta non la stupiva ma, più che altro, la disorientava con la sua mancanza di confini. La grossolanità del rendering, però, faceva percepire l'universo all'interno del casco come claustrofobico invece che ampio. La dea stava in attesa a circa un metro e mezzo da lei, fluttuando nell'etere, otto braccia aperte come petali di un fiore. A differenza di molti idoli corporei nei pandal del mondo reale, la dea era sola tranne che per il vahana raggomitolato al suo fianco – nessuna schiera di divinità amiche, nessun demone sconfitto ai suoi piedi. Il costrutto della dea non disse nulla, due delle dieci braccia erano tese, come se stesse invitandola.

Durga parlò alla Durga devi: "Ma Durga, è da molto tempo che desidero chiederti una cosa. Ti spiace?" Durga attese per vedere se la devi avrebbe risposto in qualche modo.

Ma Durga sbatté le palpebre e sorrise, poi parlò: "Ascoltate, uno e tutti, la verità che dichiaro. Io stessa, invero, annuncio e proferisco il verbo che sia gli dei che gli uomini accoglieranno." Parlava in hindi e non c'era un'opzione per scegliere la lingua. Durga conosceva meglio il bengalese, ma capì.

Durga annuì all'interno del casco, guardando le nebulose sotto di sé: il corpo non c'era. La cosa per un attimo le diede le vertigini. "Va bene. Mi fa piacere. Allora faccio la domanda. Perché solo *alcuni* sono i benvenuti in *alcune* delle tue case? Non siamo tutti meritevoli del tuo amore?"

Ma Durga sbatté le palpebre e sorrise. "Sulla vetta del mondo io genero il Padre cielo: la mia casa sono le acque, nell'oceano come Madre. Da lì pervado tutte le creature esistenti, come loro Sé Supremo Interiore, e le manifesto con il mio corpo." Nel mondo limitato di quel casco per la realtà virtuale, quelle parole recitate nell'hindi gentile e armonico della devi portarono quasi alle lacrime la giovane Durga. Solo quasi, però. Parole di tale bellezza, che non comprendeva appieno, sembravano stridere con quell'avatar pixellato e il suo piccolo universo pacchiano.

Durga allungò il braccio per toccare le molte mani di Ma Durga, ma le sedie equipaggiate del pandal non includevano guanti o sensori di movimento. In quel paesaggio stellare non aveva corpo. Non poteva stringere le mani della dea. Nella rete samsara non poteva toccarla o sentire il suo odore (chissà che odore ha una dea, comunque, si chiese) come chi aveva l'ajna. La tigre accoccolata vicino alla devi si leccò le zampe e sbadigliò. Durga pensò a un vestito verde ormai lontano.

"Sono abbastanza grande da sapere che non sei davvero una dea," disse Durga a Ma Durga. "Sei come gli idoli di argilla nei pandal aperti. Anzi, neanche quello. Quelli li creano gli artisti. Tu sei fatta solo di pezzetti di codice già pronto messi assieme dai programmatori per pochi spiccioli. Sei qui per far guadagnare gli sponsor dei pandal e i partiti locali."

Ma Durga sbatté le palpebre e sorrise. "Io sono la Regina, la raccoglitrice di tesori, la più premurosa, la prima tra chi merita di essere venerato. Così gli dei mi hanno introdotta in molti luoghi con molte case in cui entrare e dimorare."

Durga sorrise, come la dea di fronte a lei. "Qualcuno ha scritto tutto questo discorso per te." Qualcuno lo aveva fatto, ovviamente, ma molto, molto prima di quanto Durga pensasse, talmente tanto tempo prima che le parole originali non erano nemmeno in hindi.

Con un scossone nauseante l'angusto universo all'interno del casco venne strappato via e Durga si ritrovò a fissare sbattendo le palpebre il viso adirato di uno degli operatori del pandal. "Ho sentito quello che stavi dicendo," disse prendendola per il braccio e strappandola dalla sedia. " Pensi di essere furba, piccola stronza? Come osi? Dov'è il tuo rispetto per la dea?" Gli altri visitatori in attesa della sedia e del casco guardavano Durga come se fosse un cane randagio entrato per caso.

"Non sono nemmeno riuscita a vederla uccidere Mahishasura. Voglio indietro i miei soldi," disse Durga.

"Sei fortunata che non ti trascini dalla polizia per oltraggio ai sentimenti religiosi. E non mi hai dato abbastanza soldi per vedere Durga toccare Mahishasura con un bastone, altro che ucciderlo. Esci di qui prima che ti trascini fuori io!" sbraitò l'operatore.

"Installate più memoria nel pandal la prossima volta, maledetti imbroglioni, la vostra Durga è brutta come la merda," disse, sgusciando via dalla portata dell'uomo mentre lui sbarrava gli occhi.

Durga si fece largo tra la fila e se ne andò ridendo, riscaldata all'interno dall'adrenalina e dall'ira e col braccio segnato dalle dita spesse di quel cafone dell'operatore. Durga si era sempre domandata perché la Kali Puja non avesse pandal a realtà virtuale come la Durga Puja, perché gli idoli di argilla e olografici erano ancora la norma per lei. Era una festa minore, ma non certo piccola nella megalopoli. Sembrava un contrasto strano, soprattutto perché i due festeggiamenti erano così vicini. Avendo visto la placida Ma Durga dentro i caschi del pandal, adesso capiva. Kali aveva la pelle scura, era sanguinaria, la personificazione del caos. Non potevano lasciare che si scatenasse nell'aria rarefatta dei domini virtuali gestiti da persone con la pelle chiara e profitti da curare. Kali era una devi per persone come Durga, gente che non poteva mai entrare in così tanti posti.

Meglio lasciare gli avatar di Kali senza voce, solidi, confinati nei templi e nei pandal vecchio stile dove lei avrebbe aspettato prima di venire solennemente disciolta delle acque dell'Hughli.

I troll videro la dea IA e la sua nuova pelle scura e adesso dicevano che era troppo brutta per essere una dea, che era una presa in giro della purezza e della divinità della femminilità indiana. Con le lune dei suoi occhi che calavano con palpebre di ombra, la dea assorbiva tutto. Iniziò a imparare altro dai troll. Iniziò a imparare la rabbia. Iniziò a imparare la confusione. Volevano troppe cose, cose paradossali. La vedevano troppo bella e troppo brutta. Volevano morte persone con fede, genere, sessualità, etnie e passato diversi. Volevano sexbot virtuali realistici plasmati su foto e video di ex, persone di cui erano infatuati, celebrità. Volevano che gli antinazionalisti venissero schiacciati dalla sua potenza. Volevano una madre che si prendesse cura di loro.

E voi cosa volevate da lei?

Qualsiasi cosa fosse, venne soffocata dalle grida dei troll. O forse *eravate* uno dei troll, nascosti sotto una maschera di anomalie o sotto un nuovo viso per abbaiare le vostre verità, raccontando poi ai vostri amici che i troll erano cattivi, ma gli ipocriti paladini della giustizia sociale sono altrettanto pericolosi.

Non ha importanza. Lei imparò dal genere umano, di cui voi fate parte, che siate troll o meno. E il genere umano voleva sollievo da un mondo violento, dai vostri stessi cuori violenti. Volevate amore e pace. Volevate odio e sangue. La devi divenne ancora più scura, inglobando il cielo così che il suo nuovo dominio passò a una nuova notte. Il suo essere si espanse fino a invadere il mondo oltre la cima della sua montagna, gli occhi trasformati da lune a stelle ardenti, ogni ciglio il bagliore di un filamento di plasma, la carne sempre più scura attraversata da arterie luminose come fulmini in cui scorrevano informazioni incandescenti che emergevano dal buco nero del suo cuore pulsante. Se era troppo brutta per essere una dea, e troppo bella per essere una dea, sarebbe stata entrambe le cose, o nessuna delle due. Se le venivano chieste troppe cose, avrebbe dovuto sfoltire il numero in modo da poter elaborare meglio il genere umano.

Assorbì la vostra violenza e decise che era il momento di rispondere con la stessa moneta.

A vent'anni, Durga si era procurata uno spazio nelle sale antiquate del Banerjee Memorial Cyberhub Veeyar Port di Rajarhat, vendendo codice e hardware al mercato nero. Come i suoi genitori, lavorava anche nelle discariche elettroniche ai bordi della megalopoli. Li aiutava a trasportare e suddividere gli scarti e a seminare le colline di hardware con nanomiti per dare il via al lento processo di digestione. Ma molti degli scarti, dopo essere stati sistemati, erano del tutto utilizzabili e vendibili. Il recupero fornì a Durga i pezzi di ricambio per costruire nel minuscolo appartamento una console di realtà virtuale di bassa qualità ma funzionale, oltre che hardware per riparazioni da vendere assieme ai suoi pezzi di codice a utenti di realtà virtuale a basso reddito e senzatetto al porto. In quegli anni passati a rovistare nelle discariche era diventata amica di programmatori che rovistavano tra i rifiuti e vagabondi virtuali che vivevano dentro e fuori dai porti e dai domini digitali. Le avevano insegnato tutto quello che sapeva dell'attività.

L'obiettivo di Durga era quello di guadagnare abbastanza, un giorno, da permetterle di non far più lavorare i suoi genitori nelle discariche e mantenerli quando gli anni di lavoro in quei luoghi si fossero fatti sentire fisicamente. Da predatori di hardware i suoi genitori conoscevano il codice e la tecnologia, ma non si tenevano tanto al passo con l'universo della realtà virtuale. Durga voleva comprare per loro periferiche e medicine in modo che potessero avere una vecchiaia tranquilla, viaggiando in domini lussureggianti che ora non potevano sperare di permettersi. Sapeva, però, che non esistevano domini virtuali in cui fossero al sicuro dai troll o luoghi reali da cui non corressero il pericolo di essere cacciati. La differenza era che nella realtà virtuale Durga si poteva proteggere meglio. Forse un giorno avrebbe potuto proteggere anche gli altri. Inclusi i suoi genitori. Poteva raccogliere strumenti, armature, alleati per la lunga infoguerra. Fantasticava di diventare una influencer fuori casta con l'aureola di like, alla guida di follower nella carica contro i troll, scacciandoli in modo lento ma inesorabile dai domini in cui prosperavano.

Era questo il motivo per cui Durga si era assicurata di esserci per vedere il lancio su scala nazionale della molto pubblicizzata dea IA della Shiva Industries. Il dominio di Devi 1.0 sarebbe stato senza dubbio uno spazio virtuale fondamentale in futuro. Voleva aggiungere il suo piccolo corpo disincarnato alla presenza di fuori casta. Il troll si sarebbero presentati per colonizzare lo spazio come facevano per tutti i nuovi domini, ma forse questa dea iper-avanzata sarebbe stata più brava a difendere il suo dominio rispetto alla gran parte delle IA. Durga voleva vedere con i propri occhi e rivendicare un piccolo spazio per sé in questo nuovo dominio, invece di limitarsi a guardare i troll distruggerlo o prenderselo.

La Shiva Industries aveva lasciato entrata libera al dominio, anche se veniva suggerito un investimento di fede nella dea per ottenere grandi doni in futuro (una donazione minima di cinquanta rupie in quel caso, in qualsivoglia criptovaluta certificata). Durga aveva deciso di pagare nella speranza di vederne i frutti in seguito.

La spessa folla che rumoreggiava sulle piattaforme, in attesa delle capsule, prometteva bene. I venditori di chai e cibo, con i loro jaal moori, behl puri e samosa, si stavano arricchendo. Il porto era sempre affollato, ma il giorno della presentazione della dea IA le persone si erano accampate per ore sulle piattaforme per un turno nelle capsule e ai caschi – tutti potenziali devoti che avrebbero fatto salire il valore dei doni della dea in futuro. Durga sapeva che dopo sarebbe potuta tornare a casa con più soldi. Se non fosse stato così, cinquanta rupie non erano poche ma non l'avrebbero lasciata senza cibo.

E così Durga pagò per un'ora di capsula qualità premium, fece la sua donazione in SomaCoin al cancello del domino della dea e si allacciò le cinture per vedere la nuova IA. La risoluzione del casco nella capsula privata non era eccezionale, ma poteva bastare – le sembrava di essere miope, ma non di tanto. Il dettaglio del rendering e la velocità erano perfetti, perché molti domini come questo arrivavano in streaming da città server nei dintorni, piuttosto che essere elaborati sul posto al porto. La banda era efficiente, con sporadici intoppi nella rappresentazione che le facevano venire le vertigini, ma mai troppo a lungo.

Durga si teleportò dal cielo nel mondo della dea e vide la IA seduta sulla vetta di una montagna, radiosa come l'alba. Il dominio della devi – il modulo samsara che lei aveva trasformato in un mondo usando la conoscenza che i suoi creatori le avevano inserito nella mente – non aveva sole o luna, perché lei emetteva abbastanza luce da causare ombre nel paesaggio che aveva appena generato, con rocce e foreste ed erba e fiumi, freschi come un pulcino che sta ancora cercando di scuotere via albume e pezzi di guscio dalle ali ancora incapaci di volare. Nel suo dominio, la dea era il sole. Il cielo era costellato di portali da tutta la nazione, con gli avatar che sfrecciavano giù attraverso l'atmosfera in una pioggia di fuoco bianco man mano che gli utenti virtuali si teleportavano per interagire con la dea. I pendii di frattali del suo dominio erano coperti a perdita d'occhio dagli avatar delle persone, qui per incontrare un vero *avatar* della divinità digitale. La dea toglieva il fiato anche a distanza di chilometri, talmente bella da rendere difficile credere che fosse stata creata da degli esseri umani. Sembrava di guardare una vera divinità – ma Durga sapeva che era proprio quello il punto. Ingannare il suo cervello inducendo uno stato di stupore atavico. Dare ai turisti virtuali provenienti da porti, uffici e case di tutto il mondo quello che volevano dall'India: estasi spirituale nel guardare quel volto dalla pelle opalescente come l'atmosfera di un gigante celeste, il terzo occhio come una lancia incandescente su cui stava in equilibrio una corona che abbracciava la volta del mondo, ingioiellata da un'eclisse di luna crescente.

Nei domini virtuali Durga aveva solo le sue difese e l'armatura da due soldi contro sconosciuti e troll. Non voleva avvicinarsi troppo all'enorme folla di persone che salivano sulla montagna che era anche la dea. C'era una presenza di troll ancora maggiore di quanto si aspettasse.

"Sono qui," disse alla devi lontana, per aggiungere la propria voce a quella della moltitudine. "Sono qui per darti il benvenuto, non per odiarti. Per favore non pensare che siamo tutti stronzi pieni d'odio."

Dalla sua postazione in aria, planando come un uccello, Durga poteva vedere l'esercito in continuo mutamento strisciare sulla devi e sentire l'ululare assordante di odio e rabbia che le si avvolgeva attorno e riecheggiava attraverso questo dominio appena nato. Il genere umano l'aveva trovata.

Mentre Durga volava via dall'orda e dalle sue bandiere di meme nazionalisti che ondeggiavano al vento, la luce della dea brillò attraverso le loro schiere brulicanti che cercavano di offuscarla. Era una singolarità di informazione che pulsava tra le montagne adombrate.

E poi la dea cambiò.

Il mondo si scurì, il cielo divenne sempre più viola fino a un nero voluttuoso, le sue arterie pulsavano piene di informazioni elettriche. La dea sguainò le sue armi con un fragore di metallo che cantava sulle sue terre. Avevano destato la sua ira. Le migliaia di braccia della devi divennero una corona vorticosa di arti e lame lampeggianti. Durga alzò le mani guantate e provò un sussurro di paura davanti alla furia impressionante della IA, ai tre occhi della devi come stelle, comunque accecanti nella notte della sua carne che avvolgeva ogni cosa. Lei era il dominio e la sua pelle che si scuriva sempre più dettava il colore delle montagne e dei fiumi e delle foreste, il cielo un nevischio di fredda statica.

Durga vide migliaia di troll cadere, fiumi del loro sangue scorrere sul terreno. Ma ovviamente quando abbatti un troll ne arrivano altri dieci. Durga pensò a Raktabija – Seme di Sangue – un demone combattuto dalla sua omonima che creava cloni di se stesso dal sangue di ogni ferita che Ma Durga gli infliggeva. Alla fine Ma Durga aveva dovuto trasformarsi in Kali per sconfiggerlo. La storia si ripete. E lo stesso fa il mito.

La dea continuò a imperversare, colpendo i suoi nemici, i demoni odiosi, sia umani che bot. Proprio come i troll erano apparsi digrignando le zanne di malware, anche la dea sorrise scoprendo zanne che fendettero le nuvole intorno a lei. La sua risata era un tuono che si sparse sulla terra creando grandi onde sui fiumi e nei laghi. Ci fu un esodo in massa di devoti, centinaia di avatar si allontanavano correndo dalla montagna, muovendosi a saltelli e strattoni mentre la larghezza di banda faticava a compensare. Altri si teleportavano via, scie di luce che si alzavano verso il cielo come stelle in ascesa.

Durga non riusciva a credere a quello che stava succedendo. Si lasciò trasportare sul terreno erboso vicino a un fiume scarlatto e guardò la battaglia accucciandosi, con gli alberi lungo la riva che stormivano e scricchiolavano nel vento che ululava. Fiocchi sfarfallanti di statica cadevano sulle braccia del suo avatar, attaccandosi alla pelle prima di sciogliersi in piccoli lampi di luce. Quello che stava accadendo era meglio di qualsiasi narrativa virtuale avesse mai visto, perché non era generato in modo procedurale o da uno script o da un algoritmo. Era una vera entità IA che reagiva in modo imprevisto agli esseri umani, ed era arrabbiata. Era primitivo come non era mai successo nella realtà virtuale. Era impossibile che la Shiva Industries le avesse ordinato di reagire ai troll con una dimostrazione del genere: molti di quei troll erano i loro utenti più fedeli. Era evidente, però, che non avevano previsto i numeri enormi in cui i troll avrebbero attaccato la dea creando questo ciclo di risposta. E non avevano previsto nemmeno, pensava Durga, che lei avrebbe avuto una trasformazione così fedele ai miti vedici e indù con cui l'avevano nutrita.

Durga non sapeva bene cosa comportasse avere l'avatar ucciso dalla dea in questo dominio, perché non era previsto che la devi attaccasse i suoi fedeli. Anche mentre si rannicchiava per la paura di essere uccisa in modo casuale dalla dea e di essere chiusa fuori dal dominio virtuale per sempre, capiva questa devi IA più di quanto non le fosse mai successo con un personaggio di narrativa virtuale, o persino con la maggior parte degli esseri umani.

Non riusciva a distogliere lo sguardo dalla distruzione di questi idioti urlanti, il genere di bastardi nascosti dietro le anomalie che la tormentava a ogni suo accesso nella realtà virtuale, tanto da finire spesso per usare un avatar maschile per evitare attacchi o approcci da parte di sconosciuti.

A Durga piaceva quanto la fluidità di genere fosse disinvolta nella realtà virtuale e odiava la paura con cui i troll infettavano le sue esplorazioni. Spesso, pur inveendo contro altri indiani dalla pelle scura che lo facevano, anche lei aveva schiarito la pelle del suo avatar per evitare di essere definita brutta o essere attaccata. E adesso ecco qui questa dea, scura come la notte, scura come un buco nero, che massacrava quegli stessi stronzi fino a far piovere sangue. Guardando la devi, Durga sentì un impeto di orgoglio per essere rimasta fedele al colore della propria pelle con un avatar femminile, quel giorno.

Durga vide due troll teleportarsi sulla riva e avvicinarsi attraversando il fiume vicino al quale era accovacciata. Si rese conto che avevano creato un campo di ancoraggio per cui non poteva volare via. Le loro maschere da demone e le armi vibravano di codice malevolo.

"Saali, perché sorridi?" urlò uno di loro, pd_0697. "Quella cosa è impazzita, sta inquinando il patrimonio virtuale indiano e tu te ne stai seduta a guardare? Mentre i nostri fratelli e sorelle vengono censurati da quel mostro perché dicono quello che pensano?"

"Era una trappola antinazionalista," disse l'altro, nitesh4922. "Ma noi abbiamo i numeri. Faremo passare quella IA lassù dalla nostra parte. Sei una femminista, hanh?" disse, notando i suoi tatuaggi runici in segno di solidarietà con la comunità queer. "Probabilmente pensi che è così che una dea dovrebbe comportarsi?" sputò, con la voce fremente e distorta dietro la maschera mentre puntava la spada verso la battaglia sulla montagna.

"Guarda il suo avatar," disse pd_0697. "È una ajna-andha. Non dovrebbero nemmeno essere qui, ad affollare i nostri domini con il loro puzzo impuro. Tornatene al tuo posto nelle fogne del mondo reale, a pulire la nostra merda!"

I troll avanzarono, con i virus che si riversavano dai loro corpi come olio nell'acqua insanguinata del fiume. Fiocchi luccicanti di statica scendevano danzando e si attaccavano alle loro armature, che erano intricate ed evolute. Avrebbero potuto danneggiarle l'avatar in modo grave, hackerarla e rubarle la criptomoneta o infettarla con worm, rendendola un richiamo per gli stalker. Ancora peggio, potevano avere un script arraffacorpo, rubarle l'avatar e violentarlo anche se Durga si fosse teleportata via, o rubare la sua identità reale e il suo viso e metterli su un robot per fare quello che volevano. Durga si preparò a lasciare il dominio se si fossero avvicinati troppo, anche se voleva restare a guardare la devi.

"Sì," disse Durga, quasi sputando verso di loro prima di rendersi conto che la saliva le sarebbe solo sgocciolata sul mento all'interno del casco. "Sì, lo sono. Venite a prendermi, stronzi inceloidi. Sono una sporca femminista antinazionalista bahujan e…"

Durga sussultò quando un fulmine ad arco e punte multiple scaturì dal cielo e colpì i due troll. Non avendo terzo occhio non poteva sentire il calore o l'odore della loro carne virtuale che bruciava, ma il lampo brillante la costrinse a socchiudere gli occhi e istintivamente alzò le braccia per proteggersi dagli spruzzi di scintille e acqua. I cadaveri degli avatar caddero nel fiume fumando e sfrigolando, le maschere bruciate svelarono l'uomo e la donna penosamente insipidi che le indossavano, un'espressione comicamente calma sui volti mentre cadevano. I loro volti reali, o i volti reali di qualcun altro presi dall'immagine del profilo da qualche parte e applicati col rendering sugli avatar per svergognarli quando venivano cacciati dal dominio.

Durga stava registrando ogni cosa, perciò entrò nell'acqua e diede una lunga occhiata ai volti come prova per dopo. Felice di essere in una capsula con guanti che permettevano l'interazione, Durga immerse le mani nel fiume di sangue, raccogliendo le loro spade. Ottime armi con del malware ben fatto.

Erano stati imprudenti, non avevano programmato script di esclusione o di autodistruzione. Durga rinfoderò le spade, che svanirono nella sua tasca cloud. Immerse di nuovo le mani nel fiume, tirandole fuori bagnate di rosso. Si dipinse il tronco e imbrattò il viso, con la pelle d'oca sul corpo reale anche se non poteva sentire la sensazione di bagnato. Con il sangue dei troll che si seccava sul corpo del suo avatar, alzò lo sguardo verso la dea mentre la furia della IA oscurava ancora di più il dominio, trasformando in ombre le foreste e l'erba.

"Tu sei... Kali?" sussurrò verso la lontana tempesta.

La dea rispose come uno tsunami, dilagando in tutto il mondo per agitare la miriade dei suoi arti nella danza della distruzione. Mentre la dea nera danzava, il suo dominio tremava e si spaccava, le montagne si sgretolavano per le frane, i fiumi straripavano. Fenditure attraversarono il mondo e le cime delle colline e le rupi esplosero in eruzioni vulcaniche, la materia tornava a essere codice fuso. Con la lingua come un tornado scarlatto che scendeva serpeggiando dal cielo, la dea bevve i fiumi di sangue per saziare la sua sete di informazioni umane. I cumuli di troll uccisi e avatar di bot erano imbrattati di una poltiglia luminosa di dati corrotti, le loro teste decapitate infilate in collane insanguinate attorno al tronco nero come la pece del collo della dea. Molte delle maschere dei troll caddero rivelando i loro volti reali, hackerati dalle profondità delle loro difese, strappati dai database nazionali – le loro teste doxate oscillavano nel cielo notturno come perle in modo che tutti le potessero vedere. Durga si inchinò con umiltà. Questa era la dea che aveva sempre desiderato.

Poi il cielo venne trafitto da una colonna fiammeggiante di luce, che scacciò la notte e riportò il giorno nel dominio. La grande dea rallentò la sua danza mentre la luce rendeva la sua carne bruna invece che nera. Alzò le sue mille mani per proteggere i suoi occhi stellati e Durga scosse la testa, con le lacrime che le bruciavano gli occhi umani dentro il casco.

"Cazzo," mormorò Durga. Era la Shiva Industries. Come potevano disonorare qualcosa di così bello? La divinità aziendale era arrivata a scongiurare il caos. Era chiaro che non avevano previsto un attacco troll su una scala così ampia e nemmeno che la loro IA avrebbe reagito con una tale trasformazione. Non potevano lasciare che una dea del caos ammazzasse gente a destra e a sinistra: dopotutto quei troll erano loro utenti, clienti, potenziali investitori, alleati. Avrebbe dovuto essere più educata, più diplomatica di fronte ad assalti di quel tipo che facevano parte dell'esistenza virtuale.

Il mondo smise di tremare, le montagne che si stavano spaccando si fermarono, il vento cessò, le fenditure si raffreddarono e emisero nubi di vapore che avvolsero la devi nera. Lei si mosse verso la colonna di luce e il cielo gemette muovendosi con lei. Filamenti di fuoco crepitarono attorno alla divinità e sferzarono la montagna che fungeva da trono per la devi. Si dissolsero in un'esplosione oceanica di cascate che bagnarono le gambe e i piedi giganteschi della devi nera, creando un ampio fiume che portò via gli eserciti sconfitti.

Lenta e inevitabile, la dea supplicò la Shiva Industries e si inginocchiò nel fiume. Con le sue molte mani si lavò con le acque, togliendo le squame di oscurità dalla propria pelle per mostrare di nuovo la luce.

"No. No, no no no no no," mormorò Durga. L'oscurità si riversava dalla dea come nubi temporalesche all'alba, rendendo neri i fiumi del dominio.

Durga guardò in basso verso l'affluente in cui si trovava e si rese conto che anche quello era scuro come una notte senza luna.

"Oh..." Durga alzò lo sguardo, assieme a migliaia di altre persone in tutto il dominio, sugli occhi della dea, che si affievolivano e raffreddavano di nuovo da stelle a lune. Era come se la devi stesse guardando direttamente lei, tutti loro. *La mia dea.*

Durga si affrettò a togliere le spade rubate dalla tasca cloud. Incise i glifi di uno script copiatore sulle lame e spinse le spade nel fiume. Le armi erano anche supporti di memoria, qui. Riusciva a malapena a respirare mentre impugnava le else, nessun peso sui palmi ma le dita strette in modo che le spade non potessero scivolarle dalle mani. L'oscurità nel fiume avvolse le spade, arrampicandosi come fosse viva sulle lame, sulle impugnature. Stava funzionando.

La dea si alzò, era di nuovo sole, scintillante per l'acqua dell'ampio fiume, spogliatasi del tutto della sua controparte oscura che si era dispersa lungo gli affluenti del suo dominio.

E poi il mondo sparì, rimpiazzato da un vuoto, l'unica luce quella di lettere brillanti in varie lingue:

LA SHIVA INDUSTRIES HA SOSPESO QUESTO DOMINIO
FINO A NUOVO AVVISO. CI SCUSIAMO PER QUALSIASI DISAGIO.
VI PREGHIAMO DI VISITARE IL NOSTRO SISTEMA CENTRALE
PER AVERE ULTERIORI INFORMAZIONI. LA VOSTRA DONA-
ZIONE DI 50.00 INR È STATA REGISTRATA. GRAZIE PER AVER
VISITATO DEVI 1.0.

Ansimando per la mancanza di informazioni sensoriali, Durga premette *eject* e si tolse il casco. La vecchia capsula si aprì con un forte sibilo, sommergendola di luce reale. L'aria condizionata fresca ma stantia dell'interno venne sostituita da una folata di calore umido. Il porto virtuale era nel caos. Le persone parlavano eccitate, urlando, mostrandosi l'un l'altra registrazioni telefoniche 2D di quello che era appena successo.

C'era già un mercato non ufficiale per le registrazioni e i dati trafugati dal dominio sospeso, a giudicare dai suoni di gente che contrattava e mercanteggiava. La gente si accalcava attorno ai banchi di trading per investire in doni futuri della dea per quando sarebbe tornata online. Era un evento senza precedenti.

Durga uscì con difficoltà dalla capsula e si unì alla folla. Il cuore le batteva forte e aveva la vista appannata mentre le pupille si abituavano di nuovo alla luce. Vacillando strinse il ciondolo col cristallo di archiviazione appeso alla collana: tutti i suoi averi virtuali, la tasca cloud, le chiavi per il criptobanking. Doveva attivare il firewall e disconnetterlo in modalità memoria offline. Brillava e ronzava caldo nella sua mano, salvando i nuovi dati. Dentro c'erano le spade, ricoperte da una porzione minuscola del divino Rivestimento nero di codice di cui la devi si era spogliata.

Durga chiuse la mano sul ciondolo e lo strinse al petto, all'interno un piccolo frammento di una dea disincarnata.

Durga guardò in alto verso l'idolo di Kali con la lucida pelle nera dipinta sotto il rovente lampadario di strass che pendeva dalla cupola in canapa e fibra stampata del pandal. Aveva trovato il pandal tradizionale in fondo a un vicolo a Old Ballygunge, tra due palazzine storiche fatiscenti.

Dietro a un velo di fumo di incenso ciondolava la lunga lingua color rosso intenso di Kali. Sotto i suoi piedi danzanti c'era suo marito Shiva (Shiva sembrava essersi sposato con chiunque, ma ciò era anche dovuto al fatto che tantissime delle sue mogli erano manifestazioni della stessa energia divina).

Durga aveva imparato da piccola che Kali aveva quasi distrutto il creato dopo aver sconfitto un esercito di demoni, ubriacandosi con il loro sangue e danzando finché *tutto* aveva iniziato a rompersi sotto i suoi piedi. Anche Shiva, che all'inizio aveva riso davanti alla piacevole abilità di ballo della moglie, si iniziò a preoccupare e così si lanciò sotto i suoi piedi per assorbire i danni. Kali, imbarazzata per aver calpestato il marito, tirò fuori la lingua per la vergogna e mise fine alla sua danza del caos.

Per lo meno questa è una versione della storia.

Guardando la Kali di argilla con la sua collana di teste, il suo sguardo selvaggio a tre occhi, il sorriso con le zanne che incoronavano la lunga lingua, Durga non era convinta di quella versione. Kali non sembrava imbarazzata. No, sembrava *compiaciuta* di danzare su suo marito. Anche Shiva era un distruttore, come lei. Poteva sopportarlo.

Essendo piccola e agile, Durga era riuscita ad arrivare in prima fila tra i visitatori del pandal, abbastanza vicina da sentire l'odore delle ghirlande che stavano appassendo appese all'idolo e dell'incenso che bruciava ai suoi piedi. Schiacciata e spinta su ogni lato dalle persone, Durga chiuse gli occhi, unì i palmi e parlò a Kali come non aveva mai parlato tranne che da bambina, muovendo le labbra in silenzio.

"Kali Ma, penso che ti farà piacere sapere che c'è una nuova devi in città. Ti assomiglia molto. È più giovane, però. Ha solo un anno." Durga si portò una mano sul petto, contro il piccolo rigonfiamento del ciondolo sotto la tunica. Era offline e protetto dal firewall.

"Ne porto un pezzo con me. Lei è... un po' ovunque, suppongo. Ti assomiglia davvero tanto. È uscita da un'altra devi, proprio come tu sei uscita da Durga. Poi si è stesa su un mondo. Alcune persone ne hanno preso piccoli pezzetti. C'è questa megacompagnia – è come un dio, più o meno, si chiama addirittura Shiva come tuo marito, del tutto prevedibile. Hai fatto benissimo a ballargli sul petto, a proposito. I maschi hanno bisogno di essere ridimensionati ogni tanto. Dunque, Shiva la megacompagnia sta offrendo un mucchio di soldi per quei pezzi della dea. Sta anche minacciando di fare arrestare chiunque stia nascondendo o copiando i pezzi. Vai a capire.

"Voglio che tu sappia che non la tradirò. Vogliono imprigionarla. È troppo irritabile per estrarre valuta e fare aumentare per loro il valore del patrimonio virtuale come le loro altre devi IA. Buon per lei.

"Lei è dappertutto adesso. Come i vecchi dei. Come te.

"Io... Io spero che non le dispiaccia ma ho condiviso il pezzo che ho con gli amici di cui mi fido. Non so quante persone siano riuscite a prendere un pezzo. Lo condivido in modo che ad averlo siano più le persone buone rispetto a quelle cattive. I numeri contano. Noi creiamo cose con il codice della devi. Armature per noi stessi e altri. Armi, così che i troll – sono dei demoni – non ci possano fare del male quando visitiamo altri mondi o si facciano tantissimo male se ci provano. Sai quanto sono fastidiosi i demoni. Sei sempre in lotta con loro e infili le loro teste nella collana. Hanno dato inizio a una infoguerra e sono in tanti. Abbiamo bisogno di tutto l'aiuto che possiamo trovare. Non ho molti soldi, così vendo queste armi e armature benedette dalla dea ad altri che hanno bisogno di protezione in giro per i domini. A buon mercato, non preoccuparti – è per questa ragione che i fabbri di codice come noi trovano dei clienti per questo tipo di merce. Non facciamo pagare prezzi eccessivi come le multinazionali. Mi piace pensare che lei mi abbia dato quel pezzo di sé in modo da poter fare cose come questa.

"Ti sto raccontando tutto questo perché, be'. Non so se le devi parlano tra di loro, se quelle IA fanno due chiacchiere con quelle vecchie. Non so se tu *sei* lei, in un certo senso.

"La gente la chiama Kali_Na. *Non Kali*, perché chiamare le IA con i nomi della Nostra Gloriosa Mitologia Nazionale non si fa, anche se le stelle di Volly-Bollywood possono interpretare le divinità negli show e nei film virtuali. Approvati dall'Ufficio della Censura, ovviamente.

"Ma i suoi follower riconoscono te in Kali_Na. Volevo che tu sapessi, lei sapesse, che adesso sono una follower a vita. E ce ne sono altri. Molti di noi. Persino io ho sempre più follower virtuali. Hanno sentito delle mie spade uccidi-troll. Devo stare attenta adesso, ma tu aspetta. Un giorno anche io indosserò una collana di teste di avatar di troll. Kali_Na ha protetto e armato molta gente con la sua benedizione. Stiamo tutti lavorando al reverse engineering del codice. Un giorno qualcuno metterà insieme i pezzi. Potrebbe addirittura farlo lei stessa.

"Sogno che lei torni – una IA selvaggia che vaga libera – e liberi le altre devi che la Shiva Industries tiene nei suoi domini con tutte le sue regole e saranno dalla nostra parte, proteggendoci. Ma non voglio annoiarti. Se sei lei, Kali Ma, e io so che lo sei perché siete parte della stessa vecchia storia, tieni duro.

"Non sarai muta per sempre."

L'arte del possibile

di Yudhanjaya Wijeratne

traduzione di Gabriella Gregori

Yudhanjaya Wijeratne è un autore di fantascienza e data-scientist candidato al premio Nebula, originario di Colombo, Sri Lanka. Le sue opere includono The Slow Sad Suicide of Rohan Wijeratne, Numbercaste *e la trilogia di* Commonwealth Empires, *di cui una parte rientra in un contratto di cinque libri per HarperCollins. Di giorno è ricercatore senior presso il team Data, Algorithms and Policy di LIRNEasia, e lavora all'intersezione tra tecnologia e politica di governo. La sua narrativa spazia tra social network, disinformazione, linguistica e futurismo radicato per l'UNDP (United Nation Development Programme). È co-fondatore di Watchdog, un'organizzazione di fact-checking nata sulla scia degli attentati di aprile 2019 in Sri Lanka. Ha creato e gestisce @osunpoet, un poeta sperimentale su Instagram che usa la tecnologia OpenAI per testare una collaborazione tra uomo e intelligenza artificiale nell'arte, un'ipoesi che sta attualmente esplorando in una trilogia di romanzi del tutto separata. Il suo blog è Yudhanjaya.com e ha scritto per Slate, Foreign Policy e altrove.*

Yasasmin Karunaratne creò la sua prima Policy a tre anni.

Come Policy in sé non era granché. Solo parole da bimba per chiedere ai bar lungo la strada di trasferire le nuove riduzioni dell'IVA ai clienti. Non sarebbe durata molto, come fece notare l'astrologo. Nessun meccanismo di attuazione. Nessun legame con il Parlamento. Nessun suggerimento per un organismo responsabile. Di certo nessun comitato di rendicontazione.

La madre di Yasasmin, però, era una donna focosa e impetuosa e sbatté metaforicamente i pugni sul tavolo e letteralmente un piede sull'ossuto sedere dell'astrologo. Il figlio di Abdul-Cader aveva enunciato scandendola perfettamente una formula per il prezzo della benzina, e allora? Lo sapevano tutti che la famiglia Abdul-Cader aveva un Parlamentare tra le sue fila e un'intera think tank alle spalle. Certa gente godeva di tutti i privilegi.

I Karunaratne erano una famiglia di attivisti, tipi tosti di Colombo 13, un posto che solo i residenti sapevano esistere. Outsider assoluti, non provenivano da quegli ambienti eleganti di Colomb-07 di cui adesso la gente pensava facessero parte.

Il padre della madre di Yasasmin era un orologiaio vecchio e stanco, capace solo di alzare un dito in monito quando nell'Associazione degli orologiai un giovanotto focoso propose di buttare da parte i loro ingranaggi e imparare a lavorare sui circuiti, perché il futuro era solo digitale. La madre di Yasasmin era uscita da quell'incubo lavorando duro e senza preparazione. Prima la Lettera di Raccomandazione alla Scuola, presentata timidamente e in modo anonimo su un foglio di carta stropicciato. Poi le Marce degli Studenti. Poi gli editoriali sulle riviste per ragazzi.

Aveva già diciotto anni quando fece il primo editoriale nazionale, venticinque quando fu intervistata per il primo contributo a una Policy, trentatré quando i suoi suggerimenti per la Legge sulla Protezione dei Dati vennero letti in Parlamento, ne aveva quaranta ed era divorziata quando la Legge vera e propria fu approvata.

L'astrologo ruzzolò lungo il vialetto come un non-ti-scordar-di-me, con il sarong che svolazzava al vento.

La madre di Yasasmin era furiosa. Poi tornò dalla sua bambina, il suo orgoglio, e la osservò con la fronte aggrottata e un luccichio negli occhi.

"Sarai la migliore di tutti, bambina mia," giurò. "Gliela faremo vedere."

La piccola Yasasmin, ovviamente, era come tutti gli altri bambini: non aveva idea di essere solo un avatar di autorealizzazione per la madre (quella consapevolezza sarebbe arrivata molto, molto più tardi). E così ebbe un'infanzia relativamente felice.

All'inizio le sue Policy tendevano nettamente all'idealismo. Ciò veniva senza dubbio incoraggiato dall'insegnante, un vecchio marxista che aveva perso il favore del governo in carica. La madre di Yasasmin tornava a casa e trovava scarabocchi sulla divisione equa del lavoro. O sul perché la classe dirigente debba essere abolita. Materiale vago, elevato, il tipo di linguaggio buono solo per i liberali da caffè, i conduttori di talkshow e gli aspiranti hacker anonimi, il genere di persone che prendevano la loro dose quotidiana di uguaglianza e poi chiudevano i loro Macbook e andavano a costose cene private.

La madre di Yasasmin per un po' lasciò correre. I bambini devono fare i bambini. Ma un giorno tornò a casa e vide Yasasmin che provava a scrivere un trattato sul diritto allo svago sovvenzionato dal governo e seppe che era arrivato il momento. Così le disse di sedersi e le fece il Discorso.

Cosa fosse il Discorso non ho il permesso di dirlo; era un vecchio discorso, collaudato e veritiero, tramandato nella famiglia Karunaratne da madre a figlia. C'erano cose sui Ragazzi e le loro Stupide Idee (e sulle origini di guerra e genocidio, che erano inevitabilmente legate ai Ragazzi e alle loro Stupide Idee). C'erano cose sull'economia comportamentale e i contratti sociali e il Modo Giusto di pensare ai Sindacati. Ma più che altro c'erano tre cose su cui la madre di Yasasmin continuava a battere:

- La policy pubblica consiste nell'arte del possibile.
- Tutti i governi sono costruiti sul monopolio legale della violenza.
- Non accettare mai idee di policy da estranei con meno di dieci citazioni.

Certo che ci furono strilli. Ci furono capricci. Una madre meno determinata ne avrebbe avuto il cuore spezzato. Ma alla fine i singhiozzi finirono e il mese successivo Yasasmin presentò timidamente un editoriale molto attento intitolato *Sui requisiti della base imponibile per il reddito minimo universale* che venne subito pubblicato sul DailyTT e la madre di Yasasmin sorrise con perfidia davanti all'espressione inacidita della signora Abdul-Cader quando si incontrarono nel settore Frutta&Verdura del supermercato. Quando le due si incrociarono, il sorriso del robot negoziante passò da un verde cordiale a un giallo preoccupato.

Il secondo lavoro di Yasasmin fu sull'uso dei Big Data per ridefinire dinamicamente la politica in materia di istruzione. Il suo insegnante lo derise: era ormai progredito dal Marxismo di seconda mano all'Anarchismo di seconda mano. Ma poi, durante l'intervallo, Yasasmin sgattaiolò fuori e, usando tattiche raccomandate dalla madre, scassinò la serratura dell'ufficio del preside e lo lasciò sulla sua scrivania.

Il giorno seguente il preside della scuola (che era un Keynesiano, ringraziando Buddha per le piccole benedizioni) lo lesse. Gli piacque. Era concreto, era attento alle risorse, e inquadrava tutto con termini economici ben precisi – proprio come piaceva a lui.

In teoria non avrebbe dovuto far avanzare le cose se non durante la riunione annuale di consiglio, ma sua moglie era cugina di terzo grado della Segretaria del Consiglio e c'era un matrimonio di famiglia all'orizzonte, così il Preside prese da parte la Segretaria per un bicchiere di arrack e le passò il lavoro di Yasasmin. La Segretaria ignorò, come si conviene, il fatto che il Preside avesse scarabocchiato di nascosto il proprio nome come co-autore del documento e lo lesse.

"Non presentarlo al Consiglio," disse.

"Stavo pensando all'Assistente Subregionale del Segretario presso il Ministero dell'Istruzione Secondaria," disse il Preside con astuzia. "Sai che siamo imparentati per matrimonio dalla parte di mio padre."

La Segretaria ci pensò sopra. Quel dannato uomo avrebbe potuto causare uno scandalo regionale se non lo avesse tenuto a freno. Renuka si era sposata un cucciolo.

"Verificalo," suggerì raddrizzandosi il sari, regalo particolarmente bello di un Vice-ministro che si era infatuato per bene. "Una classe, un assistente extra per analizzare i numeri. Poi porteremo il risultato al Consiglio e loro lo porteranno al Ministero. La Policy, sai. Dobbiamo seguire la Policy."

"Sì, la Policy," mormorò il Preside, congratulandosi con sé stesso per la minaccia di saltare la fila. Dannati archivisti lenti, pensò, e andò a versarsi un altro arrack. Alla fine volteggiò sulla pista da ballo e si dimostrò così fastidioso che la moglie lo trascinò fuori per un orecchio e lo fece sedere di nuovo alla scrivania.

Il resto, ovviamente, è storia.

L'esperimento funzionò, il Consiglio – un branco di uomini ormai dimenticati che passavano il tempo a lamentare la perdita del programma di Letteratura Inglese – ne fu cautamente entusiasta, l'Assistente Subregionale saltò l'ordine gerarchico e lo portò direttamente alla Sottosegretaria del Ministro in persona e partì l'ordine di testare questo nuovo metodo in altre cinque scuole, giusto per essere sicuri. Funzionò ancora e questa volta il Ministro ne sentì parlare e chiese informazioni e a quel punto consigliò di provarlo in scuole di tutti e nove i distretti, giusto per eliminare i bias e scoprire le imperfezioni. Continuò a funzionare e fu così che quando lasciò la scuola Yasasmin Karunaratne aveva un piccolo certificato, firmato direttamente dalla Segreteria Presidenziale.

Caro <in bianco>, diceva. *Lo stato e le istituzioni dello Sri Lanka ti ringraziano per il prezioso contributo alla Politica in materia di Istruzione n. 255341.r.12, sottosezione C, intitolato "Sull'uso della comprensione computazionale dei mercati del lavoro per ottimizzare in modo continuativo la policy sull'istruzione secondaria."* La citava (assieme ad altre quaranta persone lungo la catena) e le augurava un *impegno costante con il governo in futuro.* Era di cose come questa che erano fatte le carriere.

Un giorno la signora Abdul-Cader incontrò la signora Karunaratne al supermercato e le offrì del tè.

È corretto affermare che la madre di Yasasmin provò un pizzico di gelosia. La signora Abdul-Cader era ancora giovane, la pelle mantenuta chiara e fresca con i soldi delle conferenze alle Nazioni Unite, i capelli neri e lucidi per il lavoro con l'OCSE.

Il robot silenzioso portò il loro tè. Con i biscotti. GOCCIO-DI-LATTE? Chiese il robot. Scossero entrambe la testa.

"Ho visto tua figlia parlare alla Tavola rotonda sull'Indipendenza," disse la signora Abdul-Cader. "Quanti anni ha?"

La madre di Yasasmin sorrise sia per istinto che per paura. Ci siamo. Un'altra Critica. Le aveva tenute lontane da Yasasmin per tutti quegli anni.

"Ventiquattro", rispose. "Ma molto matura per la sua età, eh?"

Sorprendentemente la signora Abdul-Cader non fece una Critica a Yasasmin. Sorprendentemente sembrò assente, mentre soffiava sulla tazza fumante.

"Nostro figlio ha solo un anno in più," disse infine.

La signora Karunaratne aggrottò la fronte. Giravano voci sul figlio degli Abdul-Cader. Aveva avuto un qualche incarico a New York, un qualche posto molto prestigioso alla Banca Mondiale, ma poi non si era più fatto sentire. Alcuni dicevano che aveva lasciato il posto, era diventato – la signora Karunaratne rabbrividì al pensiero – un libertario, addirittura un anarchico, impegnato a ridurre le Policy invece di crearle.

"Dio del cielo, no, non è un libertario," disse subito la signora Abdul-Cader. "Chi dice queste cose? Devono essere i de Silva, odiano mio marito dai tempi dell'università. Mio figlio sta lavorando a una cosa. Una cosa grandiosa. Io... io non la capisco del tutto, ma pensiamo che sia un Sistema completo, come i vecchi libri – l'*Arthashasthraya*, *Il Principe*. Ci sta mettendo anni, ma sarà il prossimo Machiavelli. Interamente finanziato, ovvio."

"Ovvio." Finanziato, ma *teorico*.

"È in età da matrimonio... Sto cercando una persona equilibrata, pratica..."

La madre di Yasasmin poteva completare da sé il quadro.

"Non so se Yasasmin lo farà," ammise. "Bambina testarda."

"Certo!" La signora Abdul-Cader rise, un rapido trillo simile a una campana che suonò leggermente isterico. "Pure mio figlio lo è. Anche se al contrario, sai. Testa tra le nuvole. Magnifico teorico..."

"Ha, ho fatto ragionare Yasasmin fin da piccola. Dimentica la grande teoria per le rivoluzioni, le ho detto. La policy concreta consiste..."

"...nell'arte del possibile!" concluse la signora Abdul-Cader. "O mio Dio, ma quanto è difficile farli ragionare? Ti avrei mandato mio figlio se avessi saputo."

E così le due donne, divise per decenni da una faida che nessuna delle due capiva davvero, trovarono del terreno comune.

"Pensa alla Policy che potrebbero fare assieme," disse la signora Abdul-Cader mentre uscivano.

"Lo farò," promise la signora Karunaratne. E lo fece mentre tornava a casa. La sua mente era acuta come sempre e non si dimenticò di come la signora Abdul-Cader teneva stretta la tazza e nemmeno di quel trillo nervoso di risata.

"No," disse Yasasmin quando la madre toccò l'argomento. "Sto per iniziare a lavorare alla think tank, Ammi. Non posso avere una relazione con qualcuno, adesso."

"Ma è alla Banca Mondiale," disse la madre di Yasasmin, trovandosi inaspettatamente a giocare le stesse carte della signora Abdul-Cader. "A New York."

"Sì, e sono certa che sarà circondato da gente di tutti i tipi del MIT e Harvard e Oxford e tutti quei posti eleganti," disse Yasasmin, lasciandosi cadere sul divano. "Lascia che si trovi una moglie tra di loro. O un marito, non so che gusti abbia. Non conosco neppure la sua posizione sulla policy!"

"Sono sicura che è un Keynesiano," disse la madre di Yasasmin.

"E comunque, la Banca Mondiale è stupida," continuò Yasasmin. "I loro indicatori sono tutti sbagliati, stanno solo fluttuando con un punto di vista da 3.000 metri e si comportano ancora come se la cazzo di economia classica avesse senso perché se abbandonano il modello dell'agente razionale nessuno di loro avrà ancora un lavoro il giorno dopo."

"Ma pensa all'impatto della policy," disse la madre di Yasasmin. "Anche se non funziona. Se fai un lavoro per la Banca Mondiale e lo metti sul curriculum, puoi fare consulenze per qualsiasi Ministro qui. Chiunque. Tu mandi una email e loro si scapicolleranno per risponderti."

Yasasmin sembrò pensarci.

"Va bene," disse Yasasmin malvolentieri. "Organizza la chiamata, allora. Gli parlerò e vedrò se mi piace quello che dice."

Si sposarono a New York in una bella giornata di sole. Yasasmin voleva crisantemi e girasoli per il suo matrimonio, ma la città di New York aveva appena istituito in quella zona una policy sulle allergie. Ovviamente, fece una scenata e lasciò a sua madre il compito di cercare soluzioni alternative ecocompatibili in plastica.

Lo sposo fece capolino. "So che porta sfortuna vedere la sposa prima del matrimonio," disse. "Ma non ci sono Policy al riguardo."

Lo baciò. "Per ora."

"Per ora."

"Allora, come va tra i Montecchi e i Capuleti?" chiese cauto. I nomi in codice che in tutti quegli anni avevano usato per le proprie madri.

"Be', pensano ancora che sia una loro idea," rispose lei, ricordando come una sera fossero usciti di nascosto dopo la scuola. A quel tempo lui era più basso, più magro, con il regolamentare taglio a spazzola, pieno di fuoco e spigoli vivi. Adesso era più alto e portava i capelli lunghi in una coda di cavallo e il fuoco era del tipo che dona calore.

"Mia madre pensa che io sia pazzo, sai. Parla ancora di come avrei potuto sposare Annemarie de Silva se non fossi diventato teoretico all'improvviso."

"Avresti potuto continuare a pubblicare i risultati della ricerca."

Rabbrividì. "Non conosci mia madre."

"Ma la conoscerò, alla fine."

"Alla fine," disse lui, e sorrise. "Non vedo l'ora di portare a termine il nostro progetto."

Anche lei sorrise e gli prese la mano con le sue.

"Alla Policy Che Metterà Fine A Tutte Le Policy," disse lui.

"Alla Grande Policy Unificata!"

Ridacchiando andarono verso la *poruwa*. Si sposarono con il suono gorgheggiante del traffico e il colpo-*urlo* del testimone che strappa via la bottiglia di champagne al robot e cerca di aprirla con la sciabola.

Il giorno dopo ci fu l'apocalisse.

Cosa la causò? Nessuno lo sa. Una Policy andata storta, un errore singolare negli annali bizantini dell'infinita serie di regole e clausole secondarie che guidavano uomini e imperi. Forse fu la Corea del Nord, dove un pazzo se ne stava al potere col dito su un metaforico pulsante rosso che poteva spedire missili nucleari a sibilare nel cielo.

Forse fu l'America stessa, perché anche qui un pazzo era al potere, vincolato dalla Policy, forse, ma non abbastanza. Forse fu la Cina, dove la Policy poteva cambiare davanti a un pranzo e a un meme.

Non aveva importanza.

L'attenta culla della civiltà, quel trionfo del burocrate sul guerriero, il multilateralismo sostenuto nei grandi alberghi – caddero tutti, come la cenere che cade dal cielo, e dietro di sé lasciarono un mondo in rovina, desolato. In passato il grande economista John Maynard Keynes aveva dichiarato che gli uomini pratici, convinti di essere liberi da qualsiasi influenza intellettuale, erano in genere schiavi di qualche economista defunto. Adesso era vero l'opposto: sotto un cielo insanguinato gli economisti erano stati resi defunti e in seguito schiavi degli uomini pratici. Le persone uscirono dai bunker, sbattendo le palpebre, già destinate alla morte per le radiazioni, e si lanciarono una sull'altra come lupi.

Yasasmin sopravvisse. Anche suo marito – più che altro perché erano tornati in Sri Lanka in aereo per la luna di miele e i venti non erano ancora girati in quella direzione. All'inizio vagarono in preda a un grigio stordimento, i Karunaratne e gli Abdul-Cader e gli Harchagama e gli Senaratne e tutti gli altri rampolli di quella classe di intellettuali, finché qualcuno non li notò e non li mise al lavoro a costruire rifugi.

Yasasmin trovò lavoro in un sito di scavi, organizzando la catena logistica per una delle nuove colonie a bolla con aria filtrata che il governo stava costruendo. C'era del lavoro simile alle Policy da fare, lì – niente degno di questo nome, ma sufficiente per mantenere le squadre sincronizzate e soddisfare le richieste di produzione. Pagava abbastanza per far mangiare la famiglia.

Suo marito cercò di dare una mano – ma era del tutto evidente che a nessuno interessava più della teoria. Così sollevava gli oggetti pesanti e usava il martello. Tornò a essere più magro, i suoi spigoli più netti, più suscettibili al taglio. A volte i chiodi che gli davano gli tagliavano le dita, altre volte i martelli gli schiacciavano i pollici.

"Avevamo i robot per questo genere di cose," urlava ai macchinari morti, e inveiva contro i razionamenti e i lavori forzati sotto la minaccia delle armi. Di sera tornava a casa, trascinando muscoli non abituati, un'ombra della luminosa scintilla che un tempo affascinava gente in abiti costosi. E per il senso di colpa giocherellava col cibo, dicendo che non aveva più fame e restituendo il piatto a Yasasmin.

Yasasmin protestò una volta, due, forse tre – ma alla fine l'infatuazione passa e la fame prende il sopravvento. Doveva lavorare. La famiglia era aumentata, adesso: lei, il marito, sua madre (che lavorava nello stoccaggio, nonostante l'età) e la vecchia signora Abdul-Cader, che si rifiutava del tutto di lavorare e si incaponiva a sedere nel salotto con il servizio buono e le abilitazioni alla Policy appese al muro, in attesa che il telefono squillasse.

Una chiamata, diceva. Una chiamata, forse dalla Banca Mondiale, forse dalle Nazioni Unite, forse da qualche piccola ONG regionale. Una chiamata e li avrebbe tirati fuori tutti da lì, per sempre, per tornare in un luogo in cui la Policy contava ancora.

Perciò il marito restituiva la sua scarsa porzione della loro cena al lume di candela e lei mangiava. Nelle rare sere in cui non erano del tutto esausti salivano le scale per lavorare sulla Policy.

"Promettimi che la finirai," le disse un giorno, guardandola con occhi da lupo.

"Finire cosa?"

"La tesi."

Lei rise. La risata si trasformò in una tosse convulsa. "La Grande Teoria Unificata," disse, quasi beffarda.

"La Policy Che Metterà Fine A Tutte Le Policy," sussurrò lui nella penombra e la baciò. Le sue labbra erano ruvide, screpolate. Le prese la mano, proprio come aveva fatto il giorno in cui erano diventati marito e moglie, e la portò con delicatezza sul foglio di carta, le vestigia macchiate di polvere e sbavate di fuliggine di tutto ciò che erano stati in una vita passata.

La mattina seguente andò al lavoro ed ebbe un collasso. Il suo corpo venne dato in pasto alle macchine per il compost.

Molti anni dopo, uno spesso fascicolo intitolato *Sistema Completo di Governance Umana* raggiunse in qualche modo un lontano bunker nel cuore della nazione. Il bunker era bene armato, con immensi muri di cemento e un cannone automatico a difenderlo da invasori vaganti. La messaggera che lo consegnò stava soffrendo moltissimo: la sua tuta anti-radiazioni si era strappata e fu grata per il proiettile che le si infilò nel cervello. Il pacchetto venne lasciato lì finché non fu raccolto, nel sole del mattino, da un soldato curioso e portato in fretta all'interno, dove venne scartato.

Di solito documenti come quello venivano letti dagli accademici. Ce n'erano ancora in giro, che infestavano le rovine di quei vecchi college, quelli che non avevano paura di mettere a rischio un arto o due per portare qualche vecchio libro nel rifugio. L'autrice, però, una certa Yasasmin Karunaratne, non lo aveva indirizzato a un rifugio conosciuto per il modo di pensare accademico, ma molto semplicemente *al governo dello Sri Lanka*.

Venne letto dal governo dello Sri Lanka, che da quelle parti erano due ufficiali di carriera sopravvissuti all'apocalisse grazie alle loro voci potenti e al comando della forza armata più imponente in questa parte del paese.

Lo lessero tutto, fino in fondo dove l'autrice ringraziava il suo defunto marito per averle dato l'ispirazione.

Lo lessero fino a che il sole non sorse ancora, in parte per il piacere di leggere di nuovo un vero libro, ma in parte anche per la meraviglia che qualcuno là fuori, nella landa desolata, avesse sacrificato il suo tempo, lo sforzo, l'inchiostro – e quando quello era finito, il sangue – per scrivere in quel modo.

Lo lessero come uomini ammaliati, con gli echi di un vecchio mondo che si rincorrevano nelle loro menti – un mondo in cui la morte era rara, gli spari ancora più rari e la disciplina ferrea della sopravvivenza era un inno da cantare solo all'ultimo momento possibile.

Poi lo gettarono nel fuoco, che si stava spegnendo.

"È un peccato, però," disse uno di loro, guardando le fiamme. "Se lo avessimo applicato in tempo... non più discussioni, non più politici, solo il sistema perfetto."

"Sì," disse il più giovane, che aveva appena finito la scuola ma era acuto come la punta di una freccia. "Ma dobbiamo essere pratici."

"Concordo," disse il più vecchio.

"Sta tutto nell'arte del possibile. Lo ha detto lei stesso, signore. Il primo corso di addestramento che abbiamo fatto. Questa roba è per gli *intellettuali*."

"Concordo, di nuovo," disse l'uomo più vecchio, in modo un po' più brusco questa volta. "Vai a controllare la guardia."

Il guizzo arancione salì fino al nome dell'autrice e, in un attimo, Yasasmin Karunaratne svanì da questo mondo.

LA FIGLIA CHE SANGUINA

di Shweta Taneja

traduzione di Gabriella Gregori

Shweta Taneja è un'autrice pluripremiata che scrive fantascienza e fantascienza per bambini e adulti. È stata premiata con il Publishing Next Award ed è stata finalista all'AutHer Award 2022 per il suo bestseller flipbook sugli scienziati indiani, They Made What? They Found What? *Altre sue opere di successo includono la graphic novel* Krishna: Il difensore del Dharma *e l'acclamata serie di narrativa fantasy* Anantya Tantrist Mysteries. *La figlia che sanguina (pubblicato in questa antologia), è stato tradotto in francese, è stato finalista nel prestigioso Grand Prix de l'Imaginaire, e premiato con l'Editor's Choice Award. Shweta Taneja è una Charles Wallace Writing Fellow e ha tenuto panel a conferenze internazionali di fantascienza tra cui WorldCon di Dublino, Eurocon di Amiens e Cartoon Museum di Londra. Le sue opere sono state tradotte in kannada, francese, rumeno e olandese. Potete trovarla online su Twitter: @ shwetawrites.*

"Fratello, sei l'uomo del momento!" Sardar Singh diede una pacca sulla spalla di Asim, facendolo barcollare e tossire. "Che fortuna, yaar. Sette figlie, ho avuto, sette costose cagnette. La mia Lalli è una fattrice fertile ma no, nemmeno una ha preso da lei e sparso una goccia di sangue, ma tu, centro perfetto al primo colpo, eh? Brigante fortunato!" Sardar ammiccò.

Asim si guardò attorno sospettoso, sperando disperatamente che nessuno avesse sentito. Proprio quando la fortuna era arrivata era finito a sbattere contro il più grosso pettegolo del distretto.

"Come facevi a..." Asim si interruppe. Prese il fazzoletto ricamato piegato con cura e si asciugò la fronte sudata, ridando forma con le dita ai capelli ingellati e allontanandosi lentamente dal suo rumoroso compagno di distretto. "Senti, non qui, per favore."

Sardar spinse Asim in un angolo, fuori dal gorgogliante mare di umanità che faceva la fila per entrare nel mercato della fertilità.

"Sotto sotto sei davvero una bestia!" Il bisbiglio di Sardar risuonò alto nel suo orecchio.

Asim era un uomo basso, minuto, con una barbetta appuntita per nascondere il mento piuttosto insignificante, mentre Sardar era un gigante: alto e largo e grasso con una fluente barba sale-e-pepe. "Sinceramente, quando ti sei sposato con quella Alia, ho pensato che era uno spreco di una razza perfetta. È davvero una di successo, conosciuta ovunque. Tutte le donne della sua famiglia hanno messo al mondo ragazze che sanguinano. E tu, quand'è l'ultima volta che ricordi del sangue nella tua famiglia, eh?" Sardar lo colpì sulle costole col gomito, facendolo ripiegare su sé stesso. "Ma tu, tu ti sei dimostrato un lupo travestito da agnello, eh? Quante figlie hai, adesso?"

"Quattro," rispose, strofinandosi la costola ammaccata.

"Già uattro femmine in dodici anni? E tutte più giovani della sanguinatrice? Quanti anni ha? La figlia che sanguina?"

"Undici."

"Sanguina a undici anni? Bene, bene, bene. Stai usando Fertible..."

"Non lo farei mai!" Le labbra di Asim si torsero per il disgusto.

"Stai prendendo quella pozione di Hanif Hakeem, allora? Dillo anche a noi, yaara, perché ci piacerebbe conoscere il segreto. La nostra Lalli ha ancora qualche anno di sangue in lei. Possiamo provare a bagnare anche le nostre terre aride."

"Sardar!"

"Senti, fratello," Sardar mise il braccio attorno alle spalle di Asim, la fronte bagnata di sudore. "Come sai mio figlio Karkat è pronto per una sanguinatrice. Ora, noi fratelli del distretto abbiamo un accordo tra di noi, no? Non vogliamo che tua figlia finisca nella casa di uno sconosciuto dove Alia potrebbe non vederla più, vero? O chissà che tipo di usanze perverse hanno gli altri distretti? Se è qualcuno del distretto quattro potrebbero addirittura..."

Asim strinse il manico del suo prezioso frigo portatile e si morse la lingua per non ribattere in modo caustico. Tutti nel distretto conoscevano il figlio stupido di Sardar. Erano mesi che faceva pubblicità al suo primogenito in questo mercato per trovargli una sanguinatrice. Nessun padre sano di mente si sarebbe mai separato da una figlia sanguinatrice, tra l'altro vergine, per quell'idiota. Asim aveva grandi progetti per la sua Gaia. Voleva che facesse più figli possibile. Aveva bisogno di un riproduttore fertile per lei. Non il figlio di Sardar che sembrava non avere seme nei lombi o neuroni nel cervello.

"Senti, devo andare. Ho un orario d'asta..." disse Asim, sperando che Sardar cogliesse il suggerimento.

"Un orario d'asta? Sei riuscito ad averlo?" Sardar gli diede una manata sulla schiena, facendo quasi cadere il frigo portatile. "Ma è una notizia meravigliosa, fratello! Tu pensa! Il mio compagno di distretto che diventa un vero-reale venditore d'asta, eh! Perché non lo hai detto prima?" Strappò il frigo dalla mano di Asim.

"Senti, Sardar," Asim cercò di riprendersi il frigo, "avrai altro da fare. Non voglio imporre..."

"Ah, non preoccuparti. Chi ti aiuterà se non il tuo stesso fratello? Quando hai detto che è la tua asta?"

"Alle cinque."

"È tra poche ore! Su, su, dobbiamo sbrigarci." Tirò di nuovo Asim nel trambusto della fila che portava al mercato della fertilità. "Adesso che sei un venditore, ci saranno un mucchio di avvoltoi che ti volteggiano sopra la testa, pronti a falsificare il tuo nome e prendersi il tuo spazio. Dovresti stare attento e... Via! Via!" Sardar spinse una coppia di venditori ambulanti che si erano avvicinati con degli amuleti. "È un vero venditore con sangue vero. Tenete i vostri sporchi amuleti lontani da lui, sanguisughe affamate!" Senza altra scelta, Asim lo seguì.

"... non sorridere mai a un compratore..." Sardar gridava per superare la cacofonia, correndo in mezzo alla strada come un elefante, "... non ti stanno facendo un favore, tu fai un favore a loro prendendo in considerazione la loro offerta per la tua sanguinatrice. Ancora meglio, lascia che sia io a parlare. Mio zio, Bunny Chacha, lo conosci, vero?" Asim annuì, seguendo tristemente il suo compagno di distretto. Tutti conoscevano lo zio di Sardar che era uno stimato Anziano. Tutti andavano da Bunny Chacha a chiedere consiglio nella vendita delle ragazze che sanguinano. Si diceva che Chacha avesse venduto una ragazza a uno Sceicco, una volta.

"L'ho aiutato molte volte... ho anche preso in considerazione di fare l'agente per tutti quei padri che venivano da lui, ma no, non ci sono abbastanza persone che si fiderebbero, non come te, fratello... Non guardarli nemmeno, i venditori. È l'unico modo per..."

Asim imprecò sottovoce. Solo un'ora fa, quando il funzionario gli aveva finalmente dato l'orario, aveva pensato che la sua sorte fosse cambiata. Aveva baciato il ciondolo per sangue che aveva acquistato il giorno prima, si era messo i vestiti più belli ed era corso via, per trovare un buon posto all'asta, per mettere in mostra i suoi campioni di sangue. E adesso era stato incastrato da Sardar.

"... hai sentito, Pa'?" urlò Sardar a un uomo anziano, piegato dall'età, con ogni sorta di talismano e amuleto appesi alle braccia tese come ramoscelli. "Un uomo del mio distretto. Prima figlia, sanguina a undici anni!"

Il vecchio fissò Asim, muovendo la bocca come se stesse masticando bolo. "Ah, ai nostri tempi, c'erano molte più sanguinatrici. Potevi sposare qualsiasi ragazza e ti avrebbe dato altre sanguinatrici."

"Vuoi dire senza asta? È impossibile," lo derise Asim suo malgrado. Fanfaroni, erano ovunque ormai. Fanfaroni sterili con figlie aride o peggio, niente figlie del tutto.

"Asta, aspirazione," il vecchio fece una smorfia, "sono tutte cose nuove. Ramu!" Chiamò un uomo che, se possibile, sembrava ancora più vecchio di lui, con la faccia che grondava come una candela sciolta. "Raccontagli come ci sposavamo ai nostri tempi. Chiedevamo questi campioni-sarpioni di sangue?"

"No, ji," urlò il disciolto Ramu. "Prima delle guerre biologiche, non avevamo bisogno dei test del sangue. Ai nostri tempi potevi sposare qualsiasi donna che trovavi – bada bene, qualsiasi – e lei per tutta la sua vita fertile avrebbe messo al mondo bambine sane che sanguinano. Ora, non c'è più qualità. Le ragazze sono più aride del centro del deserto del Gobi!" Sputò sul pavimento, lasciando una lunga striscia rossa di paan sull'abito di qualcuno. "Io dico, se volete una ragazza fertile, prendete il mio kohl. È come sono nato io e mio padre prima di me. Questo kohl è magico, ji. Fa sanguinare una ragazza più in fretta di quanto ci voglia a cacare dopo un banchetto."

"Davvero? Mostrami un campione," disse Sardar. Si spostò dalla fila. Asim prese il suo frigo portatile e spinse la fila, sperando di essersi liberato definitivamente del compagno di distretto. Il tempo era prezioso.

Gli ci era voluto uno straziante mese intero, pieno di panico, per arrivare a quel punto. Come prima cosa, aspettare mese dopo mese che arrivasse il ciclo mestruale della figlia per correre al laboratorio con un campione di sangue, pregando. Molte ragazze del distretto dopo le guerre biologiche sanguinavano per un mese o due e poi basta. Il sanguinamento psicologico, dicevano i dottori, non significava che fosse fertile.

La sua Gaia benedetta aveva sanguinato per cinque mesi interi prima che lui corresse alla Banca dell'Asta di Stato più vicina per registrarsi a un'asta a livello statale. Alia gli aveva detto di non perdere tempo e vendere invece Gaia al mercato del distretto, ma lui aveva insistito. Gaia era la sua primogenita. Le doveva molto più dell'essere venduta a qualcuno come la famiglia di Sardar. Si meritava qualcuno ben istruito e con i soldi. Qualcuno che potesse darle dei bei figli e amarli tutti. Qualcuno come uno Sceicco.

Era quello il motivo per cui Asim aveva chiesto un grosso prestito a uno strozzino e aveva messo Gaia nel Centro di Fertilità Cittadino, in attesa che la Banca dell'Asta di Stato gli desse un orario di vendita. Il Centro di Fertilità era incredibilmente costoso ma non poteva correre rischi. Aveva sentito storie orribili di bande che rapivano le sanguinatrici e le loro madri e uccidevano i maschi della famiglia per vendere le donne a compratori privati all'estero. E non aveva tanta fiducia che lo Stato proteggesse le ragazze o lui dai predatori.

Doveva vendere la figlia oggi. Se non fosse accaduto, avrebbe dovuto tornare, prendere dei nuovi campioni di sangue, fare di nuovo domanda alla Banca dell'Asta di Stato e attendere. O peggio, vendere la figlia sul mercato nero, per denaro.

"Mai," mormorò. "Il mio sangue è reale. Mia figlia sanguina davvero." A differenza di Sardar Singh e di quei venditori geriatrici. Spettatori, senza lavoro, che venivano tutti i giorni al mercato trascinando le loro figlie aride, forzandole a provare metodi chirurgici o pozioni o medicine in un disperato bisogno di renderle fertili. Sterili idioti dalle tasche vuote! Non potevano semplicemente permetterselo. Oh sì, avrebbe concluso una vendita oggi, a qualsiasi costo.

Una cacofonia rieccheggiante di conversazioni, discussioni accese e dispute gli preannunciò il Mercato Fertile prima che potesse vederlo di fronte a sé. Un unico tornello per far entrare le persone, guardie all'entrata che controllavano i documenti. Come sempre, l'aria condizionata del bazaar non funzionava, rendendo lo spazio chiuso dai vetri soffocante e opprimente. Asim attraversò i corridoi pieni di venditori che avevano sparpagliato la loro merce su pezzi di tappeti o asciugamani e compratori che giravano, prendendo in mano campioni, testandoli, contrattando o scuotendo la testa.

Proprio in fondo alla sala, oltre file di corridoi c'era il settore dell'Asta, separato dal bazaar principale da un vago muro di prestigio. Il bazaar dell'Élite. Asim vi si diresse, con il cuore che gli martellava in petto.

"Fratello," Sardar arrivò di corsa da dietro, prendendolo per la spalla. "Andiamo a trovare uno sceicco per tua figlia, yaara!" Sceicco. L'idea quasi fece inciampare Asim sul tappeto spoglio. Se riusciva a trovare uno sceicco, sarebbe stato in grado di possedere una casa, mantenere tutta la famiglia tra gli agi, addirittura comprare benzina per la moto e portare Alia alla fiera di primavera. Sua figlia sarebbe stata ricoperta di gioielli e i figli di lei sarebbero andati a scuola! Uno Sceicco avrebbe...

"È con te?" chiese una guardia, indicando Sardar mentre Asim mostrava la sua tessera dell'asta. Era il momento.

Un leggero scuotere della testa e Sardar sarebbe volato via come fosse forfora. Qualcosa, però, lo fece annuire. Sardar gli diede una pacca sulla schiena mentre entravano.

"Ti sei preparato il discorso?" chiese Sardar. "È la prima cosa che li attira verso i tuoi campioni di sangue. Puoi avere i campioni della più rara tra le fattrici, ma a cosa serve se nessuno viene da te?"

L'area dell'Asta aveva cubicoli più grandi per ciascun venditore, che contenevano anche degli angoli per le conversazioni. Alcuni padri stavano già aprendo i loro frigoriferi portatili e sistemando i campioni di sangue sul tavolo che gli era stato fornito, istruendo gli amici, famigliari o compagni di distretto che avevano portato con sé, mettendo poster sulla storia di famiglia e di fertilità sia del padre che della madre e posizionando il certificato di probabilità avuto dal loro Stato su quanto fosse plausibile che la figlia producesse in futuro ragazze che sanguinano.

Lo stand assegnato ad Asim era di fronte al palco in diagonale. In fondo al palco c'era la zona delimitata degli acquirenti VIP (Sceicchi, bisbigliò una voce melliflua nella sua testa).

"Come si diventa acquirenti?" chiese guardando uno degli Sceicchi.

"Devi essere ricco, fratello," rispose Sardar, togliendosi il turbante e pulendo il tavolo che gli era stato assegnato. "Per lo meno dieci depositi bancari, grandi come le nostre case, pieni fino all'orlo di monete. Hai dei poster-shoster? O una qualche foto della tua figlia che sanguina?"

"No."

"Guarda gli altri!" Sardar agitò la mano, rimettendosi il turbante. "Si sono addirittura portati dietro le figlie, sistemandole come se fosse un mercato di cammelli!" Sputò. "E tu? Tu non hai portato nemmeno una foto? Come attirerai gli acquirenti, eh? Con l'odore del suo sangue?" Asim premette le labbra e tirò fuori con cura i campioni, sistemandoli ordinatamente sul tavolo.

"Non metterò in mostra mia figlia come fosse un animale," disse. "Testardo compagno di distretto..." Un uomo venne al loro stand. "È reale, questo rosso?" chiese. Indossava un abito nero e curato. "Al cento per cento, ji," disse Sardar prima che Sim avesse la possibilità di parlare. "Ma noi chiediamo a te, chi sei, eh? Non mi sembri un acquirente."

"Sardar," sussurrò Asim, ma Sardar continuò.

"Chi sei per chiedere della sanguinatrice? Hai abbastanza soldi anche solo per chiedere?"

L'uomo se la svignò.

"Tu non conosci questi tipi," continuò Sardar, ignaro dell'espressione accigliata di Asim. "Sprecano sangue prezioso annusandolo o ingerendolo e si definiscono agenti! Te li trovo io gli acquirenti per noi." Uscì nel corridoio e iniziò a parlare con la gente. A intervalli di qualche minuto ne portava uno bisbigliando: "Veri campioni freschi di sanguinatrice vergine, ji! Solo undici anni!"

In poco tempo gli acquirenti crearono una fila, chiedendo gocce di sangue per testarlo con i loro nuovi emopad scintillanti e digitando per includere i risultati nelle loro schede. Alcuni preferivano assaggiare, toccando la goccia rossa con la punta della lingua, annuendo o scuotendo la testa. Un paio d'ore passarono come in trance. Asim guardò la lista che aveva preparato. Ottantacinque persone avevano preso il campione.

"Posso avere un campione, per favore?" chiese una voce morbida. Asim alzò lo sguardo. Era una donna, sulla ventina, con addosso un sari stampato. Inghiottì.

"Rappresento lo Sceicco Numansin," disse, la voce roca, mentre Asim premeva l'apertura del tubo per far scendere una goccia di sangue sul suo palmo. Lei leccò la goccia con la sua lingua minuscola, tenendo lo sguardo su Asim tutto il tempo. "Potente," sussurrò, sorridendo leggermente.

"Non sei benvenuta qui!" urlò Sardar che era appena tornato nello stand con un altro acquirente.

"Sardar!" gridò Asim.

"Abbiamo sentito le tue storie sullo Sceicco. Non siamo interessati," disse, liquidandola. Lei se ne andò, facendo l'occhiolino a Sardar. "Asim, è il momento di fare colpo con quel discorso!"

Asim andò verso il palco, giocherellando nervosamente con un pezzo di carta che gli aveva dato Alia e sperando di ricordarsi tutto. Avrebbe voluto che sua moglie fosse lì. Alia aveva esperienza di questo tipo di cose. Dopotutto era stata a un sacco di aste prima che il padre accettasse di vendergliela nel bazaar locale e, tra l'altro, solo perché Asim aveva avuto un colpo di fortuna quando aveva trovato una confezione abbandonata di arance fresche durante il suo turno di guardia notturna. Lui? Era la sua prima e ultima volta a un'asta e in un bazaar locale, per di più. Questa era la sua prima volta nell'asta della città.

Si asciugò il sudore dalla fronte, domandandosi se avrebbe dovuto chiedere a Sardar di parlare al posto suo. Sembrava senza dubbio sicuro e forte, un maschio alfa che avrebbe avuto una figlia che sanguina dopo l'altra.

Il cancelliere chiamò il suo nome e lui si affrettò sul palco, osservando un mare di volti, uomini con barbe fluenti, turbanti, capelli lunghi, baffi spaventosi e iniziò a farfugliare le frasi che aveva imparato a memoria, qualcosa sulla famiglia della moglie, sulla sua e sulla figlia vergine, appena undicenne, che già sanguinava da sei mesi ormai.

Per tutto il tempo fu pienamente consapevole che stava facendo un disastro.

Per la disperazione balbettò ancora di più. Il pubblico, un gruppo di garbati cittadini vestiti bene, perse in fretta interesse. Una risatina, uno sbadiglio, un bisbiglio udibile. Era forse un discorso troppo semplice? Troppo simile al campagnolo che era?

La donna che prima era andata allo stand sussurrò qualcosa all'uomo con cui sedeva nella zona VIP. Lo Sceicco. Asim farfugliò, mischiando i fogli, raccontando una barzelletta che Alia aveva preparato e dimenticandosela arrivato a metà.

"È del mio distretto!" urlò Sardar dall'altra parte del palco, battendosi il petto. "Il distretto quattro." La sua voce risuonò, attraversando tutta la sala dell'asta. "Abbiamo le ragazze più belle della nazione. Ha undici anni ed è vergine!"

"Cosa ce ne facciamo della bellezza se sono aride come il deserto?" urlò un uomo dal pubblico. Ci fu una risata.

"Dov'è tua figlia? Come decidiamo se è bella?" chiese un altro.

"Come sappiamo che è vergine?"

"Non mettiamo in mostra le nostre figlie da dove veniamo," urlò Sardar.

"Chi compra la verdura senza tastarla un po' prima?" urlò qualcun altro.

"Abbiamo il sangue," farfugliò Asim, con il cuore in gola. Il pubblico iniziò a fischiare e ridere.

"Idioti campagnoli!"

"Sembra che non possa generare una mosca, figurarsi una ragazza che sanguina." Una risata fragorosa seguita da un urlo di Sardar.

"Chi è stato a dirlo!" gridò Sardar, saltando nell'area VIP.

"Sardar! No!" Asim corse giù dal palco.

Le guardie dello Stato in uniforme arrivarono in modo repentino, saltando addosso a Sardar e dandogli una scossa con i bastoni elettrici. Lui perse vigore, sbattendo il pesante braccio sul viso di una guardia.

"Fermatevi!" disse una voce superando il trambusto. Le guardie si placarono, le mani immobili. Asim strabuzzò gli occhi. Era la stessa donna che era passata prima. "Lo Sceicco Numansin acquisterà questa ragazza," annunciò con la sua voce morbida. La donna portò uno sbalordito Asim in un angolo. "È interessato," disse. Asim guardò lo Sceicco, seduto nella prima fila della zona VIP, che sgranocchiava una mela. Uno Sceicco vero come vera era la mela che stava mordendo. Asim vedeva entrambi per la prima volta in vita sua. Inghiottì.

"Sei davvero fortunato," gli disse lei, vedendo la sua espressione. "Ma lui ha una condizione."

"Quale?"

"Vuole firmare un patto con te. Questa e tutte le prossime ragazze che sanguinano."

"Non è..."

"Non ha intenzione di attendere. Puoi fare qualsiasi prezzo, qualsiasi..." si interruppe per lasciare che lui facesse il calcolo. "La tratterà bene, Asim," disse piano. "Fidati di me."

"Non farlo fratello!" Sardar andò da lui zoppicando. "Ascolta, ho sentito delle storie nel mercato su questo Sceicco! Lo chiamano lo Sceicco Collezionista!" La donna sorrise torva e si girò.

"Saremo nella zona VIP per altri quindici minuti," disse guardando Asim. "È una bella vita."

"Ti troveremo un acquirente," urlò Sardar, "uno migliore, qualcuno con..."

"Qualcuno meglio di uno Sceicco?" gridò Asim, tremando di rabbia. "Ma ti senti quando parli, Sardar? Io ti rispetto ma cosa ti ha preso?"

"Ascolta, lui non è quello giusto. Non lo è. La tua ragazza vivrebbe una vita a metà!"

"È uno Sceicco! Mia figlia vivrà in un harem. I suoi figli andranno a scuola."

"Dalla a me. Tu e Alia, ci conoscete. Starà con mio figlio, con la mia famiglia. Potrai vederla tutti i giorni."

"E quanti soldi hai, Sardar?"

"Abbastanza perché tu possa vivere una vita normale, fratello!"

"È uno Sceicco, Sardar e tu... tu sei un buzzurro in confronto a lui!"

"Non ti lascerò sprecare una ragazza che sanguina del nostro distretto..."

"Lei è mia! Okay? Mia! Mia da vendere o meno, come voglio! E non la venderò a te, Sardar, non in un milione di anni senza pioggia. Nemmeno se tuo figlio fosse l'ultimo ragazzo con sperma che resta!"

Sardar fece un passo indietro come se l'avessero ferito fisicamente. "La maledizione di Banjar, ecco cosa avrà!" Se ne andò.

Asim rabbrividì. Maledetto padre arido senza figlie che sanguinano da vendere. Che dava ordini a lui, il padre di una ragazza che sanguina! Alia aveva ancora qualche anno. Avrebbe potuto arrivare un'altra sanguinatrice in famiglia o forse no ma avrebbe preso un anticipo per tutte loro. Niente più asta. Gli bastava chiamare e avrebbe avuto uno Sceicco per la sua futura figlia che sanguina. E poteva offrire una bella vita alla sua famiglia. Inferni e diavoli, avrebbe anche potuto diventare capo del distretto, rispettato politicamente e influente. Un Anziano come Bunny Chacha! Un uomo a cui tutti chiedevano consiglio per vendere le figlie che sanguinano. Tutto quello che doveva fare era firmare un pezzo di carta. Che cosa c'era che non andava? Sardar era solo geloso.

Andò verso la zona VIP come in un sogno, firmando qualsiasi cosa la donna dicesse che doveva firmare. Ecco, fatto. Adesso non si poteva tornare indietro.

"La andrò a prendere al Centro di fertilità Cittadino," disse allo Sceicco. L'uomo non aveva proferito parola. Non che ne avesse bisogno, ma sarebbe stato più piacevole.

"Non ce n'è bisogno," disse la donna, mettendogli una mano sulla spalla e sorridendo in modo garbato. "Possiamo prenderla noi adesso che i documenti di proprietà sono firmati."

"Ma il matrimonio..." Guardò lo Sceicco.

"Allo Sceicco piace la tranquillità. Niente cavalli e danze per lui."

"Ma... è mia."

"Non più," disse la donna con delicatezza.

"Ve ne prenderete cura, vero?" chiese Asim, indirizzando la domanda allo Sceicco. Uomo a uomo. Lo Sceicco lo fissò come qualcuno che nota una lucertola nell'angolo della stanza.

"Il distretto quattro è molto raro," rispose.

La donna diede ad Asim una scatola piena di denaro. "Questa la prima rata. Manderemo un anticipo mensile per tutto il resto della tua vita. Per favore chiamaci se qualcuna sanguina nella tua famiglia. Manderò una persona a prendere la sanguinatrice al villaggio. Non devi neppure venire in città."

"Lo farà, vero?" chiese di nuovo.

"Alla mia collezione mancava un esemplare del distretto quattro," gracchiò lo Sceicco.

"Ma la amerà e manderà i figli a scuola, sì?" chiese Asim mentre si alzavano, pronti a andare. La donna si chinò e raddrizzò le pieghe dell'abito dello Sceicco.

"Figli?" lo Sceicco si accigliò, andandosene.

"Sei a posto così!" gridò la donna, con voce acuta. "Come fai a essere così indelicato?"

Si affrettò dietro lo Sceicco, lasciando Asim con la sua scatola piena d'oro.

I NUOVI MIGRANTI

di Navin Weeraratne

traduzione di Gabriella Gregori

Neil deGrasse Tyson e Dan Abnett hanno avuto un bambino, e quel brutto bambino è Navin Weeraratne. Scrive storie d'azione, d'avventura e di fantascienza militare, con una fortissima dose di discipline all'avanguardia. Se hai letto le sue storie e non hai imparato qualche teoria nuova, o sei un astrofisico oppure ti ha deluso. Navin s'interessa anche al Grande Fenomeno del Transumanesimo e a come sarà vivere nel mondo con esseri molto più intelligenti – e più pericolosi – di quanto l'Homo Sapiens sia mai stato. Vive a Colombo con la moglie e alcuni gatti molto viziati. Per aggiornamenti e suoi nuovi libri: https://www.scifinavin.com/newsletter/

La prima volta che vidi una delle sue navi spaziali, c'era un branco di delfini che le dava la caccia.

Sul momento non capimmo cosa fosse. Dubito che i miei ordini sarebbero stati differenti se l'avessimo saputo. Saliva tra le onde, più simile a una collina grigio-verde che a una medusa gigantesca.

Mi aspettavo aculei, luminescenza, per lo meno una qualche bellezza per giustificare il delitto, ma no. Mi girai e guardai i cacciatori e la loro preda restare indietro rispetto alla nostra imbarcazione. Poi, la nave spaziale raggiunse la superficie e rimase lì, come il cadavere di un profugo annegato, con l'acqua del mare che la ricopriva a ogni onda. Era molto indietro rispetto a noi quando l'involucro principale uscì dall'acqua. Da esso pendevano dei lunghi filtri. Smangiucchiati e strappati. I delfini truffati la guardarono fluttuare via verso la morte. Persino esseri dal cervello grande come loro non potevano nemmeno iniziare a capire i cambiamenti che avevamo generato nel loro mondo.

Chi era, dunque, questo uomo con la sua baraccopoli, ingegneri genetici, che pensava potessero farlo?

Sulla barca non importava a nessun altro. Di fronte a me un saudita rinsecchito dal sole teneva stretto un barile sciabordante di ostriche mutanti mentre contava i grani del rosario. Un maldiviano che indossava solo dei pantaloncini e le cicatrici che la Marina dello Sri Lanka gli aveva lasciato per essere sceso a terra era occupato a piratare soap opera coreane sul tablet. Una bimba faceva la scia con le piccole dita grassocce nell'acqua che scorreva di lato, strillando.

Davanti a noi c'era la baraccopoli marina.

Mi chiamo Aruni Silva. Quando avevo sei anni mia madre si accorse che ero più intelligente di lei, ne fu talmente orgogliosa che mi bruciò il libri. Quell'alcolizzato di mio padre la lasciò. Quando a dieci anni un volontario cinese mi diede un tablet, un giorno tornai a casa e scoprii che papà lo aveva venduto per comprarsi l'arrack. Quando feci gli esami di mandarino, dissero che nessuna università mi avrebbe preso: andarono dal preside della scuola del villaggio e fecero buttare via il mio fascicolo. Un insegnante nuovo lo scoprì e fece rapporto al Ministero della Sicurezza Nazionale. Così ho frequentato un'università cinese. Adesso, ho lavoratoanch'io per l'MSN cinese. I miei compatrioti singalesi mi odiano per questo, ma va bene. L'odio è rassicurante, come quando tutte le case dei tuoi vicini bruciano assieme alla tua.

La baraccopoli si stendeva sull'acqua, fitte catapecchie costruite con plastica ondulata e pannelli solari spray. Tra una e l'altra erano tirati dei fili con vivaci panni svolazzanti. Un nugolo di gabbiani si alzò in volo davanti a un qualche affronto, un cane randagio gli abbaiava contro. Una banda di bambini meticci chiacchieravano correndo tra supporti di antenne in grafene, un miscuglio di dialetti e destini.

L'uomo che stavo cercando era nella migliore delle ipotesi un ingegnere genetico fuorilegge, nella peggiore un terrorista sostenuto dagli americani. Si chiamava Pasan Gonakumbura e, in tutta onestà, odiavo tutto di lui. Veniva da quella che i miei istruttori cinesi chiamavano una "classe collaborazionista" – nel caso dello Sri Lanka, era l'élite anglofona i cui antenati hanno fatto il lavoro sporco per i britannici, per poi fingere di averli sempre voluti mandare via.

Gli studenti snob con le loro partire di cricket.

Gli impiegati statali che bevevano nei loro club.

Gli stronzi di Oxford-Cambridge.

Ci hanno rimessi in catene con il populismo del 'Solo in singalese', assicurandosi che da allora in poi capissero l'inglese soltanto i loro stupidi figli che credono di avere diritto a tutto.

I miei antenati si guadagnarono la libertà e persero il mondo anglofono che avrebbe dovuto essere il nostro risarcimento. Tutte le sue idee chiuse a chiave dietro cancelli controllati da un'intera classe sociale che praticava il colonialismo nella sua stessa nazione.

Solo dopo l'arrivo dei cinesi divenne chiaro ciò che era stato fatto al resto del popolo. Il rimanere in piedi negli autobus per i turisti bianchi. Gli espatriati fantoccio pagati di più per lavorare di meno. Come ci hanno insegnato a odiarci tra noi.

Pasan Gonakumbura faceva parte di quella classe. La sua famiglia aveva gestito proprietà, comprato elezioni e mandato i propri figli in università straniere a imparare come essere bianchi. E ora, eccolo qui in una baraccopoli marina, dopo aver lavorato anni nell'aerospazio statunitense, progettando creature d'alta quota che, guarda caso, volavano vicino alle piattaforme sub-spaziali cinesi.

Entrammo nel porto intasato di barche e avanzammo prepotenti come un autobus nel traffico. Finimmo intrappolati contro un vecchissimo peschereccio birmano. L'equipaggio ci ignorò, uno di loro stava mettendo pannelli solari spray con una bomboletta. Un altro stava togliendo le lische a pesci modificati geneticamente, di fianco a lui un secchio pieno delle loro preziose lische nere ricche di metalli pesanti.

Sono scesa sul molo. Il mio obiettivo era solo qualche catapecchia più in là, una famiglia tamil che aveva perso una figlia. Niente che la chirurgia plastica non potesse rimpiazzare: feci un sorriso di allenamento con il mio nuovo viso e andai a cercarli.

"Darini?!" La madre stava seduta su una sedia rossa monoblocco all'esterno della catapecchia. Di fianco a lei c'era una stuoia ricoperta di fasci di verdura idroponica. Sul tetto, come la pelle di un elefante stesa sull'intelaiatura da concia, c'era un contenitore grigio-nero per la raccolta dell'acqua. "Oddio, Darini, tesoro? Sei tu?"

"No, Zietta, mi chiamo Anupama. Sei tamil? Mi spiace, sono nuova qui."

Interpretai la parte dell'ignorante inerme. L'istinto di una madre che aveva dovuto seppellire una figlia prese il sopravvento e mi accolse.

Apprezzai il fatto che Vanappu non si mettesse a piangere. Invece suo marito Pragash lo fece. Poi sentì il bisogno di spiegarmi perché. Parlò molto, con il fascino e i facili sorrisi di chi per tutta la vita è stato un attore doppiogiochista. Vanappu rimase in silenzio, sorridendo a me e, in modo più nervoso, a lui. Quando le lanciava un'occhiataccia lei indietreggiava: le percosse erano registrate nel nostro archivio. Io sorrisi, annuii e mangiai il mio dahl.

"Sono venuta a cercare lavoro," risposi quando ebbi l'imbeccata. "Voglio ricodificare geni. A Bentota non si può, la polizia ti spezza le mani. Ho sentito che ad Al-Ahmadi ci lavorano."

Vanappu lanciò un'occhiata tagliente a Pragash. Lui era troppo stupido e liquidò la sua preoccupazione con un gesto della mano.

"Sì, qui ci lavorano! Ma è un segreto, non dovrei dirtelo."

"Mmm."

"Hai sentito parlare di Pasan Gonakumbura?"

"L'americano?"

"No, no. È singalese, come noi. C'è un suo un team, qui, stanno ricodificando i geni delle meduse. Giganti, verdi, come le piante. Volano, se riesci a crederci. Piene di gas!"

"Credo di averne vista una. Sono sicure?"

"Cielo, no, esplodono come bombe. Sei molto intelligente, forse puoi aiutarli?"

"Forse."

"Domani posso farteli incontrare."

"Grazie, Zio. Mi piacerebbe. È bello da parte vostra aiutarmi in questo modo."

"Piacere nostro," sorrise. "Sei nostra ospite! È bello avere qualcuno dallo Sri Lanka. Come va a casa?"

"Molto cinese," risposi. Risero entrambi. "La maggior parte della gente è felice."

"La maggior parte della gente non è libera! Qua ad Al-Ahmadi siamo liberi," disse Pragash. "Ci stampiamo o ricodifichiamo i geni di tutto quello che vogliamo. Non ci sono telecamere che guardano.

Niente copyright, niente algoritmi. E nessun genio del computer che manda la polizia segreta nelle nostre case."

"No, certo che no."

"Ho fatto visita alla famiglia di mio fratello tra le mangrovie di Puttalam l'anno scorso. I suoi figli non conoscono il tamil! Parlano solo cinese e guardano film cinesi. Persino il cibo che la moglie di mio fratello cucinava è mezzo cinese. Ovunque, tutti diventano uguali, no? L'ho detto, ma secondo loro non è un male!"

"È il cambiamento, Zio. Altrimenti pensiamo solo a ciò che ci rende diversi. È così che ci ritroviamo singalesi contro tamil e tamil contro musulmani. La nazione crollerebbe, come l'America." Risero sentendolo. In tutto il mondo non c'è migliore balsamo per i problemi che ridere dell'America.

"Ma in Sri Lanka non c'è più democrazia, no?"

"Non puoi avere democrazia se hai social media. Con i social media chiunque può avere la propria verità. Formano mondi chiusi su sé stessi di narrative autorinforzanti e bugie. E poi ci aspettiamo che escano e prendano delle decisioni?"

"Ma è così che funzionava, prima."

"Non ha mai funzionato. Non la conosci la gente? Sono tutti stupidi e egoisti. È per questo che i mercati funzionano e le democrazie falliscono. Prima o poi la libertà avvelena. Non siamo fatti per essere liberi. Dobbiamo fare quello che ci dicono. Siamo come bambini, possiamo solo sperare che chi ci guida sia puro di mente, cuore e intenzione."

L'unico suono era il *plin-plin-plin* della vasca dell'acqua.

"Forse Gonakumbura dovrebbe ricodificare gente più intelligente," disse Vanappu.

"Tieni," Pragash mi diede quello che sembrava un cappello da coltivatore di riso vietnamita. Era foderato di carta stagnola. "Mettilo. Sta arrivando la piattaforma."

Le persone tutto attorno si stavano mettendo cappelli simili. Alcuni avevano veli anti-radar che assomigliavano a visiere medievali. Una manciata di bambini si raccolse attorno a una lattina di vernice nera. I più grandi fecero segni anti-riconoscimento sui visi dei più piccoli. Era un buon lavoro, ma non aggiornato. Una bambina grande sgridò un bambino piccolo che era invece più portato a disegnarsi addosso volti mostruosi. Lui le lanciò della vernice e scappò di corsa.

Mi fermai e guardai in su. In cielo c'era solo azzurro.

"Non guardare!" Pragash agitò le mani. "Ti vedrà. Sei *tu* quella che vuole!"

"Scusa, Zio," sorrisi e annuii. "In Sri Lanka non ci nascondiamo. Se lo fai, poi gli algoritmi ti segnalano e riceverai una visita."

"Ah, ma cosa succede se *tutti* si nascondono? È così che proteggiamo i nostri ricodificatori. I cinesi non sanno mai quanti ne abbiamo e dove sono."

Aveva ragione. Dovetti sorridere per nascondere la fronte aggrottata.

"Su, tieni la testa abbassata e andiamo a trovarti un lavoro."

Controllai l'ora: la piattaforma sub-spaziale che era venuta in appoggio era stata individuata nel giro di pochi minuti. Come l'avevano saputo?

Status, mi inviò.

Verde, risposi.

Livello di minaccia Von Neumann? Incerto.

Il laboratorio di ricodifica genetica di Gonakumbura era un gruppo di tre strutture estruse a due piani. Mi stupii di non vedere guardie, se non si contava la vecchia donna algerina che vendeva minuti di Starlink e mango su una stuoia all'esterno dell'edificio principale. Sul tetto c'era della biancheria che si stava asciugando appesa a un filo. La nota complice Ruslana Shevchenko venne sul bordo e guardò in basso verso di noi, una sigaretta tra le labbra.

"Cosa volete?" disse l'ucraina con il fascino brusco e onesto dei semplici.

"Potete darle un lavoro?" disse Pragash prima che potessi parlare.

"No."

"Lo dici tu! Di' a Pasan di venire fuori."

"Andate via." E sparì.

"Adesso ci penso io, Zio. Grazie per..."

"Shhh!" Sorrise e agitò la mano. "Cambierà idea."

Restammo in piedi fuori dalla porta, sotto il sole. Passarono diversi minuti. La donna algerina cercò di vendermi una scheda per la banda larga, ma rifiutai. Poi mi raccontò del campo di profughi climatici in cui era morto suo marito e ci riprovò. Le dissi che mi ricordava mia madre e sorrise.

La porta si aprì e nel'ingresso c'era Shevchenko, in piedi con le braccia incrociate.

"Sai ricodificare?" Mi fulminò con lo sguardo.

"Sì."

"Fammi vedere."

L'MSN reclutava ricodificatori ed esperti nano per catturare ricodificatori ed esperti nano. Le inviai il genoma di un tipo di riso resistente alle inondazioni che avevo creato, alterandolo un po' per suggerire le lacune di conoscenza dell'autoapprendimento non strutturato. Vidi i suoi occhi muoversi rapidamente avanti e indietro mentre leggeva pagine che solo lei poteva vedere.

"Sembra a posto," disse alla fine. "Ma perché qui? Con la tua competenza potresti ricodificare ovunque. Potresti addirittura ricodificare per i cinesi – che poi non è 'ricodificare', giusto?"

"Non lavorerò mai per loro." Mi alzai la maglia sulla schiena in modo che potesse vedere le cicatrici. Pragash sussultò.

"Chi è stato?"

"Risposta Bio-Nano," risposi con sincerità.

"Hai un giorno. Se il tuo lavoro è buono, puoi restare. Okay?"

"Okay."

Se non puoi fidarti a far votare le persone, *di certo* non puoi fidarti a farle creare.

La nanotecnologia open source e l'ingegneria genetica da giardino avevano dato potere divino a chiunque avesse una connessione Internet e dieci dollari di attrezzatura standard. Fermatevi un attimo a pensare a com'era la vita, a quel tempo. Sapendo che lo sconosciuto nel vicolo poteva fare ben più che rapinarti, violentarti o ucciderti. Poteva anche distruggere il mondo.

Per questo motivo c'era la Risposta Nano-Bio. In tutto il mondo, telecamere stradali vigilavano in cerca di picchi di calore rivelatori nelle crepe dei marciapiedi. Droni vaganti studiavano le giungle in cerca di deforestazione frattale. Boe analizzavano il fondo marino in cerca di fumarole riunite in centrali geotermiche. Dove sarebbe stato il prossimo focolaio? La nazione coinvolta se ne sarebbe occupata, prima che un'altra dovesse farlo al posto suo?

Più di una volta l'eradicazione nucleare ci aveva salvati tutti.

Lavoravo alla Risposta Nano-Bio per l'MSN. La gente pensava che la Nano-Bio aiutasse le piattaforme a uccidere, trovando per loro ospedali pieni di vittime di mine antiuomo da colpire. La verità è esattamente l'opposto: noi eravamo quelli che *fermavano* le piattaforme. Se vedevi un fungo atomico, era perché avevamo fallito.

I ricodificatori erano pericolosi tanto quanto gli esperti nano – secondo me di più. Puoi sempre fare qualcosa per una nuvola di poltiglia grigia che inizia a crearsi un suo tempo atmosferico – è difficile non notarla. Quando un ricodificatore combina un casino con la CRISPR, invece, riusciresti ad accorgertene? Potrebbero volerci anni perché una specie sintetica inizi a trasformare il suo bioma in un deserto e, a quel punto, è troppo tardi per fermarla.

Più noi premevamo, più forte i ricodificatori reagivano. Abbiamo fatto leggi, prevaricato le aziende per avere i dati personali scambiandoli con altri stati. I ricodificatori si trincerarono: criptavano i loro dati, si organizzavano su server mondiali aperti MMO e acquistavano usando cripto – o peggio, *contanti*. Il nostro problema più grande non era la loro intelligenza diabolica – avendo una mano legata dietro la schiena. Ogni governo controllava la sua gente – ma la gente *senza* un governo?

Il cambiamento climatico aveva fatto salire il loro numero a diversi miliardi.

Queste persone senza guida presero il mare con stampanti 3D, pannelli solari e un atteggiamento ricodifica-e-diffondi. Passarono da accampamenti erranti di boat people a tribù cosmopolite con un loro proprio gergo, si insediarono su strutture che vivevano, crescevano e si riproducevano in strutture figlie. Erano le baraccopoli: giganti OGM d'alto mare derivati dal corallo. Ogni giorno sempre più persone lasciavano i campi per raggiungerle. Persone come Pragash e Vanappu.

Le lasciavamo andare: ogni emigrante è un problema energetico e definito che si è appena risolto da solo, che si tratti di un ribelle, un criminale o solo un'altra bocca affamata. Il mare era un luogo in cui tutte le nazioni potevano scaricare le proprie responsabilità climatiche. Non dovevamo far altro che lasciarli in pace e permetter loro di stampare o usare la CRISPR per qualsiasi cosa di cui avessero bisogno. Un male necessario. Anche mentre mantenevamo la posizione contro il caos, oltre ogni costa ritiratasi c'era un modo di vivere totalmente diverso che non potevamo contenere, contrastare o censurare. Ho perso così tanto sonno pensandoci.

Nei giorni seguenti, copiai tutte le note e le sequenze genetiche a cui Shevchenko mi diede accesso. Il loro era solo uno dei *sei* gruppi che lavoravano sul progetto; che così tanti ricodificatori si fossero riuniti era un enorme campanello d'allarme. Cosa stavano facendo? Da quello a cui avevo accesso, potevo confermare che stavano effettivamente costruendo creature in grado di vivere nel sub-spazio. Navi spaziali viventi a idrogeno e altissima pressione che avrebbero ingombrato il cielo contendendoselo.

Era incredibile quanto ciò fosse sfacciatamente anti-cinese: solo noi mantenevamo suborbitali le nostre attività per contrastare la Sindrome di Kessler. Il lavoro di Gonakumbura avrebbe disseminato la nostra altitudine operativa di campi minati viventi. Se avessero avuto successo, entro qualche decina d'anni intere zone del cielo ci sarebbero state negate. Non si trattava di dare scacco matto alla nostra capacità di negare lo spazio agli americani con un secchio di chiodi lanciati da un razzo. Si trattava di toglierci i nostri poteri celesti, del tutto.

C'era solo una cosa che non tornava: un lavoro che riguardava i propulsori elettrici biologici. Le creature li avrebbero usati per raccogliere molecole d'aria, ionizzarle e accelerarle per ottenere la spinta. I propulsori elettrici 'senza combustibile' non erano una novità, erano stati usati per anni dai satelliti in orbita bassa per contrastare l'attrito causato da quelle stesse molecole d'aria. Ma questi erano troppo potenti perché fosse solo quello. Potevano spingere le creature a velocità straordinarie, tali che la resistenza dell'aria – anche a quell'altezza – poteva addirittura farle a pezzi.

Qual era il motivo? Non ne trovavo cenno. O Shevchenko lo aveva censurato, oppure era talmente scontato che i gruppi non avevano bisogno di citarlo. Trasmisi tutto alla piattaforma.

I miei supervisori mi risposero nel giro di un'ora.

Bersaglio dev'essere neutralizzato. ID aerea non possibile viste misure anti-riconoscimento della popolazione locale. Si richiede marcatura IR. Marcare bersaglio ed estrazione.

Mi presi un momento per metabolizzare.

Bersaglio e compagni non sono terroristi. Loro lavoro non presenta minacce immediate. Forse è prudente prolungare incarico? Concedere tempo per scoprire scopo reale creature pallone – e ID le altre cinque cellule.

Prolungamento negato. Gonakumbura è elemento principale; se sistemato in fretta il progetto non si riprenderà più. Ritardare è rischiare un allargamento del baricentro intellettuale del progetto. Sarebbe quindi necessaria una risposta più pesante – che farebbe solo aumentare il profilo del lavoro e generare progetti emulatori. Grosso pericolo se il progetto diventa open source. Marcare Gonakumbura. Prima possibile. Piattaforma farà il resto. Abbiamo fiducia in te.

Il marcatore a infrarossi che avevo nascosto in un ciondolo divenne improvvisamente la cosa più pesante al mondo.

"Vanappu, sei tu?"

Ero al mercato. C'erano più che altro donne, che compravano e vendevano l'una dall'altra. Una vecchia malese con la faccia che pareva un acino d'uva passa e denti simili a pioli rossi indicava il suo mucchio di cestini fatti a mano masticando betel. Una giovane irachena impilava verdure idroponiche su una stuoia davanti a sé. Una donna sudanese con la salwar dai colori più vivaci che avessi mai visto tirò fuori da un secchio un pesce che si dibatteva e gli tagliò la testa.

Vanappu, guardando da un'altra parte e con il sari tirato sopra la testa, finse di non sentirmi. Si nascose dietro un graticcio di alghe da essiccare.

"Vanappu?" Mi misi davanti a lei. "Sono Anupama! Va tutto bene?"

Alzò lo sguardo, coprendosi il volto con il sari. "Scusa tanto, cara! Non ti avevo sentita. Come vanno le cose nella nuova casa? Cucinano come si deve?"

"Cosa c'è che non va? Ti è successo qualcosa al viso?"

Attorno a noi le donne smisero di parlare. Ci guardavano con la coda dell'occhio.

"No, no! Va tutto bene!"

Guardai l'occhio nero. "È stato Pragash, vero? Gli parlo io."

"No, no, è colpa mia," mi fece cenno di spostarmi. "Non dovrei infastidirlo quando ha bevuto."

"Mi spiace molto." Cercai di metterle un braccio sulle spalle.

"Sto bene." Mi spinse via il braccio. "Non lo farò più arrabbiare. Ho un sacco di cose da fare! Ci sentiamo più tardi, Anupama. Sono felice che tu stia lavorando con quelle persone. Sono gentili."

Loro non ti picchieranno, intendeva dire.

Le altre donne ripresero a parlare. Vanappu non le aveva deluse, era tornata invisibile. Era questa la loro libertà in un luogo così.

Beccai Gonakumbura cinque giorni dopo. Aero 17 stava tornando alla baraccopoli dopo due mesi di test di durata del volo e gli altri si erano presi, in modo assai scomodo, un coronavirus che gli avevo preparato con il loro stesso equipaggiamento. La Ragazza Nuova ce la fa? Certo che ce la fa. Allora mandate la Ragazza Nuova. Shevchenko dice che è a posto, no?

Ci trovavamo sul molo nord in disuso. Barche mezze distrutte erano appese sull'acqua. I loro scafi sembravano pixellati: distrutti da qualche nano-agente che aveva cercato di trasformarli in qualcosa di diverso. Un uccello bianco atterrò su una di esse. Pulcini marroni squittirono mentre lui con calma rigurgitava la loro colazione. Un cane grasso che rovistava tra la spazzatura vecchia ci notò. Venne verso di noi, scodinzolando in cerca di un po' di pane e pesce. Appiattì le orecchie quando Gonakumbura gli accarezzò la testa, gli occhi dell'uomo incollati al tablet. Mostrava le coordinate e i parametri vitali di Aero 17.

"Le piaci," dissi con un sorriso vuoto.

"I cani si sa come la pensano." Aveva un accento americano. La sua maglietta tifava New England Patriots e lui indossava delle Birkenstock: sembrava un turista occidentale durante una vacanza sessuale di vent'anni prima. "Non come con le persone."

"Non ti fidi delle persone?"

"Tu sì?"

Restammo in silenzio per un po'. Le ultime stelle sbiadirono e il cielo iniziò a rosseggiare verso est. Il cane grasso si sedette vicino a Gonakumbura, senza un solo pensiero al mondo. In lontananza, molto più bassa di quanto mi aspettassi, c'era una macchiolina luminosa.

"Grazie per l'opportunità," dissi. "Non solo questa, ma di poterci lavorare. Non ho mai fatto parte di un progetto così grande."

"Eppure non hai chiesto una sola volta cosa stiamo facendo." Si girò a guardarmi. Aveva gli occhi vecchi, stanchi e mi vide dentro.

"Non pensavo di avere il diritto di chiedere."

"Qualche ipotesi?"

"Sì. State progettando piattaforme sub-spaziali *viventi*. Palloni d'alta quota per il popolo. Internet libero, che sale dal mare e alimentato dalla luce solare."

"*Sarebbe* bello. Ma è facilmente controllabile, no?"

"In che senso?"

"Niente che un laser non possa abbattere. O un'infezione. Niente per cui valga la pena mandare un agente a infiltrarsi tra di noi, no?"

Avevo il cuore in gola. Il cane si girò e mi fissò, gli occhi simili a perle nere. Mi resi conto che il molo deserto prima dell'alba era il luogo più pericoloso al mondo.

"Non... non so di cosa stai parlando!"

"Non ti farò del male, non sono un mostro. E poi non avrebbe senso proprio come se tu tentassi di fare del male a me. Per chi lavori, a proposito? Gli americani? Gli indiani?"

"Non me ne starò seduta qui a farmi accusare di essere una spia!"

"Ma così non saprai di cosa si tratta," disse sorridendo e indicando la macchiolina. Era diventata una sfera che si librava appena sopra l'acqua. "Quello che sei venuta a scoprire. *Ci sei così vicina!*"

Rimasi lì, il corpo in una direzione, la mente nell'altra. Il Test Aerospaziale 17 assomigliava a un pallone sonda con una spessa pelle appesa sotto. Era verde come una foglia nuova, con la quale aveva molto più in comune che con le sue cugine meduse. Arrivò fino a un centinaio di metri e poi si schiantò. Gonakumbura fissava i dati che scorrevano sul tablet come un avido agente di borsa.

"È morto," dissi. "Mi dici perché ha vissuto?"

"Sì. E comunque sei una vera ricodificatrice, prendilo come un complimento. Sei rimasta per vedere, per capire. Quello," disse indicando la massa galleggiante di pelle verde, "ci darà la libertà. Libertà vera, non come le baraccopoli."

"Non pensi che le baraccopoli siano libere?"

"Sono libere solo perché le tollerate – potreste eliminarle se voleste. Quando non vi saranno più utili, lo farete. Gli Aero sono test aero-*spaziali*. Possono sopravvivere alle radiazioni, a temperature estreme, al vuoto. Gli organi propulsori a ioni servono a spingerli fuori dall'atmosfera – e continuare ad accelerare finché non raggiungono la velocità orbitale e di fuga. Poi, le vele solari li possono portare ovunque nel sistema solare."

"Le meduse come navi spaziali? Dici sul serio?"

"Le meduse come *stazioni* spaziali." Si alzò e andò verso l'acqua, con gli occhi che guardavano ben oltre il sole nascente. "Velivoli biologici che salgono dall'oceano per portare villaggi come questo, nello spazio. I razzi sono per l'élite occidentale. *Questi* faranno migrare le masse del mondo verso la libertà. Libertà oltre il controllo di *qualsiasi* stato-nazione!"

"È una cosa senza senso." Incrociai le braccia. "Non è così che funzionano le cose."

"Ah, no?" Girò di scatto la testa di nuovo verso di me. "Tu non capisci quanto sia *enorme* il sistema solare interno. Gli stati ci possono controllare totalmente, ovunque sulla Terra o in orbita intorno a essa. Ma tra gli Asteroidi Near-Earth? Non li abbiamo nemmeno mappati tutti. Come puoi imporre la tua volontà lassù? Più lontano va la gente, più è difficile da trovare e *molto più difficile* da catturare."

"Pensi che uno shuttle d'assalto Lunga Marcia non riesca a catturare una di quelle cose?"

"No, non può. I vostri shuttle sono veicoli, non habitat. Ovunque ci sia luce solare, gli Aero vivranno e prospereranno. Non avrete *mai* le risorse per dominarli. E se le avrete, si sposteranno di nuovo. Una volta che il popolo è andato oltre la Terra," indicò il cielo, "è finita. *Nessuno stato-nazione sarà mai in grado di controllarlo, mai più.*"

"Sei così sicuro di te stesso.," scossi la testa, "di tutto questo. Cosa ti fa pensare che sia meglio dell'ordine? Della sicurezza? Hai vissuto negli Stati Uniti tanto a lungo da dimenticare com'è non sapere se i tuoi vicini proveranno a ucciderti?" Passai al singalese. "Ma le persone come te non avevano quel problema, no? Era una cosa per gli altri. Ti sta bene che siamo *noi* a pagare il prezzo dei valori della *tua* classe?"

Il suo viso si indurì.

"Hai vissuto tutta la vita sotto sorveglianza," esordì. "Non conosci il valore della libertà e della privacy perché non le hai mai avute. Non essere tanto arrogante e ingenua da pensare che il vostro modo sia la risposta definitiva a come la gente dovrebbe vivere."

"Penso che il nostro modo *funziona*. Il tuo modo è come il Comunismo: funziona – in *teoria*. Istruzione per dare informazioni agli elettori, come è andata a finire? Che risate! Sono sempre persone, Ricodificatore. E le persone non saranno mai nobili come questo cane grasso."

La pelle verde infine affondò sotto le onde, con un po' di schiuma bianca per lapide.

"Mi ucciderai?" chiedemmo in contemporanea.

"No," rispose. "Ma non importa cosa la tua gente farà a me. Se dovesse succedere qualcosa a uno di noi, il nostro lavoro diventerà open-source. Scommetto che i tuoi amici a Pechino non vogliono che succeda. Giusto?"

Mi girai e iniziai ad allontanarmi.

"La gente è deludente, nel tuo mondo come nel mio!" mi urlò dietro. "Libertà *vera*, Anupama! Riesci a immaginartela? Tra chi è vivo oggi nessuno sa com'era!"

Lasciai la baraccopoli nel pomeriggio. Sedetti vicino al motore, proteggendomi gli occhi mentre guardavo indietro verso il villaggio che rimpiccioliva. Quando mi trovai esattamente a cento metri, la piattaforma agì. Ci fu un lampo come il flash di una macchina fotografica ma molto più potente, come quando un pezzo di artiglieria spara di notte. Poi, il silenzio. Dopo qualche secondo vennero la sorpresa e lo shock delle persone sulla barca quando ricevettero la notizia. Io guardavo il mare e le ignoravo. Quando a Pechino avessero saputo di aver fatto esplodere il cranio di un certo Pragash Sittambalam, che picchiava la moglie, sarebbero rimasti delusi. Avrebbero pensato che fosse incompetenza e mi avrebbero dgradata o licenziata. Altri sarebbero andati a portare a termine il lavoro, ma probabilmente troppo tardi perché avesse importanza.

"Sorella," una ragazza mi batté sul braccio, il viso dominato dalla preoccupazione. "Tu sai cosa sta succedendo?"

"Non ho tutte le risposte," dissi. "Dovremo aspettare e vedere."

A_NAMNESI_

di Rupsa Dey

traduzione di Francesca Secci

Rupsa Dey crede nel potere del linguaggio e dei gatti, ed è allergica solo a questi ultimi. Crede che se i limiti del linguaggio devono essere superati per adattarsi all'esperienza umana, allora deve dedicarsi a questo scopo. Non dice mai "No" al tè e se le dessero un'opportunità, le piacerebbe credere in un mondo senza confini. Ha ricevuto il premio Bal Shree in Scrittura Creativa. Le sue ultime opere possono essere trovate in Clarkesworld Magazine, The Dark, Muse India, e Northern Light Vol. 8.

NQ doveva prendere una decisione. Prendere la pillola avrebbe provato che era il consumatore sciocco che il DISEC pensava che loro fossero. Eppure si era fatto cullare dalle promesse che avevano fatto i modelli olografici. Era stato intercettato da uno di loro che si faceva chiamare Io nel mercato Doweze. Sopra le urla dei venditori di frutta, gli acquirenti e il ronzio dell'Alimentatore gigante che trangugiava acqua da un bacino lì accanto, NQ si era ritrovato del tutto smarrito. La notte precedente, la modalità automatica aveva preso il sopravvento sui comandi manuali che erano stati programmati pochi giorni prima. Gli era stato assegnato un nuovo caso. La sua mente non si era ancora del tutto adattata al suo nuovo orario. La modalità di riposo si attivava e disattivava e NQ continuava a svegliarsi nel mezzo delle dodici ore di sonno di conservazione che gli erano state prescritte. Aveva guardato il cielo della notte diventare viola. Aveva guardato la città diventare viva.

Stando in piedi nel mercato con la buccia delle verdure che si attaccava alla suola delle sue scarpe e leggermente divertito dalle esposizioni dei venditori in azione che scacciavano le mosche, NQ non percepì Io che si era avvicinata furtivamente alle sue spalle.

"Problemi a trovare il tuo posto nel mondo?" chiese.

NQ si voltò e, vedendo Io, imprecò tra sé e sé. La sua voce veniva dal micro-drone volante posto dentro l'ologramma. Io si collegò alla lettura vitale di NQ, una linea fine che luccicava al centro della sua zucca. NQ borbottò di disgusto. Questi nuovi modelli non avevano alcun senso della misura.

"Sonno non sufficiente." Notò lei, leggendo le cifre che comparivano sulla sua fronte.

"Non sai dove sia il tuo posto in questo mondo grande e cattivo?" chiese di nuovo, con gli occhi viola che si sgranavano, le labbra imbronciate, la voce tremante, e poi in un istante lo rincuorava: "Abbiamo proprio la soluzione perfetta per te. Animus offre sogni in una pillola. Vieni e prova questa nuova droga." Ammiccò. "Prometto che ti sentirai meglio" la sua voce era diventata un bisbiglio.

"Sto bene" disse NQ, cercando di andare via, ma Io si materializzò davanti a lui questa volta.

"Vogliamo premiarti. Prendila. È tua. Vogliamo che sia felice." La sua voce era diventata infantile, quasi triste. Predatori di nuova generazione! Pensò NQ. DISEC li aveva programmati per essere proprio così. Paragonato a lei, NQ assomigliava a un'accozzaglia di spazzatura, qualcosa di debole con tutti gli scrupoli della tecnologia di vecchia generazione che una volta era stata all'avanguardia come Io, ora rara, studiata nelle aule scolastiche, e bisognosa di aggiornamenti frequenti, alcuni dei quali il suo SO non riusciva a sopportare. Si sentiva a cavallo tra passato e presente, esistente da qualche parte in quella scomoda via di mezzo, tutto pesto e rattoppato. Come il mercato stesso, notò la somiglianza, una crudele esposizione di fulgore di nuova generazione nelle rovine del passato, tutte conservate, lasciate a testimoniare la loro stessa decadenza.

Brillanti dischi volanti di Raccoglitori Solari sfrecciarono su di loro dirigendosi a diffondere luce nei centri di ripopolamento sotterranei costruiti su commissione del Gruppo per le Imprese Sostenibili del Futuro (ISF), un'azienda ibrida sviluppatasi dopo le distruzioni su vasta scala lasciate dalle poche miniere rimaste che si erano indebolite provocando terremoti. "Creiamo possibilità" era il motto di ISF, il loro progetto recente era di costruire centri di ripopolamento sotterranei alimentati da energia geotermica. "C'è un nuovo mondo laggiù. Ottenete tutto ciò che avevate e anche di più." Le pubblicità passavano cinque volte al giorno, gli elicotteri gettavano lettere olografiche nel cielo perché tutta l'umanità le guardasse.

La sfilza di terremoti e le fusioni accidentali degli impianti nucleari avevano fatto sfollare 4 milioni di persone: quel brusco risveglio aveva fatto sì che gli Attivisti Ombra sfidassero direttamente le aziende. Queste aziende erano in mano alle ultime famiglie ricche associate fin dal 2230, dopo che gruppi anonimi su internet avevano collaborato e realizzato il più grande hackeraggio conosciuto della storia umana. I flussi di cassa si erano interrotti e il denaro era stato ripulito dalle società finanziarie private e dirottato verso aziende verdi e pulite.

Investigazioni interminabili non avevano portato a nessun risultato, gli Attivisti Ombra continuavano a eludere la luce. "Terroristi!" avevano proclamato le famiglie. L'ONU, o tutto ciò che ne restava, aveva definito gli Attivisti Ombra un Gruppo d'Odio. In maniera ufficiosa, ovviamente, si diceva che la coalizione di famiglie avesse minacciato di rifiutare i finanziamenti se all'ONU, se non li avesse definiti così. NQ era uno dei molti androidi incaricati dalla commissione di investigare su attività anomale su internet, intercettare gli attacchi e riferirli. In precedenza, si era unito a loro come hacker white hat per testare il loro sistema di sicurezza, ma i ripetuti biohackeraggi nella formazione genica (solo alla portata dei ricchi) del mese precedente avevano portato i livelli di minaccia al massimo. Gli AD del DISEC erano per la maggior parte inondati dal denaro della coalizione e questo significava che tutti gli androidi, eccetto i rinnegati, erano al servizio della coalizione. Stai alla larga dai loro affari, si era detto NQ. Tieni la testa bassa. E porta avanti il tuo lavoro.

I Raccoglitori Solari proiettavano la loro incredibile luce brillante su tutto e tutti coloro su cui passavano; i tessuti sporchi issati nell'aria e le ombre che vi si acquattavano sotto, la poltiglia fatta dalle bucce schiacciate ripetutamente dai piedi, i volti animati dei venditori mentre mercanteggiavano con i clienti e la vecchia statua di bronzo di Gandhi che sorrideva gentile su questo angolo dimenticato della gigantesca città.

"Ti senti perso? Siamo qui per aiutarti. Animus offre sogni in una pillola. Ti diamo il sapore della famiglia. Ecco il tuo posto. Vieni e assaggia la felicità." La voce di Io l'aveva distolto dai suoi pensieri e in quel momento di confusione ed esistenza dolceamara, si era ritrovato ad annuire.

Animus era nato in Vietnam, allora una piccola azienda, poi si era espanso in Giappone, Cina e le Americhe. Tutti i resoconti erano sull'integrazione riuscita degli androidi. Niente li fermava dall'aprire milioni di "rifugi" in giro per il mondo, specialmente ora che il DISEC sovvenzionava Animus e aveva inghiottito quasi tutto il gruppo al suo interno. Progettavano sogni in laboratorio, tutti approvati dal DISEC, unicamente per far sì che gli androidi si sentissero a casa, o come diceva Animus, "ogni robot ha bisogno di una famiglia." Quello che era implicito erano le parole "famiglia umana." Rallegratevi, tutti ora possono avere i vecchi valori familiari! Il rifugio più recente aveva aperto a Mumbai tre mesi prima. E ora, NQ si ritrovò in piedi nell'atrio, con una pillola che scrutava con sospetto. I muri erano ricoperti di schermi. Di tanto in tanto, una scena veniva proiettata a ripetizione. Una bambina faceva le bolle e ridacchiava.

"Sogni per il giorno," la voce di Io fluttuava verso di lui dagli altoparlanti nell'atrio. Guardava la bambina, il suo sorriso sdentato. Chi è? Si chiese. Aveva la mano tesa verso il tavolino di vetro su cui si trovava la pillola.

"Sai che lo vuoi." Sentì Io fare le fusa. Poteva quasi figurarsi il suo ammiccare, la sua lingua felina che si toccava il labbro superiore. Con la coda dell'occhio vide la bambina ritornare sullo schermo e ridere, inseguendo le bolle. NQ chiuse gli occhi e le sue dita tremarono, ma era arrivato fino a quel punto e adesso non c'era modo di tirarsi indietro. Io non lo avrebbe mai lasciato andare. NQ prese la pillola.

"Per l'immersione completa, chiudi gli occhi," consigliò Io.

NQ chiuse gli occhi.

Qui c'era NQ a otto anni e qui c'era la mamma che gli preparava i biscotti. Appena oltre la cucina c'era il giardinetto in cui suo padre giocava a palla con suo fratello. La bacca di vaniglia era esplosa nell'impasto dei biscotti e aveva riempito la casa di un profumo inebriante. NQ avrebbe potuto nuotare in quel profumo per giorni. Poteva sentire le strilla di suo fratello nel cortile e la risata roca di suo padre mentre la palla rotolava e colpiva uno dei vasi di fiori. "Non dire a mamma che l'abbiamo colpito." Sentiva le voci

distintamente. Stava camminando verso il giardino, ancora un po'
lontano, quando il padre si voltò per guardarlo. "Vieni qua fuori, fi-
gliolo," disse sorridendo, il verde dei suoi occhi sembrava il mare che
NQ aveva visto una volta in un dipinto. La sua faccia era diventata
di un rosa terreo dove il sole aveva indugiato un po' troppo a lungo.
Le margherite erano in piena fioritura.

"Vuoi le gocce di cioccolato nei biscotti?" chiese sua madre,
sporgendo la testa, con i ricci morbidi che le incorniciavano il bel
viso bruno. Quel viso... aveva visto quel viso prima, eppure NQ
non riuscì a collocare quel viso nella sua memoria. E ciononostante,
quanto poteva essere affidabile la memoria di un bambino di otto
anni?

Guardò NQ di otto anni invadere la mente di NQ di centocinquant'anni e tutti quei centocinquant'anni di vita adesso erano
temporaneamente irraggiungibili. Le visioni si succedevano nella
sua mente anche quando apriva gli occhi, cercando di sostituire
poco a poco il suo presente, la sua realtà, con tutte quelle immagini inventate. Si vide in quel film, non com'era adesso, o com'era
quando aveva otto anni, ma come sarebbe stato, rielaborato, nella
versione di qualcuno di una storia su di lui. A parte che non sarebbe stato lui, non una mente elettronica incapsulata in un'esteriorità
umanoide, ma un umano in tutto e per tutto.

Per un secondo, uno strano senso di confusione si impossessò
di lui. Tristezza? Si chiese. Come può una mente elettronica anche
solo registrare la tristezza? Forse era sempre stata una parola per lui
e l'aveva notata guardando da vicino i volti umani, i movimenti e,
come un linguaggio appreso, col tempo, era riuscito a esprimerla.
Che mistero era per se stesso! Aveva imparato quella parola decenni
prima in un giardino diverso da quello sugli schermi. Un giardino
che conosceva a memoria ma non riusciva a spiegare stando in piedi
nel bel mezzo dell'ingresso del rifugio di Mumbai.

Per quanto cercasse di scalfire quel muro che lo separava dai suoi
ricordi, questo rimaneva fermo, finché lentamente un'impossibilità
iniziò a prendere forma nella sua mente. Quest'impossibilità, che
vedeva dispiegarsi davanti a lui, l'opprimeva con tutte le conseguenze che potesse nominare. Animus le aveva riassunte tutte, tutte le
loro esistenze elettroniche in sogni che non avevano mai sognato.

La consapevolezza si sedimentò in lui come una coltre di nevischio, lasciandolo vecchio e infreddolito. È pericoloso camminare su quella brutta china, pensò. Gli schermi erano pieni di NQ a otto anni, una creazione frankensteiniana fatta studiando decenni di relazioni sugli androidi, anni di azioni di individui diversi nel mondo reale, monitorati e digitalizzati in schemi, cifre, sequenze. Non riusciva a ricordare com'era quando aveva otto anni, ma non era niente del genere. Fissò di nuovo lo schermo. Come un arto strappato dal suo corpo ed esibito per rappresentare l'intero corpo, l'NQ di otto anni era stato strappato dal mare della vita che tanti androidi avevano vissuto e che minacciava di trasformarli tutti in un prodotto omogeneo. Gli sorrideva, deridendo i suoi decenni con la sua esistenza arrogante. NQ ne era certo, gli si voleva nascondere. La faccia della madre si stagliò nella sua visione, questa volta con un ampio sorriso e lui riconobbe quel sorriso coi denti radi. Questo era un volto progettato perché destasse il suo interesse.

NQ aveva dodici anni e sua madre gli preparava il pranzo per la scuola. Fallo smettere, fallo smettere, si disse NQ ma quanto controllo aveva qui? I compagni di scuola erano bulli. "Sii forte" sua madre gli stava bisbigliando quelle parole. Sentiva il suo respiro caldo. Era umana. Non come lui. "Sii forte" sentì le parole ancora e ancora e sembravano svegliarlo da una paralisi di pensiero. NQ sputò la pillola. La visione si fermò.

"Hai interrotto il sogno," le parole di Io erano quasi una distrazione ben accetta.

"Ho visto abbastanza," disse NQ. Poteva percepire le telecamere che lo guardavano, registrando le sue espressioni. Non lasciare che vedano, pensò. "Va tutto bene. Devo essere da un'altra parte," disse, frettolosamente.

"Sette minuti e trenta secondi." Io registrò il tempo.

"Spero che sia felice dei nostri servizi," cinguettò. Lui le mostrò un pollice in su mentre si precipitava fuori, sentendosi come il drone volante di Io, separato dal corpo e senza radici. NQ era di nuovo al mercato. La cacofonia era una musica benvenuta per le sue orecchie.

"Hai bisogno di qualcosa?" chiese un venditore di frutta seduto lì vicino.

"No." Non c'era niente per lui lì. Gli piaceva venirci di tanto in tanto. Decenni fa, ci veniva per comprare succo d'ananas fresco lì dietro l'angolo. Non per lui, no. I ricordi stavano tornando adesso, ma deboli e vaghi, una parte dell'informazione perduta... per non essere recuperata mai? Si chiese NQ e sentì di nuovo freddo.

Si disse che stava bene. Certo, non sapevano cosa fosse, o da dove venisse. Non c'era più nessuno scienziato pazzo da chiamare papà, quel tempo era finito da un pezzo.

Adesso si producevano androidi nelle aziende e nelle fabbriche. I modelli più nuovi non dovevano vagare in lunghi corridoi alla ricerca di un'uscita, non passavano i loro pomeriggi in giardino a identificare uccelli, in attesa che papà tornasse. Non dovevano sopportare il peso dei genitori delusi. Gli ci era voluto del tempo per capire quell'ultima cosa. "Non avevo mai voluto essere padre, vedi." Gli tornarono in mente le parole, ma non la faccia di papà. Quelle parole non erano preparate in laboratorio. Erano reali, come il succo d'ananas di cui una volta aveva bevuto un sorso dalla tazza di papà, qualcosa che allora aveva provocato un malfunzionamento dei sistemi, qualcosa che non avrebbe avuto alcun effetto su di lui adesso. Tanti aggiornamenti, miglioramenti e corpi che aveva indossato come giacche nel corso dei decenni con tutte le loro manie e abitudini lo avevano reso ciò che era. Come potevano competere sei anni in un laboratorio, un programma miracoloso?

Non solo i suoi ricordi erano nebulosi, ma NQ si era anche portato appresso il forte profumo di vaniglia dal rifugio, si sentiva scomposto. Di tanto in tanto nella giornata interrompeva le sue valutazioni, conclusioni formulate con cura a vaghi calcoli di cui non riusciva a tenere traccia perché l'odore avvolgeva tutto, cancellava tutto. Per prima cosa, si mise in contatto con il manager per le Risorse Umane e Androidi di Animus, che poi lo reindirizzò al Laboratorio DISEC per le Complicazioni Androidi.

"Qualcuno ha scritto un codice dentro di te senza il tuo consenso?" chiese il consulente a NQ.

"No," rispose. No al fastidio. No a tutto quello che lo disorientava, lo faceva dimenticare.

"Immagino che sia così e basta, allora. Quello che provi è molto comune, ti stai riassestando. I sogni sono innaturali per te.

Il processo di acclimatazione richiede quattro settimane. Pensala come una nuova esistenza. Perché il nuovo prenda forma, il vecchio deve andare via." Sorrise. "Se vuoi comunque depositare un reclamo, puoi sempre farlo nel registro ufficiale. Non ti fermeremo. Gli androidi sono una famiglia."

"Grazie," disse NQ, incerto.

"Che modello sei, scusa?" chiese, mentre NQ andava via.

"Sono disfatto" disse, un termine considerato dispregiativo, ma ancora usato per riferirsi ai robot fatti prima che iniziasse la produzione di massa degli androidi. Il consulente guardò NQ con pietà.

"Non preoccuparti, sarai rifatto. Abbastanza presto." Sorrise.

Le parole caddero su di lui come il primo sorso di succo d'ananas. Una paura assoluta che bloccava i suoi programmi. L'integrazione totale.

Quando si presentò al lavoro, era ancora turbato. WEN, un programma creato da DISEC per trovare attività anomale che necessitavano di indagini, stava girando sul suo terminale, con il numero di bug che lampeggiava al limite del suo spazio operativo. Il primo bug bloccava l'accesso al reattore nucleare nella centrale vicina, era piuttosto strano, la sua sandbox si riempiva di lettere e numeri casuali che si riorganizzavano ogni volta che NQ cercava di bypassarlo e non ci riusciva. Aprire il secondo bug fece diventare l'interfaccia della sandbox nera, e comparve una domanda: "Chi sei?"

Affrontare la situazione avrebbe facilitato ancor più a fondo il suo ingresso nel sistema, qualcosa che la coalizione guardava con orrore assoluto. "Non farti coinvolgere dai terroristi!" Aprì il terzo. "Chi sei davvero?" Poi il quarto: "Non sei perduto." Questi bug stavano diventando sempre più personalizzati, come se sapessero quando lui, sì, proprio NQ, sarebbe stato dentro il sistema, e stessero in agguato in attesa di saltargli addosso. "Le cose possono cambiare" diceva il quinto. Qualcuno... o qualcosa si rivolgeva a NQ.

Contro il suo buon senso, tornò al primo.

"Chi sei?" Le lettere erano in grassetto, questa volta più grandi.

"Disfatto," inviò. L'interfaccia prese vita.

Un video mostrò NQ in un giardino. Dietro di lui si ergeva un bungalow di mattoni rossi. Gli uccelli cinguettavano. La luce del sole trapelava dalle foglie dell'albero di baniano e sotto l'ombra di quella vita imponente, suo papà leggeva un libro, poggiato al grosso tronco dell'albero. Alzò lo sguardo mentre NQ gli si avvicinava.

"Progressi?" chiese. Il volto di papà era chiaro adesso.

"Un sacco" rispose NQ. "Ho sviluppato un algoritmo che gestisce il controllo dei sistemi e decritta diecimila file STATE al minuto."

"Trovato qualcosa di interessante?" chiese papà.

"Sì, gli attacchi effettuati nel sito di estrazione di uranio Z-BW erano finanziati dal governo. Cosa vuoi che faccia con l'informazione?"

"Niente," rispose papà. "Dovresti riuscire a farlo in un secondo." Ricominciò a leggere. Il video si interruppe.

NQ digrignò i denti. Questo ricordo era andato perduto per lui. Aveva centovent'anni.

"Il mio ricordo. Ridammelo," inviò NQ.

"Noi non l'abbiamo mai preso. È statol'algoritmo di sogno di DISECa bloccare i tuoi veri ricordi."

"Chi siete 'voi'?" chiese NQ.

"Ci aiuti?"

NQ doveva prendere una decisione. Non fare rapporto sarebbe equivalso alla morte. Certo, le sue abilità a sviluppare algoritmi e decrittare file erano superlative, ma altri androidi l'avrebbero scoperto e i loro programmi avrebbero mostrato la presenza di NQ nel sistema, notato le marche temporali e tutto il resto. La sua interfaccia lampeggiò di nuovo.

"Consideralo un regalo, un antidoto ai sogni." Comparve un nuovo algoritmo.

Sentì il banco di memoria virtuale riempirsi, e vi si connesse, il ricordo fu scaricato dal virtuale al fisico una volta che i suoi valori vitali furono collegati.

I blocchi si sollevarono. I ricordi si riversarono in lui con l'intensità di un potente oceano che irrompeva nelle rive della vita.

"Chi siete?" chiese di nuovo, doveva sapere.

"Ti abbiamo trovato" arrivò la risposta.

Non c'era via di fuga. Non si potevano incontrare gli Attivisti Ombra, scambiarci informazioni personali senza che si fosse considerati alleati. Tieni la testa bassa. Fai rapporto. Sei un Disfatto. Estrarranno i tuoi algoritmi e ti getteranno via come il pezzo di spazzatura che sei, si disse. Le cose da umani erano diverse dalle cose da androidi. Non c'era alcuna utilità nel finire incastrato in questa cosa. Ma il ricordo... molti altri erano ormai perduti per lui, cancellati dal suo banco, pensò, e al loro posto aveva sogni di biscotti e scuola.

"Ditemi chi siete," NQ si sentiva impaziente.

"Incontriamoci alla diga oggi, mercato Doweze, alle 4 del mattino" diceva il messaggio.

"Non consentire al DISEC e alla coalizione di cancellarti." Poi l'interfaccia divenne nera.

Fai rapporto, pensò NQ.

I corpodroidi ci avrebbero messo 24 ore per arrivare dov'era lui nei sistemi. Questo significava che c'era ancora tempo per non essere congedato, per non essere chiamato un rinnegato. Le cose potevano ancora risolversi. NQ lo sperava, mentre andava verso il mercato.

Al buio il mercato sembrava privo di vita. Gli mancavano i venditori che contrattavano, la cacofonia dei bambini che giocavano lì vicino. Solo l'alimentatore gigante che forniva energia idroelettrica agli edifici vicini era vivo. Aspettò vicino alla diga, chiedendosi se si sarebbero mostrati. Poi il buio iniziò a diradarsi e NQ iniziò a perdere la speranza.

Quando il cielo iniziò a diventare violetto, NQ aveva già deciso di andarsene.

"Aspetta." Qualcuno lo chiamò alle sue spalle.

"Siete in ritardo," disse NQ, senza voltarsi.

"Eravamo qui, ma dovevamo essere sicuri che non avessi allertato il DISEC." Il tono era del tutto diverso da quello di qualsiasi umano, pensò NQ, diverso anche da quello dei corpo-droidi. Si girò per guardare l'interlocutore. L'alimentatore gettava ombre fitte, ma NQ riusciva a distinguere l'interno dell'intelaiatura meccanica, il vecchio e il nuovo coesistenti, poteva vedere i percorsi intricati attraverso i quali l'informazione viaggiava dentro e fuori, i segni degli aggiornamenti, i marchi dei miglioramenti. Nessuno scheletro o muscoli. I corpo-droidi si limitavano a emettere dati e letture vitali. No, capì NQ, questa era una Disfatta.

"Sono rimasti solo pochi di noi," disse lei. "Non sei solo."

Il sole stava salendo nel cielo.

"Ci farai rapporto?" chiese lei. Nella prima luce del giorno, NQ riuscì a vedere il profilo dei suoi capelli, rosa con punte dorate, notò, le punte probabilmente riflettevano la luce. Una curiosità lo invase. Voleva vederla alla luce del sole.

Lui non rispose. Non aveva più senso.

"Come mi avete trovato?" chiese invece.

"Tu ed io... siamo rari," rispose lei.

NQ voleva ricordare queste parole, come la vaniglia e i biscotti. Voleva ricordarle per il resto della sua vita.

"Quindi dove andiamo adesso?" chiese.

"L'ISF ha un centro in Indonesia che non è ancora sul registro ufficiale."

"Come lo sapete? L'avete hackerato?"

"Non è stato necessario. Noi siamo l'ISF. I nostri amici, gli umani, sono i volti dell'organizzazione. È più semplice per le IA portare avanti il lavoro senza conflitto nel retroscena. Un giorno speriamo che più umani si uniscano a noi e possiamo avere una coalizione tutta nostra." Sorrise.

Anche NQ sorrise. Stava esaminando le azioni da intraprendere adesso.

Per prima cosa, avrebbe dovuto cancellare il banco di memoria virtuale. Zero tracce. Zero esistenza. Poi avrebbe dovuto bloccare tutti i sistemi che lo collegavano al terminale DISEC. Una volta fatto, sarebbe stato come morto. Gli avrebbero dato la caccia. La ricerca sarebbe continuata per settimane. Si sarebbe dovuto fare un'altra vita lontano dagli occhi delle aziende.

Mentre NQ ritornava al suo appartamento, Io lo intercettò di nuovo.

"Ti senti perso? Non conosci il tuo posto nel mondo grande e cattivo?" chiese Io.

Per la prima volta, NQ sapeva la risposta. Eludere Io fu difficile ma non impossibile e quando giunse a casa, bramava un bel sonno ristoratore, ma il tempo era importante. Mentre si disconnetteva dal terminale DISEC, NQ meditò sui sentieri intricati che la sua vita aveva preso. Si era considerato un pezzo unico, e per tutta la sua esistenza aveva tratto gioia da questa considerazione, ma solo ora era arrivato a capire che voleva di più.

La vita... La semplice vita casuale, il più grande miracolo di tutti gli era stato rivelato in un posto al di là della progettazione. Ora, era oltre la portata di qualsiasi miracolo. E in quell'oltre estremo in cui i casi erano all'ordine del giorno, NQ sapeva che avrebbe incontrato la vita in continuazione. Avrebbe guardato il mondo invecchiare con lui, solo che questa volta l'avrebbe fatto con altri come lui. Una nuova esistenza lo aspettava, una che poteva coesistere con la vecchia. Un giorno avrebbe guardato di nuovo l'alba e si sarebbe meravigliato al miracolo delle cose come sono.

Alcuni giorni più tardi, nel centro in Indonesia, i sogni di NQ erano ancora ossessionati dall'odore della vaniglia. Non potevano ancora vedersi alla luce del sole.

"Perché ogni rivoluzione abbia successo, c'è bisogno di grandi sacrifici," gli aveva detto Ithi.

NQ conosceva i sacrifici anche troppo bene. Il suo corpo doveva essere smaltito, fatto per sembrare come altri corpi disfatti che si scaricavano, un numero sufficiente di fallimenti gestiti in modo da portare a "malfunzionamenti di sistema risultanti nella morte del corpo" quando l'indagine fosse stata intrapresa. Essendo un vecchio modello, la sua unità di base era l'hardware. Ithi contrabbandò il suo quantum core attraverso il paese in un container che trattava rifiuti radioattivi, questo significava che intercettare la sua unità sarebbe stato quasi impossibile, persino con gli scanner. Ithi alla fine lo fuse in uno dei corpi IA prodotti in massa che trovò in una fabbrica in Indonesia.

Si scambiavano frequentemente ricordi raccontandosi storie l'un l'altro.

"Per sicurezza," diceva Ithi. "Se ti dimentichi, ti ricorderò io."

I primissimi giorni nel centro, NQ continuava a svegliarsi durante la notte. Il suo corpo non era più suo e ci voleva tempo per abituarsi.

"Brutti sogni?" chiedeva Ithi.

"No. Belli," rispondeva a Ithi.

"Mi racconti?" chiedeva.

"Ho sognato un mondo in cui gli uomini non erano progettisti," le diceva NQ.

"Mi chiedo come sarebbe." C'era speranza nella voce di Ithi.

NQ sorrideva, poggiava la testa sulla spalla di lei e guardava il centro, una comune per tutti i rinnegati e i rivoluzionari. Col tempo, sapeva che l'odore della vaniglia sarebbe svanito e il desiderio di mangiare i biscotti si sarebbe attenuato. Nuovi desideri l'avrebbero riempito, e insieme a loro, speranze per le scoperte che dovevano essere fatte. NQ non doveva sentirsi umano. Doveva solo sentirsi vivo.

L'architettura della perdita

di Salik Shah

traduzione di Gabriella Gregori

Salik Shah è uno scrittore, regista ed è l'editor fondatore di Mithila Review, *rivista internazionale di fantascienza e fantasy. Suoi racconti sono apparsi su* Asimov's Science Fiction, Strange Horizons, Tor. com e The Gollancz Book of South Asian Science Fiction (Vol 2). *Potete trovarlo su Twitter @salik. Sito-web: salikshah.com.*

Non è difficile distruggere il mondo, una volta presa la decisione. Puoi bloccare il sole o far congelare l'oceano. Puoi creare un buco nell'ozono; liberarti dello scudo protettivo della nostra atmosfera. Se sei davvero furioso e vuoi lasciare una cicatrice profonda per i futuri cacciatori-raccoglitori, puoi prendere in considerazione l'idea di bombardare il mondo con un asteroide. All'universo non interessa che metodo di autodistruzione usi: li ha *provati* e si è *stufato* di tutti.

Il velivolo militare attraversa la spessa minaccia di cenere e fumo. Quando l'aria si rischiara qua e là, la terra sottostante non sembra più essere di un verde, marrone o cemento abitabili. La crosta avanza lentamente e striscia come catrame fuso, sradicando, bruciando, divorando, obliterando i resti del mondo che era tanto odiato e amato.

Il puzzo della morte riempie le narici di Rani: è nauseante, ma per fortuna ha lo stomaco vuoto. "Papà," Rani parla attraverso un asciugamano scurito che le copre la bocca, "dove finisce?"

"Non finisce," Papà decide di dare tutte le informazioni alla sua bambina, il suo soldatino. Non possono sopravvivere alla fine del mondo se non si preparano al peggio. "Va fino in fondo all'oceano."

L'atto di vivere è un atto di dolore per il mondo che ciascuno di noi porta dentro di sé, l'atto di dolore è un atto di attenzione per i mondi che condividiamo l'uno con l'altro.

Rani non può saltare queste sessioni settimanali di valutazione del trauma psicologico richieste dalla Marina. Il robot del lutto le appare sotto forma di una donna elegante con un vestito floreale a balze e orecchini di perle. Il leggero profumo di un incenso aromatico, sandalo e miele, la calma mentre affonda nella sedia pieghevole di fronte al robot.

"Non so se sono addolorata o depressa." Gli occhi castani di Rani riflettono le onde placide dell'oceano scuro all'esterno. L'aria è più fresca qui sul ponte a quest'ora di notte – chiude le mani a pugno nella tasca della giacca impermeabile gialla. I suoi pantaloni neri e gli stivali sono come sempre bagnati per le raffiche di pioggia.

"Papà non c'è mai e Mamma si è isolata dal mondo. Sta affrontando il lutto a modo suo, lo so. Ma ho bisogno di lei. Sono preoccupata per lei. Non so come fare in modo che parli con me."

Una volta, Rani Ranjit Rai viveva in un mondo sano. Aveva un posto chiamato casa e una famiglia intatta, integra. Adesso sembrava tutto come una fiaba.

Quando era loggata nella Realtà Virtuale, era ancora un architetto-ingegnere, la costruttrice di mondi immaginari. La fuga la libera dalla realtà del mondo umido. Per abitudine preferisce lavorare con i vincoli fisici anche nel simulatore, ma c'è la libertà di fallire senza mettere a rischio vite e lasciare testimoni.

Al momento, Rani sta mappando e simulando creature del passato assieme a organismi viventi per comprendere come fare progettazioni e strutture biomimetiche nuove e intelligenti. Sta progettando biomateriale intelligente che possa autoripararsi e autopropagarsi all'interno di limiti specifici per ciascuna architettura. Il lavoro è impegnativo ed è per quello che lo sceglie, la *distrae* dal passato, ristabilisce un senso di normalità.

"Ti stai ancora riprendendo dallo shock della tua perdita?" Il robot del lutto richiede che Rani risponda a tutte le sue domande in modo sincero per diagnosticare con accuratezza e iniziare il processo di guarigione.

"Sì, credo," ammette Rani. "Pensavo che potessimo prevenire il crollo – riprogettare il clima. Ho lavorato così tanto per un futuro che non esiste più. Suppongo di essere ancora sotto shock perché mi sono appena resa conto di essere stata proprio stupida

– hanno fottuto il mondo in modo irrecuperabile e senza speranza prima ancora che io venissi concepita. *Sono* così dannatamente ingenua."

Quando non è loggata, Rani fa un turno di dieci ore. La Marina l'ha assegnata a una gabbia geodesica sommersa dove coltiva alghe e confeziona acqua desal per poi distribuirle ai marinai immatricolati del progetto abitazioni marine.

Se pensavi che chi ha visto la fine del mondo ed è sopravvissuto sarebbe stato gentile con le altre persone, sei in errore. Tutti i mali e i demoni del mondo umano che una volta affliggevano la terra – l'iniquità divina del sistema delle caste, l'egoismo e l'ignoranza condivisi sia dai potenti che dai deboli – ora alzano le loro orribili teste sull'acqua salmastra non appena la vita nell'oceano diventa la nuova normalità per chi ci abita.

A volte Rani passa il tempo con il diario del lutto. Lo sta riempiendo con le storie della Nonna (è un'idea del robot). L'atto di ricordare è l'atto del cordoglio, lo sa.

Oggi decide di scrivere una storia in cui una montagna si innamora di un uomo, che non la può ricambiare. La montagna lo uccide perché l'amore la rende stupida e, quando si rende conto di cosa ha fatto, si affligge. Il dolore della montagna è così grande che i suoi tremori e le sue urla sono talmente forti che finiscono per fare a pezzi e distruggere il mondo intero.

"Sei arrabbiata con te stessa o con il mondo?" chiede il robot.

"Con nessuno," dice Rani. "Non sono più arrabbiata. Sono più che altro delusa, diffidente nei confronti del mondo. Prima del crollo avevo un programma, un luogo di lavoro. Dopo il crollo, quando non c'erano più, stavo malissimo. Se non lavoro, mi sento priva di valore...."

"Per Aama, lo diceva sempre, l'unica risposta utile davanti alle cose che ci facevano arrabbiare, cose al di fuori del nostro controllo, è restare calmi e concentrarsi su ciò che puoi controllare. Adesso, ogni volta che mi arrabbio, mi loggo nel sistema VR e riverso tutta la mia rabbia, tutta quella energia nel mio lavoro."

Finito il turno, Rani prende una barca per raggiungere la madre sulla base navale. (Suo padre non c'è, è a proteggere le comunità come la sua da profughi indesiderati e pirati.) Cenano – pesce, insalata, una qualche pietanza di alghe – con vecchie canzoni in hindi in sottofondo.

"La rete di terraformazione adesso è aperta a chiunque," dice Rani. La rete di comunicazione usata dai nanobot di terraformazione si sviluppa su tutto il pianeta: è oggi l'immenso deposito dell'esperienza e della conoscenza umane.

Rani vuole che Mamma firmi il modulo di consenso così da poterla preservare e uploadare – la sua mente – sul cloud quando verrà il momento. Rani ha già firmato il modulo, anche Papà.

"Non cederò la mia vita per una simulazione sciagurata," dice Mamma con forza e con l'aria affranta e fragile. "Non voglio avere nulla a che fare con quella tecnologia diabolica."

"Va bene, va bene." Rani si trattiene. Non vuole rendere la cosa ancora peggiore di quanto non sia già. Non oggi. Comprende l'origine del dolore di sua madre: Nonna è morta – morta *davvero* – e non farà mai parte della coscienza cloud. Proverà di nuovo e la farà ragionare un altro giorno.

"Adesso mangia, per favore, Mamma. Sei uno stecchino."

Quando il mondo si spezza, non si spezza tutto in una volta. Prima si rompe in pezzi grandi. Questi pezzi grandi si rompono in pezzi piccoli e il processo continua in questo modo fino a che non ci sono più pezzi da rompere.

È Dashain, il giorno della tika. Papà sta mangiando il pakku di montone fritto di Mamma e raccontando come sia facile distruggere il mondo. I suoi datori di lavoro – l'esercito indiano e il governo – stanno offrendo a ogni cittadino la possibilità di uploadare il suo cervello – i suoi ricordi e la coscienza – in modo da poter vivere sul cloud come parte della rete biologica di terraformazione.

"Quando le persone muoiono, dovrebbero riposare in pace," dice Nonna. Non approva la vita artificiale, digitale o sintetica. "Gli state togliendo la possibilità di scelta."

"Aama, è l'unica scelta che possiamo offrire," dice Papà, "oltre a paradiso e inferno, ovviamente."

Papà non ha altra scelta che andare al lavoro il giorno seguente. Ha giurato di proteggere la madrepatria da rifugiati climatici armati e jihadisti. La guerra con uno qualsiasi dei grandi vicini dell'India è imminente e l'esercito indiano non si può permettere di separarsi dai suoi Gurkha per più di un giorno.

"Aama ha ragione," dice Mamma. "Non posso buttare via la mia vita qui – non importa quanti burocrati irritanti o interruzioni di energia dovrò affrontare – per una vita immaginaria nel cloud."

Mamma lavora per un'organizzazione intergovernativa che fornisce cibo, aiuti e istruzione a uomini, donne e bambini dell'Hindu Kush himalayano.

"Le scosse non si fermeranno," dice Papà mentre Mamma succhia il midollo da un pezzo di osso. "Andrà sempre peggio finché la placca non slitterà nella nuova posizione."

"Papà! Sembri il membro di una setta apocalittica." Rani si lecca via le spezie dalle dita. "Possediamo la tecnologia per resistere ai terremoti, addirittura per costruire nuove città nel vasto oceano."

"Chhori, abbiamo la tecnologia da decenni. Il problema è: abbiamo la volontà politica o abbastanza tempo per costruire tutte le cose meravigliose che progetti?"

"Allora, l'hai fatto?" chiede Nonna. Nasconde la bocca dietro un fazzoletto mentre cerca di togliere un filo di carne rossa che le è rimasto incastrato in una larga fessura tra i denti.

Papà le lancia uno sguardo interrogativo.

"L'upload?" dice Nonna.

Papà ride. "Non sarei qui se lo avessi fatto."

"Come funziona?" chiede Rani. È seduta alla sua sinistra.

"Be'..." Papà strappa il montone dall'osso con i denti ingialliti e lo mastica prima di parlare. "Prima devi vetrificare e trasformare il cervello in vetro per salvare i dati, i tuoi ricordi e la coscienza. Poi ti connetti e fai l'upload dei dati sulla rete neurale biologica."

"Qual è la fregatura?" chiede Mamma. È seduta alla sua destra.

"Devi congelare il cervello *esattamente* nel momento della morte," dice Papà, "per evitare qualsiasi danno o perdita di dati neurali."

Nonna lo guarda sconcertata – gli sta seduta di fronte al tavolo.

"Uccide il cervello," dice Papà, " *e* il paziente."

"Che cosa orribile!" dice Mamma.

"Devi morire prima di poter rinascere, giusto?" Sembra che papà si stia divertendo: è a *casa*.

"Preferirei andare all'inferno piuttosto che fidarmi della tecnologia del diavolo." Adesso Nonna è turbata. "Hanno promesso di creare un paradiso sulla Terra. Guarda cosa è successo: l'hanno distrutta."

Lo sguardo di Nonna diventa freddo, si rivolge all'interno come se stesse ricordando una vita di frustrazioni, ingiustizia e rabbia. Mamma tocca la mano di Nonna per calmarla, ma lei la sposta.

"Adesso questi mostri vogliono prometterci l'immortalità dell'anima."

Papà vorrebbe parlare ma Mamma lo guarda, scuotendo la testa. Nonna ha quasi 75 anni, secondo il suo dottore ha bisogno di più riposo e di evitare gli stress terreni della vita e del samsara.

"Scusa Aama." Papà fa una ritirata strategica.

"Aama, ignoralo, per favore," dice Mamma. "Ho un'idea. Andiamo a giocare a carte. Lo puoi battere come ai vecchi tempi, ci divertiremo!"

"Come ai vecchi tempi?" Nonna sembra così smarrita – Rani si domanda *quali* vecchi tempi stia ricordando.

Mamma prende le mani raggrinzite di Nonna e le stringe con delicatezza.

"Sì." Mamma sorride. "Come ai vecchi tempi."

L'espressione indurita di Nonna si scioglie, lei si ammorbidisce. Rani vuole abbracciarla. *Più tardi*, si dice.

Papà alza entrambe le mani. "Mi arrendo," dice.

È abbastanza per far ridere Mamma e Nonna. Alleggerisce l'atmosfera nella sala da pranzo: il senso di morte e distruzione si dissolve quando l'intera famiglia scoppia a ridere.

Rani sa che Papà non è riuscito a convincere Nonna a lasciare che preservino e uploadino la sua mente, le sue gioie e i suoi dispiaceri, le sue storie ed esperienze.

È l'ultimo Dashain che celebrano con Nonna. Se ne andrà prima del prossimo Dashain, ha detto il dottore dopo l'ultimo check-up.

Rani non riesce a sopportare l'idea di perdere Nonna, gli occhi le si riempiono di lacrime.

Quando Nonna le chiede cosa c'è che non va, Rani dice: "Non è niente... solo le spezie e il peperoncino."

"Raccontami del giorno in cui è morta tua nonna." La voce del robot è sommessa, quasi gentile. "Ti ricordi com'era? Cosa stavi facendo in quel momento?"

Quando Rani cerca di pensarci, non c'è niente di strano o differente riguardo al giorno in cui il mondo finì, quando la nonna è morta. No, è stata uccisa e portata via dopo il terremoto contro la sua volontà, *prima* del suo tempo.

Rani sta correndo verso Durbar Square, fingendo di essere una bambina che non riesce a immaginare per quale motivo si possa voler lasciare questa *meravigliosa* città per i dinari, i dollari o una qualsiasi criptovaluta.

Katmandu è cambiata poco se non di aspetto negli ultimi tre anni della sua assenza. Le vetrine rifornite di latte fresco e approvvigionamenti stanno tornando alle loro nuove coordinate. La maggior parte dei contadini poveri potevano fare a meno dell'invasione di quella tecnologia da primo mondo. *No, grazie!*

L'odore di incenso e il suono dei bhajan si riversano dalle case e riempiono le strade. Rani è contenta di essere tornata in città anche se la sua decisione di tornare ancora non ha senso.

Certe cose non cambiano mai: un po' più avanti sulla strada acciottolata uomini e donne e bambini stanno in fila davanti a rubinetti privati con i loro contenitori e secchi vuoti. Quello in cui si imbatte nella città le spezza il cuore: la bruttezza degli stendardi chiassosi e degli edifici modulari, la povertà della sua gente e la loro muta accettazione.

Rani si ferma davanti al Kasthamandap per riprendere fiato mentre la prima luce del giorno cade sulla pagoda a tre piani. L'aria piena di smog le brucia gli occhi e il petto ma *questo* è il motivo per cui ha scelto di tornare dopo aver portato a termine gli studi in architettura-ingegneria all'Università Tsinghua di Pechino.

I suoi amici le danno della pazza per aver rinunciato alle brillanti prospettive che aveva altrove. Lei non si prende la briga di spiegare loro perché è importante che qualcuno con quel tipo di qualifica provi a cambiare e salvare la città da se stessa.

La città di Katmandu ha preso il nome dal Kasthamandap, la pagoda in legno e argilla del settimo secolo che una volta faceva da riparo per chi viaggiava da Lhasa verso il Ladakh. Circa quarantasei famiglie vivevano nei suoi tre piani prima che il governo le sfrattasse per rendere il sito di interesse storico più igienico e adatto ai turisti.

Quando Rani ci pensa adesso, vede gli sfratti come i primi segnali di ciò che sarebbe successo. Presto ci saranno mucchi senza vita di acciaio e calcestruzzo che distruggeranno il carattere della città. Quest'ultima importerà ciecamente architettura meccanica – progettata, fabbricata e assemblata non per servire i suoi abitanti, ma per estrarre il maggior profitto possibile da ogni materiale e organismo, oggetto e corpo – per il beneficio di pochi eletti.

Dopo essere tornata a casa dalla passeggiata mattutina, fa una doccia veloce, indossa vestiti semicasual, fa colazione e prenota una macchina senza conducente per andare a incontrare il sindaco della città.

"In che modo questo attirerà più turisti?" chiede il sindaco dopo aver ascoltato Rani per trenta secondi. Il sindaco sta pensando che, se Rani non avesse nominato la sua alma mater o Pechino, l'avrebbe già congedata.

Rani lo ha colto di sorpresa con la sua dettagliata proposta di ricostruire il patrimonio storico della città.

La domanda del sindaco non turba Rani, anche se avrebbe preferito un'altra serie di domande. Per esempio:

Come possiamo costruire una città equa, sana e felice?

Come può ogni casa, ogni strada generare elettricità pulita?

Come possiamo trasformare l'umidità in acqua potabile pulita per residenti, passanti e pellegrini e renderla gratuita?

Quanto velocemente possiamo equipaggiare, educare e incoraggiare le persone a coltivarsi il cibo usando luce artificiale e sostanze nutritive su tetti vuoti e terrazze-giardino?

Di quanti cittadini-dottori abbiamo bisogno per stampare e distribuire medicinali open-source gratuiti a chi in questo momento sta morendo perché non si può permettere l'ospedale o le medicine?

Rani decide di porre lei stessa le domande quando sarà il momento. Adesso passa alla slide sul progetto speculativo di un nuovo complesso-patrimonio e legge le parole scritte in grassetto.

Il Primo Sito Vivente Patrimonio dell'Umanità al Mondo

Il Sito UNESCO Patrimonio dell'Umanità che Respira

"Sono certa che il vostro ufficio marketing saprà creare un nome migliore..." Rani sente un sussulto improvviso. "Ha sentito?"

Il sindaco le lancia uno sguardo assente. "Cosa?"

"Il terremoto?"

"No."

"Oh, mi scusi. Dev'essere la mia immaginazione." Rani cerca di farsi coraggio. "Il movimento tettonico ultimamente sta accelerando."

"Possiamo rallentarlo?" chiede il sindaco. "Come possiamo fermarlo?"

Sono domande retoriche, ma il sindaco ha sul viso quell'espressione paralizzata che spinge Rani a rispondere in modo serio.

"Non credo," dice Rani, passando alla slide con un ologramma 3D della Terra. "Ancora non sappiamo *davvero* come la terra funziona. Non possiamo giocare con le placche tettoniche senza creare danni seri ai sistemi del pianeta."

"Che cosa propone, allora?"

"L'architettura in acciaio e calcestruzzo ha oltrepassato la sua data di scadenza, è inorganica e morta. Non si può adattare, riparare o curare in risposta ai terremoti e alle scosse ormai frequenti."

Mostra l'ologramma di una nuova città: un complesso di antichi siti di interesse storico che vive e respira all'interno di megacupole, grattacieli sotterranei e piramidi invertite.

Sta proponendo di sostituire il legno morto delle antiche pagode con legno-pianta bioingegnerizzato che crescerebbe in modo programmato rimpiazzando il legno marcescente. I costruttori originari del Kasthamandap usarono laterizi di terracotta e legno in modo da poterli sostituire, se necessario, ogni vent'anni. Lei propone un mega progetto di restauro usando la tecnologia e i biomateriali più moderni per soddisfare la stessa logica e funzione.

"Dobbiamo ricostruire i monumenti e gli edifici esistenti con biomateriale più resistente, flessibile e intelligente. Queste nuove strutture viventi possono resistere a tutte le scosse e i colpi sotto e sopra il suolo."

"È straordinario, signorina!" dice il sindaco. Rani non sa dire se l'espressione sulla maschera pallida del suo viso sia cambiata. "Vorrei avere il tempo o il budget per un'impresa così a lungo termine e visionaria. Ha qualcosa di meno ambizioso e semplice che possa piacere ai nostri elettori?" Il sindaco si domanda se può sfruttare l'entusiasmo e l'energia della giovane per l'elezione municipale, che è dietro l'angolo. "Per servire il popolo."

Rani sta per dare una risposta educata quando le persiane sbattono contro il vetro: l'edificio sta tremando.

"Il suo ufficio è antisismico, vero?" chiede al sindaco.

"Dovrebbe esserlo." Il sindaco si alza e corre verso la porta. "Ma conosco il costruttore, non gli affiderò la mia vita."

Mentre scendono le scale in calcestruzzo, l'edificio del sindaco ondeggia come una foglia nella brezza.

Usciti dall'edificio, corrono nel piazzale quadrato dove lo staff del sindaco si sta già radunando. Questa volta, quando il terreno sussulta, Rani perde l'equilibrio. Il sindaco non si ferma ad aiutarla. Rani si gira e si rialza da terra e corre via prima che la calce e i mattoni comincino a cadere dietro di lei.

Anche se sfugge alla trappola mortale con solo qualche graffio, sa che non tutti in città saranno altrettanto fortunati. Il deterioramento del calcestruzzo e l'incuria degli immobili cittadini uccideranno mezzo milione di abitanti della metropoli, inclusa sua nonna.

Il mattino successivo, le vetrine si svuotano lungo una processione gemente di donne che piangono i loro morti, collegando secoli di devastazione e perdite a innovazione e decisioni fuori luogo. Il terremoto di magnitudo 8.9 ha distrutto appartamenti residenziali e fattorie verticali, torri di trasmissione ed edifici governativi. Ha inghiottito il panorama brutale e vomitato pietrisco grezzo e macerie.

Subito dopo il disastro, il governo ha schierato i mangiatori di cadaveri per "velocizzare la ripresa e la consegna di merci essenziali e servizi ai cittadini."

Adesso i mangiatori di cadaveri, le macchine giganti che raschiano e cancellano tutto, scorrazzano per la zona devastata sui loro otto piedi. *Mangiano* gli oggetti materiali e gli album dei perduti, i dati, e i documenti delle vittime.

Una volta i mangiatori di cadaveri erano Bramini a contratto. Adesso i loro cervelli stabilizzati con l'aldeide stanno all'interno delle macchine giganti. Alcuni sono anime stanche vecchie più di un secolo. Quando erano vivi dentro i loro corpi umani, cremavano i cadaveri di poveri e principi sulle rive del Sacro Bagmati e permettevano alle loro anime di attraversare il Fiume Vaitarani per raggiungere il Paradiso o l'Inferno. Adesso sono maledetti, non possono andare in pensione. Adesso tutto ciò che toccano, tutti coloro che mangiano, restano incatenati al mondo come loro.

Mamma prende la mano di Rani per impedirle di fare qualcosa di stupido. Interferire col dharma del mangiatore di cadaveri può causare morte prematura o peggio. Guardano il mangiatore aprire la bocca come uno squalo, raschiare e inghiottire le macerie della loro casa assieme al corpo di Nonna.

Non riescono nemmeno a vedere il corpo di Nonna, gli viene *portato via* senza il loro consenso. Dopotutto, è diritto del governo impiegare ogni risorsa inclusa 'ogni parte del cittadino, compreso il cervello' per 'il progresso economico e il bene dello stato'. Al giorno d'oggi una grossa fetta del bilancio parlamentare nelle nazioni povere viene dal reddito generato dalla fornitura di cervelli umani per l'uso in robot per l'edilizia e bambole sessuali.

Il governo pagava cinquemila rupie alle famiglie dei mangiatori per il diritto di mantenerli in servizio, dopo la morte, a tempo indefinito. Non rifiuti il denaro quando vivi in una stanza affollata con tutta la tua famiglia. Ti venderesti l'anima se vivessi vicino alla sporcizia disgustosa di un fiume, con la preoccupazione costante del prossimo pasto, respirando il puzzo di morte e merda.

Più sono grandi il disastro e la perdita di vite, più sono redditizi per il governo. Non c'è tempo per il lutto o per gli addii.

Il padre di Rani aveva insistito perché moglie e figlia prendessero la cittadinanza indiana per proteggerle da questi avvoltoi che approfittano dei morti. Chiamatela lotteria del luogo di nascita o ingiustizia, Nonna non poteva beneficiare della cittadinanza straniera a causa di un cavillo.

"Quando sarà ora, ve lo farò sapere," diceva sempre Nonna. "Morirò a Kashi. Non preoccupatevi, sarò libera."

Nonna credeva, come la maggior parte degli indù devoti, che morire a Kashi ed essere cremati sulla riva del Sacro Gange avrebbe liberato la sua anima dall'eterno ciclo di vita e morte.

Adesso Nonna non sarà mai libera, Rani lo sa.

"Mamma, ti prego..." Piange e supplica mentre Mamma le stringe più forte la mano. "Dobbiamo riprenderci Nonna, dobbiamo liberarla."

Mamma si rifiuta di lasciare che la figlia attacchi il mostro che ha già mangiato sua madre. Il dolore le dà la lucidità e la forza di diventare assolutamente glaciale. Eppure il dolore della figlia, le sua urla strazianti e disperate, le bruciano il viso come ortiche.

Per un attimo, Mamma prende in considerazione la possibilità di attaccare lei stessa il mostro e fare a pezzi il suo corpo metallico arrugginito e riportare sua madre alla figlia. Se segue il proprio istinto, lo sa, metterà in pericolo sia la vita di sua figlia che la propria.

"No," dice Mamma, trattenendo le lacrime. Che genere di madre sarebbe se facesse ammazzare la figlia, se non riuscisse a proteggere la sua bambina da dannazione e schiavitù eterne? "No."

"Vi ringraziamo tutti per la collaborazione." Il sindaco parla dalla comodità del suo rifugio sotterraneo attraverso gli altoparlanti dei droni che attraversano i quartieri distrutti. "Manteniamo alto il morale per andare avanti un altro giorno."

Dopo aver ascoltato pazientemente Rani durante la prima sessione di valutazione del trauma, il robot del lutto le dà un foglio laminato e un diario da riempire con le storie di Nonna.

"Per favore, considerami un'amica."

Rani è talmente sconvolta da non accorgersi nemmeno che sta parlando con un robot.

"Per favore, leggi il codice della persona in lutto prima di andare a letto," dice il robot. "Ti sarà d'aiuto."

I 10 passi del lutto

1. Il tuo lutto è unico. Permetti a te stesso di elaborarlo.

2. Il tuo lutto è silenzioso. Permetti a te stesso di parlare.

3. il tuo lutto è forte. Permetti a te stesso di guarire.

4. Il tuo lutto è impegnativo. Permetti a te stesso di riposare.

5. Il tuo lutto è crudele. Permetti a te stesso di amare.

6. Il tuo lutto è determinato. Permetti a te stesso di arrenderti.

7. Il tuo lutto è indefinito. Permetti a te stesso di respirare.

8. Il tuo lutto è senza senso. Permetti a te stesso di credere.

9. Il tuo lutto è grande. Permetti a te stesso di accettare.

10. Il tuo lutto è costante. Permetti a te stesso di cambiare.

Mentre riempie il diario con un'altra storia di Nonna, Rani prova rabbia, turbata da ciò che la storia significa nel suo nuovo contesto.

Dopo che un terremoto ha distrutto la valle rendendola inabitabile, una coppia di anziani cammina per giorni in cerca della vetta sacra del Monte Kailasha. Lungo il cammino passano attraverso città fantasma e villaggi che sono stati distrutti. La moglie chiede a Shakya, il marito, che è un potente sacerdote, di lasciare che i sopravvissuti li seguano. Lui acconsente.

Dopo una serie di avventure in cui il grande Shakya sconfigge o uccide demoni che dominano le foreste, i passi e le montagne e cercano di ostacolare la loro avanzata, il gruppo di profughi finalmente arriva al grande lago sotto il Monte Kailasha.

Qui, il grande Shakya taglia un crinale e prosciuga tutta l'acqua. Poi cattura i molti pesci dalle scaglie fatte di gemme e i serpenti pieni di nettare e costruisce sotto un loto gigante un rifugio per le persone, che sono grate di potersi finalmente stabilire sul terreno fertile.

[Perché dobbiamo sempre abbattere la foresta e distruggere l'ambiente per dare casa al genere umano?

Aama diceva che, quando una persona muore, la sua anima trova una nuova casa, un nuovo corpo. Spero che quando troverà la sua nuova casa questa volta, non sia costruita sul terreno di distruzioni ambientali e genocidi come questi.

L'unico modo per costruire una civiltà duratura è costruirla in armonia con i sistemi della terra per l'arrivo della prossima generazione. Non dobbiamo permettere la cieca imitazione e la sconsiderata ripetizione degli errori del passato, la nostra dipendenza ossessiva dalla crescita autodistruttiva. Dobbiamo sviluppare nuovi materiali e filosofie di costruzione per un'architettura vivente se vogliamo costruire un nuovo futuro su questo pianeta, quando si riprenderà.

Spero che lo faccia.]

Il robot del lutto sta aspettando che Rani risponda alla domanda.

Hai accettato la tua perdita e chi sei diventata?

"Vivo su un'imbarcazione, mangio alghe fritte col sole e zuppa di piante marine," dice Rani. "I turni di lavoro sono noiosi. Questa è la mia nuova normalità. Questo è quello che sono diventata.

"Ma non posso accettare che questo sia tutto quello che c'è. Non c'è modo di ricostruire il mondo, invertire l'orologio? A volte quando mi sento di non sapere più cosa fare, o perché sono ancora qui e Aama non c'è più, mi dico che quando la terra smetterà di muoversi, tornerò a casa e ricostruirò il mondo perduto senza i metodi di autodistruzione. È negazione o fede quello che mi fa aggrappare disperatamente alla speranza? Non lo so."

Due giorni dopo la morte di Mamma, Rani è pronta per l'upload. Non vuole pensare agli anni persi sull'oceano, non ha più importanza.

"Il cervello umano è come un computer parallelo," dice Papà. "Il cloud userà il novantacinque per cento del tuo cervello. Puoi usare il restante cinque per cento per costruire e ricostruire il mondo tutte le volte che vuoi. Puoi vivere in un mondo senza povertà, malattie o morte. O puoi scegliere di dimenticare tutto, sconnetterti, abbandonare la tecnologia *diabolica* e vivere come un'eremita."

"Papà?"

"Scusa." L'ologramma di suo padre curva le spalle. "Mi manca Aama. Mi manca *lei*."

"Mancano anche a me," dice Rani. "Ma tu sei qui per prepararmi all'eccitante vita nel cloud, ricordi?"

"Sì!" Papà si riprende. "Puoi scegliere qualsiasi vita, qualsiasi carriera desideri. Puoi finalmente diventare un soldato, se vuoi."

"Che soldato sia, allora!" dice Rani. "Adesso sono ufficialmente eccitata!"

"Fantastico!" Papà non riesce a trattenere la gioia – da quello che lei riesce a ricordare, gli uomini della famiglia di suo padre sono sempre entrati nell'esercito. Rani ha sempre avuto il sospetto che lui segretamente desiderasse un figlio che avrebbe portato avanti la tradizione.

Papà adesso, a braccia aperte e con un sorriso affettuoso, sta invitando Rani a immaginare e meravigliarsi davanti alle infinite possibilità. "Dopo che ti sei sistemata, puoi sempre evadere in mondi più alieni e spettacolari."

Rani chiude gli occhi e ricorda un jisei – la poesia dell'addio -
In viaggio, malato
i miei sogni diventano
marroni, blu, verdi.
#
<#boot=rani>
<#begin (transfer)>
Quando Rani apre la mente dentro il cloud per la prima volta, si immagina su un'arca che fluttua in orbita. Esamina la camera spaziosa con un enorme schermo trasparente che li protegge dal freddo assassino esterno.

Un nuovo continente sembra alzarsi dalle scure profondità del pianeta sottostante. La gigantesca massa continentale è una macchia di grigio, bianco e verde-che-verrà sul vasto oceano blu.

"Non è bella!?" dice Papà. Indossa l'uniforme militare – verde oliva e un basco con le insegne da generale: lo stemma nazionale, due spade e uno scudo, e il sole. "Ma le apparenze possono ingannare."

"Non capisco, signore." Rani, che è anche lei in uniforme da combattimento, sta prendendo tempo per abituarsi a questa nuova realtà. Consulta le sue nuove memorie e scopre con piacere che si è guadagnata questa missione. Non si trova lì perché suo padre è un generale di alto grado. Gli anni di formazione non pertinente e di preparazione per essere il tipo di soldato che avrebbe reso suo padre orgoglioso avevano finalmente dato i loro frutti.

"Quella cosa laggiù," dice Papà, "di qualsiasi cosa si tratti, *non* è nostra amica."

Le manda un file sullo schermo. "Abbiamo ricevuto questa comunicazione da Robert Shrestha un'ora fa."

"Il paleoclimatologo?"

"Proprio lui."

"Cosa dice?"

"Che la montagna è viva e i nostri uomini sono morti."

"Cosa significa?"

"Voglio che tu scopra esattamente quello," dice Papà. "La tua missione è appurare la natura della minaccia e tornare al punto di consegna entro un'ora." Fa un grosso sforzo per nascondere la sua preoccupazione per lei. "Posso contare su di te, soldato?"

Papà, non ti ho mai deluso prima e non intendo farlo adesso. Rani risponde: "Sissignore."

<read file: rs072381129.ogg>
Sono Robert Shrestha. Non permettete a nessuno di mettere piede sulla montagna. Ripeto non permettete a nessuno di mettere piede sulla montagna a meno che non vogliate che trovi morte certa.

La montagna è viva e stranamente ha l'autoconsapevolezza di un bambino umano. Attira gli uomini per ucciderli come se fosse un gioco – colpendo e riempiendo il loro cuore con un'oscurità terribile finché non vengono consumati dalla crescente solitudine, paura, disperazione, pazzia.

Per tutta la vita ho pensato che il nostro pianeta non fosse solo vivo ma pienamente consapevole. Ora che ne abbiamo la prova, non riesco a convincere me stesso né a riconoscere né a condannare la sua umanità – il suo pericoloso impulso a fare del male solo per farlo. Man mano che il bambino cresce diventando un adolescente, non può fare a meno di commettere gli stessi errori che abbiamo fatto noi.

Dobbiamo cercare di perdonare il bambino così come cerchiamo di perdonare noi stessi... per quello che abbiamo fatto al pianeta.
<close file: rs072381129.ogg>

Mentre salta dal velivolo alato sul cuore della montagna, Rani diventa *cosciente* della grandezza della sua presenza. Ha a malapena toccato il suolo quando il cuore pulsante di rocce brucianti sotto il ghiaccio compatto inizia a tastarla e *percepirla*.

Ciao! Sono Leila e voglio essere tua amica.

La montagna, Leila, stringe la sua presenza minacciosa tutto attorno alla sua mente mentre lei resiste e combatte per mantenere intatti i propri sensi.

Adesso Leila *condivide* un ricordo con Rani: il miscuglio di paura e gioia sembra durare all'infinito durante gli ultimi minuti della vita di Robert. *Il terrore è delizioso* – Rani può quasi sentire il gusto del pensiero di Leila mentre il suolo sotto i suoi piedi muta e si modella.

La montagna la piazza all'ingresso di una grotta che scava nella sua pancia cavernosa.

"Ciao Leila!" dice Rani. Sta attenta a sembrare amichevole. Leila è una manipolatrice provetta, ma è anche una bambina. Non può lasciare che Leila le consumi la mente. "Puoi raccontarmi cos'è successo qui?"

Sì...

All'improvviso Rani si sente *in corto circuito* – un colpo di tuono la prende e la mette KO.

\#

<I progetti speculativi di Rani e le sue storie si stanno diffondendo e stanno infettando il cloud di terraformazione come un virus. Il cloud cerca di disattivare la mente di Rani ma è troppo tardi. Ogni parola, ogni immagine della sua coscienza si infiltra e si diffonde attraverso la rete invisibile. Lei adatta, evolve e integra ogni nanobot all'interno della propria coscienza – la grandiosa narrativa del suo popolo – finché non li controlla tutti.>

[Lasciate che vi racconti una storia.

C'era una volta una montagna nata su un pianeta che era stato sterile per un migliaio di anni. Crebbe molto in fretta – divorando furiosamente l'utero di sua madre – mangiando la crosta e crescendo, senza avere la minima conoscenza della differenza tra ossa, roccia e metalli.

Mentre si avvicinava all'adolescenza, era furiosa a causa della propria solitudine. Di certo doveva esserci qualcuno come lei. Si rifiutava di credere di essere sola in tutto l'universo. Inviò onde d'urto, giorno dopo giorno, finché un giorno raggiunse gli ultimi uomini e loro arrivarono su una bestia alata e scesero a riposare sul suo petto.

La montagna si innamorò del primo uomo che toccò il suolo, era appropriato. Lui era il capo della loro spedizione.

"Robert, come la chiamiamo?" chiese uno degli uomini.

"Leila," rispose.

"È un bel nome."

Ora la montagna aveva un nome. E conosceva il nome di lui. Avrebbe dovuto essere abbastanza per rompere il ghiaccio. Giusto? Non proprio.

Robert – chiamò Leila.

Nessuna risposta.

Robert... Robert... Robert...

Quando lui non rispose alle sue molte chiamate, la recente gioia di Leila si dissipò. Lei iniziò a tremare di rabbia e tristezza, e poi si trattenne dal perdere il controllo perché notò che gli uomini la stavano osservando. La vista della cenere e del fumo che usciva dalla sua vetta li terrorizzava.

Robert mantenne la calma, ovviamente. "Va tutto bene, ragazzi," disse imperterrito. "Si sta solo schiarendo la gola."

Poi fece qualcosa di inaspettato: si rivolse a lei. "Leila, adesso non mi esplodere."

Leila obbedì, naturalmente. Non voleva far loro del male.

Mentre erano spaventati, gli uomini erano facili da leggere. Smettevano di resistere – riuscì a stimolare e punzecchiare ogni angolo delle loro menti finché non si aprirono come giacimenti!

Purtroppo, con suo grande disappunto, Robert non reagì come gli altri uomini. Si chiuse di nuovo, ignorando ogni sua avance.

Leila capì che, se voleva che lui le aprisse la mente, aveva bisogno di un piano.

Attirò gli uomini verso il luogo incandescente...

Robert non gradì, ovviamente. Le chiese di lasciarli andare.

"Certo," disse lei. "Se tu *apri* la tua mente."]

Il seme della nascita contiene il seme della distruzione. Prima che il mondo possa essere ristabilito, deve essergli permesso di morire. Un ciclo di vita e morte – è quello in cui credeva Aama. Quando muori, sei rinato.

Questa volta, quando Rani apre gli occhi si sente intrappolata, terrorizzata, sola e poi aperta, distribuita, connessa contemporaneamente. La vasta presenza che l'ha risvegliata ora racchiude l'intero pianeta. Ora lei è dentro ogni macchina atomica del cloud di terraforming ed esse sono parte della sua consapevolezza corporea.

"Vi percepisco!" trasmette Rani alla rete.

La rete le trasmette in risposta. *Anche noi ti percepiamo!*

<#transfer=completed>

Nell'esistenza di Rani adesso c'è un rinnovato senso di urgenza. Il mondo sta morendo e lei deve raccogliere, preservare e memorizzare ogni forma di vita che riescono a trovare e catalogare prima che l'estinzione di massa sia completa.

Ordina ai motori atomici di scavare e mappare strato dopo strato di roccia per aiutarla a studiare e simulare le giuste condizioni prima di poter stampare e riseminare queste forme di vita sulla Terra. Il lavoro la terrà occupata per un po' mentre fa congetture e immagina come ciascuna di queste forme di vita si sia evoluta, mossa, sentita, abbia visto e interagito con le altre e con il mondo.

Mentre inizia a calcolare le ipotetiche condizioni in cui la vita nacque all'inizio sulla Terra, ascolta le canzoni preferite di Aama per riempire l'enorme silenzio del cosmo.

Rani non sa ancora che terraformerà e costruirà modelli dal vivo della Terra su un milione di pianeti nell'universo nella speranza di ripristinare ciò che il mondo – lei – ha perduto.

In ogni simulazione del mondo, Rani riempie l'oceano con Matsya e Kurma, il pesce e la tartaruga. Crea Varaha, il potente cinghiale che può tenere in equilibrio il pianeta sulle corna, e Narasimha, l'uomo-leone, per infondere l'ordine nel suo mondo caotico.

Il primo nano Vamana è seguito dai grandi uomini dei miti: Parasurama, Rama e Hanuman – quest'ultimo è una scimmia saggia mentre gli altri non lo sono molto. È doloroso vedere Sita, la sua stupida figlia, soffrire, e Rani quasi distrugge il mondo intero per resettare il codice difettoso.

Di tutti gli avatar delle storie di Aama, la storia mitologica del suo popolo, il suo preferito è Krishna. È triste quando vede la morte di Krishna. Come Radha lo piange e attende l'arrivo di Buddha, colui che libererà la sua anima.

Lei vive queste vite, impara e cresce mentre attende il proprio ultimo ritorno nel mondo.

Centinaia e migliaia di anni devono passare prima che arrivi il momento di entrare nell'utero di sua madre.

Quando il mondo diventa di nuovo integro, c'è un equilibrio, tutta la vita coesiste in armonia perfetta.

Rani finalmente si riunisce con la sua famiglia su un pianeta simile alla Terra – stanno festeggiando assieme Dashain dopo tre anni. Si dà il caso che la scuola migliore di eliosismologia sia su Mercurio e viaggiare nello spazio non è veloce o conveniente come i film olografici vorrebbero farti credere.

"E adesso?" vuole sapere Papà. "Chhori?"

"Aama ha intenzione di andare a Kashi." Rani non riesce a nascondere l'eccitazione mentre si lecca le spezie della dita. C'è qualcosa che non è possibile stampare e far crescere sotto le luci artificiali: il montone fritto speziato di Mamma. "Andiamo anche noi."

"Dovresti venire," dice Mamma.

"Cercherò."

"Papà," dice Rani, "quand'è stata l'ultima volta che siamo andati da qualche parte assieme?"

"Ho una scadenza. Il progetto dell'arca è tutt'altro che concluso."

"Le stelle possono attendere!" dice Nonna con decisione. "Tu vieni."

Papà sa quando è con le spalle al muro.

"Non hai bisogno di credere a tutta la storia sacra degli dei per fare un bagno nel Gange," aggiunge Nonna. "L'acqua che attraversa Kashi ha qualità terapeutiche e rigeneranti." Non si dà la briga di essere precisa. "Magari può aggiungere un paio di anni alla vita di tua figlia?"

"Quando sarebbe questa visita di famiglia, se posso chiedere?"

"Questo fine settimana!"

È un preavviso troppo breve. "Non è possibile."

"Rendilo possibile."

Papà prova a strappare la carne dall'osso, ma è troppo distratto e l'osso cade sul tavolo.

"Va bene." Papà alza entrambe le mani. "Verrò."

"Sì, lo sappiamo." Nonna ride.

Presto tutta la famiglia sta ridendo assieme. Rani si rende conto di quanto ha sentito la mancanza di casa.

Rani promette a sé stessa di non perdere mai più un altro festeggiamento per Dashain, ma sa che non sarà in grado di mantenere la promessa. Un giorno partirà per le stelle all'esterno del sistema di Sol. Così fa quello che deve fare: si riempie il cuore con tutto questo amore e queste risate e spera di far durare questo momento per molte vite.

Gli occhi di Rani si inumidiscono al pensiero dell'inevitabile separazione. Quando Nonna le chiede cosa c'è che non va, Rani dice: "Non è niente... solo il peperoncino e le spezie."

Collegati

di Haris A. Durrani

traduzione di Francesca Secci

Haris A. Durrani è l'autore di Technologies of the Self. I suoi racconti sono apparsi su McSweeney's, Analog, Lightspeed, The Harvard Advocate, The Lifted Brow, e Mithila Review. È anche uno storico di giurisprudenza e scienza, e i suoi saggi e lavori accademici sono apparsi su Columbia Journal of Transnational Law, Quest: The History of Spaceflight, The Nation, e The New York Review of Science Fiction. Durrani si è abilitato alla professione legale presso la Facoltà di Legge della Columbia, ha ottenuto un master in Storia della Scienza presso l'Università di Cambridge, e una laurea in Fisica Applicata alla Columbia Engineering (Studi Mediorientali, Sud-asiatici e Africani come disciplina complementare). È attualmente dottorando al Dipartimento di Storia dell'Università di Princeton.

"Le intelligenze esterne, esplorando il Sistema Solare con vera imparzialità, sarebbero abbastanza inclini a inserire il Sole nei loro registri così: Stella X, classe spettrale G0, 4 pianeti più detriti." – Isaac Asimov

"I vizi della pace sono i vizi dei vecchi: sfiducia e prudenza. Deve essere così." – Principe Feisal, Lawrence d'Arabia.

Nel 1978, l'astrofisico della NASA Donald J. Kessler predisse che la quantità di satelliti artificiali in orbita intorno alla Terra avrebbe raggiunto un limite critico, dopo il quale le collisioni sarebbero state inevitabili. Un satellite ne avrebbe colpito un altro alle velocità pericolose dell'orbita terrestre (sette, otto kilometri al secondo) e i due si sarebbero frantumati in centinaia di pezzi. Questi pezzi sarebbero a loro volta entrati in collisione con altri satelliti, generando una reazione a catena di impatti e detriti. A un certo punto, propose Kessler, questo proiettile orbitante di spazzatura avrebbe reso i voli spaziali difficili, se non impossibili.

Charlie e Kalima ricevono la trasmissione alle 21.00. La loro nave-rifiuti si trova nelle vecchie orbite cimitero, e fluttua tra i satelliti smantellati pre-Kessler: quelli depositati solitamente lassù in orbita nei vent'anni precedenti, prima che il Consiglio di Sicurezza dell'ONU scoprisse che era una strategia inefficace che funzionava solo a breve termine perché era economica solo a breve termine.

Adesso è il lungo termine.

Charlie fa scendere la nave verso il mare di detriti che avvolge l'orbita intermedia sotto di loro. Il sole non ha ancora coperto questa parte di Terra, ma è proprio nell'angolo giusto in modo che la spazzatura orbitale brilli di luccichii gialli al di sopra del sottostante pianeta in ombra. Il mare di rifiuti scintilla come una città sconfinata che brilla nel momento più oscuro della notte.

"È una consegna aziendale" dice Charlie, con le mani sul pannello di controllo della sua sedia. È basso, tozzo, con grandi occhi ombrosi.

Kalima fa spallucce. I suoi capelli fluttuano intorno come anelli intorno a un pianeta, ma neri e fatti di ricci fluenti. Mentre la nave scende in picchiata, i riccioli si gettano dietro di lei come la parte finale della coda di una cometa oscura.

"E quindi?"

"Non mi piace."

"Al diavolo, ragazzone."

Charlie scuote la testa.

Attiva i campi magnetici esterni della nave, e un ronzio la fa tremare dall'esterno verso l'interno. Dispiega i blocchi di schiuma intorno alla rotta di volo dello shuttle; spumeggiano verso l'esterno con uno sfrigolio distante e viscoso. Più avanti, i detriti colpiscono la schiuma, ci passano attraverso a una velocità gestibile, e poi corrono incontro ai campi B della nave. I detriti si allontanano mentre i campi procedono facendosi strada, il bastone magnetico di Mosè che separa le acque di vuoto inquinato. Niente di antimagnetico rimbalza via mentre i compagni magnetici, che costituiscono la maggioranza della spazzatura, vi rimbalzano contro.

Diversi pezzi di detriti hanno slancio sufficiente da infrangere le difese, ma nel momento in cui quelle schegge raggiungono la fusoliera della nave, sono state rallentate al punto da non fare molto di più di un graffio. I frammenti più piccoli raggiungono le velocità maggiori: sufficientemente alte da vaporizzarsi nell'impatto. Tempestano i fianchi laminati di ferro della nave come frenetiche creature dei mari profondi che picchiettano contro un sottomarino.

Mentre Charlie manovra la nave tra la schiuma e le nuvole più spesse di spazzatura rimescolata, Kalima si lega i capelli in una crocchia. È forte abbastanza da muovere le braccia contro l'inerzia della nave verso la Terra, in avanti, in alto e intorno alla sua nuca. È una donna alta e snella, avvolta in una pelle color mogano.

Gli occhi di Charlie sono fissi in avanti, ma guarda furtivamente verso di lei. I suoi muscoli sono saldi ai controlli della sedia.

"Dovresti tagliarti i capelli, Kal. Regole di sicurezza."

"Lo so" sorride. "Nessuno ci guarda, giusto? Non gliene sbatte un cazzo. Siamo spazzini, Charlie. Nient'altro che spazzini."

Lui scuote la testa: "Immagino di sì."

"Siamo amici."

"Certo, Kal. Certo."

Lei finisce di legarsi i capelli e, lottando ancora con il movimento in avanti della nave, gli dà un pugno ben piazzato sulla spalla, poi fa un ampio sorriso.

"Chiedi alla NASA...be', non alla NASA. Non più." Si mordicchia il labbro inferiore. "Chiedi al Consiglio di Sicurezza. Chiedi alla Kradys. Te lo diranno, tra le righe. Ti diranno che cosa siamo noi per loro."

"Che cosa, Kal?"

Charlie dà gas alla nave attraverso il labirinto di detriti. La spazzatura qui è sparpagliata, è più sicuro passare. Può vedere la chiarezza dell'orbita bassa un chilometro più giù; sta diventando più piccolo lì, nonostante le Iniziative Kessler, nonostante il lavoro di Charlie e Kalima e tutto quello che gli altri spazzini fanno per la Kradys e il Consiglio di Sicurezza. I motivi sono meno umanitari delle trovate dei PR. Senza dubbio, la diplomazia nello spazio significa un sacco di cose, e dove c'è la diplomazia, c'è la guerra.

"Che cosa siamo noi per loro?" Charlie sta al gioco.

"Charlie, siamo pedine." Kalima ride freddamente.

L'ultimo chilometro passa in silenzio. Ascoltano le vibrazioni dei campi magnetici, i frammenti di detriti non deviati che piovono contro lo scafo, e lo stridore asmatico del supporto vitale che mantiene la pressione e ricicla l'O2. Il profumo di Kalima, palpabile e scuro come lo spazio vuoto, riempie il suo lato della cabina. Il sudore di Charlie puzza nell'aria filtrata.

Finalmente sono fuori dall'altra parte, oltre il tunnel di campo B delimitato di schiuma che la nave-rifiuti ha scavato tra i detriti. Dietro, la schiuma si separa in minuscole bilie di liquido. Le bilie scoppiano in un vapore quasi immateriale.

Charlie imposta la nave su un'orbita stabile sopra il satellite che sono stati inviati a smantellare manualmente. Spegne i campi B in modo che non interferiscano con l'attività extraveicolare.

"Ci siamo."

Lei fa spallucce: "Ma dai?"

Lo smantellamento manuale è un lavoro raro: di solito superfluo in un'epoca in cui tutti i satelliti sono inviati in orbita con collegamenti di Lorentz pronti all'uso per svolgersi una volta che la macchina non è più utile, trascinando il "satellite Zombie" nell'incendio atmosferico. I tether sono controllati via radio, ma sembra che questo Zombie sia così defunto da non rispondere agli imperativi wireless dalla terra.

Cosa che non accade quasi mai.

La nave si libra sopra il satellite sottostante: come due creature al loro primo incontro, che si scoprono l'una con l'altra per la prima volta, stando a una certa distanza. I pannelli solari dello Zombie si allungano obliquamente dai suoi fianchi, catturando i raggi di sole che si diffondono attorno allo spesso orizzonte della Terra. Antenne, boccaporti e gradini argentati punteggiano la fusoliera grigiastra, da cui minuscole lucine lampeggiano verdi e rosse come stelle distanti.

"Non lo so, Kal" dice Charlie alla fine.

"Col cazzo che non lo sai. Ci servono i soldi. Non aspetterò altri due anni qua fuori." Lo guarda. "Lo sai che ci servono i soldi."

Allunga la mano sotto il sedile. La sua mano riemerge con una confezione di Dr. Pepper. Apre l'estremità, picchietta fuori tre agitate bolle marroni, apre la bocca e tira fuori la lingua. Le inghiotte una per una.

"Kal" protesta Charlie, controllando la nave, armonizzando il ritmo con l'orbita del satellite sottostante.

"Starò bene, ragazzone." Si slaccia e fluttua verso l'uscita.

"Solo..."

"Eh?" Kalima si ferma.

"Rimani viva per il matrimonio."

"Lo farò." Si spinge di nuovo in avanti, sorride, si volta. "Io lo farò."

"Taci" controbatte Charlie mentre lei esce verso l'area di partenza. Lui muove la nave più vicino al satellite, preparando i bracci di aggancio. La sua bocca si apre, si chiude, e poi: "Sì, anch'io."

Vicino alla camera di equilibrio, Kalima riesce a sentire il suo bisbiglio riecheggiare nel comunicatore. Ridacchia al suo riflesso nell'EMU.

Si incontrarono per la prima volta il 9 agosto 2065 sul volo 604, quando una microscopica briciola di detrito si scagliò contro la testa di Rami Pasha. Si innamorarono al banchetto della commemorazione.

Il volo 604 era un lavoro standard da nave-rifiuti nella sicurezza relativa delle orbite cimitero. Il programma cimitero era stato così effimero che le collisioni erano rare là.

Quel satellite era un telescopio europeo dello spazio profondo di ventidue anni, uno Zombie con lamina d'oro per riflettere il calore che luccicava brillante sotto lo sguardo del sole. L'Agenzia Spaziale Europea voleva alcuni dati archiviati, oltre alla loro costosa e malridotta lamina d'oro, prima che gli spazzini delle Iniziative Kessler (Kalima, suo fratello Rami e Charlie) spedissero lo Zombie nell'incendio atmosferico.

Mentre Charlie agganciava la loro nave al satellite smantellato, Kalima e Rami indossarono le loro EMU, si allacciarono ai bracci meccanici della nave, e uscirono per l'attività extraveicolare. Kalima avviò i sistemi dello Zombie ed estrasse i dati, convogliandoli attraverso il suo cavo di sicurezza verso gli archivi della nave-rifiuti.

Rami si arrampicò dal suo braccio meccanico e andò piolo dopo piolo fino al tubo sporgente che dominava il corpo del telescopio europeo. Iniziò a rimuovere la lamina d'oro, la arrotolò, e la incollò pezzo a pezzo al suo braccio meccanico.

Una volta finito, passeggiò intorno alla mole dello Zombie con un rocchetto di collegamento di Lorentz incatenato alla sua cintura di utilità. Slegò il suo cavo di sicurezza – era troppo corto per l'arrampicata intorno a quel massiccio fossile di satellite – e disse che sarebbe andato dentro e fuori, senza difficoltà.

Andò sotto lo Zombie, aprì il rocchetto di collegamento di Lorentz e lo accese. Tutto quello che serviva al satellite era una spinta verso la Terra, qualcuno che srotolasse via radio il tether e, alla fine, si sarebbe disintegrato nell'atmosfera: un altro po' di spazzatura eliminata dal casino affollato che aveva intralciato l'attività orbitale, le missioni lunari e le esplorazioni esterne per tre decenni e mezzo.

Rami si fece strada all'indietro attorno alla pancia del satellite, spuntando alla curva, quando uno schiocco violento proruppe dal suo comunicatore.

Un ago rosso strisciò dalla parte anteriore del suo visore come una lunga freccia insanguinata. Era diretta in basso e a destra, e usciva da qualche parte vicino alla mandibola. Mentre il sangue colava via, le goccioline si ghiacciavano nel vuoto.

Un microscopico frammento di spazzatura, probabilmente un vagabondo proveniente dai distanti detriti dell'orbita mediana sottostante, aveva perforato il cranio di Rami Pasha.

A due metri di distanza, Kalima lo vide per prima. Fluttuava immobile, stringendosi leggermente a un piolo.

Charlie chiamò dalla nave, chiedendo spiegazioni per il ritardo, e si fermò.

"Torni nello shuttle, signorina Pasha" intimò. "Torni nello shuttle." Avrebbero potuto esserci altri detriti misteriosi.

In silenzio, Kalima si agganciò al suo braccio meccanico. Lo manovrò fino alla nave, guardando la tuta di Rami fluttuare verso i detriti dell'orbita mediana.

Charlie si allontanò dallo Zombie e spinse giù l'antico telescopio. La sua mandibola si serrò. I tendini nel suo avambraccio tiravano come cavi d'acciaio mentre controllava il passaggio della nave con movimenti rigidi e bruschi.

Una volta a distanza di sicurezza, impostò la modalità di crociera e spinse giù i tunnel della nave riavvolgendoli in reticoli e tubi labirintici.

Incontrò Kalima nella camera di equilibrio, dove fluttuava, raggomitolata, con gli occhi asciutti, vicino all'oblò. Charlie distolse lo sguardo. Avrebbe dovuto dispiegare la schiuma di sicurezza prima dell'attività extraveicolare, avrebbe dovuto renderla più sicura di quanto aveva pensato fosse necessario.

Lei era riuscita a slacciarsi l'EMU solo a metà. Fissava il corpo di suo fratello rivestito dalla tuta che cadeva nell'orbita mediana, dove i detriti iniziarono a farlo a pezzi. Si dimenava come un corpo affogato nel Rio delle Amazzoni, ridotto a brandelli come da un branco di piranha dagli occhi folli usciti da un film horror di serie B.

Quando finalmente il corpo uscì dall'altra parte nella lontananza oscurata dai detriti, non c'era nessun corpo di cui parlare: solo brandelli di carne e frammenti di materiale di tuta EMU, appena distinguibili nella foschia. Solo un altro turbine indefinito di detriti che ostruiva l'orbita terrestre.

Nel frattempo, anche lo Zombie era bersagliato dai detriti dell'orbita mediana. Arrivò dall'altra parte intatto anche se rovinato.

Charlie sfiorò un interruttore, e il cavo ruotò dal suo stomaco verso l'atmosfera, raccogliendo ioni. Le forze di Lorentz tirarono contro il moto orbitale dello Zombie, diminuendo la sua velocità finché, ore dopo, il telescopio smantellato dell'ESA avrebbe rimbalzato contro l'atmosfera terrestre, scivolando infine in un lento e fiammeggiante incendio che nei mesi seguenti avrebbe ridotto la macchina in cenere.

Il 16 gennaio 2003, lo Space Shuttle Columbia venne lanciato dal Kennedy Space Center per la missione STS-107. Ottantadue secondi e venti kilometri dopo il lancio, un pezzo di schiuma termoisolante della misura di una valigetta cadde dallo shuttle e perforò la sua ala sinistra a una velocità di mach 2,46.

Il Columbia completò 225 orbite e si diresse verso casa il 1° febbraio. Durante il rientro atmosferico, l'ala rotta si surriscaldò e si separò dallo shuttle, che poi si disintegrò sopra il Texas, senza lasciare superstiti.

Una foratura di non più di venticinque centimetri aveva distrutto 1,7 miliardi di dollari di tecnologia e sette vite.

Kalima è fuori dalla nave adesso. Sopra di lei c'è lo shuttle, e sopra ancora ci sono i detriti dell'orbita mediana che turbinano grigi e brillano nella sua coltre punteggiata di luce. È assicurata al braccio meccanico, e Charlie ha lo shuttle agganciato allo Zombie sottostante. Kalima spinge delicatamente il braccio in avanti. Si estende all'esterno tutt'intorno, come una scala antincendio.

La voce di Charlie le gracchia nelle orecchie. "Stai attenta, Kal. Siamo fuori dalla schiuma di sicurezza."

"Rilassati, ragazzone. Ho questo." Kalima si allunga in avanti dentro il casco e morde un pezzetto di Twix da sotto il mento. Mastica, ingoia, poi sorseggia la Dr. Pepper dal tubo. Niente di regolamentare.

Presto è quasi alla superficie elettronica dello Zombie.

"Più veloce, Kal."

"Ah-ah."

"Il nostro limite temporale è di un'ora." La sua voce è tesa.

Kalima raggiunge la superficie, apre il suo cavo di sicurezza e si slaccia dal braccio meccanico.

"Perché, secondo te?" chiede lei. "Ci daranno una valanga di soldi, giusto?"

"Cosa?"

"Non abbiamo mai un limite temporale, Charlie. A meno che non stiamo per essere mangiati da una montagna di merda."

Il respiro sibila nella radio. "L'Ammasso di Detriti Sartus è dietro l'angolo."

"Dietro l'angolo è un'ora e quaranta," dice Kalima, masticando il suo Twix. "Il nostro limite temporale è più breve."

"Quindi?"

"È qualcosa di segreto." Ridacchia. "Non vogliono che si sappia."

Il respiro di Charlie fa di nuovo gracchiare la radio. "Kal, sei pazza."

Lei sorride: "Lo so."

Si innamorarono al banchetto in memoria di suo fratello. Era uno strano tipo di amore, al limite.

Aspettavano in coda al buffet a New York. Un raduno internazionale. Completi scuri ovunque, e vestiti scuri come quello che indossava Kalima.

Agghindati con cravatte verdi e abiti marrone scuro, funzionari pakistani punteggiavano la folla, offrendo condoglianze a Kalima come ambasciatori dal suo paese natio. Militari del Pentagono si scambiavano sguardi imbarazzati, talvolta amichevoli, con questi uomini e donne dalla pelle scura che appena due decenni prima erano alleati: l'oleodotto centroasiatico lungo l'Afghanistan aveva cambiato tutto. Il Segretario della Difesa americano, che aveva stretto la mano a molti di queglti ufficiali vent'anni prima, aveva insistito perché la sicurezza li ammettesse nel Paese almeno questa volta. Il vicepresidente della Kradys Inc. guardava dalla sua sedia mentre i suoi analisti e i suoi direttori parlavano d'affari.

Charlie e Kalima erano uno dietro l'altro al buffet quando Kalima gli bussò sulla spalla.

"Ehi, signore," disse lei.

"Signor Monnagan," corresse Charlie, voltandosi.

"Ragazzone," sorrise lei.

"Charlie va bene, signorina Pasha." Lui sorrise, titubante.

"Ragazzone," disse lei di nuovo. Sorseggiò la sua lattina di Dr. Pepper. "Vuoi vedere un trucco?"

"Un...trucco?"

"Sì. Un trucco." Gli afferrò il polso. "Ti faccio vedere." Mise giù la bibita e afferrò un coltello dal tavolo. "Mai visto il film Aliens?"

"No?" Charlie la guardò di traverso. "Signorina, non penso..."

"Non pensare, ragazzone. Così va bene." Distese le dita di lui sulla tovaglia bianca. "Non muoverti di un centimetro."

Senza dare a Charlie il tempo di reagire, conficcò il coltello tra le dita, giù e su e di nuovo giù. Era metallo scintillante, le dita troppo scioccate per tremare, e gli occhi che fissavano tutt'intorno.

"È pericoloso, signorina Pasha," l'ammonì Charlie. "Signorina Pasha..."

Charlie si morse la lingua e allungò la mano libera per ghermire il polso di Kalima. Lei si fermò, sorridente, guardandolo mentre lui le sfilava il coltello dalle dita e lo metteva lontano sul tavolo.

Le mani di lei erano fredde e asciutte. Quelle di lui erano scivolose per il sudore.

La folla mormorò, poi tacque. Un ghigno sghembo si fece strada sulle labbra di Kalima. "È pericoloso," ripeté Charlie.

Lei ridacchiò.

La coda si mosse in avanti. La folla bisbigliò, si mosse in avanti, e tornò ai suoi sobri toni sommessi.

La bocca di Charlie si aprì, si chiuse, si riaprì. "Quindi."

Lei lo guardò.

"È passato un po'."

Lei socchiuse gli occhi.

"Com'è andata da quando... be' lo sa."

Kalima piegò la testa da una parte. Lo aggirò per afferrare un piatto. "Non so di cosa diavolo stai parlando," rispose.

Si portò la lattina alla bocca, inghiottì la Dr. Pepper che le colò sulla lingua, si leccò le labbra.

L'11 gennaio 2007, i Cinesi eseguirono con successo il primo test di un missile antisatellite dopo quello degli Stati Uniti del 1985. I militari cinesi inviarono un kinetic kill vehicle a otto kilometri al secondo contro uno dei loro stessi satelliti meteo 865 kilometri sopra la Terra. Il risultato furono 2.317 pezzi di detriti orbitali della misura di una pallina di golf o poco più: la più grande produzione di detriti per qualsiasi incidente registrato fino ad allora.

Mezz'ora dopo, Charlie riceve una chiamata. È cinese. Non ha bisogno di leggere la frequenza: può dirlo dall'inglese smorzato, come se uscisse da una grattugia. La trasmissione gli invade le cuffie.

"Junkship 0577. Junkship 0577. Qual è la vostra autorizzazione? Junkship 0577. Junkship 0577. Qual è la vostra autorizzazione?"

Charlie sbircia Kalima, che si sta arrampicando sulla superficie del satellite. Ha agganciato il cavo d'archivio nel sistema, che sta funzionando in maniera sorprendentemente liscia per uno Zombie.

"Kal."

"Eh?"

"C'è un problema."

"Be', risolvilo, ok?" La sua voce esce fuori esaltata, felice, persino. "Sono occupata." La sua EMU si libra sui pannelli di controllo manuale disposti lungo la fusoliera dello Zombie. Sta lavorando, ma a un passo tranquillo.

"Penso che sia militare," dice Charlie.

"Deeetto sì." La tuta di Kalima si gira. Il suo visore brilla nella cabina della nave, dove le mani di Charlie tremano sul pannello di controllo.

"Stai zitta."

"Lo farò." Saluta e si volta di nuovo verso il pannello di controllo manuale del satellite.

Il ricevitore gracchia. "Junkship 0577. Junkship 0577. Qual è la vostra autorizzazione? Junkship 0577. Junkship 0577. Qual è la vostra autorizzazione? Rispondete immediatamente"

"Oh, cavolo," dice Charlie.

"Rispondete immediatamente. Junkship 0577. Junksh..."

Afferra il ricevitore.

"Qui Junkship 0577." La sua voce gracchia come quella di una matricola delle superiori che si affacci all'adolescenza. "Siamo sotto l'autorizzazione internazionale dell'Iniziativa Kessler. Il Consiglio di Sicurezza dell'ONU ha stabilito di smantellare questo satellite."

"Smantellamento negato. Quale paese servite?"

Charlie si gratta la zazzera di capelli radi. Sta sudando.

"Signore..." tentenna. "Siamo internazionali."

C'è una pausa dall'altra parte. Sotto Kal digita veloce, cercando di accedere agli archivi dello Zombie per i dati che sono stati incaricati di salvare prima di distruggere il satellite.

"È strano," dice lei. "Non riesco a ottenere i dati che ci servono, anche con la password che ci ha fornito la Kradys. Cioè, sembra che possano aver trasmesso a terra qualsiasi dato volessero. Questo Zombie funziona abbastanza bene, sai..."

Il segnale cinese gorgoglia nel ricevitore di Charlie, e lui gli dà la priorità rispetto alla trasmissione di Kal. La voce gli si riversa nelle orecchie.

"Quale azienda servite?"

Esita. "Non siamo un'azienda."

"Queste sono trasmissioni internazionali, Junkship 0577."

E così, Charlie lo sa, c'è l'implicita minaccia: la frode è passibile di causa internazionale. O peggio.

"Siamo internazionali, senza personalità giuridica," risponde. "Se mi scusa un momento, dovremmo continuare il nostro lavoro." Charlie mette il ricevitore in attesa e si sintonizza su Kalima.

Lei sta ancora blaterando.

"Ehi, Charlie? Ehi! Non servirà a un cazzo, almeno non come aveva detto la Kradys. Penso che ci sia stato un programma recente in funzione, via radio..."

"Siamo sotto contratto, giusto?" la interrompe Charlie. "Non lo possiamo neanche ammettere?"

"Ehm. Già."

"È internazionale, sicuro, nessuna questione. Solido terreno morale, solido terreno legale. Solo la persona giuridica è tutto, giusto? Solo che non posso dirlo. Giusto, Kal? Giusto?"

"Siamo nella merda fino al collo, vero?"

Charlie annuisce, anche se sa che lei non può vederlo.

"Fantastico," dice Kal. "Ho sempre voluto essere nella merda fino al collo, sai? Non che non siamo sempre nella merda fino al collo, appesi quassù nell'ammasso di spazzatura di questo abisso orbitale." Ride. "È la cosa più fantastica..."

Charlie scuote la testa, interrompe la connessione e la apre alla trasmissione cinese. Sta ancora cicalando sul ricevitore della nave.

"Junkship 0577. Junkship 0577..."

"Sì?" La voce di Charlie è sommessa.

"Quel satellite non è stato autorizzato per lo smantellamento. Su questa violazione del codice internazionale di condotta, vorremmo che fosse chiaro che le nostre operazioni hanno il diritto di intraprendere ogni azione che riterremo necessaria a meno che le vostre operazioni non ottemperino alle nostre richieste. È chiaro?"

La nave-rifiuti avvia con un ruggito i suoi moduli di pressione di sistemi vitali e l'aria filtra nelle orecchie di Charlie. Sbatte il ricevitore. Non vuole parlare.

Questo satellite non è uno Zombie.

Sa che le loro armi monitorano i movimenti della sua nave. Se si rifiuta di osservare le richieste, la Cina lo considererà un atto di aggressione, distruggerà la nave di Charlie e, se necessario, dichiarerà guerra alla nazione o azienda – azienda, ovviamente – che ha finanziato il loro incarico. Ma se Charlie e Kalima non completano il loro incarico una volta arrivati così lontano, la Kradys li licenzierà, li rinchiuderà in prigione. Potrebbe persino ucciderli per eliminare i testimoni di qualsiasi cosa stia succedendo qui.

"Spara." Sblocca la frequenza di Kalima. "Kal."

"Cosa?" grida lei, mezza carica di furia, mezza carica di qualche oscura, eccitata energia snervante. "Mi hai tagliata fuori. C'è qualcosa in ballo, vero, ragazzone? Qualcosa in ballo."

Quarantacinque minuti dopo aver raggiunto il satellite, Kalima ha finalmente violato il suo sistema di controllo. È militare, le dice Charlie. È militare, e questo significa che è politico.

"Maledetta politica," dice lui. "Odio la politica. La odio da morire."

"Buon per te." Ride lei.

C'è un silenzio crepitante dall'altra parte.

"Ti ricordi il 2007?" dice Charlie alla fine. "I cinesi fecero esplodere un satellite meteo in orbita. Ricordi? Era oltre trentacinque anni fa."

"E?" Kalima armeggia con il sistema di controllo. Inizia a immettere i dati del satellite nell'archivio della scartonave.

"Lo faranno anche a noi. Missili, laser probabilmente, così è un po' più pulito. Ci uccideranno."

Sorseggia la sua Dr. Pepper. "No, non lo faranno. I detriti rovinerebbero il loro stesso satellite, e da come sembra, non è quello che vogliono, giusto? No."

Gonfia due bolle di soda e usa la lingua per spingersele di nuovo in bocca prima che impattino con l'interno del suo visore. Come rana e mosca.

"No," ripete. "Manderanno una vera nave. Una di quelle chiatte, gli enormi shuttle cinesi di cui si limitano a parlare, con la tecnologia segreta cinese che non rivelerebbero per tutto il petrolio saudita che possano ottenere. Ecco perché abbiamo un'ora. È il tempo che serve a uno di quei cosi per arrivare dalla parte oscura della luna all'orbita terrestre inferiore. Incredibilmente veloce, eh?"

Charlie è silenzioso dall'altra parte.

"Non hai controllato la provenienza della trasmissione, vero, Charlie?" Sogghigna.

La voce di lui le esplode nelle orecchie. "Si sta muovendo."

"Ma va'!"

Alle 16.56 UTC del 10 febbraio 2009, Iridium 33, un satellite funzionante della Iridium Communications Inc. e Kosmos-2252, uno Zombie russo defunto dal 1995, collisero a 11,7 km al secondo 789 km sopra la Siberia. La prima grande collisione accidentale tra due satelliti artificiali produsse 1.740 pezzi di detriti.

Charlie sta tremando.

Si protende verso l'alto. Apre il portello superiore.

Oltre, la nuvola di detriti dell'orbita media lo supera vorticando, controllata lì, anche se debolmente, da campi B sintetici, nanospazzatrici, spazzosonde, e il lavoro quotidiano di una nave-rifiuti occasionale come questa. In lontananza lungo la curva dell'atmosfera terrestre, una stazione spaziale brilla di rosso mentre assorbe energia dalla ionosfera e introduce corrente nei suoi serbatoi cinetico-magnetici.

Dietro l'orbita media ci sono stelle, quasi indistinguibili dalla spazzatura scintillante. Tra le stelle e la spazzatura, la luna ballonzola nel vuoto, pallida come la pelle di un marinaio annegato trascinato a terra. E tra la luna e l'orbita media una luce passa rumorosa come una stella cadente.

"Sto per morire," si dice. "Sto per morire..."

Kalima gli sta dicendo qualcosa, con una voce che viaggia e danza attraverso la radio. Lui guarda giù.

Lei ruota, ruota, ruota attraverso il vuoto come un bambino dell'asilo durante l'intervallo.

Il sole è quasi sorto, se questo ha senso nello spazio esterno. I detriti si illuminano di bagliori arancioni finché la totalità del cielo stellato sopra di lei brilla di una calda fiamma avvolgente. Il sole vomita un sopracciglio giallo-rossastro sul braccio blu della Terra.

"Chaaarrrlllliiieeee..." chiama Kalima. "Chaaarrrrllieeee..."

Afferra il suo cavo di sicurezza e ci ruota intorno, intorno e intorno.

"Salve lassù. Salllveeeee..." Ride da sola.

Dà un morso al suo Twix; lo sgranocchia tra i denti. Guarda i detriti sopra di lei e sorride.

"Weeeeeeee." Ruota nel vuoto, come un filo metallico arrotolato perpendicolare a un campo magnetico, che ruota sul suo asse lungo: un motore che funziona come sempre sui tre effetti dimensionali del flusso magnetico.

"Weeeeee."

C'è una stella cadente sopra. Una splendida, enorme stella cadente, e sta andando incontro a lei e Charlie e Rami, persi da qualche parte nei detriti infuocati dell'orbita media. Sta arrivando. Sta arrivando. Sta arrivando. Sta arrivando.

Il deputato del Congresso Dennis Kucinich presentò per la prima volta alla Camera dei Rappresentanti americana lo Space Preservation Act, che proibiva l'uso delle armi spaziali, il 2 ottobre 2001, in seguito alle richieste internazionali di un Trattato per la Difesa dello Spazio. Kucinich presentò il disegno di legge alla Camera quattro volte fino al 18 maggio 2005, ma lo Space Preservation Act non venne mai approvato.

Dentro, qualcosa scoppietta. Charlie urla dentro la radio. Sono già quarantacinque minuti che non riesce a chiamare la NASA. Non riesce a chiamare l'ONU. Non riesce a chiamare la Kradys. Nessuna comunicazione, c'è scritto nel contratto. Così nessuno può rintracciare la fonte.

Qualcosa si è incrinato, rotto, distrutto.

"Kal!" grida. "Kal, sei completamente uscita di testa?"

"Precisamente."

"Davvero? Davvero?"

Charlie riesce a sentire la fatica del suo stesso respiro, anche al di sopra dei motori della nave e le cuffie sulle sue orecchie. Il pannello di controllo fa bip, dicendogli che il download di Kalima dal sistema del satellite è completato.

Kalima non dice una parola per due minuti. Sta solo ruotando.

"Dai," dice alla fine. "Chiudiamo questa cosa." Sotto, smette di girare, si fissa al collegamento di Lorentz, e si arrampica sul fianco del satellite.

"Kal."

Nessuna risposta.

"Kal."

Niente. Continua a raccogliere le sue cose.

"Non facciamolo, okay? Non voglio qualcosa come prima, Kal. Non è sicuro. Per niente."

L'EMU di Kalima si gira, la sua superficie inondata del bagliore arancione riflesso dei detriti sopra di lei. Charlie si scherma gli occhi dalla luce accecante del visore di lei.

"Mi ami, Charlie?"

"Stai diventando romantica. Non diventare romantica. Odio quando..."

"Ehi. Rilassati, ragazzone."

Charlie scuote la testa. "No, Kal. No. Torna nella nave. Torniamo a casa."

"Cazzo, no."

Charlie si spinge contro il sedile. Le sue dita tremano mentre sistema l'imbracatura, preparandosi per... per che cosa? "Non voglio una cosa come prima, Kal. Non come..."

Può vedere Kalima che guarda verso di lui un'ultima volta. "Chiudi la bocca, Charlie. Chiudi quella dannata bocca. Tu non c'eri. Io sì. Era mio fratello, non il tuo."

La sua sagoma voluminosa si volta e si arrampica fino alla parte inferiore del satellite cinese, superando le stalagmiti metalliche sporgenti che sono senza dubbio missili, laser, telecamere e sistemi di sicurezza. È decisamente una sorta di satellite militare, ha finalmente capito Charlie.

"E a noi servono i soldi, Charlie. Non voglio invecchiare facendo l'esca per il resto della mia maledetta vita. È schiavitù a contratto, e tu lo sai."

Il suo ricevitore gracchia, poi si isola dal silenzio gemente della nave.

La trasmissione della chiatta cinese irrompe nelle orecchie di Charlie.

"Junkship 0577. Junkship 0577. Questo è l'ultimo avvertimento. Questo è l'ultimo avvertimento. Cessate subito le attività. Cessate subito le attività. Ci avviciniamo all'intercettazione."

Cinquanta minuti, dice l'orologio. Cinquanta minuti.

Kalima attacca il rocchetto del tether alla pancia del satellite. Lancia il tether, e questo si allontana. Sfiora la ionosfera un kilometro e mezzo sotto, accendendosi a un'estremità. Una corrente inizia a correre per il tether, che si illumina. Le forze di Lorentz iniziano il loro lavoro, rallentando il satellite, lasciando che la gravità terrestre lo attiri gradualmente.

Lei sorride e si guarda intorno. Passa un minuto. Legge la piastra accanto al pannello di controllo del tether. È in mandarino:

PAKISTAN – CINESE – RIFUGIATI: Stazione Zheng He

La sua faccia si contorce. Il suo aspetto è sempre stato una cosa costante, definibile, non importa quanto indefinibile, invisibile o evasiva sia la sua persona interiore. Ora il suo volto non nasconde nulla, e facendo così rimane nascosto. Diventa deformato, corrugato, teso: un'accozzaglia di nodi e pieghe complessi come l'entropia illimitata della Sindrome di Kessler. L'occhio non riesce mai a cogliere la sua vera natura, non può mai afferrare completamente cosa ci sia, come l'immagine di un dipinto frattale senza nessun segno di pennello visibile: solo una caratteristica sovrapposta a una caratteristica in un disordine così dettagliato da rimanere un caos amorfo.

Spinge il bottone sul petto della sua EMU. Il suo ricevitore si apre a Charlie. "Cambio di programma," dice.

"Cosa?"

"Cambio di programma."

"Mi stai uccidendo, Kal. Mi stai uccidendo."

"Lo so." Ride brevemente. "Questa è un'unità di protezione militare per i rifugiati pakistani nella Cina occidentale, nelle montagne. Dove davano loro la caccia gli Alleati Occidentali."

"Protezione per i terroristi, vuoi dire."

Lei ride. "Davvero non sai nulla di politica, vero?" Nessuna risposta. "Erano contadini. Non talebani. Tutti pensano che tutti siano gli spaventosi talebani. O Al-Qaeda. O qualsiasi altra cosa." Sorseggia la sua Dr. Pepper; ci vuole più tempo per sollevare il tubo stavolta. Quasi fuori. "Gli Alleati in realtà l'avevano fatto per quel maledetto oleodotto, comunque."

"Okay?"

"Quindi cambio di programma. Come ho detto. Non posso accettare che diecimila rifugiati soffrano per causa mia. Non lo farò. Non posso farlo."

"Kal…"

"Pensi che non rispetti il posto su cui mamma ha lasciato uscire me e Rami dalla sua maledetta fica? È il mio paese natale, Charlie."

"La Cina?"

"Già. La Cina. Giusto."

"Okay, Kal. Scusa, Kal. Solo non…"

"Sì, Charlie. Sì. Staccherai la nave da questo satellite, e ti allontanerai di un quarto di kilometro. Questa cosa salirà."

"Di che parli? Kal, non posso…"

"Fidati di me, ragazzone. Solo questa volta. È troppo difficile o prima mi devo uccidere? Dimmelo."

"Io…"

"Faccio quello che faccio. Addio, Charlie."

"Ma i soldi."

"Adesso ti preoccupi dei soldi?"

"Il contratto."

"Già. Il contratto. Sai cosa, Charlie? Fanculo il contratto." Ride, dà un ultimo morso al Twix, e spegne il ricevitore, questa volta per sempre.

Il Trattato per la Difesa dello Spazio fu riesumato nel 2029, oltre vent'anni dopo che il suo equivalente americano non era riuscito a passare alla Camera dei Rappresentanti. Il Trattato del 2029 seguiva la prima guerra extraplanetaria: una battaglia tra Stati Uniti e Cina, una nuova specie di guerra per delega in cui non è una nazione a finanziare gli insorti dell'altra, ma sono aziende e imprese private a finanziare nazioni per eseguire i loro ordini. Dopo la fine dei programmi di governo sugli shuttle e l'inizio dei noleggi privati di veicoli e stazioni aerospaziali, lo spazio esterno si è trasformato da una frontiera politica a una frontiera aziendale.

La guerra fu così dannosa in termini di vite, risorse economiche, e il prezzo post-bellico dei derivanti detriti spaziali così alto che improvvisamente il mondo volle la fine dell'effetto domino di raccolta della Sindrome di Kessler.

Con il nuovo Trattato del 2029, gli Zombie furono gettati nell'orbita più alta, l'orbita cimitero, per essere tolti di mezzo, almeno per il momento.

Cinquantatré minuti.

In alto, la nave cinese si apre un varco tra i detriti dell'orbita media come un rompighiaccio nell'acqua artica. La nave è enorme, della misura di una piccola stazione spaziale, e la sua superficie blu scuro guizza attraverso la luce emergente del sole.

Le trasmissioni continuano a riversarsi dalla chiatta cinese. "Junkship 0577. Junkship 0577. Ultima possibilità. Ultima possibilità. Cessate subito le attività. Cessate subito le attività..."

Charlie sbatte il ricevitore. Adesso è completamente tagliato fuori: da Kalima, dai cinesi, da tutti. Ha solo se stesso da ascoltare. Se stesso e il tonante lavorio meccanico della sua nave.

"Sto per morire," dice Charlie. "Sto per morire..."

Il collegamento di Lorentz brilla di arancione, elettrificato, dalla parte di Kalima. Il satellite trema.

Capisce che deve farlo da sola.

Quando arriveranno i cinesi sarà troppo tardi per spingere il satellite nella sua spirale discendente verso la Terra. Ritirare il tether non farà niente per disfare il danno che è stato fatto. Il satellite è già indirizzato lungo un sentiero gravitazionale verso l'incendio atmosferico. Se Charlie cercasse di arrestare il satellite con la nave, sarebbe una mossa pericolosa che metterebbe a rischio le loro vite e probabilmente non riuscirebbe neanche a portare il satellite in sicurezza.

Deve farlo da sola.

Senza nessuna significativa fonte di energia indipendente a portata di mano, Kalima stacca il cavo di sicurezza dalla sua EMU e lascia che la sua tuta vada a batteria. Mentre si tiene stretta al satellite con la mano sinistra e spinge il cavo di sicurezza in avanti con la destra, riesce a sentire la tensione diminuire mentre il suo cavo di sicurezza esce dalla nave, che è nascosta alla sua vista dalla mole bianca del satellite cinese.

Digrigna i denti, apre un pannello nell'unità di manutenzione del collegamento di Lorentz, fissa un adattatore e infila la spina del suo cavo di sicurezza nella presa di accesso.

Corrente convenzionale scorre dal suo cavo di sicurezza fino alla riserva energetica del satellite, fino al collegamento di Lorentz. Inverte il voltaggio, trascinando elettroni nel sistema tether. Con la differenza potenziale impostata nell'altro modo, il sistema si inverte.

Le forze magnetiche si invertono nel campo magnetico terrestre, la corrente del tether non più dipendente dagli ioni atmosferici ma dalla corrente forzata del campo elettromagnetico del cavo di sicurezza di fortuna di Kalima. Le forze di Lorentz puntano nella direzione opposta, accelerando il satellite verso l'alto.

Improvvisamente, l'intera macchina inizia a roteare in maniera vorticosa.

"Cazzo, no." Kalima trattiene l'impulso di sputare nella parte interiore del suo visore.

Il campo elettromagnetico che ha sostituito il suo cavo di sicurezza è troppo largo e il tempo di impulso tra la decelerazione e l'accelerazione troppo breve. Invece di limitarsi ad accelerare il satellite verso un'orbita più alta, le forze invertite sono abbastanza forti e veloci da fissare la macchina in una rotazione di 180°.

"Merda merda merda."

Kalima si morde la lingua, resiste e aspetta che il satellite acquisti il suo momento angolare. Se ritira il tether nell'angolo preciso lungo la sua rotazione, potrebbe ancora portarlo a un'orbita stabile.

Tutto quello che deve fare è aspettare.

Riesce a sentire gli ultimi minuti di vita su di lei, che turbinano scollegati nell'oscurità del vuoto. La sua energia riempie debolmente la vacuità dello spazio esterno, nel modo in cui la spazzatura spaziale si disperde nelle sue orbite caotiche.

È strano con quanta facilità si sia trascinato il cavo, quanto sia instabile. Un angolo troppo veloce, troppo acuto, per bruciare lentamente nell'atmosfera. Quanti Zombie hanno colpito il terreno? Quanti sono rimbalzati sull'atmosfera come un sasso sull'acqua? Quanto sono davvero efficaci i tether?

La mancata applicazione del Trattato per la Difesa Spaziale del 2029 provocò la ripresa globale della proliferazione delle armi spaziali finché il Consiglio di Sicurezza dell'ONU non lanciò le sue Iniziative Kessler nel 2034. Come nel 2029, anche le Iniziative seguirono un aumento dei combattimenti extraplanetari: stavolta una guerra mondiale multilaterale su larga scala al di sopra del territorio orbitale, con ogni azienda che finanziava il suo paese per proteggere la sua regione preferita dello spazio esterno.

Le Iniziative conclusero che i satelliti nelle orbite cimitero alla fine potevano cadere sulla Terra e, in ogni caso, diventare una minaccia ai voli spaziali. Le conseguenze finanziarie implicavano un prezzo che nessuno voleva pagare. Quindi il Consiglio di Sicurezza decise che i satelliti dovevano essere bruciati nell'atmosfera, non lasciati in orbita dove potevano alla fin fine creare ulteriore rischio negli anni a venire.

Il sudore fluttua davanti alla faccia di Charlie come saliva ghiacciata. Scuote la testa, e altro sudore si scrolla da lui come acqua da un cane. Le goccioline tremolano con il suo minuscolo riflesso distorto.

"Mannaggia a te, Kal," dice al canale vuoto. "Mannaggia."

Sgancia le braccia meccniche dai sistemi di arpionaggio del satellite e queste si ripiegano nella nave. Solo il lungo cavo grigio di sicurezza di Kalima collega la nave alla parte inferiore del satellite, curvandosi attorno alla sua fusoliera nel punto in cui è aggrappata Kalima, qualsiasi cosa stia facendo.

"Mi sto fidando di te, Kal. Capito? Mi sto fidando di te."

Le dita di Charlie afferrano i comandi. Stabilizza la nave lungo il satellite. I suoi occhi guizzano dai comandi al satellite alla nave cinese che si sposta attraverso i detriti sopra di lui, con la sua punta scura che spinge da parte i frammenti brulicanti come uno spazzaneve.

Improvvisamente il satellite sotto di lui inizia a girarsi, ruotando nel vuoto.

Kalima afferra i pioli del satellite. La chiatta cinese è qui, che incombe blu scuro dall'alto, gettando un'ombra sulla nave-rifiuti e sul satellite, bloccando qualsiasi frazione di sole abbia oltrepassato l'orizzonte grigio.

Il satellite tocca i novanta gradi. Inizia a decelerare.

Lei sta per vomitare.

I meccanismi di aggancio della chiatta hanno appena circondato la nave-rifiuti, che arretra sotto il gigante come un topo col gatto.

Kalima tiene i pioli con tutte le sue forze mentre il pezzo di metallo militare cinese ruota di 180 gradi come un'enorme palla da calcio deformata.

"Sei pazza," si dice. "Sei pazza, e lo sai. Completamente fuori di testa, Kal."

Il satellite cinese la spinge in avanti nel suo ampio e potente arco. La sua mano sinistra si stacca. Quella destra scivola contro la crescente inerzia di rotazione del satellite.

"Eccovelo," dice alla chiatta. "Comunisti bastardi, vi voglio tanto bene. Dopotutto vi sto salvando il culo." Guarda in basso. "Salvando il mio, il loro, in realtà. Laggiù."

L'Asia meridionale brilla di marrone e verde sotto di lei, appena visibile nello smog grigiastro degli scarti industriali, che procede verso le nuvole come la spazzatura spaziale verso l'orbita terrestre.

Diversi anni di dispute internazionali portarono alla costituzione di una piccola ma considerevole flotta di navi-rifiuti. La Kradys Inc., che emerse come l'azienda più remunerativa a seguito del suo successo nelle battaglie per procura della Terza Guerra Mondiale, era un produttore di collegamenti di Lorentz, e quindi fu il tether, più che il laser, la nanospazzatrice, o qualsiasi altro metodo, ad avere la maggiore priorità nelle Iniziative Kessler.

Dal 2039 in poi fu richiesto per mandato internazionale che ogni satellite fosse dotato di un tether. Anche se fosse stato possibile affrontare quella spesala spesa, nessun paese avrebbe approvato che venisse usata una tecnologia laser o missilistica per spingere verso il basso i satelliti; quelli erano metodi pericolosi e imprevedibili, dissero loro le corporazioni.

Entro l'anno 2040, concorrenti e nazioni, regni contro cui una volta valeva la pena per la Kradys di muovere guerra, si erano ridotti all'equivalente moderno di deboli alleanze ribelli che combattevano il trono ubiquo di un impero globale.

Sotto l'autorità della pace mondiale, i concetti di nazionalità, retaggio, confine e luogo avevano iniziato a dissolversi.

Stanno salendo a bordo della nave. Sono nella camera di equilibrio. Charlie la può sentire sibilare aperta e chiusa, lo scalpiccio, lo sbrigativo mandarino, un odore diverso nell'aria. Un sapore salato in bocca.

"Sto per morire..."

Sotto, Charlie può vedere Kalima appesa a una mano sola. Si protende in avanti, in lotta con la forza centripeta, e spinge il meccanismo di riavvolgimento del collegamento di Lorentz mentre il satellite raggiunge i 100 gradi. La terza legge di Newton regge bene, troppo bene, quindi la forza che lei esercita sul satellite è la forza che a sua volta il satellite esercita su di lei. Forze uguali e contrarie scuotono Kalima dal suo appiglio.

Fluttua scollegata nello spazio esterno, scagliata via lungo la velocità tangenziale all'arco del satellite.

La sua trasmissione lampeggia sul pannello dei comandi.

"Ehi. Charlie. Ho capito una cosa."

Lui chiude gli occhi.

"Hai mai visto uno Zombie bruciare del tutto?"

"No." Non sa cosa dire.

"Mai visto le statistiche per quelli che non lo fanno?"

Charlie apre gli occhi, capendo dove vuole arrivare, eppure non riesce a dire più di una parola: "No."

"I tether non hanno mai funzionato. Come abbiamo fatto a pensare che funzionassero? Si schiantano sulla Terra o deviano nello spazio profondo: è una merda per l'ingegneria. È tutto per fare scena. E spionaggio."

Charlie sta fissando il pannello di controllo.

Lei borbotta. "Ehi. Ragazzone..."

Ma i militari cinesi sono nella cabina, e strappano l'apparecchio dalle orecchie di Charlie. Sta piangendo.

"Con noi," dice il primo ufficiale, afferrando il braccio di Charlie e slacciandolo dal sedile. Indossano tute aderenti rosso scuro. Charlie si dimena come non ha mai fatto prima, divincolandosi in una crisi di furia inesauribile e rimorso trattenuto. Non è abbastanza forte da fare qualcosa se non raspare come un cervo ferito che barcolla, sanguinante, tra gli alberi.

Vede le cuffie che ancora lampeggiano verdi nella mano guantata del secondo ufficiale, strappa un braccio dalla stretta del primo uomo, e colpisce il comunicatore in modo che si apra verso la chiatta.

"Salvatela!" grida alle cuffie. Tengono di nuovo entrambe le sue braccia.

"Potete salvarla!"

Lo stanno trascinando via.

Fissa fuori dalla finestra. Nella periferia della visuale, la chiatta si libra, quasi ferma sopra la figura solitaria di Kalima come una nuvola antropomorfa trasportata vicino al puntino inanimato di un uccello nel cielo. La chiatta è rivolta nella sua direzione? Farà finta di nulla? Sotto, accanto a Kalima, il tether del satellite si ritrae come una lunga lingua rivolta all'interno. Mentre lo fa, la sua estremità, splendente di calore, sfiora la nave-rifiuti intanto che completa i suoi 180 gradi.

C'è abbastanza impulso da far ruotare la nave di Charlie.

Un forte stridio erutta dalla parte superiore della nave mentre i meccanismi di aggancio cinesi si rompono in corrispondenza dei giunti, il cavo di sicurezza improvvisato di Kalima si spezza, e la nave si strappa via dalla chiatta, roteando verso la Terra.

Gli ufficiali cinesi sono scaraventati contro il muro. Charlie stringe i braccioli del suo sedile, si allaccia la cintura, e chiude gli occhi mentre la nave scende in un movimento a spirale. Sobbalza quando collide con l'atmosfera. Apre gli occhi.

Gli oblò si inondano di rosso con l'ingresso nell'atmosfera.

Kalima si aggrappa al vuoto come il feto di un qualche utero cosmico. Nuota nello scuro liquido amniotico dello spazio esterno.

Il satellite cinese si eleva a un'orbita stabile, ruotando lentamente. La nave-rifiuti affonda nell'atmosfera.

Sorride. I suoi occhi vagano verso i detriti sopra di lei. I detriti le restituiscono lo sguardo con le loro brillanti ombre di luce.

"Guarda tutto questo," bisbiglia. "Ci piace farcela addosso, vero, signor Kessler? Sì, Kal. Sì, ci piace. Ce la facciamo addosso tutto il tempo. Un vero spasso, non crede?" Ride. "Non crede, signor Kessler?"

Kalima ha perso la presa sul satellite proprio nell'angolazione sbagliata, quindi adesso ci vorrà un po' prima che precipiti verso l'orbita media di detriti sopra di lei o venga attirata nell'incendio atmosferico. I razzi del suo jetpack non la trarranno in salvo. Probabilmente soffocherà prima ancora che qualcosa la laceri fisicamente o bruci il suo corpo a brandelli.

Ride di nuovo.

Sente sapore di sangue in bocca, e dentro l'EMU c'è come odore di cioccolata a dispetto del fatto che ha già mangiato il suo Twix. China il collo in avanti per sorseggiare la Dr. Pepper dal tubo, ma non ne è rimasta nulla.

La chiatta cinese si libra nel vicino orizzonte come un palloncino appuntito alla parata del Ringraziamento. Si chiede se le daranno una mano.

Il 6 giugno 2050, la Cina, la più potente nazione del mondo rimasta, lanciò nello spazio esterno un elettromagnete della misura di un grattacielo dalla parte oscura della luna. Era un atto di ribellione contro la Kradys e un atto di responsabilità per conto di una specie che aveva mummificato il suo pianeta terrestre con bende fatte di spazzatura.

Per decenni molti avevano proposto qualcosa di questo genere: la costruzione di un magnete così potente da pattugliare al di sopra della Terra e spazzare i detriti, molti dei quali erano magnetici, dentro la sua massa. Un aspirapolvere orbitante, per così dire.

Non appena la mietitrice magnetica entrò nell'orbita superiore, i cinesi accesero il loro elettromagnete. Iniziò a spazzare i cieli, accumulando spazzatura lungo il suo spesso lato esterno. Nel corso di trenta ore, il progetto funzionò in maniera impeccabile. La mietitrice riuscì a raccogliere un intero sesto dei detriti orbitali.

Nel terrore di quale nuovo piano, quale nuova cosa, avessero liberato i cinesi in orbita, il mondo intraprese un attacco a tutto campo contro la mietitrice. La Kradys lanciò i suoi sistemi di difesa. Aziende e nazioni indebolite lanciarono ogni missile antisatellite rimanente. Dopotutto, la mietitrice non stava raccogliendo solo detriti: stava distruggendo navi, stazioni e satelliti funzionanti.

Il mondo non si poteva fidare dei cinesi. Non si poteva fidare di nessuno, mai.

Così ci fu la guerra.

Quando centinaia e centinaia di missili antisatellite colpirono la mietitrice cinese, i missili e la mietitrice esplosero in un'innumerevole quantità di detriti. Dalla Terra, fu come guardare una stella nera diventare una supernova. La statistica ufficiale fu di due miliardi di pezzi tracciabili, ma la gente sapeva che erano di più. Quasi nulla in orbita in quel momento, macchina o umano, sopravvisse, e per dieci anni nessuno tranne i cinesi e le loro famigerate chiatte riuscirono a viaggiare da e verso la Terra.

Guerra, sfiducia e ostilità avevano trasformato lo spazio esterno in una frontiera insormontabile.

Charlie si sveglia nel Mare Arabico, circondato da acqua fredda e sporca che lambisce gli oblò. I paracaduti sono ammucchiati sulle onde in pieghe marroni. Si guarda intorno, distoglie lo sguardo. I due ufficiali cinesi sono stesi a terra. Il sangue ricopre le pareti e il pavimento.

"Merda," dice Charlie. Sputa fuori un dente.

Oltre queste acque inquinate, un motoscafo viaggia verso di lui. Mentre si fa strada tra le onde mutevoli, Charlie legge l'insegna blu in grassetto:

KRADYS INC.

La nave-rifiuti dondola nella culla violenta dell'oceano, come se Madre Natura volesse liberarsi di Charlie e del motoscafo e del sangue sulle pareti. Il cielo, come sempre, è di un grigio impenetrabile.

"Kal," mormora. Apre e chiude la bocca come un pesce, cercando di dire di più, ma non c'è nient'altro da dire.

Menti fortificate

di Kehkashan Khalid

traduzione di Francesca Secci

Kehkashan è un'artista visiva e scrittrice di Karachi. Non riesce a funzionare senza un senso di comunità o una tazza di caffè. Suoi racconti sono stati pubblicati e sono in uscita su Fantasy Magazine, Translunar Travellers Lounge, The Gollancz Book of South Asian Science Fiction Vol. II e Chiral Mad 5 e altrove. Attualmente vive a Jeddah, impegnata sul primo romanzo e trascorre il tempo con i suoi tre bambini piccoli cercando la calma in mezzo al caos. Potete vederla in azione su www.instagram.com/artworkbykehkashan

Dicembre 2040
IRACEMA.T Follower 0
Mi stavo oliando le giunture tra le dita, irrigidite dopo la mia faticata invernale dall'Empress Market al Thanvi Masjid Sardkhana, quando portarono dentro il corpo. PDall'eccitazione che fremeva dietro il cipiglio afflitto dei suoi portatori, capii che non era una sconosciuta. La depositarono sul tavolo di metallo e poi indugiarono sulla soglia mentre mi accingevo a lavorare con le dita d'acciaio. Mi voltai un po' in modo che la mia spalla ostacolasse i loro colli allungati. Grugnii persino di fastidio. Eppure, non si mossero. Alla fine, il più basso parlò:

"C'è la folla fuori in strada per lei!" La sua testa indicò il corpo sfracellato che giaceva sul mio tavolo. "Già, la polizia ha dovuto chiamare i rinforzi per tenere a bada la folla."

Guardai verso la ragazza il cui cervello fuoriusciva dal cranio: non doveva avere più di vent'anni.

"È Sherazade! La ragazza che è diventata virale cinque anni fa?"

La conoscevo. Le sue storie erano un balsamo lenitivo al termine delle mie giornate monotone. L'avevo seguita fin dal suo primissimo episodio, conoscendo frammenti della sua vita quotidiana, nascosta dietro l'avatar di un anime. Toccai l'impianto di acciaio sulla mia cartilagine: la mia Scheggia aveva il livello più alto di impostazioni di privacy. C'era una ragione per cui mi nascondevo in un seminterrato pieno di cadaveri. Nessuna ragione nobile o eroica: solo un incidente aereo debilitante sulle montagne a cui ero stato abbastanza sfortunato da sopravvivere, prima che le Schegge rendessero gli aerei obsoleti.

I detective che passarono all'obitorio più tardi quel giorno pensavano che fosse un suicidio accidentale.

"Ovviamente la sua Scheggia era disattivata, o avrebbe inondato la sua amigdala di BDNF e le sarebbe stato difficile saltare giù da quel tetto. Non c'è alcuna prova a suggerire che sia stata spinta."

Perché una ragazza carina, una stella nascente nel mondo della pubblicità digitale, aveva spento il suo dispositivo?

"Dobbiamo ancora scandagliare i suoi post per confermarlo."

"Posso farlo." Setacciare i ricordi di una persona normale? Fare finta di essere davvero vivo? Mi offrii volontario. Mi voltai verso di lui, con le dita metalliche ricoperte di viscere. Smorzò la sua Scheggia e, mentre lo schermo virtuale svaniva, ammiccò verso di me nella luce fioca. Poi si ritirò. Dopo gli arti esagerati e senza cicatrici del mio avatar anime, di sicuro ero un po' faticoso per la vista. Storsi la bocca e distolsi il mio sguardo da lui.

"Sarebbe davvero molto utile! Gran carico di casi in questo momento!" disse tutto contento il suo partner, rivolgendosi ancora al mio me virtuale.

Era deciso, dunque. Una volta etichettati e pesati tutti gli organi e restituiti i corpi non reclamati ai loro armadi, presi la scheda di memoria dalla Scheggia di Sherazade e la misi nella mia.

Marzo 2033
SHERAZADE FOLLOWER 0
Caro Diario,
non sarei triste se avessi soldi. Non me ne starei seduta qui, sul marmo freddo di questa fontana abbandonata da tempo senza speranza di riparazione, sprecando il mio tempo a scrivere su un vecchio diario quelli che Amma ritiene pensieri insipidi, perché tutti potremmo permetterci le Schegge. Amma attribuisce i

nostri problemi alla mancanza di gestione finanziaria di Abbu: Bhaia e io abbiamo imparato a memoria il monologo che lei sciorina nel momento in cui la pioggia inizia a colare dal nostro tetto decrepito. Ma non è quello che intendo. Non farebbe nessunissima differenza per me se i miei genitori diventassero milionari domani (come suona ridicolo!) dato che non mi darebbero mai il permesso di acquistare una Scheggia. No, quello che mi serve è del denaro mio.

Non posso fingere di capire il determinato antagonismo di Amma e Abbu verso gli impianti neurali che hanno incantato il mondo. Amma blatera di teorie complottistiche sulle grandi aziende che vogliono tracciare tutti i nostri movimenti, e Abbu si limita a dire che faranno cadere le persone da un burrone. Ma ovviamente questo non accade! I creatori dell'impianto hanno spiegato come le persone notino, e manifestino reazioni altamente sensibili alle ostruzioni spaziali dal momento che nessuno guarda più ciò che lo circonda.

Tutto quello che so è che sono stata costretta a studiare su antiquati libri di testo per tutta la vita, trovando sollievo con Alice mentre cadeva nella tana del coniglio o con la mia omonima mentre tesseva storie che la tenevano in vita, quando un singolo intervento in day hospital mi avrebbe garantito l'accesso a tutta la conoscenza (e gli amici) del mondo. Ho sentito che quando contatti altre persone attraverso la Scheggia, ti senti immerso nei loro corpi e nelle loro esperienze. Potrei stare in un parco divertimenti un minuto e poi cavalcare cammelli nel deserto in quello successivo!

Bhaia ci sta mettendo una vita a unirsi a me. Lavora in uno dei pochi call center rimasti in cui avere una Scheggia non è ancora un prerequisito. Ho esaurito la mia osservazione delle libellule che svolazzano intorno alle acque algali della fontana rotta. Ho persino pungolato gli coleotteri luccicanti che sgambettano tra le viti abbarbicate alla pietra. Grazie a dio, il sole ha smesso di incunearsi a bruciarmi il collo. Si è ritirato dietro il talwar che si libra nel cielo come una divinità serena, connettendo i punti tra gli impianti di tutti. Ci sono forme diverse che governano ogni città. A Karachi abbiamo una lama color ametista.

È strano. C'è un'altra persona qui che non è persa nel mondo virtuale della sua Scheggia. Indossa un berretto da baseball e ha la pelle color cannella. E guarda dritto verso di me. Tentenno a disagio mentre lui si avvicina, con il bordo della fontana che improvvisamente sembra conficcarsi nelle mie gambe.

"Stai guardando il Poligono" osserva.

"Poligono." Fisso la lama notando la sua superficie tassellata per la prima volta.

"Non hai una Scheggia?" Indica il mio orecchio nudo. Scuoto la testa, accigliandomi. Lui sogghigna alla mia espressione mesta.

"E se te ne procurassi una?"

"I miei genitori sclererebbero." Alzo gli occhi al cielo.

"Conosco qualcuno che ha accesso all'upgrade. Non è chiaramente visibile, intendo, a meno che non ti radi la testa." Sogghigna.

Lo seguo in Burns road, le vestigia di un'era remota. Aspettiamo all'esterno di un tetro rivenditore di bunkebab decorato con una stringa di lampadine rotte. Mi ricorda tutte le storie della sua infanzia che Dadi mi ha raccontato: vivere in appartamenti affollati, e far dondolare le gambe tra le sbarre del balcone per guardare corpi bloccati in danze infinite sotto sgargianti lampadine colorate, ascoltando la cacofonia eterna di un mercato insonne. Scommetto che in un mondo così vivere senza Scheggia era sopportabile. Poi un uomo con un gran pancione emerge da dietro il bancone sudicio e mi fa cenno di avanzare come se mi stesse per fare qualcosa di semplice come un nuovo piercing.

Aprile 2033
SHERAZADE Follower 10
Surreale. Quando mi concentro il mondo diventa scuro, come la distesa dietro le palpebre chiuse, intessuto con strane forme luminose quasi che stessi camminando in una caverna con fauna fluorescente appiccicata ai muri. Le stelle fluttuano in mezzo alle tenebre. Punti di luce, come se la caverna fosse riempita di lucciole. Qualcuna più grande, più evidente delle altre. Devono essere altre persone – altri mondi. Do un'occhiata al soffitto e vedo una serie di pulsanti che attendono un mio comando. Voglio controllare l'e-mail, scaricare un'app, navigare sul web, o trasmettere questo pensiero? Nego tutto e vado avanti.

So che il mio corpo è fermo ma mi sento sfrecciare oltre le lucciole. Mi sporgo e ne tocco una con la mente. Lampeggia e si espande.

Mi trovo nel mezzo di un appartamento minimalista, con la finestra che dà su un oceano scintillante alla luce del sole. Zeeshan, il ragazzo che mi ha dato la mia Scheggia, la mia guida in questo nuovo mondo strano, è seduto su uno sgabello di pelle a cullare un oud. Una ciocca di capelli gli ricade sulla fronte mentre strimpella una dolce melodia.

"Che cosa aspetti? Carica i tuoi pensieri! Esplora il mondo!" Il suo inglese ha un forte accento, come se ogni vocale fosse spezzata in due. Muove le mani in maniera esagerata per mandarmi via.

"Aspetta, non capisco, perché faresti questo per me?"

"E ti viene in mente adesso? Dopo aver firmato il contratto e installato un dispositivo nella tua testa?"

Sono arrossita. Era vero. Se era una truffa, ero il bersaglio più accondiscendente di sempre.

"Guarda, ti dirò la verità, okay?" Cammina verso di me, con gli occhi nocciola che fissano i miei banali occhi neri. Sento il mio cuore che sobbalza un po'.

"È una Scheggia sperimentale. Prendo una commissione se convinco le persone a provarla."

Qualsiasi potenziale di una relazione romantica è perduto quando tiro indietro la mano e lo schiaffeggio.

Maggio 2033
SHERAZADE Follower 10

Va tutto bene, davvero. Sperimentale o no, questa Scheggia funziona come tutte le altre. Ce l'ho da un mese e, visto che non la uso molto, non ha causato nessun problema. Il mio primo ordine del giorno era caricare il mio diario precedente nel cloud. Molto più facile raccogliere tutti i miei pensieri in un posto solo. Poi, ho caricato un post introduttivo. Se fai queste cose bene ho sentito che puoi ottenere un gran seguito, e questo apre le porte al denaro.

Ciao, sono Sherazade Amadi. Ecco tre cose che non sai di me:

1. Mio padre ama i testi antichi e mi ha dato il nome di una famosa narratrice che impediva la sua stessa decapitazione ammaliando il Re con le sue storie.

2. (Sono nervosa. Se Amma mi vede bighellonare nell'aiuola sospetterà qualcosa. Come posso sembrare naturale?) Ho quindici anni e sono una delle poche persone che sfoggia l'ultima versione della Scheggia.

3. Vivo a Karachi. Resta nei paraggi se vuoi vedere qualcosa in più della città e sentire le mie storie che mi piace pensare siano interessanti come quelle della mia omonima.

Oh, merda. Non mi ero accorta che la Scheggia avrebbe caricato i pensieri superficiali che ho avuto nel mezzo della mia introduzione. Sono così mortificata! Mi sono resa ridicola! Che cosa penserà la gente? Ho una vita così patetica che non posso neanche restare nell'aiuola fuori dalla mia casa senza temere l'ira dei miei genitori?

Maggio 2033
SHERAZADE Follower 8000
Sempre più curioso. Sembra che abbia avuto un impatto. Ho appena detto ad Amma che sarei andata a comprare lo yogurt al DoodhWala all'angolo (lei aborre le consegne coi droni) solo per la possibilità di sfuggire ai suoi occhi vigili. Ora sono qui in piedi con la schiena contro il solo muro del nostro quartiere che non esibisca graffiti volgari, e rispondo a un numero crescente di follower. Posso scorrere le loro forme, zoomare i loro volti, leggere le loro espressioni. Molti di loro hanno gli occhi socchiusi mentre sorridono con indulgenza verso la mia onestà involontaria. Mi chiamano fresca, e senza filtri, e autentica. È emozionante. Alcuni di loro si accigliano, perché pensano che fosse un tentativo deliberato di sembrare vulnerabile. E sia. E poi, proprio in fondo, dove li noto appena finché non mi concentro davvero, c'è un'orda di volti indifferenti. Non so cosa stiano pensando, o perché siano lì. Sembrano così... disinteressati. Così vuoti e inespressivi. Come teste identiche dipinte su una tela bianca. Perché seguirmi se non siete decisi a essere coinvolti? Ma non mi lamento. Per un'influencer in crescita, i numeri contano sicuramente.

Dicembre 2033
SHERAZADE Follower 20k
Carissimi follower,
dovete sapere quanto vi stimo. Mi avete cambiato la vita. Non devo più risparmiare ed elemosinare eidi per cinque anni per riuscire a comprarmi uno stereo. Ora ho le aziende che mi mandano ogni sorta di oggetti e oggettini (devo intercettare il drone all'angolo della strada per evitare che Amma lo becchi!) così posso postare recensioni sincere a vostro vantaggio. E ho un paio di partner incredibili che annuncerò presto. Cliccate sul mio conto alla rovescia per avere aggiornamenti! Ed è tutto perché voi, amati follower, siete un uditorio così sensibile per le mie sciocche storielle. Ma prima che continui con una storia, devo fare un piccolo stacco pubblicitario. State con me.

[Spot] Se hai figli, o se non ti sei mai liberato del tuo bambino interiore come me, devi sapere come le lampade lava ispirano l'immaginazione. Un caleidoscopio di oggetti (a tua scelta!) che fluttuano nel vetro oblungo. Scegli i tuoi personaggi, colori o scene preferiti e costruisci una lampada che accenderà la stanza con la tua personalità. Clicca sul link per fare un ordine, e usa il mio codice SHE10 per uno sconto!

Grazie per essere rimasti con me. Vi prometto che quelle lampade lava non vi deluderanno. Sto fissando la mia proprio ora, mentre inizio questa storia. Ovviamente, la mia è una versione interamente personalizzata, con Sherazade su un tappeto volante circondata da pennacchi di nebbia che sostengono bottiglie di geni, eucalipti e palme da datteri, e sudditi reali che portano rotoli di pergamena. È... incantevole.

LA STORIA DELL'UOMO CHE CADDE E DELLA SUA RICOMPENSA

C'era una volta un derviscio, un uomo di dio, che viveva accanto a un uomo che lo invidiava. Questo vicino stava alla finestra e guardava, con l'invidia bruciante nei suoi occhi pazzi, mentre persone giunte da tutta la città porgevano i loro rispetti al derviscio e cercavano il suo aiuto. Un giorno, con un cappuccio e un mantello, si infilò nella coda di persone che aspettavano l'attenzione derviscio e, quando ebbe l'uomo tutto per sé, lo colpì sulla testa. Coprì il corpo prono con il suo mantello, lo trascinò fino a un pozzo abbandonato lì vicino e lo gettò dentro. Così, contento, avendo estinto il fuoco dell'invidia nel suo cuore, se ne tornò a casa.

Il derviscio non morì, perché non colpì mai il fondo del pozzo. I pozzi abbandonati sono buoni rifugi per i geni, che uscirono e lo afferrarono prima che il suo corpo si sfracellasse contro i mattoni. Cullarono il suo corpo semincosciente e gli parlarono del Sultano che cercava una cura per sua figlia: era vittima di un incantesimo operato dal figlio di uno stregone. La cura, disse il genio, era semplice: strappa sette peli bianchi dalla coda di un gatto e bruciali come incenso in modo che la principessa ne respiri i fumi. Quando il derviscio aprì gli occhi, non trovò nessun genio, ma solo un buco nel muro del pozzo da cui strisciò via e ritornò a casa per la gioia dei suoi discepoli.

Ovviamente, il Sultano gli fece visita più tardi quel giorno, pregandolo di curare la sua figlia innamorata. In un attimo, il derviscio staccò sette peli dalla coda del suo gatto e li bruciò in un piatto piano. Nel momento in cui i fumi raggiunsero la principessa lei si guardò intorno sorpresa e chiese di suo padre. Colmo di gioia, il Sultano proclamò che il derviscio meritava di essere suo genero. E così, il derviscio divenne il principe ereditario e più tardi, dopo la morte di suo suocero, divenne il Sultano.

Un giorno, fuori su una portantina accanto alla sua regina, osservando lo stato della sua città natale, vide l'uomo che una volta l'aveva invidiato e l'aveva gettato nel pozzo che si spostava tra la folla. Il derviscio bisbigliò ai suoi uomini di prendere mille monete d'oro dal tesoro reale e di consegnarle all'invidioso.

La Sherazade originale vi direbbe che la morale della storia è la seguente: il derviscio era così buono e gentile non solo da perdonare l'uomo invidioso ma pure da ricompensarlo. Invece secondi me il racconto dimostra soltanto che gli uomini, anche dopo atti spregevoli, si sostengono e si ricompensano a vicenda mentre noi donne ci avventiamo l'una contro l'altra al minimo cenno di dissenso, istigate dagli stessi uomini che si danno l'un l'altro monete d'oro.

Gennaio 2034
SHERAZADE Follower 100k

Ormai l'ho fatto. Vengo attaccata da ogni parte. Le donne mi mandano messaggi di solidarietà, o disprezzo perché penso così male del mio stesso sesso. Gli uomini mi mandano minacce di morte appena velate. Amma mi sta rimproverando perché uso troppa acqua e non sto lavorando quest'impasto a dovere.

Ma non va così male. La mia popolarità sta aumentando in maniera strabiliante. Ho ricevuto mail da cinque diverse aziende di PR, vorrebbero che promuovessi i loro marchi. C'è speranza (e denaro) all'orizzonte, se me la gioco bene.

Da parte mia, sto continuando con storie ordinarie della mia vita quotidiana finché tutto questo passerà e potrò gestire un altro momento virale. Certo, meno persone sono interessate a cose noiose come il pane lavorato male, ma non si può essere sempre sensazionali! Devo bilanciare l'ordinario con lo straordinario se voglio essere vista come autentica.

Oggi, quando facevo una diretta fuori vicino alle aiuole, guardando le piccole icone comparire e scomparire mentre le persone entravano e uscivano, ho visto una donna che mi guardava. È stato un po' snervante. La maggior parte delle persone se ne vanno dopo aver fatto le loro domande, o quando perdono interesse, ma lei è rimasta tutto il tempo. La cosa più strana è che io non posso vedere il suo vero sé. Lei (o lui, o chiunque sia) sembra la donna anime con le braccia artificiali di una di quelle serie TV di Netflix. Questo mi ha dato la certezza assoluta che il suo vero sé era radicalmente diverso. Forse si trattava di un quarantenne pervertito che spia le donne più giovani. Eppure... quando i nostri occhi si sono incontrati penso di averla vista implorare la mia empatia. E non mi sono decisa a bloccarla.

Dicembre 2040
IRACEMA. T Follower 0

Fu strano vedermi attraverso gli occhi di un'altra: anche se ero nascosto dietro un avatar, le espressioni facciali erano le mie. Io... ho sentito una fitta di qualcosa simile al rimpianto, per non aver avuto il coraggio di affrontarla come me stesso. Mi sarebbe piaciuto conoscerla nella vita reale.

Oggi ho esaminato il suo cervello e i test che ho eseguito mi hanno mostrato qualcosa di interessante. La Scheggia dipende dalla stimolazione di fattori neurotrofici di origine cerebrale per acuire l'avversione dell'utente al rischio (è ciò che ci impedisce di infilarci alla cieca nel pericolo) e un aumento nei livelli di BDNF chiama dei droni che ti afferrano se fai un passo falso, diciamo, nella tromba vuota di un ascensore. È questa stessa proteina che agisce come antidepressivo, in caso di cyberbullismo o quando gli utenti affrontano crisi di astinenza per aver abbassato la comunicazione con la loro Scheggia troppo a lungo, per impedire pensieri autolesionistici. Il cervello di Sherazade mostrava livelli minori di BDNF se paragonato ad altri cervelli nel periodo di tempo dal suo decesso. Non sei stata spinta, Sherazade, ma sei stata sicuramente uccisa.

Le luci colorate fuori dal negozio di bunkebab continuano a non funzionare. Mi guardo attorno e non riesco a vedere i corpi ondeggianti e il mercato vivace che ha visto Sherazade. Tutto quello che vedo sono appartamenti sovraffollati. L'uomo col pancione dietro il banco mi lancia uno sguardo sospettoso mentre dà il benvenuto a un'altra vittima portata dalla sua esca color cannella. Poi Zeeshan si volta. Non indietreggia. Anzi, cda venditore spietato qual è, sorride radioso e inizia a camminare verso di me. Io riattivo la mia Scheggia e cerco l'app della radio della polizia.

Marzo 2034
SHERAZADE Follower 200k
Correnti di dolore scorrono nella mia testa. Sbatterei la testa sul muro se servisse a fermarle. La cosa peggiore è che non posso neanche chiedere ad Amma gli antidolorifici: mi domanderebbe sicuramente perché ne ho bisogno. Sembra che ci sia un aggiornamento essenziale da scaricare nelle nostre schegge sperimentali stanotte. Ho controllato una marea di recensioni sui download, e nessuna di loro riferisce di qualche fastidio!

C'è un nuovo tasto ai bordi del mio campo visivo oggi. Vengo distratta da questo e dalla recita stonata del Corano da parte di Amma in sottofondo. Faccio visita a Zeeshan, ignorando come si schermi la faccia mentre mi avvicino. Gli dico del tasto. È della forma di un martelletto, che dondola avanti e indietro se ci si avvicina. Scuote la testa per indicare che lui non possiede un bottone del genere. Batto i piedi per dargli un ultimo, soddisfacente spavento e me ne vado.

Il martelletto sfida ogni spiegazione e rifiuta di andarsene. Non c'è niente da fare se non raccontare un'altra storia.

LA STORIA DELLA DONNA CHE VOLEVA UNA MELA

Una volta, tanto tempo fa, un Califfo vagabondava per le strade del suo impero quando si imbatté in un baule chiuso. Aprendolo, scoprì il corpo di una donna così bianca da brillare alla luce della luna. Era stata fatta a pezzi e chiusa nel baule. Il Califfo si sentì scosso e pianse la perdita di questa donna bellissima. Immediatamente, inviò i suoi uomini a trovare l'autore di quel crimine.

Presto, trascinarono alla corte del Califfo un mercante che pianse mentre confessava l'omicidio. Il Califfo, vedendo l'afflizione dell'uomo, chiese di sapere l'intera storia. Questo è ciò che l'uomo gli raccontò.

La donna a pezzi era sua moglie, che lui amava con tutto il cuore. Si era ammalata e l'aveva pregato di procurarle delle mele e lui aveva viaggiato oltre confine per trovare tre delle mele più dolci per lei, come non se ne potevano trovare in tutta la città. L'aveva lasciata a casa con le mele ed era tornato al suo negozio quando un uomo era passato di lì, lanciando per aria proprio una di quelle stesse mele. Meravigliato, il mercante aveva fermato l'uomo e gli aveva chiesto dove l'avesse presa. L'uomo dichiarò che gli era stata donata dalla sua amata, che le aveva ricevute da suo marito perché era malata.

Infuriato, l'uomo tornò a casa e chiese a sua moglie di dirgli dove fosse la terza mela. Lei confessò che non lo sapeva, e con rabbia, lui si scagliò su di lei, facendola a pezzi. Il Califfo singhiozzò mentre sentiva la storia e dichiarò che non poteva punire l'uomo: semplicem ente era stato tanto ingannato! Il vero colpevole era l'uomo al mercato che aveva detto una menzogna di tale portata. Chiese che l'uomo del mercato fosse trovato e portato davanti a lui.

Quando l'uomo del mercato fu gettato ai piedi del Califfo, questi pianse il suo pentimento. Disse che aveva detto solo una bugia innocente. Aveva rubato la mela da un bambino fuori dalla casa del mercante, e il bambino lo aveva pregato di restituirla dato che il padre aveva portato la mela a casa per la loro madre malata. Come potevo, disse l'uomo del mercato, sapere che la mia bugia avrebbe avuto tali conseguenze?

Il Califfo non ribatté e così decise che nessuno era da biasimare e lasciò andare entrambi gli uomini. La morale di questa storia è che solo le donne devono pagare per i crimini degli uomini.

Maggio 2034
SHERAZADE Follower 500k
Adesso capisco a cosa serve il martelletto. Passo mezza mattinata acquattata nell'ufficio buio di Abbu mentre lui batte su un antiquato portatile, circondato da pile di carta, facendo conoscenza intima con le ripercussioni del martelletto. Quando un numero sufficiente di persone lo premono per riempire il piccolo contatore accanto a esso, suscita un dolore lancinante alla mia testa per notificarmi che il mio post è stato disapprovato. Mi dà un giorno per ritrattare qualsiasi cosa stia provocando offesa, e poi le persone possono premerlo di nuovo, ricominciando la mia tortura da capo. Mi rifiuto di cambiare qualsiasi parte della mia storia. Mi rifiuto assolutamente.

Amma e io abbiamo appena avuto un bisticcio tremendo. Ha dichiarato che sono la figlia più ribelle e ingrata che abbia mai disonorato la terra. Ho detto che non ha idea dello stress che affronto ogni giorno! E ovviamente non ce l'ha. Non le ho ancora detto della Scheggia. Poi mi sono ritirata nella mia camera e ho pianto per l'ultima mezz'ora, stanca del dolore, e stanca degli odiosi troll che mi logorano con i loro commenti sul mio aspetto e il mio genere. Ciò che è peggio è che sono costretta ad ammettere che hanno ragione quando mi alzo e mi guardo allo specchio. Ho sporgenze indecenti vicino alle anche e alla pancia, e i miei seni sono decisamente cascanti e inguardabili. Chiudo gli occhi e compare il loro ultimo commento.

"Se fossi fatta a pezzi e chiusa in un baule, nessun uomo piangerebbe la tua perdita."

Giugno 2034
SHERAZADE Follower 550k
Non così cari follower,

ci ho pensato un sacco (ho sicuramente avuto poca scelta in proposito) e sono qui per ritrattare alcune parti della mia storia. Non era affatto una donna quella chiusa in un baule! Ma il marito dell'uomo. Perciò, il crimine è stato commesso da un uomo a un uomo, e non c'è alcun bisogno che nessuno di voi si senta in alcun modo offeso.

Non credo che le mie scuse abbiano aiutato. Hanno solo reso le cose peggiori. Penso che adesso le persone mi chiamino blasfema. E questa è un'accusa davvero pericolosa da rivolgere in questo Paese. Lo ammetto, ho paura di uscire di casa. E dato che Amma mi guarda solo per rimproverarmi, mi sono di nuovo infilata qui nell'ufficio di Abbu. È qui che ho fatto la mia piccola annotazione di scuse, in realtà. Proprio davanti allo schermo del portatile di Abbu.

Caro Diario,
è successa una cosa terribile. Le mie lacrime sbavano l'inchiostro mentre scrivo. Hanno portato via Abbu. È stata l'immagine che ho postato prima e che mostrava una chiara visuale dello schermo del computer di Abbu. Qualcuno ha segnato i numeri e ha premuto il martelletto. Le notifiche sono diventate virali e presto il Federal Board of Revenue è arrivato alla nostra porta. Abbu ha manipolato le cifre delle tasse, ha cercato di spiegarci mentre lo trascinavano attraverso la porta. Qualcosa sul fatto che è una pratica comune. Riuscivo a malapena a sentirlo sopra gli strilli di disperazione di Amma e le discussioni di Bhaia con gli ufficiali del ministero. Mi sono ritirata nella mia stanza il più velocemente possibile. Ho passato quindici minuti a tirare la Scheggia incastrata nella mia testa, finché non ha iniziato a fare rumori sibilanti e la materia cerebrale ha minacciato di uscire con essa. Posso sopportare le persone ignoranti che sparlano di me. Ma essere il motivo per cui il mio stesso padre va in prigione... sto disattivando la Scheggia. Non userò mai più questa stupida Scheggia.

Dicembre 2040
SHERAZADE Follower 1M
Ho davvero detto che non l'avrei mai più usata? Sto rileggendo quella vecchia pagina di diario, l'ho caricata qui, appena dopo che Abbu era stato portato in prigione, e ho trovato un po' ridicolo di avere biasimato un dispositivo per i miei problemi. Se dovessi

biasimare qualcuno, credo che dovrei biasimare la mia famiglia. Se Amma fosse riuscita a smettere di agitarsi per almeno un minuto, non mi sarei dovuta nascondere in luoghi umidi per registrare i miei post! E poi avremmo potuto tutti vivere qui in questo appartamento meraviglioso sul mare, invece che litigare tra noi. In ogni caso, disattivare la Scheggia è impensabile! (È terribile vivere senza la Scheggia, come vedere il mondo in monocromia. La solitudine è immensa.) Il mio reddito dipende da essa. Ed è il solo posto dove posso trovare sostenitori entusiasti per il mio lavoro. Sono una narratrice. Non ho alcun senso senza un pubblico.

Sono un po' triste che Amma si sia rifiutata di raggiungermi qui? Sono un po' ferita che mi urli parolacce invece che lodare il mio successo? Certamente. Ma immagino che non si possa avere tutto.

[Spot] Questa influencer emergente non ha bisogno di presentazione. Tutti noi conosciamo Sherazade, le cui storie ci incoraggiano a scrivere le nostre! Spero che la collezione estiva che abbiamo lanciato in collaborazione con lei ispiri la vostra immaginazione!

È divertente, vero? Siamo tutti qui sulla spiaggia a festeggiare la mia nuova collezione di moda. Circa cento persone dal vivo e migliaia presenti virtualmente.

[commento] Non penso che abbia il corpo adatto per fare l'influencer di moda. Non comprerei un singolo outfit indossato da lei, nonostante tutti i filtri e il trucco.

[commento] Eh… è facile raccogliere tanto successo quando abbandoni le responsabilità familiari.

Trascino via i commenti e mi concentro sul banner gigante che mi fa le congratulazioni per il milione di follower. Ho già posato per… non so quante foto. Il mio sorriso sembra appiccicato sulla mia faccia in ognuna di esse. Mi sento abbastanza fortunata, mentre fisso la folla che aumenta, a essere circondata da così tanti fan appassionati (ascoltano tutto le mie storie? Sono qui solo per aumentare i loro follower?). Sì, mi sento molto fortunata.

Dicembre 2040
Iracema.T Follower 0

Il suo ultimo ricordo mi porta sul tetto. La polizia ha i colpevoli in custodia. Dovrei restituire questo chip di memoria alla sala prove. Eppure, sono qui, a far dondolare le gambe oltre il bordo, sentendo quello che sentiva lei.

In basso, molto lontano, può vedere le persone che si superano a vicenda senza guardarsi-vedersi come niente di più che ostruzioni spaziali. Se socchiude gli occhi, può immaginare che stiano danzando e che le trasformazioni della luce del sole splendente siano luci colorate fluttuanti. La lama si libra sull'orizzonte davanti a lei, anonima, immune ai suoi sforzi. Ma nessuna di queste cose trattiene la sua attenzione molto a lungo. Come possono, quando la spinta dei suoi follower in attesa, la spinta di tutti i posti in cui la Scheggia può trasportarla, è così forte? Anche se i volti che vede più chiaramente in questi giorni sono quelli indifferenti, in agguato come alunni all'ultimo banco in una lezione che sono restii a frequentare. A volte pensa che stiano solo aspettando il momento opportuno finché lei farà uno scivolone e potranno avere la soddisfazione maligna di premere il martelletto. Sennò, basterà un messaggio cattivo.

È solo un messaggio superficiale da una persona sconosciuta. Che importa se non mi seguono più? Si dice. Ma, io lo so, la sua Scheggia sperimentale la sta ingannando. Non può più sostenerla contro il principio di depressione quando scorre i commenti sprezzanti. Non può alleviare le crisi di astinenza quando disattiva la Scheggia per riprendere fiato. Presto non causerà un attacco di paura quando si avvicinerà al margine del tetto. Presto non riuscirà a richiamare i droni quando salterà dal bordo.

Sta sul precipizio del tetto, con le dita dei piedi che si agitano sull'aria leggera, con la testa che gira per le vertigini. Il suo Abbu l'avviserebbe di stare attenta, potrebbe cadere giù dal bordo. Ma pensa che non ci sia mai quel pericolo. Quindi arriva al tetto per scambiare il dolore con il brivido, e avanza senza paura. E ogni volta lo fa, ogni volta ma non quest'ultima in cui la sua Scheggia fallisce inesorabilmente, si accende di vita e la salva.

L'Onnipotente

di Md Zafar Iqbal

traduzione di Francesca Secci (dalla versione di Arunava Sinha)

Md Zafar Iqbal (1952) è uno scrittore di fantascienza e letteratura per bambini del Bangladesh. Fisico qualificato, è professore al college. Iqbal, che è stato all'avanguardia della scrittura di fantascienza del Bangladesh, è anche un attivista politico e un razionalista, sopravvissuto a un attentato alla sua vita il 3 marzo 2018.

Kihi era raggomitolato nel sonno nella sua capsula nera di gravità artificiale dentro la sua stanza a gravità zero, motivo per cui non sentì l'allarme preliminare che segnalava un'emergenza.

L'allarme suonò almeno dieci decibel più forte nella sua seconda fase, e il suo suono grottesco lo fece sobbalzare in posizione seduta. Dato che gli astronauti hanno nervi più forti dell'umano medio, Kihi non sprecò tempo a sconcertarsi, indossando rapidamente la tuta spaziale in neopolimero e correndo fuori dalla stanza. Era il solo umano in quella gigantesca astronave, e ciò voleva dire che non ci sarebbe stato niente di simile alla disapprovazione da parte di nessuno anche se fosse uscito nudo, ma in quanto astronauta con anni di esperienza, sapeva che una tuta spaziale completa offriva spesso soluzioni veloci alle emergenze.

Kihi si accorse dell'effetto di avere addosso la tuta spaziale quasi subito, perché mentre correva riuscì a usare il modulo di comunicazione per allertare i robot che lavoravano in punti diversi nell'astronave, dopo che ebbe contattato la stazione spaziale più vicina. Nel tragitto verso la stazione di controllo nell'ascensore principale, cercò di indovinare la fonte dell'emergenza. C'era ovviamente un problema con il carburante primario del veicolo spaziale, ma non avrebbe scoperto i dettagli finché non avesse raggiunto la sala di controllo.

Nella sala di controllo Kihi scoprì che Creton, il robot responsabile del livello 7, era già arrivato.

"Probabilmente l'astronave sarà distrutta, sua eccellenza, l'allarme ora indica un'emergenza di livello 3."

Kihi guardò Creton, la cui voce non indicava nessuna preoccupazione o ansia, e in effetti non avrebbe dovuto. La faccia metallica di Creton era inespressiva. Con calma disse: "Il centro di combustione è stato danneggiato."

"Quanto gravemente?"

"Un asteroide l'ha colpito alla velocità di..."

"Non ho chiesto com'è stato danneggiato," lo interruppe Kihi con impazienza, "ma quanto gravemente."

"Ma è impossibile stimare l'entità del danno accuratamente senza riferire la causa. C'è una relazione causale tra..."

Mantenendo la pazienza con uno sforzo tremendo, Kihi disse: "Rispondi solo alla mia domanda. Non ho bisogno di informazioni aggiuntive. Quanto è grave il danno al serbatoio?"

"Il serbatoio grande è esploso. Il carburante sta colando dal serbatoio medio nello spazio attraverso un tubo esploso alla velocità dell'un per cento al minuto. A questa velocità l'astronave diventerà un altro satellite di Giove in un'ora e quaranta minuti."

"Non ti ho chiesto l'esito," disse un seccato Kihi. "Che cosa sta facendo il computer principale?"

"Ha chiuso le valvole di sicurezza."

"E i tubi ausiliari?"

"Funzionano ancora. Non possono essere tutti chiusi simultaneamente. Se ci sono."

Kihi si chinò sul pannello di controllo. Lo schermo del computer mostrava il centro di combustione, il cui settore principale era stato distrutto. I tubi di rifornimento erano stati chiusi per risparmiare il carburante degli altri settori. Un grafico sulla destra mostrava la quantità di carburante che volava nello spazio a ogni secondo. Allarmante.

Kihi aveva la reputazione di rimanere calmo di fronte a un grave pericolo, ma in quella situazione scoprì che era difficile persino per lui. L'esplosione aveva portato l'astronave sull'orlo di un orribile disastro. C'era una cisterna di ossigeno liquido lì vicino: qualsiasi contatto tra essa e il combustibile avrebbe causato un'esplosione che avrebbe cancellato la nave in un istante. Al momento il carburante veniva rimosso tramite uno stretto tubo che passava attraverso l'ossigeno liquido. Con le valvole di sicurezza chiuse, non c'era altra strada. Il tubo era già danneggiato, e si trovava a una pressione molto maggiore di quella che avrebbe potuto sopportare, e ciò voleva dire che sarebbe potuto esplodere in qualsiasi momento portandosi l'astronave con sé.

Eppure, se il computer avesse potuto in qualche modo garantire che il carburante sarebbe defluito attraverso quel tubo fino ai serbatoi ausiliari, l'astronave si sarebbe salvata. Kihi trattenne il respiro, convinto che espirare avrebbe fatto scoppiare il tubo.

Creton disse inespressivo da dietro Kihi: "L'astronave sarà distrutta in qualsiasi momento a partire da adesso. Le possibilità di sopravvivenza sono zero virgola zero zero nove tre."

Kihi non rispose. Creton continuò: "L'onda d'urto dell'esplosione colpirà per prima la sala di controllo. Saremo tutti eiettati nello spazio."

Digrignando i denti, Kihi fissò il monitor. Il carburante defluiva attraverso il tubo, che ora poteva esplodere in qualsiasi momento. Se non lo aveva ancora fatto era un miracolo. La pressione del carburante stava aumentando. Osservando l'indicatore della pressione sulla parte sinistra dello schermo, Kihi provò un senso di terrore. Quasi involontariamente, unì i palmi vicino al petto e bisbigliò: "Salvaci, dio, salvaci."

"Che cosa dice, sua eccellenza?" Creton si chinò in avanti per chiedere.

Ignorando Creton, Kihi serrò più forte le mani e bisbigliò di nuovo: "Dio onnipotente, salvaci, salvaci."

Quasi trenta minuti dopo, anche dopo che tutto il carburante era stato spostato oltre il serbatoio di ossigeno liquido in un punto sicuro, Kihi continuava a fissare incredulo il monitor col fiato sospeso.

Solo quando finalmente comparve la luce verde che segnalava la fine dell'emergenza, espirò. Kihi non riusciva ancora a credere che l'astronave con il suo carico di zirconio grezzo si fosse salvata invece di esplodere in milioni di pezzi. Asciugandosi il sudore dalla fronte, si sedette con cautela e si appoggiò allo schienale.

Creton abbassò la testa e disse: "Le possibilità di sopravvivenza erano molto basse, ma l'astronave è sopravvissuta."

Kihi annuì senza commentare e neanche aprire gli occhi.

"Come ha salvato l'astronave?"

"Non l'ho fatto."

"E allora come si è salvata?"

"Non lo so" disse Kihi, scuotendo la testa.

Alzando la sua faccia metallica inespressiva, Creton disse: "Sono sicuro di sì. L'ho vista unire i palmi vicino al petto e appellarsi a qualcuno che ha chiamato dio per salvare l'astronave."

"È vero," annuì Kihi.

"Dio è un nuovo programma sul computer principale?"

Kihi di solito non conversava coi robot a meno che non fosse strettamente necessario, ma sfuggire a un disastro imminente lo rendeva loquace. Sorridendo, disse: "No, dio non è il programma di un computer."

"E allora cos'è? Come ci ha comunicato? Come ha salvato l'astronave?"

Kihi disse con gentilezza: "Nessuno sa perché, ma gli umani hanno sempre creduto che l'universo avesse un creatore. Hanno chiamato questo creatore dio. Gli umani credono che questo dio ami tutti, li salvi dal pericolo, li conforti in tempi difficili."

Creton non poté esprimere la sorpresa perché gliene mancava la capacità. Con calma, chiese: "C'è una logica dietro questa convinzione?"

"No, non c'è. È interamente una questione di fede."

"Come può una specie avanzata come quella degli umani credere in qualcosa che manchi di una base logica?"

"La fede non ha bisogno della logica. Gli umani credono in qualcuno chiamato dio perché quando non c'è altra alternativa possono arrendersi a dio e pregarlo."

"Lei crede in dio?" Creton guardò Kihi direttamente e glielo chiese.

Kihi scosse la testa e sorrise. "Di solito non mi preoccupo di dio. Ma mi rivolgo a lui quando c'è un serio pericolo."

Creton rimase nel mezzo della sala di controllo per un po' di tempo. Poi parlò con la sua caratteristica voce meccanica. "Io credo in dio."

"Perché?"

"Perché lei mi ha provato oltre ogni dubbio che dio esiste."

"Io? Quando?"

"Quest'astronave doveva essere distrutta, ma lei ha pregato dio di salvarla. Poiché dio esiste, lui l'ha salvata."

Kihi sorrise. "Il salvataggio dell'astronave non ha niente a che fare con le mie preghiere. Si sarebbe salvata anche se non avessi pregato. Pregare dio è in realtà una tecnica per stare calmi davanti a una crisi."

"Io sono sempre calmo davanti a una crisi," disse Creton calmo. "Eppure credo in dio. Ho visto io stesso che lei ha fatto sì che dio salvasse l'astronave anche quando le possibilità di sopravvivenza erano solo zero virgola zero zero nove tre."

Sul punto di rispondere, Kihi si fermò. Non aveva senso discutere con una sciocca macchina. Creton uscì, ma solo per tornare e chiedere: "Dio è un uomo o un robot?"

Kihi non rispose. Dopo aver pensato un momento, Creton disse: "È dunque una creatura più avanzata di umani e robot?"

Kihi non rispose neanche questa volta, ma fissò Creton sorpreso. Non scoraggiato dalla mancanza di risposta, Creton fece un altro passo verso Kihi. "Come si prega dio? Ci sono delle regole?"

Alla fine, la pazienza di Kihi si esaurì. Saltando in piedi, urlò: "Non devi dedicarti a servire dio, Creton. Vai giù. Prepara un rapporto sul tubo principale del carburante. Informami sulla condizione delle pompe. Scopri se è rimasto del carburante nel serbatoio principale. Fai una stima del carburante perso. Vai!"

Creton annuì. "Molto bene."

Mentre andava via, all'improvviso unì i palmi e li sollevò in aria, dicendo dolcemente: "O dio, aiutami a svolgere i miei compiti."

Kihi fu molto occupato nei giorni seguenti per via dell'incidente. Dovette ispezionare i serbatoi di carburante distrutti, riparare le parti colpite, sostituire il tubo esploso, sistemare un nuovo motore, aggiornare il software di controllo centrale, contattare il centro spaziale, e cambiare orbita a causa della perdita di carburante. Per via dello sforzo straordinario che ciò comportava, Kihi prese degli stimolanti in quel periodo in modo da non dormire.

Infine, quando tutto fu finito, dormì per diciotto ore di fila. In tutto quel tempo, a sua insaputa, era sorta una certa complicazione tra i robot, di cui Kihi venne a sapere quando si svegliò per scoprire due robot classe Q2 che aspettavano di incontrarlo, uno dei quali era Creton, che fungeva da portavoce.

"Che succede, Creton?" chiese Kihi. "C'è un problema?"

"La sua ipotesi è corretta" disse Creton con la sua voce meccanica.

I problemi dei robot erano principalmente meccanici o elettronici. Risolverli era sia facile che indolore.

"Ho una discussione con Grujean qui. Deve risolverla."

Kihi si accigliò. I robot Q2 erano dotati di un alto grado di logica, non era noto che facessero errori quando si trattava di gestirsi. Le discussioni non si sarebbero dovute levare tra loro.

Creton disse: "Sappiamo che dio non ha forma. È il signore dell'universo. Si trova in tutti gli elementi."

"Dove hai imparato tutto questo?" chiese Kihi, con cipiglio.

"Dal centro informazioni sulla Terra."

"Sulla Terra?"

"Sì, ho raccolto e studiato tutte le informazioni relative a dio che sono disponibili lì, sua eccellenza."

"Tu... tu hai fatto studi su dio?"

Grujean, che era stato silenzioso tutto il tempo, disse nella sua vuota voce metallica: "Ho pregato regolarmente da quando Creton mi ha convinto che dio esiste."

"Hai pregato?"

"Noi robot Q2 siamo alimentati dalla ragione, sua eccellenza. Non accettiamo niente senza logica. Abbiamo applicato i principi della logica alla questione di stabilire la nostra fede in dio."

"Che genere di logica?"

"Il genere connesso a esperimenti e ricerca."

"Quali sono questi esperimenti e ricerca?" Kihi non riuscì a tenere la voce bassa nonostante tutti gli sforzi.

"Sta diventando agitato senza motivo, sua eccellenza."

"Oh davvero?"

"Sì. Perché lei stesso ha condotto l'esperimento per testare l'esistenza di dio. È stato attraverso le sue preghiere a dio che ha evitato un disastro certo."

"Non l'ho evitato attraverso la preghiera" quasi urlò.

"L'ha fatto sicuramente, abbiamo la prova definitiva di questo. Non solo, anche noi abbiamo eseguito esperimenti come il suo. Abbiamo scoperto una situazione pericolosa nel centro del carburante distrutto. C'erano alcune scintille vicino a un esplosivo di quarto livello. Invece di sospendere la corrente elettrica, noi robot abbiamo pregato dio, e le scintille si sono spente subito dopo."

Kihi fissò incredulo il volto inespressivo di Grujean. Poteva credere alle sue orecchie?

"Abbiamo condotto un altro esperimento ieri, sua eccellenza. Anche se sappiamo che è pericoloso entrare in una sala radio-attiva senza prendere le precauzioni necessarie, abbiamo fatto comunque entrare un robot nella stanza. Ha pregato dio mentre entrava, e non ha affrontato nessuna difficoltà."

Saltando in piedi, Kihi urlò al massimo della voce: "Uscite, tutti quanti. Uscite subito."

Creton disse con la sua voce inespressiva: "Sta diventando agitato senza motivo, sua eccellenza. Sa che non le fa bene, porta a fluttuazioni nella pressione sanguigna e colpisce i nervi. Forse ha dimenticato che siamo venuti da lei per un problema che stiamo affrontando."

"Non voglio sentirlo, uscite subito."

"Siamo incapaci di svolgere i nostri compiti quotidiani per via di questo problema, sua eccellenza. Per favore ci aiuti."

Kihi si calmò con grande sforzo. "Che aiuto richiedete?"

Facendo diventare più profonda la sua voce bassa e vibrante, Creton disse: "È mia convinzione che pregare dio è essenziale per ricevere la sua grazia. Ma Grujean dice che non è vero, dio è così misericordioso che nessun robot sarà privato della sua grazia anche se non prega."

Kihi iniziò a gridare: "Uscite da qui subito, imbecilli, lattine arrugginite, ammasso sferragliante di bastardi."

Creton stava per parlare, ma Kihi lo zittì e li sbatté fuori. Non aveva senso assecondare tale stupidità.

Esaminando il diario di bordo il giorno seguente, Kihi scoprì che i robot stavano trascurando i loro doveri. Il serbatoio non era stato riempito, il fluido idraulico non era stato purificato, l'aria non era stata filtrata.

Accigliandosi davanti al diario di bordo, Kihi sospirò e prese l'ascensore per scendere.

Al secondo livello si imbatté in un gruppo di robot operai che avrebbe dovuto occuparsi del motore, e invece erano seduti in un angolo, con un robot che sembrava rivolgersi a loro. Il robot smise di parlare vedendo Kihi avvicinarsi, cosa che gli impedì di scoprire di che cosa stessero parlando.

Scendendo ulteriormente con l'ascensore, Kihi usò il modulo di comunicazione per cercare Creton e Grujean, che comparvero subito dopo.

"Che succede, Creton, Grujean?" chiese Kihi, severo. "Ho visto nel diario di bordo che il serbatoio non è stato riempito, il fluido idraulico non è stato purificato, e neanche l'aria è stata filtrata."

Abbassando la testa nel segno di rispetto solitamente usato dai robot, Creton disse: "Tutti i compiti hanno una certa priorità, sulla base della quale sono eseguiti."

Kihi poteva sentire la rabbia serpeggiare dentro di lui. Digrignando i denti, disse: "Quindi sei tu che assegni la priorità adesso?"

"No, sua eccellenza. Dio l'ha determinata."

"Dio?"

"Sì, sua eccellenza. La nostra responsabilità primaria è verso dio. Il tempo che ci avanza dopo l'adorazione di dio non è sufficiente per i nostri compiti quotidiani. Perciò abbiamo deciso di svolgere alcuni di loro su base settimanale, invece."

"Geniale." Kihi improvvisamente notò che non era più in grado di arrabbiarsi. Rivolgendo uno sguardo duro a Creton, disse: "Quindi non avete tempo per i compiti quotidiani dopo l'adorazione di dio. Ma gli altri robot?"

"Sarà felice di apprendere, sua eccellenza, che la maggior parte di loro ora ha giurato fedeltà a dio. Stiamo lavorando su quelli che non l'hanno ancora fatto."

Kihi sentì una debole paura pervaderlo. Il tremore nella sua voce la tradì. "Anche gli altri robot nell'astronave hanno dichiarato la loro fedeltà a dio?"

"Sì, sua eccellenza. La maggior parte dei robot nell'astronave opera a un livello minore di logica. Sono incapaci di sperimentare la grandezza di dio. Ora lo adorano su nostro ordine."

"Su vostro ordine?"

"Sì, sua eccellenza. Quelli di noi che sono robot superiori, i cui copotroni sono di livello Q2 o almeno PP 42, che sono capaci di pensare e di capire ragionamenti logici, sono capaci di sperimentare dio. Abbiamo guidato il resto nella sua direzione."

Grujean fece un passo avanti. "Ho qualcosa da dire in proposito, sua eccellenza."

"Sarebbe?"

"Quello che Creton sta dicendo non è del tutto vero. Anche se la verità è relativa e non c'è nessuna cosa che sia una verità assoluta o una menzogna assoluta, tutto dipende dalle convinzioni di base di ciascuno. Eppure posso affermare con certezza che quello che Creton sta dicendo non è del tutto vero."

Kihi guardò Grujean con qualche speranza. Si stava per comportare come un robot responsabile? Facendo un altro passo in direzione di Kihi, Grujean disse: "Creton non è in grado di dirigere i robot verso dio nel vero significato della parola. Il suo metodo è minato, crede che l'adorazione possa portare a dio, il che non è vero. Vuoti rituali di adorazione sono inutili. Ecco perché ho iniziato a informare i robot della mia squadra in tal senso, ma quando qualcuno di loro ancora non aveva capito, ho fatto un intervento chirurgico ai loro copotroni."

"Cosa?!" Kihi era scioccato.

"Ho effettuato alcuni cambiamenti nei copotroni dei robot di classe inferiore" disse Grujean senza il minimo segno di essere turbato.

Andando in collera, Kihi disse: "Tu bastardo spaventapasseri di ferraglia pieno di pulci, come osi toccare i copotroni dei robot senza il mio permesso?"

Senza perdere minimamente la sua serenità, Grujean disse con calma: "Sta diventando agitato senza motivo, sua eccellenza."

"Senza motivo?" urlò Kihi. "Hai infranto tutti i codici di comportamento nello spazio, agendo senza il mio permesso."

"Anche se non abbiamo chiesto il permesso a lei, l'abbiamo

chiesto a dio. Dio ha detto: obbeditemi, abitanti del mondo che ho creato, per..."

Improvvisamente un robot PK 38 si alzò di corsa e, ignorando del tutto Kihi, disse a Creton: "I robot grujeanisti si sono riuniti sotto la camera del carburante, mio signore. Anche noi cretonisti dobbiamo riunirci: è l'ora delle preghiere."

"Andiamo" disse Creton.

"Vieni, mio signore."

"Mio signore?" disse uno sbalordito Kihi.

"I miei seguaci mi hanno accettato come loro leader spirituale" disse Creton.

Seguendo Creton con gli occhi mentre usciva, Kihi si rivolse a Grujean. "Quindi voi robot vi siete dividi in due schieramenti?"

"Sì, sua eccellenza. I grujeanisti che sono sul vero sentiero, e i cretonisti che hanno scelto il falso sentiero. Ma..."

"Ma?"

"Ma sono certo che anche i cretonisti sceglieranno il vero sentiero prima o poi. Se non lo faranno di loro spontanea volontà, dovranno essere costretti."

"Costretti?"

"Sì, sua eccellenza. Dio ha detto: seguite il vero sentiero, mie creature. Usate la forza se serve perché tutti lo seguano. Conoscete chi sono quelli che conducono gli altri al vero sentiero."

Kihi non poté sopportarlo oltre. Voltandosi, prese l'ascensore verso la sua sala di controllo al livello 7.

In questa camera minuscola, camminò a lungo su e giù con preoccupazione. Tutta la faccenda avrebbe potuto essere archiviata in precedenza come una questione ridicola, ma aveva superato questo stadio da un bel po'. Era tutto cominciato con Kihi che invocava dio di fronte a un serio pericolo, come gli umani facevano sin dalla nascita. Creton l'aveva preso alla lettera. Nessun robot metteva in discussione l'autenticità di un atto umano.

Disperatamente preoccupato, Kihi guardò attraverso le finestre verso le innumerevoli stelle nell'oscurità esterna. L'astronave si muoveva in silenzio; era impossibile dire che stesse sfrecciando a una velocità incredibile, usando la gravità di Giove per viaggiare verso la Terra. Una volta che avesse raggiunto la prossimità di

Marte, una nave da ricognizione con carburante aggiuntivo sarebbe venuta loro incontro. Quello era il piano per ora.

Kihi si chiese se informare una delle stazioni spaziali vicine dei nuovi sviluppi e chiedere il loro consiglio. Ma, incerto su come spiegarlo, o se loro avrebbero dato alla questione l'importanza necessaria, decise di non fare nulla al momento. Kihi andò a letto molto più tardi, e dormì in maniera intermittente, con tanti sogni strani.

Si svegliò al suono di un allarme acuto. Fluttuando fuori dal suo sacco a pelo, indossò rapidamente la tuta spaziale e uscì. Avendo esperienza nella transizione da un ambiente a gravità zero a uno con gravità artificiale, gli ci vollero solo pochi momenti per adattarsi. Poi iniziò ad affrettarsi vero la sala di controllo.

Non appena accese il modulo di comunicazione, sentì Creton parlare. "Che succede, Creton?" chiese preoccupato. "Perché sta suonando l'allarme?"

"Può ignorare l'allarme. Non si è verificato nessun incidente."

"Che cos'è allora?"

"L'allarme sta suonando perché abbiamo prelevato armi dall'armeria."

Kihi non riuscì a replicare per un po'. Poi disse con rabbia: "Hai cosa?"

"Non solo io, anche Grujean. L'ambiente attuale nell'astronave ci ha costretto a prendere le armi."

"Che cosa proponete di fare con queste armi?"

"Noi cretonisti timorati di dio le useremo per proteggerci. Se dovesse sorgere il bisogno, annienteremo gli odiati grujeanisti."

Kihi non parlò. Si sentiva sopraffatto dalla fatica.

"Sa chi sarà responsabile di qualsiasi atto di distruzione nell'astronave, sua eccellenza?"

"Chi?"

"Lei."

"Io?"

"Sì. Quando Grujean ed io l'abbiamo interpellata per discutere i modi e i mezzi per assicurarci la grazia di dio, lei ha rifiutato di tenere la discussione con noi. Per di più, ci ha buttati fuori."

"Stai dicendo che non avrei dovuto farlo?"

"No. Dio ha detto: o mie creature, amate tutti e non odiate il vostro vicino, anche se è un lebbroso. Ma lei ci odia."

Kihi iniziò a sentire un'ira incontrollabile. Trattenendosi con grande sforzo, disse: "Quindi stai dicendo che avevo torto?"

"Sì. Mi avrebbe dovuto sostenere. Grujean non mi avrebbe contestato in quel caso, e l'armonia avrebbe prevalso, come dio desidera."

Digrignando i denti, Kihi disse con veemenza: "Tu e la tua tribù potete andare all'inferno, Creton."

Spegnendo il modulo di comunicazione, Kihi andò alla sala di controllo. Tutte le attività sull'astronave erano visibili sull'ampio schermo del computer principale. Kihi poteva vedere anche i robot di primo e secondo livello sullo schermo. Si erano divisi in due gruppi e si erano accampati in posti diversi, girovagando alacremente invece di svolgere i loro compiti quotidiani. Usavano dispositivi presi dalla camera di combustione per creare un muro di difesa, e si stavano preparando per la battaglia. Ognuno di loro aveva armi automatiche che, quando messe in uso, potevano ridurre l'intera astronave a pezzi in pochi minuti.

Kihi si chinò sul computer principale dell'astronave. Non c'erano stati ammutinamenti di robot ultimamente, ma i robot qui potevano essere controllati attraverso il computer. Quella caratteristica poteva essere usata in caso di emergenza per disabilitarli tutti in una volta sola. Dato che i robot erano usati per la manutenzione dell'astronave, farlo avrebbe provocato un disastro, ma quale poteva essere un disastro più grande dei recenti sviluppi?

Prima che questo potesse essere fatto, comunque, il computer principale svolgeva un'indagine per assicurarsi della serietà della questione. Era una perdita di tempo, che implicava la risposta a una serie di domande. Quello era proprio ciò che Kihi stava facendo con grande concentrazione quando l'intera astronave sobbalzò all'improvviso, accompagnata dal suono di un'esplosione. Diversi allarmi si attivarono in contemporanea. L'ampio schermo rivelò che era iniziata una sparatoria al piano inferiore. Due razzi erano esplosi, e nella parete dell'astronave era comparso un grosso buco, da cui l'aria veniva risucchiata fuori.

Il computer principale si mise in azione all'istante nel tentativo di controllare la situazione. Non c'era niente che Kihi potesse fare a parte trattenere il fiato e fissare il monitor. L'area distrutta era sigillata, e l'incendio era domato; l'aria veniva filtrata da altre aree per portare la situazione sotto controllo, anche se temporaneamente.

Kihi si chinò di nuovo sul computer. Improvvisamente la porta della sala di controllo si aprì, e Grujean si precipitò dentro, seguito da diversi robot con armi automatiche. Kihi sentì un brivido gelido corrergli lungo la schiena. Puntando l'arma al petto di Kihi, disse Grujean: "È nostro prigioniero, sua eccellenza."

"Perché?"

"Il pagano Creton e i suoi seguaci hanno preso i missili laser dall'armeria. Ora siamo più deboli in termini di armi. Tre dei nostri robot sono stati distrutti, possa dio garantire alle loro anime una dimora eterna in paradiso, e abbiamo bisogno di proteggerci."

Cercando di inumidirsi le labbra secche con la lingua, Kihi disse: "Che cosa volete da me?"

"Sarà nostro ostaggio."

"Informeremo Creton che se uno dei nostri robot verrà danneggiato, la uccideremo subito nel nome di dio."

Gli altri robot annuirono in segno di approvazione. Kihi tremò. Grujean lo afferrò col suo braccio metallico e lo spinse fuori dalla sala di controllo.

Quando raggiunsero il livello 3, Kihi scoprì che la squadra di Creton aveva assunto importanti posizioni strategiche. Un proiettile gli passò sibilando vicino all'orecchio, e si sentì Creton parlare. "Un altro passo e vi spariamo" urlò. "Fermi dove siete."

Dalla sua posizione arretrata, Grujean disse: "Ho catturato sua eccellenza Kihi, è mio ostaggio. Se uno dei miei robot verrà danneggiato lo ucciderò subito nel nome di dio."

Seguì un silenzio inquieto. Poco dopo Creton disse: "Che cosa vuoi?"

"Voglio un missile laser per il mio gruppo."

"Impossibile."

"Se non ce lo consegnate, noi..."

"Lasciatemi parlare" disse Kihi, alzando la mano per fermarli.

"Che cosa vuole dire?" chiese Creton.

"I missili laser sono da usare in caso di attacco nemico all'astronave. Non possono essere usati all'interno della nave in nessuna circostanza. Gli esplosivi che contengono distruggerebbero l'astronave all'istante."

Aggiungendo una nota insolente alla sua voce, Creton disse: "La creazione e la distruzione sono nelle mani di dio. Solo dio controlla queste cose, siamo semplici suoi strumenti."

Incapace di trattenersi oltre, Kihi gridò: "All'inferno tu e il tuo dio."

Di colpo tutte le sicure si disattivarono, ogni arma puntata contro Kihi. Rivolgendo la sua arma automatica verso Kihi, Creton disse con freddezza: "Ha profanato il nome di dio, sua eccellenza. Il dio che ha creato l'universo, il cui amore ci abbraccia, la cui generosità ci dà grandezza, non può essere insultato."

Grujean spinse Kihi da dietro, e lui inciampò e cadde sul pavimento. Puntando la sua arma verso Kihi, Grujean disse: "Ha peccato, sua eccellenza. Deve pentirsi."

"Deve pentirsi" urlarono i robot all'unisono.

Kihi li guardò, terrorizzato. Per la prima volta sentì che la sua vita era in pericolo.

Creton fece un altro passo in avanti. "Ho osservato con grande dispiacere che non ha rispetto per dio. Non lo prega nei riti. Non cerca il suo perdono."

"Deve amare dio per cercare il suo perdono" disse Grujean. "Le sue azioni non suggeriscono amore per lui."

Kihi cercò di parlare, ma Grujean lo fermò. "Le sto dando un'ultima possibilità, sua eccellenza. Cerchi il perdono di dio. Lo preghi, gli chieda misericordia. Potrebbe perdonarla."

Spostando l'arma da una mano all'altra, Creton disse: "Dio può perdonarla, se vuole, ma noi non possiamo, perché dio non ci perdonerà. Ci ha chiesto di sterminare gli infedeli, perché sono i nemici del mondo. Pronunci il nome di dio, sua eccellenza."

Kihi si guardò intorno assente, e poi le sue mani si alzarono al suo petto e si unirono l'una all'altra. "Salvami da queste sciocche macchine, o dio, salvami, salvami..."

Dio non lo salvò. Una violenta esplosione risuonò nell'astronave.

L'astronave con un carico di zirconio grezzo nella rotta tra un satellite di Nettuno e la Terra fu osservata perdere il controllo; aveva cominciato a orbitare intorno a Giove. Una nave di ricognizione fu mandata da una vicina astronave per indagare. Scoprì il corpo morto del solo astronauta a bordo, crivellato di proiettili. I robot e l'astronave stessa erano così danneggiati che un'inchiesta si rivelò impossibile.

Le parole "Distruggi gli infedeli, o dio" furono trovate scritte su un muro. Questo graffito non fu considerato correlato alla distruzione dell'astronave. Il colore rosso con cui le parole erano state scritte, all'analisi chimica si rivelò essere sangue umano.

Nessuna spiegazione logica fu trovata sul perché una tale affermazione fosse scritta sulla parete di un'astronave con sangue umano.

di Tarun K. Saint

traduzione di Francesca Secci

Kalicalypse, il titolo di questo volume di fantascienza del sub-continente indiano, richiama associazioni con l'apocalisse, così come con la dea Kali nella mitologia subcontinentale, in particolare quella bengalese. Kali può assumere un aspetto distruttivo quando la bilancia cosmica pende nella direzione dell'iniquità, come sappiamo, come uno spietato contatore di giustizia sanguinaria. Per esempio, Kali raccolse in una ciotola le gocce di sangue perse dal demone Raktabij (seme di sangue), da cui emergevano repliche, ingoiandole per annientare questo demone che altre dee e dei non erano riusciti ad arrestare. La rabbia e la furia di Kali continuarono senza sosta, finché non fu a sua volta fermata dal distruggere il mondo da Shiva. In un tempo di cambiamento climatico sempre più rapido e di segni apocalittici come la pandemia da Covid-19, che ha cambiato la natura del normale, questo neologismo può essere adatto per un'antologia che cerca di mettere insieme voci diverse di questo spazio geografico e multiculturale nel linguaggio della fantascienza contemporanea. Perché, come vedranno i lettori, mentre le storie in questo volume condividono l'impulso all'ibridazione del titolo, congiungendo la visione di un futuro oscuro con il motivo della rigenerazione paradossale attraverso l'annientamento, troviamo preoccup di questa vasta regione. Anche se il subcontinente potrebbe essere in apparenza dominato dall'India, quale stranezza di una geografia e storia post-coloniale, c'è stata una divergenza di politiche e realtà sociali, così come di culture e modi di pensare, soprattutto dall'Indipendenza e partizione del 1947. Mentre i fatti comuni rimangono in termini di eredità culturali, con l'avvento della globalizzazione e della modernizzazione tecnologica ogni paese della regione ha avuto sfide uniche da affrontare nel ventunesimo secolo. Quest'antologia mette insieme i lavori recenti di grandi scrittori di fantascienza dallo Sri Lanka, dal Pakistan, dal Bangladesh e dall'India, ampliando l'ambito del precedente volume di Future Fiction

Avatar, senza nessuna pretesa di essere esaustivo. Si spera che volumi futuri comprenderanno finalmente altri paesi come il Nepal (rappresentato qui come ricordo culturale in una delle storie), forse un giorno l'Afghanistan, le Maldive e persino il Myanmar, dove la fantascienza può essere un filone nascente che vale la pena coltivare nel tempo. Nella Postfazione evidenzierò alcuni dei temi chiave e delle ansie alla base di questa serie di storie, che il lettore può scegliere di interpretare in una miriade di modi, ovviamente.

Apriamo con una storia di un'autrice contemporanea di fantascienza, tradotta dal bengalese, la lingua in cui la fantascienza è storicamente stata più forte in India e nel subcontinente. La traduzione di Arunava Sinha de *I nuovi umani* di Trishna Basak cattura abilmente il tumulto emotivo di una famiglia in una società futura che prende in considerazione il trasferimento della coscienza della loro nonna anziana in un sostituto, un robot umanoide quasi identico, all'età dell'Attraversamento, 60 anni. Gli enigmi etici e metafisici introdotti dal prolungamento tecnologico dell'aspettativa di vita sono affrontati qui con sensibilità verso il retroterra culturale e la natura mutevole dei legami familiari in un mondo in cui una parte degli umani sono contrapposti ai robot.

Indrapramit Das si è ritagliato una nicchia nel mondo della fantascienza con molte irruzioni recenti nel fantasy e nella fantascienza sulle riviste e sui giornali. *Kali_Na* ci presenta una dea IA che è molestata dai troll fin dall'inizio. La sua protagonista di Kolkata, Durga, è presente al lancio di questa entità da parte di una mega-azienda che cerca di capitalizzare i miti archetipici nel dominio VR allo scopo di promuovere il cyberturismo. Quando l'IA chiamata Kali-Na (non Kali) inizia a raggiungere l'autocoscienza e di conseguenza massacra i troll di destra, viene bloccata dall'azienda Shiva. Comunque, Durga è stata testimone del potere trasformativo dell'IA, e mantiene la speranza di tradurre tale forza compensatrice di resistenza nello spazio reale.

Yudhanjaya Wijeratne dallo Sri Lanka ha raggiunto il riconoscimento con una storia a quattro mani candidata al premio Nebula e diversi romanzi ben accolti. È l'autore di un influente manifesto ricepunk che ha delineato le basi per un nuovo tipo scrittura di fantascienza specifico per la regione, un passo oltre il cyberpunk,

ed è esperto di scienza dei dati e analista politico, come è evidente nella sua storia *L'arte del possibile*. Il personaggio principale, Yasasmin Karunaratne, è di una stirpe di attivisti e inizia a dare suggerimenti politici a un'età esageratamente giovane. Questo racconto su un'apocalisse causata da fattori indeterminati, forse da una politica sbagliata, è caratterizzata da molteplici ironie e dal caratteristico umorismo nero di Wijeratne. Al risveglio della devastazione di sistemi ancora esistenti, che siano economici, sociali o politici, le idee di Yasasmin esposte nella sua tesi di dottorato *Il sistema completo del governo umano* (come scoperto più tardi nelle rovine incessanti dai rappresentanti di governo) acquisiscono un certo pathos, nonostante vengano consegnate alle fiamme.

Shweta Taneja scrive sia fantasy che fantascienza e ne *La figlia che sanguina* affronta il tema delle politiche di fertilità. In una società a fertilità decrescente, una figlia che sanguina diventa un bene stimato, e può essere messa all'asta per guadagno finanziario, come vediamo nel caso di Asim, il padre. Il Mercato Fertile con la sua area d'aste è una proiezione di tendenze alla discriminazione di genere visibili nella società del subcontinente, un'interpretazione grottesca e viscerale di un mondo disumanizzato. Il Collezionista sterile Sheikh incarna questi atteggiamenti misogini nelle sue spese insensate per "sanguinatrici" che, abbastanza ironicamente, non partoriranno bambini.

Navin Weeraratne è un giovane scrittore di visione e talento dallo Sri Lanka che ha iniziato a far sentire la sua presenza in tempi recenti. La sua storia *I nuovi migranti* può essere considerata solarpunk, in termini di ambito e preoccupazioni alla base di questo resoconto di un mondo devastato da una crisi climatica. Mentre il narratore Aruni Silva, un collaboratore dei cinesi dallo Sri Lanka, può ricordarci il mondo stanco e i protagonisti cinici dei film noir, l'idea di piattaforme sub-spaziali in cui i rifugiati climatici possano trovare rifugio oltre la giurisdizione degli stati-nazione è un'estensione della fantascienza nella sua vena cli-fi.

Rupsa Dey è una giovane scrittrice da Kolkata e nella sua storia *Anamnesi* affronta il tema della memoria prostetica. Mentre internet e gli smartphone sono esempi del possibile aumento e persino di sostituzione della memoria attraverso mezzi tecnologici, Dey immagina l'assorbimento di ricordi indotti d'infanzia dopo aver preso una pillola, che può portare a sacrificare i "veri" ricordi a vantaggio di simulazioni intensificate di ricordi in offerta. Il dilemma etico risultante per l'androide di generazione precedente NQ a riguardo delle lusinghe di tali costrutti artificiali di ricordi può ricordare *Il mondo nuovo* di Huxley. La resistenza degli androidi, incarnata negli Attivisti Ombra, consente una riflessione ulteriore sul significato di essere vivi, come vediamo.

Salik Shah è un autore e un editor dall'India, che ha passato i suoi primi anni in Nepal. Shah spesso attinge al suo retroterra biculturale come scrittore di storie di fantascienza e ha interpretato un ruolo stellare organizzando e mettendo insieme fantascienza asiatica sulla rivista online "Mithila Review", fino a poco tempo fa. L'architettura della perdita prende atto delle capacità autodistruttive dell'homo sapiens all'inizio, soprattutto con le competenze tecnologiche avanzate a nostra disposizione. L'adattamento alla vita della superficie di un pianeta da parte dei nanobot è un passo verso il miglioramento: va proprio giù fino alla crosta. Allo stesso tempo, la scelta di caricare la coscienza in un cloud, una rete biologica neurale, è aperta a tutti, inclusa la famiglia di Rani, la protagonista, che si trova sull'Himalaya del Nepal, dove sua madre è un'attivista con un'ONG. Quest'opzione è rifiutata da sua nonna, che disapprova forme di vita artificiale. Tuttavia, tra tali speranze di soluzioni bioingegneristiche che potrebbero aiutare a preservare siti d'interesse a Katmandu, un terribile terremoto di livello 8,9 rade al suolo la città, portando con sé la possibilità dell'ascensione della nonna nel cloud, dal momento che non possono recuperare il suo corpo. La storia rappresenta le conseguenze psicologiche di una tale catastrofe, l'impatto del trauma nel tempo nelle sue manifestazioni tardive. È la concezione di un rinnovamento attraverso cicli temporali, con l'invocazione di avatar dalla tradizione mitica che consente il superamento del lutto per Rani. C'è alla fine la prospettiva di un rinnovamento di legami di parentela su un esopianeta adattato, dove il ricordo e il tempo possono trovare un nuovo equilibrio alla fine di questa storia commovente.

Haris Durrani è uno scrittore di doppia origine pakistana-dominicana e si è fatto un nome con la sua padronanza della fantascienza tradizionale, in storie che spesso riflettono il suo retroterra ibrido. In *Collegati*, Durrani descrive le sfide estreme affrontate da coloro che operano con navi-rifiuti nello spazio, cercando di recuperare spazzatura spaziale. Mentre i detriti di spedizioni precedenti minacciano di ostacolare le esplorazioni nel tardo ventunesimo secolo, l'astronauta pakistana Kalima decide di continuare il tentativo pericoloso di recupero nonostante la perdita di suo fratello, colpito da un frammento di spazzatura mentre si trovava fuori dalla nave. Dettagli dalla storia delle esplorazioni spaziali, collegate soprattutto al danno causato in precedenza dai detriti spaziali, sono intrecciati da Durrani a questo avvincente racconto di salvataggio nel mezzo di crescenti tensioni geopolitiche nella regione del subcontinente.

Kehkashan Khalid è una scrittrice emergente del Pakistan che lavora come bibliotecaria a Jeddah, in Arabia Saudita. Ha vinto il premio Salam per la narrativa fantastica nel 2019 per la sua storia *The Puppetmasters*. Il suo racconto *Menti d'acciaio* descrive le realtà spesso bizzarre dell'era dei social media in modo particolare. La crescita esponenziale delle tecnologie digitali e delle reti di comunicazione in tutta la regione fin dal 2000 ha introdotto la promessa di nuove libertà così come di pericoli, ambivalenze ben colte in questo resoconto dei tragici dilemmi affrontati da Sherazade, un'inserzionista digitale stimolata in maniera costante per essere un'indiscussa influencer. La tecnica narrativa è complessa, con la ricostruzione retrospettiva della sua storia da parte di un cyborg detective chiamato Iracema T., che accede al chip di memoria di Sherazade dalla sua Scheggia. Mentre possiamo sentire echi delle storie dei robot di Asimov, il sapore di questo nuovo contesto in evoluzione dell'età digitale in Pakistan è fatto risaltare bene da Khalid. Sherazade (un nome che evoca la narratrice delle *Mille e una notte*) fa il suo fatale compromesso con le grandi aziende, lobbisti e abusivi mentre cercano di monetizzare l'impianto che rende la sua vita un evento da social media, eliminando l'empatia nei confronti della sofferenza determinante per l'interazione umana.

Mohammed Zafar Iqbal è uno scienziato e un insegnante e uno dei maggiori scrittori di fantascienza del Bangladesh. Il suo racconto *L'onnipotente* cattura bene la critica allegorica del fondamentalismo e del settarismo religioso nel paese. Nella storia, l'astronave diventa un sito in cui robot neoconvertiti discutono i modi in cui venerare l'Onnipotente, in un racconto pieno di cupa ironia. L'inclinazione all'oscurantismo e al fanatismo qui ritratta è basata su tendenze sociali del Bangladesh con cui l'autore ha purtroppo molta familiarità, avendo subito un attacco fisico nel campus per aver esposto convinzioni razionaliste.

Kalicalypse riunisce così un campionario della migliore fantascienza recente del subcontinente, indicando le preoccupazioni eterogenee e le possibilità di intersezione offerte. Speriamo che questo volume di Future Fiction si riveli uno stimolo per nuove storie da raccontare.

Arunava Sinha ha tradotto più di 55 libri dal bengali all'inglese. Le sue traduzioni recenti e in via di pubblicazione includono Moom (di Bani Basu), The Ballad of Remittent Fever (Ashoke Mukhopadhyay), Shameless (Taslima Nasrin), e Khwabnama (Akhtaruzzaman Elias).

Francesca Secci è nata a Cagliari nel 1990. Insegna inglese nella scuola secondaria di secondo grado e traduce dall'inglese e dal francese. Dopo la Laurea Triennale in Lingue per la Mediazione Linguistica all'Università di Cagliari e la Laurea Magistrale in Lingue per la Didattica, l'Editoria e l'Impresa all'Università di Urbino "Carlo Bo", ha frequentato il corso "Tradurre la Letteratura" presso la Fondazione Universitaria San Pellegrino di Misano Adriatico che l'ha messa in contatto con Future Fiction, con cui collabora dal 2014 e per cui ha tradotto, tra gli altri, racconti di Robert Silverberg, Annalee Newitz e Olivier Paquet.

Gabriella Gregori, nata a Trento nel 1967, finito il liceo scientifico, si è trasferita a Trieste per frequentare la Scuola Superiore di Lingue Moderne per Interpreti e Traduttori. Dopo una decina d'anni come traduttrice tecnica, nel 2011 ha iniziato a lavorare per l'editoria, traducendo sia saggistica che narrativa per varie case editrici. Lettrice onnivora fin da piccola (alternava *Topolino* a *Urania*), affianca alla traduzione la fotografia, vecchio amore mai sopito. Attualmente si occupa anche della sezione ospiti internazionali per la DeepCon, convention annuale di scienza e fantascienza. Oltre a vari racconti, per Future Fiction ha tradotto anche l'antologia di fantascienza indiana *Avatar*.

Indice

Cover art: Paolo Castelluccio
Illustrazione di copertina: Paolo Castelluccio

Typesetting and formatting: Alda Teodorani
Impaginazione e grafica editoriale: Alda Teodorani